WEAVING ROOTS

Heather Wood

Finding Home Series

Until We All Find Home
Until We All Run Free
Until the Light Breaks Through
Until We All Share Joy
(stand-alone novella concurrent with Until We All Run Free)

A Gathering of Mercies Series

Weaving Roots

Copyright © 2024 by Heather Wood

All rights reserved. No part of this book may be used or reproduced in any form whatsoever without written permission except in the case of brief quotations in critical articles or reviews. This book is a work of fiction. Names, characters, businesses, organizations, places, events and incidents either are the product of the author's imagination or are used fictitiously. Any resemblance to actual persons, living or dead, events, or locales is entirely coincidental. All scripture quotations are from the King James Version of the Bible.

Printed in the United States of America.

Cover design by Hannah Linder

ISBN - Paperback: 979-8-9900837-0-7

To Heidi
because every Patrick needs a Colm,
and I'm grateful that you're mine

Blessed *is* the man that walketh not in the counsel of the ungodly, nor standeth in the way of sinners, nor sitteth in the seat of the scornful. But his delight *is* in the law of the LORD; and in his law doth he meditate day and night. And he shall be like a tree planted by the rivers of water, that bringeth forth his fruit in his season; his leaf also shall not wither; and whatsoever he doeth shall prosper.

Psalm 1:1-3 KJV

Dear Reader,

Let me be the first to welcome you to eastern U.S. city life in what is known as the Nationalist period of American history. You'll quickly realize that this underrepresented time and place didn't look like the Colonial or Victorian eras before or after it, and it matches the concurrent Regency culture of England not at all. There are a few notes on the real history represented in this story in the author's note at the back of the book, and I often share more of my research in my online spaces for those of you who are curious to learn more.

As with all individuals throughout all of history, my characters reflect opinions and beliefs in existence at their time which were of course not the only opinions and beliefs present in their people group and social circles. One of my primary purposes in writing is to explore what God was doing at different points in history, and I'm overjoyed to have the opportunity to share the truth of that with you now.

Running together,
Heather Wood

Name Pronunciations:
Betha: BEH-thah
Colm: KA-lem
Seamus: SHAYM-us

1

August 1827
Baltimore, Maryland

Betha studied the two-story brick building before her, praying that this wasn't yet another of Seamus's bad ideas.

"Are you nervous?"

Her nephew's voice pulled her gaze from the boxy red structure to the blue eyes tilted up beneath his plaid cap. A face that before much longer would stand eye to eye with her.

She smiled at how well Henry knew her, and wrapping an arm around him, she pulled him against her best mulberry-colored dress.

"Enrolling you in school oughtn't be too frightenin'." As long as they weren't making a mistake by sending him to the Oliver Hibernian Free School. It didn't matter how much she tried to convince her brother of the importance of a quality education for Henry; linen wasn't selling the way it used to, and the expense of a paid school would make things tight for them. A sacrifice Seamus wasn't as willing to make for his son as she was.

"Are you nervous?" Betha asked, turning the question around on Henry. Facing unfamiliar situations and people weren't her favorite things to do, but she wasn't the one starting a new school in a new city, and if she'd learned anything this year, it was that the ten-year-old by her side was far more resilient than she gave him credit for.

"I'd like to get it done with."

So he was nervous but carrying the brave face he'd worn since birth. Betha could only pray that this school gave Henry a new beginning as fresh as the one Seamus counted on Baltimore being for himself.

A shiny lacquered coach and four rounded the corner, and Betha pulled Henry out of the road, peering around the school at the affluent neighborhood beyond it. Despite its location, the building they now approached was obviously built more for function than to relay any grandiose sense of the high endeavor of education. Mounting the stairs, Betha felt the protective mother bear within her rise and surrendered Henry to the Lord. His new schoolmaster might be a strict, hardened old codger. He might hold Henry to an impossible standard or crush the boy's curious spirit. He might not see Henry as an individual in a crowd of rowdy boys. But at least he would never know of the circumstances of Henry's birth or call him names related to it.

No one in Baltimore would be able to hold Seamus's long-ago choices against Henry if Betha had anything to do with it. Not like New York had.

Betha sent Henry an affectionate smile. If he was going to allow courage to chase his fears away, she would do the same. She offered her hand to him. He took it, reminding her that despite what he often voiced, he was still her little boy. He still needed her. Betha didn't know what she would do if he ever didn't. Seamus might view Henry as the biggest mistake of his life, but he was the biggest blessing in hers.

"All the students here are Irish," she said brightly.

"I know, Ma. You already told me."

Betha reached for the front door and pushed it open. "It might be nice to have friends who are like you."

Henry shrugged like he didn't care either way. Betha didn't blame him with the way he'd been treated by so-called friends in the past.

A chair scraping across the floor greeted them as Betha closed the door behind Henry and turned around into a giant room filled with rows of benches. A man stood behind the desk, pulling his coat over white shirtsleeves.

"Good morning."

Betha lifted her eyes from the stacks of books and papers covering the desk to the face watching her approach. Well, she could check "old" off her list. His curious brown eyes didn't look hardened either.

"Good morning. We're here to enroll Henry in school."

"Excellent. Welcome to Oliver Hibernian." The teacher walked around the desk and extended his hand to Henry first. "I'm Mr. Gallagher, the boys' teacher."

Betha watched Henry straighten and his skinny little chest puff out as he gave a firm handshake like a man. "Henry Young."

Then Mr. Gallagher turned to her, and Betha took in the neatly combed brown hair, straight white teeth, and . . . dimples? Surely a man with dimples couldn't be a strict taskmaster of a teacher, could he? He was clean-shaven, but the shadow on his jaw and lines on the outer corners of his eyes told her he wasn't fresh out of college. Hopefully that meant he could hold his own in a classroom of energetic boys.

He reached his hand out to her with a real smile. "Colm Gallagher." His accent revealed that he was just as American as she was. Maybe he had never seen Ireland with his own eyes either. As far as Betha's da was concerned, those who had never stepped foot on the ancient land of Hibernia were lesser than. Which had always confused her, seeing as he was the one who brought Seamus and their mother to America before Betha was born.

"Betha Young," she murmured in response.

Mr. Gallagher released her hand and leaned back against the desk. "How old are you, Mr. Young?"

"Almost eleven, sir."

As if Betha needed to be reminded that he was growing up too fast. Especially when his birthday was still five months away.

"You've been in school before?"

"Yes, sir, in New York."

Betha supposed the teacher had to ask that one, as the school serviced poor Scotch-Irish neighborhoods, but at least he'd formed the question in a positive manner, assuming Henry had. Henry stood tall and brave, already so anxious to impress his new teacher.

Mr. Gallagher—or was it Colm, since he'd added that name just for her?—rounded the desk to rifle through his pile of papers. "I could place you in the level you were in in New York to start with, or if you're willing to undergo a more exacting evaluation, I'll place you in separate reading, writing, and arithmetic levels according to your abilities. That way you can simply continue your education from your current place."

"Do you do that for all your students?" Betha couldn't conceal her surprise. "Break up their academic level by subject?"

Colm didn't appear fazed by her challenge. "Yes, ma'am. I utilize the Lancaster education model, which allows for students to excel at what comes naturally to them while steadily working at what doesn't."

Whatever the Lancaster model was, it sounded newfangled, and Betha wondered what Seamus would think. But she wouldn't give away to Colm that she wished her teacher had used such a model when she was a child. Besides, Henry's dislike of writing made his eyes simply glow at the suggestion.

"I can do the evaluation, can't I, Ma?"

Betha looked to Colm.

"I could evaluate him now if you have time, Mrs. Young. It won't take long."

"Miss." Betha cringed at the implication left by Henry's address. Until now, she'd never felt obligated to correct the title he'd used for her since he was five. What compelled her to want to ensure this man knew the truth of their relationship? "I'm Henry's guardian, but in truth, only his aunt."

She noted with satisfaction that the information seemed to have pleased Colm, for he almost smiled. He stood blinking at her before Betha realized that she hadn't answered his actual question and he was still waiting.

"Yes, of course. We can do the evaluation now."

Betha wandered around the schoolroom to give them space while Colm pulled out his books and gestured for Henry to take a seat. Stopping by the window, she took in the view of church steeples and government buildings, the steady, articulated cadence of Colm's low voice wafting through the room as he quizzed Henry.

Somewhere out in Fell's Point, their neighborhood surrounding Baltimore's wharves, Seamus was looking for a flax supplier. Betha removed her bonnet from her black hair, breathing out a prayer that she and Henry would return home to good news and she could get the spinning wheel going sooner rather than later. Seamus hadn't seemed at all concerned about suppliers when he packed up his loom in New York.

"Baltimore is just as close to the Delaware Valley as New York is, Betha. It shouldn't affect our supply at all. Besides, Baltimore is half as big as New York and growing. It's the perfect place and time to establish our name."

Betha knew it was all just excuses to defend the decision he'd already made. When she'd reminded him that the new Erie Canal made New York a clearly more advantageous city for trade, he'd brushed off her concerns, pointing to the railroad Baltimore was planning to compete with the canal. It didn't matter, because they both knew cotton was overtaking linen in every market, and it wasn't a secret that behind her questions, she supported his reasons for moving. But someone had to ask them and keep Seamus's impulses in check.

She mindlessly stretched her fingers, glad for the forced break from spinning even as she welcomed the thought of returning to a normal routine. When had she ever had two whole weeks off since Ma died and Betha filled her place as the family's primary spinner? Back then, Betha wondered if she would ever be able to spin as fine a thread as her mother's nimble fingers could. Now there was no doubt that her mother would be proud of the quality of linen she and Seamus produced. Its quality had made the Young name respected in New York. Unfortunately, New York made it clear they would never extend the same respect to Henry.

Betha turned from the window when Colm and Henry's oral volley ceased and Colm came to his feet. She watched Henry beam as Colm shook his hand and said something she couldn't make out before turning his dimples on her.

"You have a bright boy here, Miss Young. He said you were the one primarily responsible for his education." He relaxed his stance, his hands in his coat pockets.

Betha dipped her head, self-conscious at the unexpected compliment. "I only helped fill in what was lacking."

"So many of our students come with little to no education, both immigrants and American-born. It's nice to have some well-educated students among them."

A thought struck Betha's mind, causing her brow to furrow. "Does the school serve both Protestant and Catholic children then?"

"All Scotch-Irish children." Colm used his whole torso to nod from the waist up. "The board is particular that the education doesn't exclude any student."

"How do you manage them all?" Was *he* Catholic?

"I manage," Colm said. He held her gaze, confidence emanating from his whole person and shutting down all of Betha's questions. He shifted his attention to Henry. "I'd like to consider you for one of my monitors. They each oversee a group of smaller boys working at the same level in a subject. Since you have an easy grasp of arithmetic, I think you could help others excel. Would you consider it?"

Henry's enthusiastic nod outpaced anything Betha had seen from him since before Seamus had him pulled from the New York school.

Colm remained as serious as a merchant striking a business deal. "Very well then. I'll announce my final monitor selections the first week of school. I look forward to having you in my class, Mr. Young."

"Thank you, sir."

Betha had grown so used to the tightness in her chest, she'd forgotten it wasn't normal until it unclenched, and she drew a deep breath for the first time in far too long. As she regarded Colm Gallagher and dipped her head in farewell, she felt the first flicker of hope fill her heart. Somehow she knew that this man was on Henry's side with her, and Henry had finally found a place to thrive.

As long as Seamus didn't mess anything else up for his son.

September 1827

Colm scratched one last name onto his list and leaned back from his desk to reread it. With the first day of the school year finally over, he had a pretty decent idea of who his monitors would be.

It was amazing what a person could learn in just one day of watching a group of children. The natural-born leaders emerged, for better or worse, and by the end of the morning's instruction, Colm had a feel for what to expect from his school year. After six years in classrooms, he was rarely surprised anymore.

His eyes landed on Henry Young's name and stopped there.

If there was a boy in his class that reminded Colm of himself, it was the serious Young boy. He had already shown himself exacting, conscientious, and eager to please. More than once, Colm had caught Henry's anxious eyes on him, as if asking, *Did I do it right, teacher?* If only he could warn the boy away from giving his allegiance too readily.

Colm shook his head, running his fingers across his forehead. Of course a student should seek to please his schoolmaster. It was the good and right order of things. It was also good and right that the schoolmaster should be worthy of that kind of respect. Not everyone was like Mr. MacMurrough. *He* wasn't. Please, Lord, let that much always be true.

Colm's mind wandered to Henry's pretty raven-haired aunt, wishing she had escorted Henry to school. Somehow in that first meeting, he'd gotten the impression that she was the type to hover over him, even if the boy was old enough to find his own way to school, but she hadn't. Would Colm's only interactions with her be reduced to school exhibition nights when all the parents were present for the children's recitations? It wasn't easy to find a good Irish girl who had decorum and all of her teeth. Betha had both, which meant that the Youngs were probably a merchant or craftsman family, not the typical shipbuilders and sailors of Fell's Point.

The front door banged open, breaking up Colm's thoughts. Betha Young's lovely image was chased away by that of his gangly brother filling the doorway.

"School's out, yet you're still here." Patrick pushed his coat open to rest his hands on his hips. His cap sat in its usual position on the back of his head, behind a mass of reddish-brown curls that had never truly been tamed in his entire life.

Colm dropped his pencil and cocked his head. "Yes, where there's quiet to get work done."

"Harsh." Patrick shot Colm a toothy grin. "Is the girls' teacher still here?"

"Miss O'Neill? I believe she's upstairs."

"Is she pretty?"

Colm narrowed his eyes. "Sarah O'Neill. You know her."

"Sarah?" A grimace crossed Patrick's face. "No then. Are you about done? I came to retrieve you."

"For what? I don't remember needing to be retrieved."

"For the freedmen society meeting." Patrick's eyes pleaded hopefully with Colm.

"I never agreed to go."

"You never agreed to go *yet*. I'm here to convince you."

"I don't have time for that, Patrick. I have responsibilities."

"You have excuses," Patrick returned. "Always more excuses."

"You have your causes, and I have mine." Colm gestured at the empty benches. "I cannot fix all the problems in the world, and neither can you. I'm doing the work I've been called to, and you need to accept that."

"Injustice is everyone's problem," Patrick shot back, his voice rising. "Where there are atrocities in a nation, everyone is affected. You can care and do something about more than one problem in the world at a time."

Colm sighed heavily. How many times had they had this exact same argument? "No, I can't. If I get involved with the freedmen society, I'll lose respect among the Irish. I won't be able to effect change from the outside any more than you could. On the inside, I can. I can teach the next generation that all men are created equal. But if I join the society, my students' parents will stop sending their children here, and I'll lose that ability to influence them for good."

"You make an awful lot of assumptions around here." Patrick scowled and started for the door. "It's really all a dung pile of your own fears. You can't influence anyone for good if you're too afraid to bring God into the classroom."

"I'm not afraid to bring God into anything," Colm snapped. "I simply teach to the specifications given by the founder, and that involves providing education for families of different beliefs."

Patrick stopped and turned back. "You're lying to yourself. And you only assume that supporting the freedmen society will lose your influence among the Irish. You don't actually know."

"I do know." Colm pushed down the ire rising in his chest as he came to his feet. "I do know, Patrick. I'm doing my job, and it's making a difference here. But don't let that stop you from doing what I can't."

"I wasn't planning on it." Patrick let the door slam shut behind him.

Colm let out a frustrated growl into the empty room and dropped into his chair. His brother was wrong about one thing.

Colm wasn't lying to himself. He knew the truth perfectly well.

He was only lying to Patrick.

2

The front door creaked, and Betha eased her foot off the treadle when footsteps sounded in the adjoining room. From his seat at the loom, Seamus offered a word of greeting. The rhythmic thumping of his loom continued, but Betha's spinning wheel stilled as she came to her feet and rubbed her stiff fingers together. She straightened, stretching her back, as Henry passed by his father and appeared in the middle room.

"Welcome home. How was school?"

"Grand." Henry set his books down and leaned in for a hug.

Betha pressed a kiss against his ruffled black hair and exhaled. As proud as she was to belong to a family of weavers, the profession was still isolating, and his hugs were a lifeline she looked forward to in anticipation every afternoon. They were the only physical touch she ever received.

"You're such a good boy," she murmured.

"Some of my boys were acting out. Mr. Gallagher wanted me to keep them in line, but they wouldn't mind."

Betha stepped back to peer into Henry's eyes. "What did you do?"

"I tried to talk to them." Henry's shoulders fell in a defeated shrug. "They wouldn't listen to me. They just act like children!"

Betha's laugh escaped before she could stop it. "They are children. And so are you, which you often forget."

Henry let out a groan. "Finally, Mr. Gallagher became stern with them and made them stay in from recess. But I didn't do my job. He wanted me to show more authority."

Betha pressed her lips against a smile. Henry had never had reason in his life to exercise authority; no one at his old school would have dreamed of giving him any. This Mr. Gallagher might be good for him.

"Did he have any suggestions to help you learn how?"

Henry furrowed his eyebrows. Shaking his head, he squirmed, and Betha knew he hadn't asked. "The other monitors just get mean and tattle. I don't want to get mean, Ma. But I sure felt like it today."

"It can be hard not to, especially when their behavior is a reflection on you to the teacher. Maybe it will help to remember when you were a squirmy little boy and what would have made you mind. Put yourself in their shoes."

Henry gave her a look. "I won't tell them they're going to hell if they don't study their lessons. Can I have a biscuit?"

He moved toward the kitchen behind her. Betha didn't stop him, although there was more of the conversation to be had. It was always a delicate balance to know what he needed to figure out for himself and when she should intervene. She still didn't understand Colm's methods for handling his classroom.

"Yes. Do your studies before the light's gone."

"I know, Ma." Henry stopped at the doorway. "I have to choose a piece to recite for the exhibition."

Betha lifted her eyebrows. "Do you have anything in mind?"

"Most everyone else is quoting the myths or the Bible."

Betha knew how he felt about Cu Chulainn, the most famous of the old Irish legends, a man who lived and died by the sword and adultery. Seamus blamed Betha's moralizing for the way his son rejected the sacred stories of their culture, but that was all Henry.

"Wordsworth, perhaps?"

Henry wrinkled his nose. "Too girly."

"Well, there's nothing wrong with quoting the Bible."

Henry's lips were pursed in thought, but a moment later they relaxed. "Daideó had a book . . . What was his name who wrote the poems . . . The butterfly one, remember? And the frog?"

"Bunyan."

"I think I could find something in there."

Betha backed toward her wheel before Seamus barked at her for talking instead of working. "I think you could."

She returned to her chair and tugged the flax fibers between her fingers as Henry slipped into the kitchen. It wasn't that long ago that Seamus was this boy, possessing childlike faith and determination to do right. Betha offered up her daily prayer that Seamus would return to that path before Henry followed in his father's footsteps and left it.

The shadows were long in the middle room, and Henry had gone out to the streets to play when Betha rose from her seat, lit a candle, and stoked the coals in the kitchen hearth. By the time the kettle sputtered, the cornmeal batter was mixed up and the kitchen warm and cozy. The loom went quiet, and Seamus's seat scraped across the floor. Betha was pouring two mugs of tea, a folded towel protecting her hand from the hot kettle, when Seamus plodded in.

He rolled his shirtsleeves down to his wrists, pausing to accept the tea from Betha. He nodded his disheveled head toward the middle room. "Is that pile all you did today?"

Betha blew on her cup and set it back down. Seamus knew perfectly well it was "all" she had done today. She'd been spinning for him for more than ten years. The butter in the skillet began to sizzle, so she dropped dollops of batter into it. Immediately the rich aroma swirled through the room.

"We need to produce more linen than we used to if we want to stay afloat in this market, Betha."

"Your loom stayed active all day," Betha reminded him. "You're already weaving for half the spinners on the street. People buy Young linen because it's quality. If I wanted to make inferior thread, I'd go work for a factory and save my ears from your complaining." She shooed at him with her hands, but he leaned his hip against the table.

"Come on, Betha. Can't you make a good quality thread just a little faster?"

"For what?" Betha crossed her arms. "So you can go spend it at the pub? I'll not work my fingers to the bone for that."

"You'll send us to the poorhouse."

That produced a chuckle Betha couldn't hold back. They were a long way from the poorhouse, and a few extra yards of thread each day wouldn't keep them out of it.

"Get on with you! You'd have no linen to sell the bleachers if not for my wheel, and you'd do well to not abuse me for it."

Seamus shook his head and sighed, but his eyes twinkled. At the end of the day, she knew he'd rather have linen he was proud to put his name behind. If he wanted a greater quantity, he could hire more spinners—and weavers.

He changed the subject. "Did Henry finish his studies?"

Betha nodded. "He's a good boy. Responsible."

Seamus indicated the woodpile. "He didn't bring in more firewood."

"Are you staying for supper?"

"I'll have some of those corn cakes." Seamus eyed the crackling pan hungrily.

"If I'm just cooking for me and Henry, I don't need a lot of firewood. But you should think about getting a stove, Seamus. It would be more efficient and take less wood." Betha slid a cake onto a plate and handed it to him.

Seamus tore at it with his fingers gingerly, allowing the steam to escape. "We'll have to see how the linen market is this month. Renting the wagon and team for the move was expensive." He shoved the cake into his mouth, and Betha turned back to the skillet.

When the second batch was frying, she reached for her tea and sipped. Seamus grabbed a second cake while she watched and retrieved his cap from the peg by the kitchen door. "Lock the door when you're inside," he said, his way of saying "I love you."

Before Betha knew it, he was gone to spend his evening jawing with the men at the neighborhood pub. He'd come home late from McColgan's with all the news, local and abroad, and dozens of other curiosity bits he'd probably forget to tell his sister. Then at first light, he'd be up again at his loom.

Betha scooped beans leftover from the midday meal next to her corn cakes. Balancing her plate and tea, she crossed through the house to the front door and sat on the stoop of her corner rowhouse. Once settled, she stared at her plate. It would be nice to have more variety in their dishes from the simple meals she'd learned so long ago from her mother. Back in New York, she'd heard about new books explaining how to prepare elegant dishes, but she never had time to go to the bookstore, and the money had always been needed elsewhere. Maybe in this new chapter of their lives, she could figure out a way to make it happen.

Through the dusk, a crowd of boys was visible kneeling in the dirt at the other end of the street, probably shooting marbles. It looked like Henry's brown cap was among them, but it was hard to say in an immigrant neighborhood. A tall, skinny German girl came by with a stick in an attempt to round up chickens, and paperboys with empty sacks waved goodbye to each other before disappearing into dimly lit houses.

She considered getting up and taking a walk, find another woman to talk to, but couldn't produce the energy to leave her step. Jealousy rose in her at the thought of Seamus at McColgan's. It was so easy for him to make friends. Even when she had the time, she lacked the spark that Seamus possessed. Seamus with his crinkling blue eyes, the thick, wavy black hair every woman coveted, and the build like a street brawler. People were just drawn to him and generally found his sister easy to overlook.

Betha finished her dinner and set aside the plate as the next-door neighbor's husband passed, tipping his hat to her. A called greeting captured her attention, and she pivoted her head to see Mrs. Oliver on her doorstep, children peering out from behind her. But Mrs. Oliver was turned away from her husband, speaking to a young couple approaching from the other direction.

Mr. Oliver met them on the street, and a friendly conversation ensued between the two couples, with Betha and the Oliver children equal spectators.

The younger woman was as pretty as she was talkative, escorted by a lanky man with a mass of russet curls who interrupted every other thing she said with a joke or added detail that brought smiles to his listeners. His companion asked about the Olivers' other children, and Mr. Oliver turned to gesture down the street toward Henry's pack.

Following his gaze, the young woman's eyes passed Betha on her stoop and then swung back again to offer her a smile of acknowledgment. Mr. Oliver noted her diverted attention and extended a hand to Betha.

"Have you met our new neighbors, the Youngs?"

"I haven't." The young woman stepped in Betha's direction, so she pressed a hand against the doorjamb and came to her feet. "I'm Maisie, and this is my brother Patrick. You're new to the neighborhood?"

Betha guessed that Maisie was a few years younger than herself, her brown hair plaited beneath a wide-crowned bonnet from which ribbons flowed modishly around her shoulders. Her dress, though simple, was dyed a blue brighter than anything Betha had ever cared enough to attempt.

Betha nodded. "Betha Young. Yes, we came recently from New York."

"What brought you to Baltimore?"

Betha swallowed uneasily. It was an innocent question, one anyone would ask a new acquaintance.

"We needed a change," she said simply. She'd have to think of a more reasonable answer to give such a question in the future. "Are you from here?"

"Lived here my whole life. Are you married?"

At that, Patrick returned to his conversation with the Olivers, and Maisie and Betha were left in privacy.

"No, I live with my brother and his son. Just the three of us are left. We're linen weavers," Betha added, nodding toward the open house.

"Oh, lovely."

Betha got the feeling Maisie would have responded the same, regardless of which industry she named. "I'm a seamstress, and Patrick's a newspaper man. But our father is a revenue officer for the city. We live on the other side of Jones Falls but are just on our way home from a meeting. Patrick likes to go to these kinds of things, and I go with him since no one else will. Have you found a church here?"

Betha clasped her hands in front of her, aware that her answer would likely determine the future of this new relationship. But the Olivers were Presbyterian, and Maisie and Patrick were their friends, so . . .

"We attended Second Presbyterian last week since it's close."

12

Maisie nodded. "With Reverend Breckinridge. You're welcome to visit First with us. My brothers might say otherwise, but you would probably like either church just as well. They split over politics, you know, before I was born. I think all the arguments are outdated now, especially since Breckinridge came to work with old Dr. Glendy."

Henry appeared by Betha's side, bringing her to the present. A quick glance around the street revealed that darkness had nearly overtaken it and all the boys were moving inside. Betha touched his arm. "Wash up; supper is waiting for you inside."

He nodded and left.

"My nephew, Henry," Betha told Maisie after he had gone. "Thank you for the invitation to your church. I've not really met anyone besides the neighbors." She thought of Colm Gallagher. He almost shouldn't count, as short as their encounter was, but for some reason, she thought of him while at her wheel more than she did the Olivers. It only made sense, since Henry was with the dimpled schoolteacher and his revolutionary ideas while she worked.

"We must change that," Maisie declared, and Betha's heart lifted. "We should meet up at the market. Oh, make sure to get your fruit from Lanahan's; theirs is the freshest."

Betha nodded, trying to keep up.

"Would you like to go shopping with us after work Saturday? We usually go to the market in the mornings before work, but Saturday night is the best time to stroll around Gaither's and do the rest of our shopping. You'll meet people in no time."

Betha cocked her head. Didn't Maisie's father do most of the family's shopping? She supposed she did have stores she wanted to explore, and if it was the best way to make friends, she should consider it. "I would like that," she said at the same moment that Patrick called Maisie's name.

Maisie backed toward her brother with one last grin for Betha. "Saturday then. It'll be grand."

Betha remained against her doorframe as the two young people ambled off into the dusk. Mr. Oliver took a deep breath and shook his head after them. "That boy is trouble," he said to his wife.

Mrs. Oliver returned with something Betha couldn't hear, and Mr. Oliver stepped up into the house. The door closed, leaving Betha alone with the quiet street, wondering about his declaration.

Patrick and Maisie seemed nice enough. Sure, but he was some kind of card, but nothing about him struck her as deserving of the label "trouble." He was even a Presbyterian. Apparently she'd have to keep her head up in this city if people weren't what they appeared to be.

3

Betha resisted the temptation to ask Maisie about Patrick on Saturday. Instead she settled for the kind of vague questions polite company were allowed to ask and did her best to listen between the lines as Maisie stood next to her at the counter of Gaither's Dry Goods.

She asked herself why she cared when Patrick wasn't the type of person she would normally befriend, but something about the duo fascinated her. And the thought of him being trouble brought a level of intrigue she couldn't shake.

Maisie's younger sister, Mor, and her friend and fellow seamstress Ava had joined them. Ava was tall, with pale skin, emerald eyes, and thick brown hair. Betha could see why they were good friends; Ava was thoughtful where Maisie was vivacious, and both had obvious respect for the other. Betha ran a finger over each of the cottons the proprietor brought out, wondering what it would be like to have a close friend. To have an outlet for her thoughts somewhere other than Seamus.

"You know, Betha and her brother are linen weavers," Maisie told Ava when the proprietor carried a bolt of linen lawn to the back.

"There is nothing like linen for the summertime." Ava met Betha's eyes over Maisie's head. "Where do you sell?"

"My brother was meeting with a bleacher today," Betha admitted. "But if you need a weaver, Seamus can take on more households."

Maisie touched the sleeve of Betha's handmade dress. "You do lovely work."

Betha dipped her head, self-conscious. "My mother taught me."

"Were your parents born here, or did they immigrate?"

"They immigrated when my brother was little, before I was born. Yours?"

Maisie nodded toward Mor and Ava. "Our grandparents all came during the Ulster persecution. The raised rents forced them off their land. They say it's because they're Presbyterian."

"My grandparents weren't allowed to marry," Ava added.

The tale was nothing new to Betha. "My da came after the rebellion. He doesn't call it that; they were just trying to reform the government. But it wasn't safe for him to stay after it failed."

The other girls grimaced, showing their empathy.

The proprietor returned with a selection of ribbon, and Ava perked up at the sight of the bright colors. Once she made her selection and completed the purchase, the group moved on to the next store. As they strolled through the streets, Maisie stopped several people to introduce them to Betha until Betha's head nearly spun.

"Do you know everyone in Baltimore?" she finally asked, and Maisie laughed.

"Not at all."

"She just makes friends wherever she goes," Ava said lightly.

Maisie tilted her face to hide her smile. "Sure, but people are interesting. They all have their own stories. And I aim to find you a husband in no time."

Betha simply stared, her face flaming red. "What makes you think I'm searchin' for one?" What would Seamus and Henry do if she were to marry? The thought was so inconceivable, she had only ever dreamed about it in far-off terms, not as something that could happen imminently.

The shocking proclamation sprouted a growing distinction between Betha and her new friends in her heart. By the time she left New York, most of her close connections had been married women. It was how she felt most days herself, as mother to Henry and in partnership with Seamus. She never sashayed through town with girls who didn't have children to think of.

"You never found me one," Ava teased. "Or your own self."

"You simply wouldn't accept the choices I gave you," Maisie retorted. "And I'm too picky; I'll probably never find one."

"Ah, so ye have a brother of yours in mind for our new friend."

"So what if I do?" Maisie squared her shoulders, accepting the challenge.

Patrick? Would now be a good time to ask what sort of trouble Patrick was, if her future was being arranged with him? Betha looked entreatingly at Mor for help, but the girl couldn't stop giggling.

"I wouldn't give Patrick to her." Ava's voice held a warning. "He's too big a task for any one woman. 'Twouldn't be fair to her."

"I wasn't thinking of Patrick for Betha. I have more than one brother." Maisie marched down the street, her chin high.

Ava lifted a shoulder and pursed her lips as though acknowledging the merit of the statement. Mor only covered another giggle with her hand.

"Ava." Betha hurried after her. "Ava, what's wrong with her brothers that you wouldn't have them?"

Ava turned, grinning, and hooked her arm through Betha's. "They're a fine family and a worthy one to marry into. It's only that I've known the boys since they were wee things. It's hard to be swept off one's feet by someone who used to put grasshoppers in your bonnet, and I want a love like Orpheus and Eurydice."

Betha bit her tongue in time before she blurted out her shock. Did women still consider such myths as something more plausible than daydreams? Wasn't everyone just looking for a man who would provide and not wander? She had all that with Seamus, and she knew what to expect with him. Sure, she'd always wanted babies—as many of them as possible—but a love like the stories . . . well, the very idea was crazy.

"What kind of trouble is Patrick?" she asked instead, then clamped her hand over her mouth. "I didn't mean—I barely met him, but I heard . . ."

Mor laughed from behind Ava, and Betha's face flamed even brighter. Somehow, she'd thought Mor had headed down the street after Maisie.

"Patrick has—" Ava stopped, considering. "Patrick has a good heart. A big heart. But it gets ahead of his head, is all. It's hard to keep up with him and his ideas."

Betha nodded, forcing herself to not ask any more questions. As she quickstepped with Ava and Mor to catch up with Maisie, one question still swarmed like a pesky gnat around her head.

What about the other brothers?

Colm finished his inspection of the spelling classes and returned to his desk. His eyes swept the noisy classroom aisles one by one.

Class one was tracing letters in sand with their fingers. Class two crowded around their monitor, copying two-letter clusters onto their slates. Class three listened for the monitor's dictation, writing on their slates in unison. Classes four and five stood in rows, reciting spelling words to their monitors. The monitor of class six made a careful inspection of his students' slates, and the upper levels gathered around the cards displaying their words to study for the day.

All was exactly as it should be. He moved his eyes to the clock. After allowing the gentle murmur to continue for five more minutes, he stood and tapped his bell. Students shuffled back to their seats, and the monitors returned their instructional cards to the nails on the wall.

"Let's begin arithmetic," he said, keeping his voice at a normal level. Joseph Lancaster said in his teaching model that the students should hear the master's voice as little as possible; thus they would attend to it when it was used.

The arithmetic monitors rose and retrieved their assigned problem cards from the wall, and the room shifted to form the arithmetic classes. Colm took the opportunity to copy out the next day's assignments for each class from Lancaster's book. Once the assignments were given, it was up to the monitors to present them to the boys, the boys to listen and obey, and him to oversee it all.

A voice rose above the scratching sound of chalk pencils, and Colm looked up. Class six, of course. It always was. Henry Young leaned across his circle, trying to reason with little Sam Wilson. Colm straightened and watched as Sam crossed his arms over his chest. Henry closed his eyes briefly and blew out his breath. When he opened his eyes, he said something that made the other boys titter but only hardened Sam's face.

At that, Henry cut his gaze Colm's way and saw himself being watched. Henry's cheeks burned red and he turned back, speaking to Sam through gritted teeth. Sam wrote furiously on his slate before turning it so Henry could see. Henry tipped his head back and sighed, then gestured for the boy next to Sam to proceed—presumably to redo the problem that Sam figured incorrectly, which was the correct move to make.

Sam muttered under his breath, the boy tossed his head in reaction, and Sam jabbed him hard with his elbow. The boy bit back a cry that was obviously more angry than hurt. Henry came to his feet, snapping about behaving loud enough to turn every head in the room.

Colm's heart sank as he stood. "Class six. Please come for your recitations." He hated to intervene and undermine his monitors' rapport with their students, but apparently after three weeks, Henry still had none.

The group obediently moved to stand in a line before his desk. With one pointed look at the rest of the room, Colm returned the other levels to their studies. From there, his eyes moved to Henry at the end of the line of class six. The boy's hands clutched the slate behind his back, his head bowed, everything from his collar up a deep shade of red. Colm moved down the line. Sam Wilson had the good sense to look scared. Everyone else stood solemn and silent, unwilling to add fuel to whatever fire was about to burn.

Colm returned to his desk and picked up his pen, poising it over a blank card. "Mr. Young, would you delineate for me please the nature of Mr. Wilson's offenses?"

"Insubordination," Henry mumbled without lifting his head.

"Excuse me?"

"Insubordination," Henry said, more clearly.

Colm wrote it on the card.

"Inattentiveness."

Colm copied it down. "And?" he prompted when Henry fell silent.

"Fighting."

Colm added it to the card, reached into his desk for a string, and tied both ends to the card.

"Mr. Wilson."

Sam dragged his feet in his approach, and Colm stood to place the string around his neck, displaying his sins on a sign over his chest. Colm tipped his head. "You can stand by my desk until the end of the day." Sam moved to the side, and Colm returned to the silent remainder of class six. "Mr. Young, I request your presence at this desk after school lets out."

"Yes, sir."

"Now let us proceed with the multiplication recitations. You may begin."

When everyone else was gone at the end of the day, Colm cleared his desk while Henry stood kneading his cap directly before it. Once everything was tidy, he retook his seat before taking a long look at the boy, keeping his face blank. His heart ached. Never before had he so wanted to see a monitor succeed. It must be why he had given as many chances as he had, because never before had he had a monitor who simply refused to follow class protocol in regards to reporting bad behavior.

What could he say that would get through this time? *Lord, grant me wisdom.*

"Mr. Young—this classroom has expectations that must be met in order to maintain decorum. I have expectations."

"Yes, sir."

"But you know this. You know the expectations."

"I do, sir."

"Which leads me to the conclusion that there should have been two boys standing by my desk today with insubordination signs around their necks."

Henry's head jerked up and down once.

Colm was sorely tempted to put him out of his misery and simply remove him from the duties of monitor. Maybe he just wasn't cut out for leadership. Or not ready. The boy was young.

"Multiplication is a valuable skill for students to master. It will serve them well their whole lives. But my particular level six class is unable to achieve mastery if they are distracted by disruptive behavior. The entire class suffers."

"If I may say, sir."

"Please do."

"Sir, Sam Wilson acts out because he's trying to prove a point. If I get him in trouble, his point is made, and he'll never come to see the real problem."

"Which is?"

"That he needs Jesus. That there's no point in just being good."

Colm swallowed, taken aback. "There's not *no* point, Son. Helping a man live a life as close as possible to God's design for their good is not completely wasted."

"But the Wilsons don't go to church, sir. All Sam really knows about it is that being religious takes the fun out of life. He thinks that God is just mean and bossy. He knows I'm a Christian. If I tattletale, he'll know he's right."

Colm felt his mouth go dry. How did this ten-year-old have a better handle on his understanding of God than Colm himself did most days? But Henry didn't have Mr. MacMurrough's voice drilled into his head, causing him to regularly confuse MacMurrough with his conscience.

"I didn't know he didn't go to church," Colm managed.

Henry sighed, his shoulders slumping. "At my old school, the teacher used to drill us in the catechism and read the Bible every day. It's just that . . . over time, it teaches boys who God really is. They'd see it for themselves. Sometimes I think every school should do that."

In other words, him. Henry was saying as respectfully as he could that Colm wasn't meeting *his* expectations.

Colm cleared his throat, feeling more uncomfortable by this conversation than he'd counted on. "Perhaps in places where that's not permitted, God places boys like you who can share His Word with those who need to hear it."

Did he seriously just tell a ten-year-old boy that it was *his* job to share the gospel with Colm's students since Colm refused to do it? But there were no rules against children reading the Bible in school. Just against Colm doing it. How did that make sense? Colm looked at Henry, serious and steady in front of him, and wondered how it was that he was the one squirming in his seat.

Colm lowered his voice. "But Henry—getting frustrated at Sam in class and allowing him to disrupt multiplication drills is not showing him God more clearly than bringing the matter to the schoolmaster's attention would, like you were instructed to do."

Henry's face now reflected the shame that Colm felt. When the boy began blinking rapidly to clear his damp eyes, Colm couldn't take the guilt anymore.

"You think it would help? For the whole school to hear from the Bible every day?"

"I know it would," Henry choked out.

Unable to sit still anymore, Colm moved around his desk to put his hand on Henry's shoulder. "I will give what you said serious thought. But despite my faults, it does not excuse the fact that I have one monitor who does not abide by the classroom rules. If you find my methods untenable, you have permission—within reason—to approach me and present your case, but no student has permission to defy the schoolmaster."

"No, sir." Henry's voice wobbled dangerously.

Colm couldn't allow the poor boy to lose his composure in front of him; neither of them would ever recover. Not Colm, and especially not the tenderhearted boy who had in the past five minutes entirely captured his heart.

"I will have no repeats of insubordination. From now on, you will report behavior issues to me like the rest of the monitors."

"Yes, sir."

Colm reached back to his desk for his hat and satchel. "We can start walking so your aunt isn't worried about where you are. I have a question I wanted to ask you."

"Sir?" Henry didn't move from his spot.

Colm crossed the floor and held the door open. "I'd like to hear more about your school in New York."

For a moment, Colm thought Henry would actually refuse. But the boy put on a resolute face, tugged his cap on, and followed Colm out the door.

"It was a normal school. Like all the others, I suppose."

"Except mine."

"Oliver Hibernian has a new way of doing things, but it's not all bad."

Colm couldn't help his laugh as he sauntered down the street by Henry's side. "You are very frank, my boy."

"Was that disrespectful? I'm sorry. I didn't mean to be disrespectful. Honest."

"Oh, I didn't doubt that. But you liked your old teachers?"

Henry was silent for a moment. "I like you better, sir. Since I'm being honest."

Colm dipped his head, pressing his lips against the smile that tempted to form. "A respectful way of stating the truth."

He heard Henry let out his breath. "Mr. Gallagher? Sometimes I think I would have been fine. But my da and ma, they wouldn't put up with the goings-on there. My ma especially—she needs to feel like she takes good care of me. So I didn't say anything when they decided to move. Sometimes I feel bad because I know moving was an expense and my da complains about it. Do you think I should have told them? That I could handle the problems at school?"

Colm put his hands in his coat pockets. "Don't you suppose they already know that? Who knows you better than your parents?"

"They seemed more upset by it than I was."

"Guess we just have to trust them then. Maybe there's more going on than you knew. Maybe even things that had nothing to do with you."

"Maybe," Henry said in a polite tone, clearly unconvinced.

When he fell silent, Colm turned to internally questioning his motives for walking Henry home. He intended to give his merciful explanation for Henry's tardiness before the boy had a chance to tell a more self-incriminating one. It was entirely in the proper order of things that a schoolmaster call on his students and meet their families. But had that really been on his mind when he grabbed his hat and led Henry out the door?

Four long weeks had passed since he'd met and last seen Betha Young. She was like a tick his skin couldn't shake off, and he had to know if his memory had gotten carried away from reality or if she really was worth the intrusive daydreams he suffered from. It didn't help that every day he grew to love her nephew a little more and attributed Henry's character to his pretty caregiver.

"Here we are," Henry said, stopping before a two-story brick rowhouse exactly like the ones most of Colm's students lived in. But there was no squalor or loud voices, crying babies, or stench coming from inside like some of the homes he'd been in.

Colm hesitated briefly before following Henry through the door. The clacking of a loom paused, and his eyes adjusted to the inside to see a man rising from behind the apparition in a cloud of dust and step around a puddle of water on the floor.

"Da, this is my teacher, Mr. Gallagher. Mr. Gallagher, this is my da."

The man stepped toward Colm, hand extended. "Seamus Young. Is there a problem?"

"Colm Gallagher." He accepted Seamus's hand. "Not at all. Henry stayed after class to explain a situation to me, and I took the opportunity to walk him home."

The inside of the house was simple, with no extra furnishings or decorations other than what a family of artisans would need to live and work. Colm remembered in time that linen required humidity before he embarrassed himself by asking about the water on the floor.

Seamus relaxed. "That's grand. Welcome. Please, have a seat. Betha?"

Colm's eyes traveled through the dust swirling in the rays from the window into the next room, where they tangled with those of Betha.

She rose from her spinning wheel in a graceful movement, wiping her hands down the front of her crisp white apron. "Mr. Gallagher. What an honor to have you. I'll bring drinks in."

"Oh, I don't need to stay. I only—"

Protesting was pointless, and Colm knew it. Besides, he had no intention of leaving, cad that he was.

"You'll stay for supper, of course. We're so pleased you came."

Her face mirrored her words, lending them sincerity, and Colm was grateful for the Irish disposition that didn't hide what it felt. He didn't have to wonder; Betha Young was every bit as happy to see him as he was to see her.

4

Betha bolted into the kitchen, her heart racing. Colm Gallagher, here. In all his tall, dimpled, and uncurmudgeonly glory. With no warning. What was she to serve for supper? She reached a hand up and patted her hair, hoping it was where she'd left it when she braided it that morning. There was little she could do about it now; he had already seen her.

She stoked the fire, put the kettle on, and poured ale into two mugs. The men were where she'd left them in the center of the front room, listening to Henry regale his father with a story about his teacher, face alight. Betha handed the mugs over to Seamus and Colm.

Colm held her gaze, thanking her as he took his.

Flustered by his nearness, Betha wiped her damp palms on her apron. "Of course. Henry, come get your milk and biscuit and let the men do the talkin'."

"What led you to become a teacher?" Seamus asked as Betha backed out of the room. She hated to miss the answer, but neither could she let their guest wait overlong for his meal. She scurried back to the kitchen with Henry behind her.

"How was school today? It's an exciting thing to have your teacher here," Betha said as she reached for her stew pot.

Henry helped himself to a biscuit and plopped into a wooden chair at the table. When he didn't answer right away, Betha sent him a glance over her shoulder. "Henry? What is it?"

"Nothing." He expelled a sigh before taking a bite.

"You're not goin' to tell me about it?"

Henry took his time chewing while Betha pulled vegetables and sausages out from the larder and crates around the room. In short order, her knife was swiftly chopping and dicing.

"I like Mr. Gallagher," Henry said. "Ma, why do you suppose he never reads the Bible in school?"

Betha blinked at Henry. "He doesn't?"

"Never."

Her mind scrambled to catch up. Surely the man wasn't an atheist? She tried to replay her conversation with him on the first day but couldn't recall exactly what was said. She must be a simpleton, because she'd apparently been blind to his real character.

"I've no idea, Henry. Do you think he believes in God?"

Henry looked at her as if she had lost her mind. Maybe she had. "Of course he does, Ma. He told me he'd think about reading the Bible. But I thought it was done in all the schools. He said something about it not being permitted."

"No, I don't suppose they do at schools where the teacher doesn't live by the book himself. I hadn't heard of Oliver Hibernian banning it."

Henry swallowed the last bite of his biscuit. "Would you rather have a teacher who lives by the book even if he doesn't read it in class than one who reads it in class but never lives by it himself?"

Like Seamus? Betha filled her pot with water and set it over the fire. "I'd rather the schools had teachers that did both, make no mistake."

Henry nodded his agreement and scraped his chair back. "Can I go back in there now?"

"After you bring in my firewood."

Henry scurried toward the kitchen door. When the woodbox was filled, he bolted back to the front room, leaving Betha in the quiet with her thoughts and snatches of Colm's deep voice in the front room. Her opinion of the teacher had plummeted since the time he entered. Maybe it was best she got Maisie and Ava's girlish ideas about love out of her head now, before she ended up doing something foolish and actually considered abandoning Henry for a man.

Seamus wasn't doing his part to raise the boy in the nurture and admonition of the Lord, and it sounded like Colm wasn't either. It was up to Betha and the Lord to fight against the apathy of the two men in the front room and keep Henry grounded in the Word of God. All her efforts for Seamus once upon a time had been wasted, and she could not fail at her post again.

Colm sat upright at the supper table, his spoon halfway to his mouth. Betha Young no doubt knew how to make an excellent stew. She must have an herb garden out back, because each bite held multiple bursts of fresh flavor. With black wisps framing her milky-white face, her eyes looked even bluer, framed by a feminine set of dark lashes.

It was unfortunate that what would have been a delightful experience was marred by this interrogation he now found himself undergoing. With the exception of his grueling teacher examination six years ago, he'd never felt so much like he was facing MacMurrough again as he did now. There was a type of conversation where people asked each other friendly questions to get to know each other. This was not that.

He'd only ever met the woman once before; where did this obvious distrust come from? She'd already asked about his education and religious upbringing, and now she was challenging the Lancaster method. What was it, she wanted to know, that induced him to utilize such a newfangled approach?

"Believe it or not, I'm not the one who chose it." Colm hoped his calm reply would smooth away some of the lines on her forehead. "Oliver Hibernian has been following the method since its inception. I studied Joseph Lancaster's writings in school, among those of other modern educators, and was intrigued by it. While it is one of the reasons I was drawn to apply for the position at Oliver, the founder, John Oliver, is the one who chose it."

Betha folded her hands in her lap. "And what is it in particular that Lancaster does better than other programs?"

Colm lowered his spoon and leaned back in his chair. "There are numerous advantages. It allows one schoolmaster to manage larger classroom sizes. It teaches children responsibility and to take ownership for their education. It reduces the amount of books needed so poor children are given an equal opportunity to learn."

"But what of the subjects taught? Does it limit what topics are presented?"

"Not at all. It focuses on spelling, reading, writing, and arithmetic. I read Morse's geography and history to the whole class, and once students know how to read, they are able to explore those topics more in depth through the textbooks available at the school."

"And what of the Bible?"

Ah. Here at last was the heart of the issue. Colm avoided glancing at Henry, who must have made a report to his aunt when he was in the kitchen.

"The absence of the Bible in the Oliver curriculum is a choice of the school board, not of the Lancaster method, ma'am."

"Of all the things! Do you agree with the decision?"

Colm looked from Seamus back to Betha. "It doesn't matter whether I do or not."

Betha Young glared at him with a ferocity that nearly melted Colm in his seat. He slowly inhaled, considering his words carefully.

"I do agree with it, to an extent. I've known teachers to use the Word of God as a weapon to ensure good behavior in their classrooms that ultimately leaves students more bitter against God than without it. Perhaps schools should best focus on the skills children need to master like reading and arithmetic and leave the Bible to their own parents and trained theologians on Sundays."

"I agree," Seamus said, placing both hands on the table. "Schools are for practical subjects. Leave the Bible for the churches."

Henry fidgeted in his seat, drawing Colm's attention. "Did you have something to say?" Betha asked him.

"It's just that I think that's what Mr. Piper did in New York. Used the Bible as a weapon."

"Your old teacher?" Colm asked, and Henry nodded. "I'm sincerely sorry that happened to you. It happened to me as a boy too. Teachers who don't understand God's Word shouldn't be the ones wielding it before children."

Betha lifted her chin. "Do you understand it?"

"Excuse me?"

"If you've been raised by a Presbyterian family in church as you claim, I should think you would be one of the teachers capable of wielding it well."

Colm briefly pressed his lips together, more than a little disquieted over the acknowledgment that Henry's response to their similar negative experience was vastly different and much more acute than his had been. And still was. "I hope so, ma'am. Although it doesn't change the school's express requirements that the Bible not be part of the curriculum." He was starting to hate the sound of the words every time they passed through his lips.

"This entire country is turning away from God to selfishness and debauchery. Every Christian in the public square has a duty to God first to teach His Word and make disciples. If you take the Bible out of schools, why—" Betha threw her hands in the air. "Who knows what will happen next?"

Seamus snorted. "You're worried over naught. There's more religious fervor than there ever was when I was a boy. You went to the camp meeting, Betha; you saw it. People coming to the altar by the hundreds. And Charles Finney is attracting giant crowds wherever he preaches. You don't have to worry that religiosity is in danger of dying out just because Colm spends his days teaching spelling instead of Psalms."

Betha huffed and stood to clear the dinner away.

"You went to a camp meeting?" Colm asked quickly before she left. She nodded.

"In New York?" Colm had heard plenty about the revivals, but most of the reports were as fantastical as they were questionable, of converts howling and writhing in the aisles.

"On the way here. We passed one in New Jersey, and I made Seamus let me go to it."

"I would be fascinated to hear about it by someone who's actually gone." Colm studied her. The little Irishwoman had surprised him, revealing acumen along with her backbone. Rather than feeling threatened by her judgment of him, he found admiration and respect prevailing.

Betha gave him a small smile. "Sure then. Come back next week, and we can talk about it. It's not something that can be summed up easily."

"No indeed," Seamus muttered.

"I will. Supper was very nice, thank you."

She gathered the empty bowls, and Colm let her go. He excused himself shortly afterward, and a few minutes later hailed a cab, on a mission.

The librarian at the University of Maryland was about to lock the library door when Colm arrived and slid inside. He strode to the education section, and it didn't take long before he had a short stack ready to check out. His errand complete, he tucked the books and pamphlets under his arm and hurried home.

5

The following Friday, Colm walked home directly after school. Before he reached his father's Georgian-style house, the savory aroma of supper preparations beckoned him inside. His stepmother was feeding the stove in the kitchen, sweaty gray wisps coming loose from her braid.

"Afternoon, Colm," Maisie called from the table, where she punched into a mound of dough. Beside her, Mor shelled beans with Lyla. Colm turned around to wink at the younger faction of half and stepsiblings strewn around the room with their samplers, slates, and books in hand.

"You're home early." Bridget straightened from the stove and wiped her dirty hands on the apron covering her stout middle.

"I'm only getting cleaned up and then will have dinner with a student."

"One less mouth to feed," Maisie teased. "Ben will eat your portion."

"He's welcome to it." Colm grinned at the boy stretched out on the floor. The redheaded youth was all arms and legs and appeared to have grown close to a foot in the past year. Colm well remembered being that age and the endless appetite that came with it.

He stepped over Ben's legs and jogged up the stairs to the room he shared with Patrick. Last Friday's dinner at the Youngs had been an impromptu decision, but this week, he had time to improve his presentation. After washing his hands and face in the basin, he reached for a towel. Mid-move, his eyes fell on the stack of books by his bed, and the words of Benjamin Rush flooded his mind:

The only foundation for a useful education in a republic is to be laid in Religion. Without this there can be no virtue, and without virtue there can be no liberty, and liberty is the object and life of all republican governments.

Colm tossed the towel aside, pulled out his comb, and set to work. *Without virtue there can be no liberty.* Hadn't history proven that too many times to count? And according to Rush, religion wasn't just something to be added to the school day; it was the foundation everything else was built on.

It was the reason for studying science and arithmetic—because they were how God structured his creation.

It was the reason for studying reading—because God gave His Word in written form.

It was the reason for studying spelling and writing—because believers were called to be preachers, teachers, and evangelists, communicating the gospel in the public sphere.

Without a foundation, what reason did boys like Sam Wilson have to apply themselves to their studies? Merely so they could grow up to have a decent job and make a living wage?

Colm tied his cravat and smoothed his hands down the front of his frock coat. Making a living wage was enough of a motivator for most boys. No one wanted to go hungry or give up their freedom to indenture themselves. He exchanged his cap for his low top hat and headed down the stairs and out into the streets, competing thoughts wrestling for the upper hand in his mind.

"Lord, lead me into a correct understanding of the place of Your Word in my school," he said aloud. He didn't hurry this time, taking care to avoid mud and slop in the streets. No need to arrive at the Youngs out of breath just to be covered in filth and smell like a barnyard.

The table was set when he arrived this time, Betha's spinning wheel set back in the corner and the piles of flax and lint tidied away. Henry took his hat and closed the door behind him, his cheeks and neck scrubbed until they were ruddy. Apparently Colm's second visit was significant to everyone.

"Come watch my da work," Henry urged. "He promised he'd do a few rows to show you."

Seamus stood from behind the loom to welcome Colm, then retook his seat as his son and guest watched. Dings and clanks from the kitchen joined with the smell of garlic and onion to tell him Betha was hard at work. Colm took in the complicated apparatus Seamus managed, lulled by the rhythm of it. The job appeared mind-numbing but also held a certain satisfaction as new rows appeared and the pattern emerged.

"I've rarely had the privilege of watching a loom of this type in action. Does Betha spin this thread?" Colm stepped around a wet spot on the floor.

"She did this one. She spins a stronger, thinner thread than you'll find anywhere else, and it makes a linen that's smooth and soft. I also weave for some of the housewives on the street."

"It was your father's trade?"

Seamus finished another row, set the shuttlecock aside, and came to his feet. "There was more demand for fine linen back when he trained me. He brought his loom in crates from Ireland when I was a wee thing. When I came of age, he built this one for me. It's lighter and faster than the one he used, which I have in storage upstairs."

"Did you lose your parents recently?"

Betha came in then in a pretty dress dyed the color of mulberries, with a white kerchief tucked into the neckline and a clean apron tied over it. "Welcome," she said to Colm and handed him and Seamus their ale. He hoped that he wasn't wrong in his deduction that the distrust of the previous week was gone from her eyes.

"Thank you. I'm honored to be invited back and look forward to hearing about the camp meeting."

"In due time." Her eyes sparkled as she backed into the kitchen again.

Seamus gulped his ale and set it down. "In answer to your question, our ma died twelve years ago, and Da's been gone about two years now."

Colm nodded his sympathy. "I lost my mother a couple years before you. My father remarried and our family size doubled."

"So it's not this quiet at your house then," Seamus said, quirking a smile.

Colm laughed. "Not at all. And you have to be careful where you step, or you'll stumble over a body."

"Where do you fall in the order?"

"First, in fact. The eldest son, at your service."

"I'll drink to that." Seamus tapped his mug with Colm's. "It was only ever me and Betha."

"But she's a very good sister who is worth more than five sisters to you," Betha called from the other room before materializing in the doorway with a full serving bowl. "Come and get your supper," she said, setting it on the table.

"Maybe four and a half," Seamus said with a grin for Colm.

Betha waited until her plate was empty before she brought up the revival, and Colm bided his time.

"I've thought all week how to describe the revival. Seamus and Henry dropped me off, so they saw it but didn't stay. I caught a ride back to the inn late that night myself. People were camped all around the meeting place as if they'd moved in for the week."

She had folded her hands in her lap, her attention fixed on Colm alone. "There was a good deal of singing in that demonstrative Methodist style before the preacher began. I had heard stories and admit that I held doubts as to the validity of the claims that the meetings are a movement of God. So when the preacher stood up, I was skeptical. But after a while, I decided that as I was hearing the Word of God, I should listen to it as such. To hear from God, not concern myself with whether or not I liked the messenger.

"He didn't say anything untrue. He presented the gospel and entreated people to repent and come to the Lord. Perhaps he did appeal to the hearers' emotions and work himself up to shouting. Dozens of people responded, and many were crying, but I didn't see the shriekin' and carryin' on that you hear about in the camp meetings out west.

"I do believe it was the Spirit of God working there. What I saw wasn't something you see men able to do. People did turn away from sin, and I found my own heart touched as well. I left with joy that God is at work. But of course I can't see into every heart there or say every repentance was true or every motive pure. I came to the conclusion that the revivals aren't something to dismiss, and I would encourage anyone to go to one if they have the opportunity."

When she finished, the table sat quiet in their own thoughts for a moment before Colm responded. "I was hoping this was the report I would hear tonight. I'm glad you were able to go, and thank you for your willingness to tell me about it."

Betha gave a small smile of understanding. "Everyone's talking about them these days. I think that style of singing would take some getting used to though. It wasn't at all orderly and proper like church singing. I liked it in a way, but not enough to induce me to become a Methodist."

Seamus laughed, which made Colm grin. Imagine becoming a Methodist. "Did you come from Ulstermen too, then?" he asked.

"That's the second time I've been asked that recently." Betha still glowed from the memory of the revival, her cheeks flushed a pretty shade of pink. "We did. Living in Ulster became untenable. Our parents left after the attempts at reforming the government failed."

It was a tale Colm had heard often. "My grandparents came to America for the same reason."

Betha leaned forward. "When faith is passed down through so many generations, sometimes we can lose sight of the urgency of it. That's what makes the camp meetings so valuable. They shake us out of complacency and refresh our desire to live for the Lord, not out of habit or because it's what our parents always did."

Colm studied her, wondering if her message was directed more at Seamus or himself. Both of them, probably. He didn't have to reply, because Seamus changed the subject and rescued them both.

Before he left that evening, Colm thanked the siblings again for their hospitality.

"You are welcome anytime," Betha said, blushing brightly.

"Have you met many people here yet?" Colm asked. With their occupation, the duo probably spent most of their time within these four walls.

"Seamus makes connections at the pub," Betha replied. "I'm still working on it."

"I should tell my sisters to come by and make your acquaintance then." A shiver of pride went through Colm at his stellar idea. If Maisie got ahold of Betha, his access to her company would break wide open.

"That would be grand then," Betha said, and Colm took his leave, already concocting a plan that would further entrench Betha Young into his life.

6

Pivoting, Betha squinted against the sun to take in the throngs of people as she followed Seamus into Patterson Park. When Maisie and Ava took her home after another evening stroll the night before, they had insisted that Sunday afternoons at Patterson were the highlight of the week.

"Everyone packs a picnic and comes," they had said.

Betha had thought "everyone" meant their friends. Had she known it was the whole city, she might have thought twice about braving the outing. The wind blew leaves across the path in front of them, and Betha had to hold her bonnet ribbons to keep them from lashing at her face. She tried to pick out the few faces she knew while Henry exchanged greetings with school friends they passed.

The foliage had begun to change, decorating the park in colors as bright as those of the many dresses and hats. Bright blue—there was Maisie in her favorite dress, waving at her.

"Over here," Betha said to Seamus. He shifted the picnic basket in his arms and looked to where she pointed across the lawn. Betha didn't hear what he grumbled under his breath and didn't care. She had stopped listening to his griping a long time ago.

Maisie grabbed her hand when she arrived. "My brother's here," she whispered.

Betha didn't dare ask which brother, instead turning to greet Ava and Mor and their friends. Her heart rate increased nonetheless. If it was Patrick, Maisie would have just said so since Betha had already met him. She also wouldn't have whispered it as if his presence was noteworthy.

Seamus had wandered away to explore the park and find his own acquaintances by the time Betha had their picnic laid out.

"Can I go play with my friends?" Henry asked, shifting impatiently beside her.

"After you eat something." Betha handed him a peeled boiled egg and gestured for him to sit on the blanket.

Henry dropped down with a huff and shoved most of the egg into his mouth. Betha caught his eye and shook her head in reproof.

"Isn't it wonderful?" Maisie gestured around her. "This park just opened earlier in the summer. I brought a raisin cake to share." She plopped onto the neighboring blanket beside two of her younger sisters, who had already tucked into their spread.

Henry's eyes lit up and he straightened, slowing to chew his bite properly.

"That's kind of you." Betha lowered to the blanket and tucked her skirt over her legs. A breeze rippled over the park, and Betha held onto the cloth napkins with one hand and her ribbons with the other. When was Maisie's brother going to make his appearance? Betha didn't want to be midbite when he arrived. She had low expectations for the romance Maisie desired to materialize, but one hated to leave a gentleman with an awkward first impression.

Colm stubbornly appeared in her mind. If she ever did have the chance to fall in love, she'd want it to be with someone like Colm anyway, respectful and steady. Maybe not him precisely—he was sure to have a lot of females trying to catch his eye—but someone like him. Betha realized she had never asked if he'd been in Baltimore long, but if he had, he'd certainly have plenty of admirers lined up.

Listen to her! Daydreaming about falling for a man as if she'd ever truly consider leaving Henry for Seamus to raise. Barely a week ago, she'd sworn to herself not to abandon her post, and here she was, allowing thoughts of a man to sweep her away.

She tore a morsel of bread off and chewed it. Listening to Maisie's description of the Female Bible Society she and Ava belonged to with half an ear, she watched to ensure Henry ate properly while scanning the crowds for her brother or Maisie's. The thought of the Bible Society was intriguing; she'd been active in the tract society in New York, but distributing actual Bibles to those without them would be all the better. She nibbled on another small bite, doing her best to keep her spine straight, her ribbons out of her face, and her skirts over her legs.

Maisie carried on, confident and at ease, as if she didn't have a care in the world. "We'd be delighted if you joined the society with us. We could raise the funds together, and my favorite part is delivering the Bibles around the community." She sliced the raisin cake and gave Henry a hefty piece, which he wolfed down. Then—"Here they come," and she jumped to her feet.

Betha swallowed and scrambled up after her, looking about until she spied Patrick making his way up the path toward them.

"Can I go play now?"

Betha's attention diverted and she glanced over Henry to ensure he'd cleared his crumbs away. "You may, but don't leave the park, and be sure to come back within the hour."

"Yes, ma'am."

She reached to tug his cap straight on his head. When she let go, he took off at a run and she returned to the situation at hand.

Ah, there was Patrick. Betha froze. Next to Patrick's ruddy face was her favorite set of dimples in Baltimore. His frock coat whipped around his legs, and he held the brim of his top hat to keep it in place.

"Colm," Maisie exclaimed, stepping forward. "My friend is here, the one I told you about."

Colm had already seen her, and his smile stretched wide. "Miss Young."

Was she blushing? An added surge of embarrassment rippled through Betha with the knowledge that she likely was.

"You know her?" Maisie's smile deflated. "This is my friend Betha."

"Hello, Betha," Patrick said with his easy grin, the wind ruffling the curls over his forehead.

"Hello, Patrick. Hello, Mr. Gallagher."

"Oh, come now!" Colm's smile darkened. "He gets called by his Christian name? If he's Patrick, you must call me Colm."

Betha blinked at him, considering his invitation as a new, different warmth spread over her. It only did make sense. "Sure then. But—you're Patrick's brother?"

Colm gestured around Maisie's blanket. "I'm brother to most of this crew. Captain of the ship. Elder statesman."

Betha looked from Maisie to Patrick. "You're the Gallaghers? I'm sorry; I'm foolish for not knowing."

"Oh don't," Maisie begged, coming near and wrapping an arm around Betha's waist. "It's my fault. I suppose I told you I have another brother and I told Colm I have a new friend, but I didn't mention names. Don't be embarrassed. We're all friends here now, and all the better."

"Maisie often forgets to mention key details," Patrick added, and Maisie swatted at him. "Did you save us some food?" He bent to Maisie's basket, grabbed a handful of grapes, and popped one in his mouth.

"You know there's plenty."

Patrick walked around the blanket and took up residence between Ava and Mor. Soon he was picking at the food in the basket and commandeering the conversation on the far side of the blanket.

Colm took a deep breath and faced Betha, turning his palms up. "Imagine my pleasure at discovering that Maisie's new friend is the same as mine. I knew she would like you."

Maisie threw a triumphant grin unashamedly at Colm before backing away toward the others, leaving him alone with Betha.

"I'm not that interesting." Betha desperately wished to disappear and for the conversation to return to another subject.

"I disagree since I've already learned quite a bit from you. Maisie said she and Patrick met you when they were on a walk one day?"

Uncertain what to do with her hands, Betha laced them in front of her and shifted her head so the wind blew the ribbons away from her face. "They're acquainted with our neighbors, the Olivers, and I gained an introduction when they stopped to visit. Have you eaten?"

Colm glanced around. "I'm not particularly hungry at the moment. Did you come alone?"

"No, Seamus and Henry are about."

"Ah. Would you care to join me for a stroll?"

Truly? Colm Gallagher was not only the attractive teacher who came to her home and asked thoughtful questions, he was also the brother her friend Maisie thought would be a good match for her. Betha had no interest in squashing the budding attraction between them, but she had some hard questions to pray about and answer to herself. Another day, because right now, the Lord had put this man in front of her with hope in his brown eyes and an invitation on his lips. Betha didn't have the gumption to turn either the Lord or Colm Gallagher down just now.

"That would be lovely."

"Well then, let's." Colm tipped his head in the direction of the path.

Betha gave Seamus only the fleetingest of thoughts before putting him and any future regrets out of her mind and taking a decisive step toward Colm.

Betha caught Maisie's eye as she moved toward the path and saw the satisfied gleam in her friend's smile. The web she was willingly entering would leave much to untangle later.

"How was church this morning?" Colm sauntered down the path at an easy pace for Betha, keeping his hands at his sides. Nothing about his carriage betrayed nervousness or whatever this inner flutter was that Betha couldn't shake.

"It was good to be in the Lord's house. I like Reverend Breckinridge. He doesn't read his sermons, just speaks from note cards, and he puts his heart into it."

"And there was none of that wild Methodist singing?"

Betha laughed, basking in the display of Colm's dimples.

"No, but he is starting a singing school to improve the worship. It's a small church and there aren't many men, so the singing leaves something to be desired."

"Dr. Glendy has been in ill health for some time, I understand," Colm explained. "But I've heard very good things about Breckinridge and the efforts he's making to revitalize the church."

"I see." Betha considered the information for a moment before opening her mouth to ask Colm about his church. He spoke again before she could.

"I'll have you know, I've been studying education philosophy again since meeting you."

"Whatever for?"

"Because, Miss Young, you challenge me."

Surely she was dreaming. "I find it sad that no one else did."

"Patrick challenges me about many things." Colm's tone had turned wry, as if he'd rather do without Patrick's challenges.

"Besides the school?"

"I regularly fail to meet his expectations."

So maybe she and Patrick had similar experiences as younger siblings. She would happily trade him Seamus for Colm.

Colm went on. "I've been reading the writings of ministers, philosophers, and leaders from over the past hundred years. And the truth is, I do agree that education can't be separated from religion. What one thinks about the Creator and how He relates to the natural world affects how they approach history, the sciences, even arithmetic. But I don't have an answer for what I ought to do about it."

"You'll get in trouble if you go against the board?"

Colm faced away from her and let out his breath. "It's quite possible. There are some on the committee who won't be happy."

"Do you think your position could be at stake?" If Colm could be removed for bringing scripture into his classroom, she'd have to face the possibility of Henry having a different schoolteacher. One that might end up less like the man next to her and more like that nasty Mr. Piper in New York. Maybe this wasn't as black and white a topic as she had originally thought.

"I wouldn't go against my conscience for the sake of keeping a job, Betha—"

"But you would lose the children you have now. I see it all better now."

"Do you?" Colm slowed, then stepped off the path and stopped. "I see it less clearly than ever."

Ah, Colm. He stood there, his heart in his eyes, and Betha barely had time to register how hard she'd fallen and stop herself from swooning into his arms.

"What does it profit a man if he gains the whole world but loses his soul?" Colm stared into the distance at a group of boys engaged in a series of foot races. Including Henry, probably. "Or loses the souls entrusted to him?"

His nostrils flared, revealing emotion deeper than what he probably wanted Betha to see. There was no mistaking how much the man loved them. Students entrusted to him, one of whom was Henry. Now Betha had to swallow to keep from weeping. How long had she prayed for this, for others willing to stand beside her as part of Henry's guard?

"You're an answer to prayer, Colm Gallagher," she said, shifting away so he wouldn't see her eyes glisten. Through the blur, she spied a familiar form beside a grove of trees and stilled. Her eyes took too long to clear, and she blinked impatiently.

It was Seamus. The coat she had made him stretched across the back of his broad shoulders, and his curly hair brushed the collar. His current orientation protected her from detection, but her gratitude at not being seen was chased away the moment she saw who he was with.

A woman clung to his arm, leaning into his hand that had reached for one of the tight brown artificially-created curls framing her face. She peered at him coyly from beneath her bonnet. What—?

"What is it?"

Betha hadn't realized the word had slipped out until Colm spoke. She nodded in the direction of Seamus, and Colm followed her gaze. "Do you know her?" she asked.

"Contrary to what you may think, we Gallaghers don't actually know everyone in the city or even Fell's Point. But I do recognize Cara. Don't know her well."

"Is she—"

"Someone your brother should be spending time with?" Colm shrugged. "I couldn't say. I was never interested enough to find out."

Betha longed to ask Colm how many women he *had* been interested enough to learn about, but she couldn't get the words past her throat. Seamus was entirely too comfortable with that woman and was making a fool of himself in public. She'd taken the first step in his direction when a firm hand on her elbow stopped her.

"Betha. Think about what you're doing."

"I don't even know her!"

"Precisely. So this moment would be her first encounter with you. And it doesn't appear as though Seamus met her today."

The dark look Betha had been shooting Seamus's way now turned on Colm. Who was he to speak to her in such a way? He barely knew *her*.

But it didn't negate the fact that he was right, and more than that, he was looking out for her. Her scowl melted away, and her shoulders slumped.

"Why am I angry that he's with a woman? I'm—I'm with you, even if it's not the same thing. But he's met you and has never mentioned a woman to me."

"It's not the same thing?" Colm frowned.

Betha stared at him, speechless. What could she say to that? *I'm simply on a walk with an uncommonly attractive friend, but she's fawning all over my brother?* "It doesn't look like it to me," she faltered.

"Do you . . . want to head back to the others?" Colm asked quietly.

Betha took a deep breath and nodded slowly. Maybe it would be best. If Seamus wanted her to meet the girl, he should know where to find her.

Colm didn't speak again until they were halfway back to the picnic. "Does he not usually keep female company?"

"Not at all," Betha said quickly and then sighed. "Not as far as I know, apparently. But in New York, someone in the neighborhood would have told me. And the way she's hanging all over him is utterly indecent!"

"Are you close with him?"

"No. We work well together and are about as close as most siblings, I think. No one knows him like I do. But we were closer and shared more with each other when we were younger. Before . . ."

Colm shifted his eyes to her when she didn't continue. "Something happened?"

It didn't matter how much she liked him; this was all happening way too fast. Maybe she wasn't close with Seamus, but she wasn't close enough with Colm to betray her brother to him.

"I said too much." Betha pressed her hand against her forehead and quickened her pace. Everything was too much. She was losing her head since Colm had walked into her life. But she didn't want to arrive back at his siblings ahead of him as if she'd stormed off, so when he didn't match her pace, she slowed back down.

"I'm sorry, Betha. You don't have to tell me anything you don't want to. I guess Maisie is better at these things anyway."

"It's not that." *It's that I like you a lot more than I should already, and I can't handle both Seamus and me falling in love at the same time.*

Falling in love? Was that really what Seamus was doing? What would it mean for Henry and for her if he did?

"I should probably find Henry," she added, stopping in view of Maisie and the others.

Colm turned to take in the distance to the foot races, his brow furrowed. The poor man was probably dizzy from trying to keep up with her changing mind. "Do you want me to come with you?"

Betha wanted to say no, to put space between them and be alone with her swirling thoughts. After all, she wasn't a little girl needing to hold a schoolmaster's hand to find her way home safely. But she was a female in a crowded, unfamiliar park in a new city, and Colm Gallagher was the only person she could claim to trust. Maisie had been elevated today due to the discovery of her relation to Colm, but she was surrounded by friends, and Colm was here, offering his services.

Betha nodded although she wanted to scream. "I'll pack up our things."

Seamus should be the one looking for his son. It was Seamus's cavorting with a woman that left Betha in such a tizzy that she needed to get home and out of the public eye to work this all out. Henry's teacher shouldn't have to be the one dealing with Seamus's mess.

Betha gathered her basket and made an excuse to Maisie, ignoring the question in her eyes. She would not be weak or emotional in front of Maisie or Colm, as kind as they were. Her family problems weren't theirs to worry about. She needed to get somewhere quiet where she could unload her heart to the Lord and find the peace she needed in His presence.

7

When Betha returned to Colm, he closed his hand over her gloved one on the basket handle and silenced the apology on her lips.

"It will be fine, Betha. We'll find Henry and then I can walk you home if you want."

Betha clenched her jaw in determination, although she allowed him to take the basket. "Thank you for understanding."

Doubtless Henry wouldn't understand though. On the long walk across the park, Colm wondered how she would convince the boy to leave early. Surely she'd need an excuse other than that she'd seen his father in the embrace of a strange woman in a public park.

She must have thought the same thing, because halfway there, she said, "I think if you just leave me down by the races, I'll wait for Henry and leave when he's ready."

"I—"

"You don't have to stay, Colm, really. I'll just stay put and we can find our way home together."

Colm couldn't make out whether he was being dismissed because she really wanted him gone or because she thought she'd already troubled him too much. He wished he already knew her well enough to know. Then he could make himself useful in what was obviously a difficult and confusing moment for her instead of being such a bumbling idjit.

He tightened his grip on the basket and didn't reply until they were almost within earshot of the parents milling on the outskirts of the games.

"Would you rather be alone?" He relinquished the basket to her, reluctant to let her go.

"I would." Betha gave him an apologetic half smile. "I thank you for your help."

"Sure. I'll see Henry in school tomorrow. And you . . ."

"Maybe next Sunday," Betha said, and the tightness in Colm's shoulders relaxed. "I wasn't done with the education conversation, you know."

"It'll all work out, Betha. If you need someone to talk to . . ."

"Then I'll let Maisie know."

Colm gave her a frustrated look that said it wasn't what he had meant, but it was, after all, the proper order of things.

"All right then," he said without meaning it.

"Go on now," Betha said. "You said it would all work out."

The corner of his mouth twitched, and he took a step backward. She found a position beneath a tree, set the basket at her feet, and crossed her arms to wait out Henry. When he was sure that he was good and truly dismissed, Colm backed away.

He understood needing space and quiet to think through a thing, and Betha obviously wasn't prepared to face the idea of another big change in her world so soon. Maybe nothing would come of the flirtation they'd witnessed, but the fact that Seamus was open to love and therefore all that came with it had big implications on Betha's life—not to mention the boy she always considered ahead of herself.

Colm gave Betha one last look before his path turned and took her from his view. She stood statue-like, her mind clearly elsewhere. If it took this much for her to wrap her mind around Seamus falling in love, what would it take for her to consider the same thing for herself? Because if Colm's hopes developed into reality, it wouldn't be long before he became someone she couldn't dismiss so flippantly.

"I didn't know you'd left." Seamus's voice held accusation as he came through the kitchen door, bringing the sharp, smoky smells of the outdoors with him in a gust of chilly evening air.

Betha stood from the straight-backed chair and put her empty mug in the dishpan. It had been a good two hours of quiet with a cup of tea and the Lord since her return with Henry late in the afternoon. She had felt significantly calmer even as she stole glances at the clock, waiting for Seamus to return and say what he had to say.

"I didn't feel like wandering all over Patterson Park searchin' for you. How was your afternoon?"

"It was as good as any." Seamus looked cool, bored even, as he examined the apples in her basket and picked one up.

Fine then if he was going to hide things from her. There was nothing cool about the way he'd been acting in the park, and she was no fool.

"You were gone a long time. We had lunch with the Gallaghers and then I went by myself to watch Henry play until he was knackered. But I'd have liked to meet your friends, you know."

"The Gallaghers?" Seamus bit into his apple.

"Colm's family. I learned that Maisie is his sister. But you go out every night, and I don't know who you're in the company of."

Seamus studied her for a length of time, chomping on his snack. "You can come with me," he finally said.

But that was just the thing; Betha didn't want to spend her evenings at McColgan's with gossiping Scotch-Irish housewives. Colm and his family were far more her preferred type of associates. Nonetheless, it would be wise for her to join him at least once so she could see what he was getting himself into and meet this Cara person. Colm was right; it was better that the meeting happen when she was prepared for it and had a clear head.

"I will then."

She moved away from him to the open back door and leaned against the doorframe. *Lord, what was this move from New York really about? Because Baltimore has turned out to be far more than what I was prepared for.*

8

The next morning, Betha watched Henry slurp his porridge while doubts arose within her whether joining Seamus at the pub was such a wise idea.

"Henry, I was thinking of goin' with your da tonight. Maybe I should see if Mrs. Oliver can keep an eye on you."

"Ma!" Henry set down his spoon, scowling. "I can take care of myself."

"I would be much more comfortable if you weren't left on your own in case something happened. There's only one of you, and it's getting dark out earlier these days."

Seamus poured his coffee and sank into the chair across from him. "Betha, the boy is ten. When I was ten, I was . . ."

"Making a living wage, I know." Betha sighed impatiently. "I don't like it, though. We've never left him before."

Seamus lifted an eyebrow that said maybe Betha had never left Henry, but he wasn't to be lumped into the "we." "You have to start sometime."

"Maybe I just shouldn't go," Betha murmured.

"Maybe," Seamus agreed.

"Nothing's going to happen, Ma. All the other women go out in the evenings anyway."

"That's hardly true." Betha fiddled with her spoon, her lips pursed. "Well, don't touch the fire."

Henry rolled his eyes.

"Henry Young! Seamus."

Seamus swallowed his coffee. "Henry, don't disrespect your ma. You owe her an apology."

"Sorry, Ma, but honest, I know to not touch the fire. I've got to get to school now." He scooted his chair back and stood.

"Be good and work hard." She opened her arms, and Henry came over for his hug.

"I will."

"We won't leave until after you get home, so I'll see you after school."

He took off, and Betha stood to gather the dishes. Her heart pulled in two different directions. Most days, it felt like she had two little boys in her care. The only difference was that one, she'd already failed, and the other, she hadn't yet.

Betha squared her shoulders and followed Seamus into McColgan's as if she'd been there before and was expected. That was the thing about the Scotch-Irish; one always knew what to expect in a neighborhood pub, regardless of what city you were in.

There'd be a couple laborers or sailors at the bar who got too deep in their cups and would get escorted outside halfway through the evening. There'd be a din of brogues discussing politics louder than need be, encircled by the quieter members of the community who insisted they came just to watch but would be in the thick of it in another glass or two. There'd be singing, always singing; it would start out jolly and without fail end with the sad songs. And threading through the whole evening would be a thick tapestry of stories of the old country woven together with the day's local news.

Betha could see why Seamus liked coming. He was only four when he left Ireland, but he'd always identified with their people and the motherland more strongly than Betha did. The pub, with its faithful community, was home to him, whether in New York or Baltimore.

His walk turned into a swagger the moment he stepped through the doors, and soon he was winking at people Betha had never met, slapping the backs of men he passed, calling names out.

"My sister, Betha," he said a dozen times with a jerk of his thumb, his accent exaggerated. Betha smiled and nodded at all the Johns and Patricks and Jameses with no hope of remembering later who was which. He stopped at Mrs. McColgan and ordered their suppers before working his way across the room.

Betha spied Cara first; or at least she thought she did. Seamus appeared to not notice her, but perhaps it was part of a game he was playing.

Cara circled a crowded table like a prowling cat, placing herself at a junction a moment before Seamus reached it.

Up close, Betha could see that she had probably been pretty once. Now, around a decade into adulthood, she had all the signs of someone who had to put a good deal of work into maintaining an appearance that had once been effortless. Betha reached up to touch her plain braid self-consciously. She didn't even own curling tongs. Her skin was only white because it rarely saw daylight; she had never spent money on face powder like Cara apparently did.

Seamus acted surprised when he stopped in front of her, which told Betha that he'd probably spotted her the moment he walked through the door.

"Good evening, Miss Murphy."

"Mr. Young!" Cara's hand flew to her throat and the tight curls framing her face bounced. "It's lovely to see you. And who do you have with you tonight?"

"My sister, Betha," Seamus repeated, giving the line more life than he had previously. Instead of jerking his thumb, he moved an arm around Betha to propel her forward.

"I'm Cara Murphy. How splendid to meet you," she said sweetly. Too sweetly, Betha thought, and caught herself. She shouldn't be so critical of someone she'd just met. It was an appalling way to behave.

"You as well," Betha said and tried to mean it.

"Seamus told me about you," Cara went on, meeting his eyes and holding them. "I feel like I know you already. Come and sit with us. Seamus, pull up an extra chair, will you? I didn't know to have an extra." Seamus obeyed, and Betha's eyes almost fell out of her head.

Women young and old gathered around a table close to the entrance of the grocery side of the establishment. Cara made introductions while Betha's head spun at the rapid-fire list of names and Seamus pushed the chair for her between two strangers. He then proceeded to move around the table and lean up against the wall behind Cara. Two other men had broken away from the conversation at the bar and wandered over to lounge beside him.

"Have we started rounds yet?" he asked, looking around the table.

"We were waitin' for you," Cara replied with a cheeky smile.

Seamus lifted a finger to the barkeep. "Soft ciders for the table."

Betha did her best to stay engaged in the conversation and take in as much as she could about Seamus and his friends, but watching him, her mind couldn't move past Henry. What if it was a huge mistake to leave him alone? What would he have to do by himself in the house? Surely he was old enough to not do anything foolish, but—

Time and again, she pushed her fears to the back of her mind and forced herself to refocus on the conversation. But she cared little for either politics or gossip about people she didn't know, and the effort to stay engaged felt monumental. Especially with Seamus across the table, leaning forward to speak in low tones to Cara and share the food off his plate.

Betha gave an appropriately-timed smile for the climax of the story the domestic beside her was telling about her employer, even while she studied Seamus and Cara. They did make a matching pair and appeared to be around the same age. Cara wasn't swarthy like Seamus was, but she was sturdily built, her dark hair and eyes complementing Seamus's coal-black mane.

Seamus seemed to actually like her. He got her a new drink when hers got low, listened intently to the things she said, and picked up her napkin when it fell on the floor.

What's more, Cara respected him more than Betha's initial impression led her to believe. She lifted a hand of resistance more than once when Seamus offered her the choice bits of meat. With a shrug, he popped them in his mouth. Maybe she had some of the same vivacity Maisie did, and maybe she flirted a little, but it was only with Seamus, who practically encouraged it.

Betha clenched her glass and prayed for peace to replace the knots in her stomach. It was supposed to feel better to know that Seamus wasn't running around with any lass who batted her eyes at him. But no, this was worse, because this looked serious.

Serious had the potential to upend everything.

At eight o'clock, Betha came to her feet and made her way over to Seamus. "We ought to be gettin' back to your son," she said just loud enough for those closest to hear.

"Oh, what time is it?" Cara asked, looking to Seamus for an answer. He must have already told her about Henry.

"Eight."

"Already?" Cara pushed her chair back. "We don't usually stay as late as the men. Seamus, will you walk us home?"

"If you wish." He pulled his cap out of his coat pocket while Cara gathered up her gloves and wrap.

"I never walk out alone after dark if I can help it," Cara told Betha as they made their way to the door while Seamus stopped to settle his account. "Good night, Mr. McColgan!"

"Stay safe, Miss Murphy. Good night, Miss Young."

Betha smiled her farewell and stepped out into the quiet street, leaving the laughter and singing behind them.

"It gets so stuffy in there. My father used to bring me when I was a girl, and I always hated how thick the smoke was." Cara blew out her breath and turned to wait for Seamus to appear and light his lantern. She took it from him and grabbed his elbow with her other hand, so Betha took his opposing arm. Behind them, more of the women spilled from the pub in pairs and trios and dissipated into the night, their lanterns swinging beside them.

"Are you coming back after you take us home?" Betha asked him.

"I might. I'll take you first, since Cara lives a couple blocks further."

Betha scowled at the darkness. Just what did he plan on doing alone in the dark with Cara?

"Oh, then I'll get to see your house!" Cara chirped.

"It looks like all the others," Betha replied. Why did she have to be so droll? The last thing she needed was for a future sister-in-law to have reason to dislike her from the start. But honestly, she wasn't such a flirt with Colm.

Betha bit her lip. Truthfully, she *would* be interested in seeing his house, but her mind revolted against the thought of making a spectacle of herself in public the way Cara did. Whatever attraction had been simmering between her and Colm didn't have a place in this new world where Seamus had a woman on his other arm, laughing and chattering with him. This was not the time to be entertaining daydreams of tall, dimpled scholars; Henry would need her and her careful attention more than ever. It was a good thing that Cara came onto the scene before things had progressed much more with Colm. Betha could see herself being in real danger of falling for him.

A shout sounded ahead on the street, and then the Olivers' oldest son came barreling toward them from the shadows.

"Mr. Young! Miss Young!" The young man gasped for breath in an attempt to get more words out.

Betha's stomach dropped, and she gripped Seamus's arm tightly. "What is it?" she asked impatiently as he gulped air.

"Henry's hurt. You need to come!"

9

Gathering her skirt in her fists, Betha took off down the street, berating herself all the way for leaving Henry. She hadn't stayed long enough to hear from the Oliver boy what had happened, and her mind imagined all the worst possibilities.

Their house was dark, silent, and still standing when she reached it. Next door, children crowded at the front door of the Olivers' in front of a blaze of light, so Betha headed there. They parted for her as she rushed into the house.

Henry was on a bed in the front room in Mrs. Oliver's arms. All Betha could see was the blood as she dropped to her knees before them. Mr. Oliver squeezed water from a rag into a bucket on the table and handed it to Mrs. Oliver, who pressed it against Henry's head and handed a bright red one back to him.

"Ah, Henry!"

His blue eyes blinked at her, so Betha took his hand and squeezed tight. "What happened, my boy?"

He opened his mouth, swallowed, and licked his lips. Betha looked around for a cup of water. One of the daughters dipped clean water into a mug and gave it to her.

"We heard him cry out," Mrs. Oliver said in a low voice. "When we looked to see where the sound came from, the house looked all dark and quiet, so John went out for a looksee. He found him out by the back door." She dropped the now-soiled rag into Mr. Oliver's hands, who exchanged it for a clean one. "We sent Little John for a physician, since I think he'll need stitches."

"Ma," Henry said, his voice so weak and pitiful that Betha almost burst into tears.

"What happened, Henry?"

"I went out to get the firewood. There was a . . . a snake came out of the woodpile and scared me. I stepped backward and tripped over the step."

"His head must have caught the doorframe just so," Mr. Oliver added. "It probably looks worse than it is. Head injuries bleed heavily."

"Can I see?" Betha moved around Mrs. Oliver, who removed the rag and parted Henry's hair at the site of the cut. The wound had swollen into a knot and displayed a nasty inch-long cut, but Mr. Oliver was right that it wasn't as bad as she first thought. Still, her stomach wrenched at the sight of it.

"I'm terribly sorry this happened. Thank you for caring for him."

"'Tis no problem at all," Mrs. Oliver said, relinquishing her position to her.

Betha settled into the seat with Henry's head in her lap. "I'm sorry for leaving you, Henry. So sorry."

"Aw, Ma. Now you'll never let me alone. It was just an accident."

"Exactly. You never know when things will happen."

"I won't get spooked by a snake again," Henry protested as the Oliver children parted again and Seamus came through with the physician and Little John.

Betha hadn't stopped to think about what had taken Seamus so long, but the sight of him with the physician was comforting.

"Where's Cara?"

"What happened to Henry? I took her home."

She retold the story for both of them as the physician came over and peered at the wound. He motioned to the lantern, and Mr. Oliver held it aloft over the bed.

"A couple stitches will do it," the physician announced. He moved to wash his hands and prepare his instruments, and Seamus stepped into the gap he'd left.

"You'll be a real man now, Henry," he said cheerfully. "Nearly every boy gets stitches at some point in his childhood. Did I tell you about the time I caught my finger in the—"

"Now is not the time," Betha growled.

"Better a few stitches than some of the accidents I see boys get into," the physician returned. "Or a snakebite. At least you still have all your limbs."

"If he's living in the woodpile, I'll go out and kill the snake tomorrow," Seamus promised Henry.

"I'll help you, Da," Henry murmured.

"Absolutely not!" Betha glared at Seamus, then gently turned Henry's head as the doctor came over to begin his work.

Henry was white-faced and sweating profusely by the time the job was finished. Betha laid him on his side against the pillows and shifted to her feet. "I'll go pull his bed out. And if you give me these soiled linens, I'll wash them."

Mrs. Oliver waved her off. "Nonsense. You just take care of the boy."

Betha offered her thanks and headed next door. Soon she had a fire lit and Henry's mattress pulled out from beneath her bed in the upstairs room. She had just finished arranging it when Seamus came tromping up the stairs with Henry in his arms.

"I was goin' to come help get him."

"I can walk," Henry said, his words slurring.

Seamus deposited him in bed, and Betha took off his shoes and tucked the blanket up to his chin. She'd check on him every couple hours to make sure he remained lucid, but for now, he could rest. His eyes were already closed when she reached forward and brushed sweat-soaked strands of hair from his face. "My sweet boy."

Seamus hesitated in the middle of the floor. Betha glanced up to see him run his hand down his lined face before turning and retreating downstairs with heavy steps. She came behind a moment later but went on to the kitchen and put the kettle on for tea. Sinking into a chair at the table, she buried her face in her arms and only then allowed the tears to come.

Colm studied class six on Tuesday morning, a crease in his brow. Henry Young was absent from school. He had seemed well the previous day, happy even. Illness had a way of striking suddenly, though, and Colm couldn't help the concern he felt for Be— er, Henry.

But Betha's panicked face from Sunday wouldn't leave him either. The moment she'd seen Seamus with Cara, her face had lost its color and her earlier conversant demeanor had fled with it. She'd closed up right before his eyes.

Sure, he didn't know her well, but anyone could read the signs: she was terrified.

He stood and called the first four-letter class up for inspection. Ten heads of black, brown, and red traipsed to the front, their owners clutching slates and pencils. When they lined up with significantly less jostling than there had been the first weeks of school, Colm rewarded them with an approving smile. He pronounced the first word, and their pencils scratched furiously as he paced back and forth before the line.

Would it be too aggressive to show up at the Youngs' after just one day of missed school? Normally, he'd save a visit until the missed days stacked up.

A few of the boys tittered, and Colm lifted his head. Ten sets of eyes looked back at him with ten slates held out before them while the schoolmaster had been lost in his head. He didn't even remember what the word was until his eyes focused on the four-letter word recorded perfectly in ten different hands.

"All correct." Lifting his book, he read the second word. The pencils were set to work again.

There was a scuffling in the first class, followed by angry whispers. Colm sent the littlest boys a stern look, checked the slates of the four-letter class, and gave them another word before heading to the sand table to investigate the problem. By then, the first class had all gathered around Charlie, whose eyes were cast guiltily onto a pile of sand on the floor. It was hardly the first time Colm had seen a youngster take a break from writing letters in the sand to see how it felt sliding through his little fingers.

"What letter are you practicing here?" Colm asked the boy.

He only shrugged.

"B," the monitor replied with importance.

"*B* as in 'broom'?" Colm lifted an eyebrow at Charlie. "You may get the broom from the corner and return the sand to the sand table where it belongs and continue with your letters. The rest of the class may proceed."

By the time he'd returned to the front of the room, the four-letter class was shifting impatiently with their completed slates. Colm examined the words, corrected the boy who had missed it, and gave the next word. By now, the three-letter class was hissing angrily at Charlie, whose control of the broom had resulted in sand spraying into their row behind his and across their bare feet.

Colm moved to quickly grab the broom handle before it rammed into the head of the boy beside Charlie. "I'll do that." With a few strokes, he had the sand corralled into the dustpan and back on the sand table.

"Mr. Gallagher."

Colm gave the four-letter class a "stay still" glance and stopped by the three-letter class monitor. "Yes?"

"Mr. Gallagher, is a word counted wrong if it doesn't have a capital letter?"

"Not usually. Why?"

"Some of the boys spelled 'God' with a lowercase *G*, but the card has a capital letter. Are they wrong?"

"Well, it doesn't get capitalized if it's referring to a false god, but for the sake of the class, we use the capital letter to refer to the one true God."

"So it's not wrong, then?"

"It is wrong since the card has it capitalized and there's only one God, but if the boys didn't know it before, we won't count it wrong this time. It should be capitalized for inspection though."

"There isn't either any God," another one muttered, sporting a slate with the lowercase *G* prominent. "They're all myths."

The four-letter class shuffled their feet, and even Colm's glare didn't temper the movements.

"I was talkin' about the idol gods," another lowercase *G* speller offered.

"How do you even know which god is right?" the first boy asked. "There's dozens in the myths."

A hand went up a few rows back. "Is 'Bible' capitalized?"

"How about 'fairy' and 'banshee'?" someone else retorted, causing a snicker to go through the room.

Colm held up his hand. "In this class, we use the capital for 'God' and 'Bible'. Please continue with your lessons."

Joseph Lancaster made it sound like having a class in the hundreds should be easy for one trained teacher, Colm thought as he returned to the front of the room. As easy as he had made Betha think it was. Somehow, Lancaster had missed the fact that monitors were just boys, too, and not every disruption was a sin that required discipline. Chances were, the methods would work better in a paid school attended by children with educated parents and a desire to learn. Wouldn't they?

But God had placed him here, on the rougher side of town, with boys who wouldn't get an education any other way. It was up to him to convince them that hard work and discipline in their education was worth it.

Without God, apparently. For a brief moment, Colm was glad that Henry wasn't there to overhear God being categorized with fairies and banshees.

He reached the front of the room in time to snatch a slate midswing on its way to the head of its owner's neighbor. The class quickly straightened into a line again, their faces flushing. Forcing himself to remain calm, Colm read the word on the slate in his hand, nodded, and handed it back to the owner. "Correct."

At a quarter past five, Colm locked the schoolhouse door, a headache sprouting at his temples. A step sounded behind him and he turned to see Miss O'Neill descend the outdoor staircase from the second floor.

"You look tired, Mr. Gallagher."

He cocked his head, taking in her rumpled dress and loose hairs. "You look about the same. I thought girls were supposed to be easier."

She laughed long, and in a not very ladylike manner. "A myth as old as the Bible." Giving him a look of challenge, she sauntered off.

Colm stared after her. "The Bible is not a myth," he ground out under his breath to her receding figure. For a moment, he stood by the door, waffling. Maybe it would be best to go to the Youngs' when he was in a less sour mood and a little more fresh in appearance and mind.

But then, the best way to change his mood would be to ease his mind about them. He would feel better once he knew Betha and Henry were fine.

With that thought, he started east.

10

October 1827

Betha concentrated on the flax running through her fingers, positioning them to allow the precise amount of tension to match the speed her foot worked the treadle. This flax was a beautiful gray color, a shade darker than the norm, and was always a treat for the eyes when she had the pleasure of working with it. Darker shades happened during rainier summers, but even so, every bag she opened had a slightly different color and sometimes feel. This gray would be lovely for curtains or a dress for a woman with the right coloring for it. Unfortunately, it would likely be bleached and dyed before it reached that point.

From Seamus's bed in the corner came the low murmur of Henry's voice as he repeated the words of the poem he was memorizing for the exhibition.

"Methinks I see a sight most excellent,
All sorts of birds fly in the firmament:
Some great, some small, all of a divers kind,
Mine eye affecting, pleasant to my mind."

Betha had it down before dinner, leaving no doubt in her mind that Henry did too. He hated public speaking, though, and would fret over the exhibition until it was over. Besides, reading was one of the few things Betha had allowed him to do today, and he'd already read the Bible to her for an hour. Next to him on the bed was his beloved model schooner, which had taken up the majority of his attention throughout the day.

A knock came on the door while Seamus was rubbing tallow on the warp threads to prevent breakage. Betha dipped her fingers in her water bowl and worked steadily on while Seamus clomped to the door.

She heard the female voice and didn't even have to look up. Seamus allowed Cara entrance, moving with her toward his loom, out of Betha's line of sight. Thankfully, they spoke in low voices and Betha didn't have to hear what they were saying—or, God forbid, doing—to each other. The thought turned her stomach.

"Who is it?" Henry asked.

"Your da's friend, Miss Murphy."

"Oh, I don't know her."

"No. We were with her last night when we found out you were hurt, so she probably came to see how you were."

Betha kept her movements measured, pulling flax through her fingers, running the treadle with her foot. What was her place in this situation? Did Seamus want her to be a proper hostess to their guest and therefore disrupt whatever rendezvous he was engaged in? Perhaps she should.

"If she came to see how I am, why haven't they come in here?"

It was a legitimate question, and Betha had no answer. She jumped to her feet. "I'll wet the tea."

The teakettle was already hot and ready for Betha's midafternoon break, so just a few moments later, she was bustling back through.

"Miss Murphy!" she exclaimed loudly, bursting into the front room with the teacup in hand. "Thank you for coming."

Seamus stood with his hand resting affectionately on the breast beam, talking to Cara, who leaned close to him, examining his work. He broke off in the middle of his sentence, and they both turned toward Betha.

"Of course." Cara stepped away from Seamus to take the teacup. "I was so worried about the boy, I had to see how he was doing."

Betha lifted an eyebrow to Seamus while Cara took a drink. She wouldn't invite this woman in to meet his son if he wasn't going to.

"I'm so thankful it was just a cut," Cara continued with a smile for Seamus.

Betha glanced toward the middle room. "Yes, we all are. 'Tis very kind of you to stop by. I know how hard it is to get away from work in the middle of the day."

"'Twas nothing at all. I had the time."

Betha waited, hoping Cara would reveal her occupation or admit to having none, but she didn't. "I love seeing your loom, Seamus. It's such a part of you, and your craftsmanship is a marvel, to be sure."

Seamus blushed. "My father provided me an excellent loom, he did. It's no doin' of my own."

"Seamus ought to be proud of his work," Betha put in. "There's none in Baltimore like it that I've seen."

"Will you train your boy on it?" Cara asked, saving Seamus from further embarrassment.

"He's been learnin' it since he was a wee thing sitting on my knee while I work."

"But the industry is changing and linen isn't as profitable as it used to be," Betha finished. "Henry has dreams of his own." Seamus needed the reminder every chance Betha had to give it.

He ignored Betha and gestured to Cara. "Come and meet him."

"Are you sure? Is he well enough?"

"I'm perfectly well!" Henry shouted from his confinement in the middle room.

Betha hurried through the doorway ahead of Seamus and Cara, her finger to her lips. "Whisht. We don't shout at our company," she hissed, straightening up his bed covers.

"Sorry, Ma, I didn't mean to shout, but it's so dull listening—" He cut off, scooting up on the pillows to stare at the stranger who entered behind his father.

"My lively son, Henry Young. Henry, can you greet our friend, Miss Murphy?"

"How do you do," Henry managed, staring. Betha winced at the view of his black hair sticking out on all sides of his bandage. He looked nothing short of a homeless waif.

"How do you do? He looks just like you, Seamus. That's a blessing."

Now Betha joined Henry in staring. How could she be so rude as to act like resembling his mother wouldn't also be a blessing—and in front of the boy?

"I've thought so," Seamus agreed, and Betha glared at him.

"Did you keep him in bed all day just over a cut? Were you mitch today?"

"Yes, ma'am." Henry looked uncertainly at Betha.

Of all the nerve! Henry had every right to be truant with an injury like the one he'd suffered. "Of course I needed to keep an eye on him, since head injuries can be so unpredictable." Betha drew herself up, forcing her hands to not knot up at her sides. This woman had no place to walk in and judge them on her first visit.

"I remember when I was a girl and wanted naught more than to stay abed on a cold winter morning. With a couple of coughs and groans, I'd convinced my mother I was quite unwell." Cara laughed at her own joke. "Thankfully, she wasn't of a mind that girls needed school anyway, so she didn't demand I go every day."

A knock came on the door, and Betha nearly ran past Cara and Seamus, grateful for the escape from the awkward turn of conversation. Her breath caught when the opening door revealed Colm on the front step, his hat in his hands. He exhaled, his shoulders falling, as if the sight of her had lifted an invisible weight.

"I missed Henry today and feared something had happened," he explained.

Betha held the door open for his entrance. "He had a bit of a tumble last night and still had a headache this morning, but I think he's recovering. Thank you for checking on him. You can see him, but we have company."

"Oh, I don't have to stay long. It wasn't serious then?"

Betha led the way across the floor. "He hit his head on the doorstep, and the physician gave him a few stitches."

Colm's hand on her shoulder stopped her halfway through the room, and she turned. "How are you? I'm sure that was frightening."

Betha swallowed, lifting her fingers to the hard lump in her throat. A reply finally formed on her lips to express her gratitude for his unexpected concern.

"Ah, Colm, come in." Seamus appeared in the doorway. "Henry will be glad to see you. He'll be back in school tomorrow."

"I just wanted to make sure no one was sick." Colm ducked through the doorway. Betha followed him, disappointment at the end of the tender moment meeting with wonder at his thoughtfulness. "Good afternoon, Miss Murphy. Master Young, class six missed you today. You got yourself a battle injury? Who were you fighting against? Napoleon? Marc Antony? Tilly?"

Cara looked fixedly at Colm as if strategizing how to gain back the attention that he had taken from her and the tales of her childhood transgressions.

Henry laughed. "A snake."

Colm pretended to draw a sword. "Like in the garden of Eden?"

"Like Saint Patrick. I drove them out of Baltimore!"

Colm sat on the foot of the bed, making himself at home. "I'm sorry I missed seeing the great battle. You'll have to share your secret to victory with us sometime."

"I must be getting back," Cara said with an affected sigh, as if conceding defeat under the rapport of the schoolmaster. "Seamus, I am relieved to see no greater harm was done. It was nice to meet you, Henry. Good day, Mr. Gallagher, Betha."

Seamus ushered her out of the room as the others murmured their goodbyes.

"I've ale for you," Betha said to Colm, taking Cara's teacup and heading into the kitchen. She returned with his mug to find him with Henry's schooner in his hands, giving it a careful inspection.

"And what are your plans for this great sailing vessel? Where are you going?"

Henry looked thoughtful. "I don't think I want to go anywhere."

"Not even old Hibernia?"

Henry shrugged. "It might be nice to see it sometime, but it sounds like a hard place to live. I like Maryland, though. Maybe when I get older I'll go west."

"West," Colm repeated, still examining the ship. "It would be hard to get there on this. You'd need a river barge or a wagon, maybe."

"Or a railroad."

"There's a forward-thinking lad now." Colm set down the ship and took the ale from Betha. "And yet a schooner is what you built."

Henry ran a finger along the bow. "They're so much prettier than steam engines, don't you think?"

"There is something graceful about a ship riding a wave on the seas," Colm agreed.

"Henry did his studies today," Betha told him, taking her seat by the wheel. "He has his poem memorized."

Colm lifted his eyes to hers and held them there. "I wasn't worried about it. I only wanted to know if the boy was well."

"Was the class good without me?" Henry asked suggestively.

"No." A smile crept up Colm's face, and the dimples appeared. "No, it wasn't the same without you. No one knew which way was up."

"My headache is gone, and I'll set them in order tomorrow," Henry said with a giggle.

"Aye, aye, captain."

The front door finally closed, and Seamus recrossed the floor. When Colm saw him approach, he came to his feet.

"Aren't you staying for supper?" Betha asked, joining him in the middle of the room.

"No, I didn't mean to stay at all. My meal is waiting for me at home."

"It means a great deal that you came." Betha turned to Henry and lifted an eyebrow.

"Thank you, Mr. Gallagher."

"I couldn't stay away." Colm reached down to pat his knee before handing Betha his empty mug.

Seamus was back at his loom when Betha followed Colm to the door. "Come again," he called as he picked up the tallow and rag.

On the front step, Colm stopped. Turning, he placed a hand over Betha's on the door latch. "I hope to talk to you soon," he said softly enough that Seamus couldn't hear. "I'd like to know about what happened since we were last together."

Betha had hoped that he would forget the humiliating scene she had made on Sunday, running around the park like an untamed filly with her emotions carried away. "You have nothing to worry about." Still, her hand warmed beneath his, and she felt his touch all the way to her heart.

"I wouldn't call it worry. I do care though."

Betha didn't know what to say. The combination of embarrassment and heightened awareness of the man in front of her left her flushed and muddle-headed, and all she could do was stare dumbly over his shoulder into the street.

"Am I allowed to care?" he asked with a gentle squeeze of her hand, drawing her eyes to his.

Could she give him that permission? If she did, it could eventually lead him to things like sparking and courting. Things that could take her away from Henry right when Seamus was already on the verge of upending the boy's life and he'd need her more than ever.

And Betha? Well, if she was going to get through the possibility of Seamus bringing a wife into the house, she'd need—

"Yes," she said.

Because she'd need someone who could listen to and think for her and who didn't always have to be right or have all the answers. Someone with a tender touch and a pair of amazing brown eyes that she'd never get tired of looking at if she lived to be a hundred. Someone who in a month was already worth more to her than all the surface friends she'd left behind in New York.

"I'd appreciate that, truth be told."

Colm was smiling at her, and she almost couldn't take it. She backed into the house, toward the injured child waiting for her with her dose of reality.

"Soon, then," Colm said.

Betha could only manage to nod, take another step backward, and shut the door in his face.

11

Colm's headache was gone by the time he reached the front walk to his own family's dwelling. Nothing but Betha had occupied his mind on the walk home. She had encouraged him with her final words to be sure, but a gentleman always had to be careful about how he proceeded when wooing a woman. He could go neither too fast nor too slow or be too vague or too overt.

He had little doubt in his mind about whether Betha Young had good character or would make an appropriate wife, but doubts about whether he was ready to take a wife were abundant. The numbers said he was—his age, his purse, the number of days per year he was hale and healthy—but it was such a big step to take. Did he have what it took to lead a wife and children in the nurture and admonition of the Lord? Most days, it still felt like he was a schoolboy in that regard.

One thing was for sure—he couldn't expect to win Betha with the matter of education still hanging over his conscience without a solution.

He stood on the walk for a moment before turning aside and continuing further up the street. At the end of the block, he reached another brick house, an exact copy of his father's, and knocked on the door.

A maid answered the door and allowed him entrance. "Good evening, Mr. Gallagher. Mr. and Mrs. Brown are just sitting down to supper, but I'll get another plate."

He thanked her and followed her into the dining room, where the older couple sat with still-empty plates listening to his entrance. Stewart Brown came to his feet when he saw Colm.

"Colm! You're just in time for supper. Come join us."

"Thank you. Good evening, Mrs. Brown," he said, nodding toward her. "I'm sorry to intrude, but I had a matter about the school that I wanted to discuss."

"Of course." Stewart indicated a chair across from himself, and Colm sat as the maid set a plate before him. "I'll say the blessing, and then we can hear what you have to say."

Colm waited until the food was served up and the Browns had begun eating before he spoke.

"It's about the absence of religious education at Oliver."

Stewart held his knife and fork in each hand and nodded for Colm to continue.

"It's become more and more untenable to teach without the use of the Bible. Joseph Lancaster recommended the use of Freame's *Scripture Instruction* and Watts's hymns in his curriculum, but the guidelines of the school require that I replace those with nonreligious works. I've followed their instruction up until this time, but as I read more on the purpose of education and spend every day with children growing up with less and less of a knowledge of their Creator, I'm finding that my conscience is no longer willing to sit by and allow me to comply. Since you're on the committee and are also an elder at my church, I value your wisdom in this."

Stewart set his silverware down and peered at Colm through his eyeglasses. "You're considering contravening the committee?"

"I'm not disposed to. That's why I'm here. Perhaps you could give me a reason to leave the Bible out of the school."

"Because it's the intent of the original founder, for one. John Oliver expressly indicated that the school was for all denominations and sects."

Colm placed his palms on the table on either side of his untouched plate and leaned forward. "And would not the children in all denominations and sects benefit from hearing God's Word?"

"You and I both know they would. The question is whether you are the one to do it, and whether this setting is the one to do it in."

"Right." Colm sighed. "I'm realizing more and more the futility of simply educating children for this world when life is so short and uncertain, their eternal souls hang in the balance, and their Father in heaven offers them mercy and grace to help through the trials of this life. Being able to do sums quickly simply pales in comparison to these weightier matters."

"I quite agree, Colm." Stewart picked his knife back up and continued to slowly work at his fish filet. "I can only imagine the challenge you face to spend time with the children day after day, likely growing in affection for them at the same time. I wish I could grant you the permission you seek, but I'm not convinced that this is the only or best way."

"I'm ready to hear what would be."

"You must consider the fact that even among the religious families, there will be an uproar over whichever version of the Bible you use."

"The English one, of course," Colm blurted out. "King James's."

"The parish will be sure to protest. The school will lose scholarships and the society will lose sponsors. I ask again, is there a better way to expose your students to God's Word?"

"Do you mean Sabbath schools?"

Stewart lifted a shoulder. "It would give you an opportunity to accomplish your purpose outside of Oliver Hibernian and still maintain the influence you have over your students. It's an option to consider."

Colm pursed his lips in thought and turned to his plate for the first time. "I will consider it." He cut a chunk off the fish and used his knife to bring it to his lips. It was tender and savory, and he took his time to enjoy it and think. At Oliver Hibernian, he had almost two hundred students under his influence. How many of those would actually come to a Sunday school? On the other hand, a Sunday school could attract children from other schools and broaden his reach.

"There's something else I'd like you to consider." Stewart continued.

"Yes?" Colm wiped his mouth with the linen napkin.

"Reverend Breckinridge is looking to start prayer meetings at Second Presbyterian, and Dr. Nevins pledged the support of our church. A group of men from First is forming that will be involved in the prayer meetings over there. I strongly encourage you to join us."

"It's weekly?"

"It will be when they get started. I can keep you informed. Your father and brothers are of course invited as well."

If Second was where Betha and Henry went, then Colm had every reason to want to see the church grow and thrive. "I will do that. Put my name on the roster." He lifted another bite on his knife.

"Thank you." Stewart placed his napkin on his empty plate. "I would advise against adjusting the curriculum of the school without the committee's approval, and although you would have mine, I can guarantee you that there are members that will never approve. I believe your best course of action would be to consider a different avenue for giving the children God's Word."

Colm nodded and swallowed. "I appreciate your consideration and advice and will pray about the best way to proceed."

"You're a gift from God to the school, Colm. I would hate to see your well-intentioned youthful zeal get you into a position in the community that I can't get you out of."

12

Only a week had passed since the first Sunday at the park, yet already, things were vastly different on Betha's second excursion to Patterson. For one, she and Henry had traipsed after Seamus up to Cara's house to pick her up before they even headed to the park.

The tidy three-story brick home Seamus stopped in front of appeared to be owned by a very respectable family, Betha would give it that. She waited out on the walk with Henry while Seamus retrieved Cara alone. By the way Cara spoke to the women who appeared on the doorstep with her, Betha gathered that she lived in the home of an aunt and uncle.

After the initial greetings, Cara walked ahead of Betha and Henry on Seamus's arm, paying them no more mind. Betha made note of the snub but couldn't bring herself to be upset by it. Cara had already made her character known, and Betha wasn't going to care about how someone of that caliber treated her.

The problem was that Seamus was smitten.

Betha tugged her shawl tight and listened to Henry chatter about the new game he'd learned from his friends the previous day. There were hares and hounds involved, and it sounded like a complicated game of chase or hide-and-seek.

"I had a red flag, since I was the whipper-in," Henry said.

Betha nodded, even though she had no idea what a whipper-in was or why they needed a red flag. She would have to talk to Seamus about Cara. There was nothing else to it. She simply was not the kind of woman that Henry needed to live with every day or continue to be exposed to, for that matter.

This time, Betha didn't even try to find the Gallaghers first. After Seamus and Cara went on their own way, she took Henry straight to the footraces and fed him his dinner while they watched the bigger youths compete.

"Can I go now?" Henry asked with the swallow of his last bite.

"'Twouldn't be wise to run until your food's had a chance to settle."

Henry must have agreed that the thought of losing his lunch wasn't a pleasant one, because he didn't protest. Betha leaned back with her hands behind her while Henry took off his cap and rested his elbows on his upraised knees. From her vantage point, she had the opportunity to look over the wound on the back of his head. It seemed to be healing well, God be thanked. It could have been so much worse, which was exactly why Betha had no more plans to let the boy out of her sight.

"Hello there."

Betha peered up at the voice to discover Colm standing over them in his greatcoat and hat. His clothing was never flashy or ostentatious, but he always appeared well-pressed and put together. Like a gentleman. Surely someone like him could do better for himself than entertaining a plain, common housekeeper like her. Had no one ever told him so?

"Hello yourself." Betha straightened, preparing to stand.

"You don't have to get up. May I join you?"

"Of course." Betha reached over to try to smooth the blanket out for him.

Colm sat with his knees raised like Henry and arranged his coat tails about him. "How are you, Henry? Having a good Lord's day?"

"Yes, sir. I started a new schooner yesterday."

"Did you? What will be different about this one?"

"I found a lovely piece of ash to make the hull out of, and it will be French."

"Indeed?"

"The *Triton*. It has seventy-four guns and is almost three thousand tons when empty!"

"That sounds like a challenge to build. You think you can do it?"

Henry shrugged. "I might need Da to help me, but I think we can."

"Hi, Mr. Gallagher." A passel of siblings Betha didn't recognize strolled by behind their parents, waving shyly at Colm. He greeted each one by name and asked about their day in his amiable way.

Henry stayed silent but waved as they turned to walk away. "Can I go play now?" He tugged his hat onto his head.

"You may. Be careful."

He ran off before Betha tried to wrap him up in padding to keep him safe from the dangers of the world. She watched him go, her heart still raw from the image of him bleeding on Mrs. Oliver's bed. At the same time, she was acutely aware of the man next to her and that for some reason unknown under heaven, she had him to herself for the moment.

"Are Maisie and the others here?"

"I believe they're in their usual spot."

"How did you end up over here then?"

Colm glanced down at her, his eyes serious although the dimples highlighted. "I figured you wouldn't want to let Henry out of your sight and would be in the area. I haven't seen Seamus."

"He's about somewhere with Cara," Betha said, the words bringing a cloud over her thoughts.

"I'll admit, I was surprised to see her in your home the other day. Was that the first time you actually met her?"

Betha shook her head. "I went to the pub with Seamus on Monday so I could gain an introduction, but then Henry got hurt while we were away. I'm afraid the incident didn't increase my appreciation of the relationship."

"Have you made up your mind about her then?" Colm tilted his head so the brim of his hat would shade his eyes from the sun.

Betha picked at the grass and watched the boys line up for the next race while she considered her answer. "It's not carved in stone where she hasn't ample opportunity to change my view, but I would prefer Henry—and Seamus—to spend their time with people who are more mindful of themselves." Hopefully that didn't sound too harsh. "I believe in extending grace, but selecting a wife and a—" She stopped. Seamus's wife would never be Henry's mother; only she could ever have that position, and she refused to entertain any other thought. "One should look for the highest character when selecting a spouse," she finished lamely.

Colm studied her as if trying to hear what she wouldn't say aloud. "Do you think Seamus would actually bring her into the household?"

"I pray not, but Seamus usually does whatever it is I wish he wouldn't, so I fear the worst."

"It seems as if you may need to prepare yourself for that possibility."

His words twisted like a knife in Betha's heart, but they were all things she'd already thought. Instead of telling Colm that she had plans to talk to Seamus, she changed the subject. "I do thank the Lord that Henry has your influence at school to help offset any negative ones. Have you thought more about religious education?"

"Every waking moment."

Henry walked by and grinned at them on his way around to the starting line. He'd done well in the last race, coming in near the front of the pack.

"I'm wondering if leading a Sunday school would be a good way to provide religious education while keeping the rules at Oliver," Colm continued.

It wasn't everything Betha wanted from him, but the idea took root. It could be a good addition to the greater hopes she had for the children in Fell's Point. "I'd like that. I could help."

"That would be wonderful." Colm beamed at her. "I'll talk to Reverend Breckinridge about hosting it at Second since it's closer to the neighborhood."

"I'll go with you," Betha said. After all, it would be best for a church member to be there to make the request.

Colm drew in his breath, then hesitated, as if weighing whether he should say something. When he didn't speak right away, Betha turned to cock her eyebrow at him.

"Of all the parents, I wonder why you are the one who cares the most about what I teach at Oliver, when you probably do the best job of teaching the Word of God in your home. You spoke to me about it even before Cara Murphy came along."

A sour feeling pulsed through Betha. Should she be bold enough to give Colm the truth? The answer was the bitterest part of her life, one she had never actually voiced to another person.

Her face flamed with a mixture of shame and anger, and she shifted away to avoid looking Colm in the eye. "My influence wasn't enough to make a difference on Seamus."

Colm inhaled with realization. "That's it then."

"'Tis."

"He's older than you?"

"Four years."

A race finished, and the gathering crowd clapped and whistled for the winner. Colm and Betha sat in silence.

When Colm spoke again, his voice was low and close to Betha's ear. "I'm sorry to say this, but I'm afraid neither of us will be enough for any of the students. There comes a point when they will make their own decisions about faith. I'm sorry that you bear the guilt for your brother's. I'm sure you can't blame yourself."

It was reassuring to hear him say it, despite the fact that she'd tried for years to believe what he said without success. "I'm not sure I could bear it if Henry went the same way." The words came out so softly, she couldn't be sure that Colm could hear over the crowd. "Not only for my sake; I've seen the pain Seamus has caused himself."

"Was he always opposed to the Lord?"

"Not at all. He was much like Henry when he was a boy. It was after our mother died that he changed. Colm, I was closer to her than he was, and I miss her every day of my life, but I never understood why her death changed him so much. People die. It's a part of life, not something to walk away from God over."

"And yet he did."

Betha threw her hands up. "Before my very eyes, and there wasn't a thing Da or I did that could stop it."

"I'm sorry, Betha. It does indeed sound painful."

How had the conversation once again turned back to the painful parts of her life? Hadn't she already moved the discussion away once? She took a deep breath and shook her head to clear it. She wasn't at all used to having someone act like they actually cared about the burdens of her heart, and the newness of the situation felt foreign and uncomfortable. "So tell me how the Sunday school will be organized and what the lessons will focus on."

13

November 1827

Colm reached home in good spirits after an invigorating day of school. The crunch of leaves under his feet and the bite of cold on his nose added a spring to his step. Not to mention that Betha had given him a little deeper peek into her heart every time they spoke, and each time, his interest and appreciation for her only grew. He opened the door of his home to find it a bustle of activity.

"Shut the door!" Maisie hissed, running up and slamming it closed behind him. Colm looked around in confusion in time to see Mor come down the stairs with her arms full of clothing. Peeking into the kitchen, he found Lyla and Bridget cooking furiously at the stove and his father standing behind Bridget, arguing with her in low tones.

"What is it?"

"Patrick," Maisie said with a sigh, gesturing toward the hall. Colm joined her in following Mor through the house. Had something happened to Patrick? Had he done something to hurt himself this time?

When they reached the back bedroom, Colm stopped in the doorway as his sisters bustled in. Patrick was on his knees by the bed, wrapping a bandage around the leg of a Black man. Beside him on the bed sat a woman darker than him, clutching a toddler on her lap. Dirt streaked their faces, and their clothes were little more than filthy rags. The man's head was shaved close to his head, but the woman wore a cloth wound around hers. All three were barefoot.

Colm's mouth moved into an *O* and remained there.

"Colm," Patrick said cheerily, leaning back on his heels. He was coatless, with his shirtsleeves rolled up to his elbows. His brown eyes sparkled up at Colm. "Meet John and Hester."

The couple stared at Colm, distrust written all over their faces. Colm realized it was probably a reflection of the look on his own and forced a smile. "Good day. I'm Patrick's brother Colm."

They only stared back at him. Mor stepped in front of Hester, holding up a dress that would fit the baby and redirected their attention. "I have diapers too," she said.

Maisie poured a steaming pitcher of water that Colm only just then realized she was holding into a washtub in the corner and squeezed past him to leave again.

"Where did you meet these . . . friends?" Colm asked Patrick.

"That, my dear brother, is not public knowledge. Suffice it to say they needed help, and we are here to give it."

"In other words, they're fugitives?"

Patrick secured the bandage and came to his feet. "They're God's children." His words were clipped.

Colm returned his look for a long moment. "Do you need me to do anything?"

"Not at present. I think we have everything taken care of."

Father appeared behind Colm, so he shifted back, out of the way.

"Patrick? A word?"

"I'll be right back," Patrick assured John. Maisie came in with more water, and Mor handed Hester a woman's dress and a pile of white undergarments.

Patrick followed Father around Colm, out of sight of the doorway.

"You cannot bring your guests here," Father wasted no time in saying.

Patrick opened his mouth, then dipped his head, as if he'd expected nothing less.

"It endangers my entire household," Father continued, and Colm had to agree. "They can stay here until dark, but this will not become the custom for my house."

"I wish you would reconsider," Patrick said in a low voice. "The Bible commands us to show hospitality and to remember those in bonds."

"You can consider that for your own household. This is mine. I have four daughters to think of as well as our legal standing, and my decision is final."

Colm watched as a battle crossed Patrick's face before he drew himself up. "Then I will be required to separate and set up my own household."

"You are welcome to do so," Father said. "You are of age. Have you considered a wife?"

"No. I'll have to do it on my own." He met Colm's eyes then and his eyes widened briefly, but he said nothing more.

Mor and Maisie backed out of the room and closed the door behind themselves. "They're going to bathe and change now," Maisie said. "We gave them corn cakes when they first arrived, but we'll have supper ready for them when they're done."

"Where will they go from here?" Colm asked Patrick.

Patrick gave Colm a skeptical look. "I'll hook up the carriage and take them out of the city. To a location that is—"

"Not public knowledge," Colm finished. "I don't know what you're thinking. It's Guy Fawkes tonight."

Patrick blew his breath out. Resting his hands on his hips, he turned to his father, a request on his face, but Father shook his head. "They have to go tonight, Patrick."

Patrick chewed on his lip and looked back at the closed door. Colm wanted to tell him that he should have thought all this through first, but he couldn't bring himself to do it. Instead he found himself saying, "I'll go with you."

"You can't know where I'm taking them."

"You're going to need a reason to be out on the burning streets alone tonight. You wouldn't go to a bonfire alone with the carriage, but together, we might."

Patrick considered, then nodded. "And we could pretend we're stuffing our effigies into the carriage, and no one will be the wiser in the dark. I'll go get dressed."

"Never again, Patrick," Father said before walking away.

But Patrick's face had lit up with what was probably plans for an epic escape. He rubbed his hands together and turned upon Colm. "The boys should come too. This will be a night to remember."

It was plenty dark at nine o'clock when Colm pulled the carriage up to the front door and hopped down. The entire family had gathered in the hall when he stepped inside.

"Are we ready?"

John was wearing an old coat and hat of Father's; the toddler wore a bonnet and dress that completely covered his skin and on the dark street would hopefully make him unnoticeable at best or one of their many cousins at worst. Patrick shoved a terrifying-looking scarecrow dressed in patched together old rags into Mor's hands. He was wearing the clothes John arrived in and looked rather like he belonged outside a tavern down by the wharf. He indicated Hester, who had a beat-up straw hat stuffed down over the scarf covering her hair.

"You and I will carry her to the carriage as if she were another effigy," he said to Colm, then glanced around. "Let's go then."

Colm and Patrick bent down and crossed arms for Hester to sit in. She sat stiffly and Maisie arranged her new skirt to completely cover her feet. Father and Bridget remained behind the door as the group paraded out to the carriage and placed Hester and the fake effigy inside. John and the baby were safely installed before Ben and Reuben came around the house with flaming torches. Colm and Patrick climbed to the front of the carriage and took the torches, and the younger boys scrambled inside before Maisie quickly shut the door. Had any neighbors seen, they wouldn't give the moment a second thought but that Don Gallagher and his boys were heading out to partake in the night's festivities.

Colm glanced over and met Patrick's eyes in the light of the torches, wide and sparkling. An excited grin stretched across his brother's face. He was having the time of his life. Colm rolled his eyes, inhaling, as Patrick clucked at the horses and the carriage moved away.

The noise was just beginning as they moved through town; at first, it was just the low voices of shadowed figures running through the streets, but further uptown, the shouts increased, accompanied by glass breaking. Soon they passed youths rolling barrels up a cobblestone street, and at the next corner, they encountered the first bonfire. With torches blazing and Reuben and Ben hanging out of the carriage windows to catch the excitement, none of the troublemakers tried to detain the carriage of revelers rushing through town.

Fireworks boomed nearby, and the horses jumped and became skittish. Patrick handled them expertly, calling to them soothingly as he navigated down a side street to avoid another bonfire up ahead. They were near the northern edge of the city when he slowed down.

"Take Guy and the boys to the bonfire up ahead. We'll say I'm parking the carriage, but I'll be back in a few minutes."

"Are you sure you'll be fine alone?"

"Quite sure. Don't leave until I come." He pulled on the reins, and Colm climbed down.

"Stay safe, Patrick." He took one of the torches.

"I will. Don't get yourself arrested." He winked at Colm as if he didn't have a care in the world.

John and Hester stayed silent and still in the shadows of the carriage as Colm opened the door just wide enough for Ben and Reuben to jump out with Patrick's effigy.

"That thing is so ugly," Colm commented after he shut the carriage door. "It looks a bit like Patrick, don't you think?"

Ben held its arms out as if to hug Colm. "What should we do to him?"

Stepping back, Colm put a hand out to stop the mannequin's romantic advances as the carriage moved away behind them.

"Light him up!" Reuben exclaimed with glee.

Ben led the way, holding the effigy out before him, as Reuben followed, quoting together, "He looks like Guy Fawkes, and of him we'll take care; And for his base crimes we will him upraise, and while he is hanging we will give him a blaze; then a halfpenny spare us to give him a light, for hang him, WE'LL BURN HIM AS SOON AS IT'S NIGHT!"

Colm brought up the rear with the torch in hand. It had been a few years since he'd last gone out on Guy Fawkes night, but he had once been the ages of his brothers and enjoyed the excitement of the bonfires. He'd felt noble at the time, listening to the speeches given about the purity of the Church and the evils of the pope. But now, nearing thirty and watching younger versions of himself carry Patrick's ridiculous scarecrow through a dark street, nothing about the event felt very noble.

He thought of John, Hester, and the baby. Despite believing in the wrongness of slavery, he would never have offered to assist fugitives on his own the way Patrick did, but he was proud of his brother. Looking into the eyes of a family risking everything for their freedom had made him realize how noble Patrick's actions really were. As they neared the bonfire, Colm offered up a prayer for safety for Patrick and those in his carriage. And if his presence at this bonfire helped them escape safely—well then, he would celebrate Guy Fawkes night to the glory of God.

Every man and boy around the fire was dressed in ratty old clothes as they were, except for the man standing on the overturned crate. His powdered wig and black hat and cloak hailed back to the preachers of old, and he kept up a steady diatribe against papism over the roar of the fire. An effigy hung from a noose in a nearby tree, and someone set fireworks off on the next street, drowning out the preacher for a time.

Colm hung back as his brothers found a couple of classmates they knew and paraded their Fawkes about together. Some of the revelers wore masks, and when he spotted a student of his with his father, he wished he'd worn one as well. What would they think to see their schoolmaster at an event mocking and condemning the faith of half his students? He turned his face further into the shadows and rubbed his hands together. It would certainly be warmer if he moved a couple of feet closer, but all he could think of was Patrick.

"You're missing all the fun."

Colm jumped at the sound of the voice close by his elbow and turned, pressing his hand against his heart.

Patrick stood there in the threadbare coat, his legs sticking out from too-small trousers, his grin unfaded.

"You're back already?" He'd only been gone a quarter of an hour at the most. "Did everything—"

"Sure did. I think the horses will be safe where I left them. Have they burned Fawkes yet?"

The drop-off location must have been close by for him to have returned so soon.

"They were waiting for you since you're the one who spent an hour crafting the masterpiece."

"Terrific." Patrick didn't wait but jogged off to where Ben stood with the Fawkes tucked under his arm, watching the fireworks with his friends.

Colm watched him go, and for a moment, he felt a pang of envy for the way Patrick lived without fear. What would it be like if he could live like that, letting go of his sense of duty and the expectations of his parents, the committee, his students' parents, society . . . and just make choices based on what he believed was right? Would he have a fraction of the joy that Patrick lived with?

His chest tightened at the thought. He could never live as irresponsibly as Patrick did. His brain would think of all possible caveats and consequences before every step he took and would never stop reminding him of his obligations. He couldn't be anything other than himself.

Besides, someone had to keep Patrick in check.

But on nights like tonight, he wished it didn't have to be him.

14

Patrick was quiet on the drive back through town. The streets were silent now that the fireworks were all over and the bonfires were dying down. Colm didn't want to know how late it was or how little sleep he'd get before he had to be up for school in the morning. There was more rubble in the street than there had been earlier, and occasionally the carriage jolted over something Patrick hadn't seen to avoid.

"Father's right." Patrick's voice broke the silence in the front seat.

"Hm?"

"I need to have my own house to continue my work."

Colm nodded sleepily in the dark, forgetting that Patrick wouldn't see it.

"Would you consider getting a house together?"

"What?" Colm jerked upright, suddenly awake.

"I need you," Patrick said softly.

"Whatever for?"

Patrick didn't reply at first. Only the horses clip-clopping over the cobblestones made a sound. After a minute, he said, "I'd need to retain a housekeeper and regularly purchase extra food and other supplies, and I can't afford all of that on my own. Not yet."

What was Patrick thinking? Colm had no interest in leaving the comfort of his father's house or Bridget's meals without having a wife waiting for him on the other side of the transition. Patrick would be hard-pressed to find a wife who would support his work, and Colm wasn't about to ask Betha to be that person.

"I'm not—"

"Just think about it, Colm, please? I don't know what else to do."

"You could wait until you can afford it yourself. Get a promotion or a better paying job." Colm gripped the seat as they bounced over a half-burned board in the street.

"The needs are here and now. It's people's lives. They can't wait."

With a statement like that, all of the reasons against it sounded selfish in Colm's mind. But was this his war to fight?

"I don't know. I will think about it though."

"Thank you." Patrick glanced at him, and by the light of the moon, Colm could see the grin and all playfulness were gone. "I wish you cared as much about the slaves as I do, Colm," he said, his voice distant.

Colm heaved a sigh. He'd come because he cared. "I know you do. And I wish you cared as much about the uneducated lower class of Fell's Point as I do."

"Fair enough." Patrick fell silent for a time.

"Patrick—"

Patrick grunted in response, so Colm continued.

"You need to figure out what it is God has called you to do and do it. You can't do everything. You can't run in circles trying to save them all. But you can't quit either, not when God has given you this much passion for their suffering."

Patrick didn't reply, but Colm knew he had a captive audience—literally. They were still a half mile from home.

"Is it the newspaper? Is it legislature? Is it having a home that's a refuge for fugitives? How can you, with the skills and resources you have, work the most efficiently to make the biggest difference? And maybe what you can't do right now are things you can work toward for the future."

Patrick didn't speak again until they reached their street and approached the livery. "I hear you, Colm. You take into account only what you can see, and you want me to do the same. But that's not faith. Considering the resources I have for God's work is not considering the resources God has. Sometimes He wants us to step out in faith and attempt something more than what we can do on our own. He's capable of so much more than I am."

He pulled on the reins in front of the livery but stayed on the seat, looking straight ahead as Reuben and Ben scrambled out and walked to the house. "You don't want to give up your comforts to buy a house with me, and that's that. It was from a lack of faith that I even asked you, trying to think of a solution on my own. But God will make a way for it to happen. I know He will."

Instinctively, Colm knew Patrick's arguments were wrong, but the inexplicable racing of his heart and their arrival prevented him from digging deeper. "I said I would think about it, and I meant it."

"Don't bother." Patrick jumped to the ground. "I know your heart's not in it, and there can only be people I trust at the refuge house."

"Come on, Patrick. Don't be obtuse." Colm landed on the street and came around the carriage. Patrick ignored him and yanked the livery door open.

Colm left him and strode home, too frustrated to stay. That was Patrick for you. Always misconstruing what was said and what other people thought, and poking annoyingly accurate fingers at tender spots in the meantime. It bugged Colm to no end. Not only was Patrick mistaken about whether he could trust him, but now Colm got the added joy of having to lie awake at night, wondering if Patrick was right about his lack of faith.

What if he did buy a house with Patrick?

Colm took the opportunity of his walk to work the next morning to keep his promise to think about it. The sun had just made its appearance, turning the dusky streets a soft gold. Normally, this was his favorite part of the day, but today, he had a load on his mind and a fuzzy head from lack of sleep.

His attention to the question might be a moot endeavor anyway, since Patrick hadn't spoken to him when he returned to their room the previous night. But a promise was a promise, and Colm only made ones he intended to keep.

So if they bought a house together, he'd give up his life with his family to live the life of a bachelor while they harbored runaway slaves on their journey to freedom. Which was a crime that came with fines and ruined reputations. Those were all the kinds of sacrifices the Bible seemed to think were normal for Christians living in obedience to God. Just the same, they were also consequences for wrongdoers.

But what would Patrick do if Colm did something like, oh, get married? He couldn't afford to buy Colm out, and Colm couldn't afford to buy a second house or entertain the idea of remaining there once married. So if Colm's personal plans came to fruition, the house situation would only work for a year or two. And it would be Colm's fault for getting Patrick into a financial situation he couldn't get out of. Unless, of course, Patrick was right about faith, and that year provided time for his income to change.

Lord, from my point of view, Patrick's request doesn't seem like something I should do. So I'm asking You—if this is what You desire for us to help people in need and further Your kingdom, please change my mind.

Colm stopped in front of the school door and dug into his pocket for the key.

And while You're at it, could You give me wisdom about the religious education of my students? I'd appreciate understanding the difference between living by faith and living foolishly in the name of faith.

He remembered that the meeting with Reverend Breckinridge about Sunday schools was today after work. All the activity of the previous day had almost made him forget it, but the thought of seeing Betha later would indeed be a boon to help him get through the day. Furthermore, the school exhibition was Friday night, giving him yet another chance to see her this week.

After placing his lunch and hat on his desk, he headed back outside for firewood and soon had the stove warming the room. Back at his desk, he stopped with his hand resting on the day's lesson books and took a slow, contemplative look around the room.

The prayers poured out more than usual—for the students, for their own encounters with their Creator and for the specific struggles Colm knew some of them faced; for their school day together and for the strength and wisdom he needed to get through it; for the connection he'd begun growing with Betha Young, and especially for Henry.

When the first students arrived, the room was warm and Colm felt more at peace than normal. He smiled at little Charlie and his askew cap and returned his greeting. Maybe it wouldn't be a bad idea to start every school day this way.

Friday was the coldest day that week, but it was nearly stifling in the schoolhouse that evening. Colm herded students into rows at the front of the room and tried not to tug at his cravat in an attempt to ease the itch that his sweat produced.

He hadn't seen Betha yet, but it would have been difficult to spot the little Irishwoman in the crush of families. Most of the students looked somewhere on the scale from nervous to downright scared, mirroring how Colm himself felt. Instructing children was vastly easier than addressing their parents. Not to mention that the performance of their little angels was a direct reflection of his competency at his job, and someone always fumbled their recitation.

Henry slid into his row and Colm couldn't stop himself from straightening and looking around. He met Betha's eyes across the room and returned her smile. Her presence was a small consolation for the absence of Patrick. Every school exhibition, he'd been there in the back, bright-eyed and enthusiastic and shamelessly stuffing himself with popcorn and cake afterward. Every student had at least one person there to support them, and Patrick had always been that person for Colm, even though neither of them had ever admitted it.

But Patrick had barely spoken to Colm all week. It was clear that he was disappointed in his brother's apparent shallowness and dismal priorities, and there was nothing Colm could say that would make him understand. At some point, he needed to tell Patrick that he'd made the decision to not buy the house with him, but every time they were in the room together, his fear of what the declaration would do to their already strained relationship kept the words locked inside.

Betha was there for Henry; Colm wasn't going to fool himself into thinking anything else, but just seeing her raised his spirits. She was dressed up, with a becoming white cap over her hair and wearing her mulberry dress. If only he could go stand by her rather than in the public eye; but with her watching him, he would do his duty to the best of his ability.

With a glance at his watch, Colm moved to his desk and rang the bell to silence the crowd. Sweat trickled down his temple as he gave the welcoming speech and called the first class up to recite.

As the night wore on, thoughts of a cool drink of water and a handful of the popcorn claimed more and more of his attention. He was every bit as bad as the children, and he knew it.

It was Henry's turn. Colm gave him a bolstering smile when he passed on his way to the front with his face contorted like he might throw up. After a long pause, he lifted his chin, looked straight at the back of the room, and recited Bunyan's "The Fowls Flying in the Air" clearly and flawlessly. Colm exhaled with relief when he finished. So far, no one had lost their dinner, but it had happened before. He was never truly safe from the threat until the evening was over.

By the time the last students of the upper class began their lengthy pieces, the aroma of over two hundred unwashed bodies competed with the heat to make even Colm nauseous. It took effort to focus on the words of Peter, one of his favorite monitors, as he quoted Psalm 46.

"The Lord of hosts is with us; the God of Jacob is our refuge. Come, behold the works of the Lord . . ."

All the students and their parents were held in captive attention as Peter spoke the words of truth in his **calm, authoritative** way. Colm felt peace settle over him. This was completely opposite of the way Mr. McMurrough had spoken God's Word in his school. These weren't words of condemnation and shame, but words of hope and rest. Why could Peter testify to who God was in this classroom but Colm couldn't? His heart ached at the difference the psalm made in the atmosphere of the room, ached at the dream of having this experience with his students on a weekday morning.

The room broke into applause, and Colm returned to the present. He did his best to make his closing remarks both dignified and brief, and when the audience was dismissed to the treats waiting in the back, he cut straight to the exit. After a glorious moment gulping in the fresh air on the step, he took up residence beside the open door to congratulate his students and greet their loved ones.

15

"**Y**ou did wonderful, Henry!" Betha hugged him tightly and took his merit ribbons in her hand to examine them. "It was splendid."

When he grinned broadly up at her, she glanced over his head at Seamus beside Cara and gave him a death glare.

"Good job," Seamus said and cleared his throat.

"Thanks, Da."

"Go with the women and get your cake now. I saw an acquaintance I need to speak to."

Henry was too excited about the cake to care and tugged Betha's hand toward the refreshments. She had no idea where Colm had disappeared to, but it was a busy, important night for him. Still, she'd like to have a turn to thank him for his work organizing the exhibition.

A bony woman with bouncing gray-tinged ringlets approached Cara. "Miss Murphy! It's so lovely to see you here tonight." Betha stopped politely beside Cara to wait for the introduction despite Henry's impatience behind her.

"Mrs. White." Cara smiled sweetly. "You as well."

"What brought you here? I didn't think your cousins attended Oliver."

"They don't. I came with a particular gentleman, Seamus Young." Cara indicated Betha. "This is his sister, Miss Betha Young. Miss Young, Mrs. White is an old family friend." She turned her back on Betha to address Mrs. White again. "Seamus has a bastard son who attends school here."

Betha gasped over the roar that filled her ears as blood rushed to her face. She stared stupidly at Cara with her mouth hanging open and felt Henry's hand abandon hers. All sense seemed to have left her, because her mouth refused to work. She stared gaping at her hand and realized that Henry had bolted.

Then the anger arrived, jarring her from her muteness. "What a *horrible* thing to say!"

Cara feigned innocence. "I didn't say anything untrue."

Although Betha wanted to tear into her with both hands, the last thing she needed was for more attention to be brought to the situation. "Henry is his *son*, and naught else. You miserable witch!"

She turned to see Seamus staring at her from a few yards away, surely out of earshot in the crowd. Betha gave him a tortured look, picked up her skirts, and dashed for the door Henry must have run out of.

She didn't see Colm through her swimming vision until he grabbed her wrist in the doorway. "Betha?"

"Let me go, Colm." Her voice remained low and steady, but she jerked her hand away and flew into the night before he had time to react.

A tremulous breath left her at the sight of Henry's unmoving form on the woodpile in near-complete darkness, his head in his hands. She picked her way over the logs, sat down beside him, and pulled him into her side. Cara had fled from her mind, along with the anger. Betha held Henry to herself, sick to her stomach.

"I know what it means." Henry's voice came muffled from between his knees.

"How—"

"I asked Mr. Gallagher one day after school."

Betha froze. Surely Colm didn't tell the boy!

"He wouldn't answer me," Henry added. "He just stood there. So I went over to his dictionary and looked it up myself."

"Did he say anything?"

Henry didn't reply, so after waiting for a minute, Betha asked, "What did you learn?"

"It's about my da and ma. My real ma."

Betha wanted to weep over the fact that she had to have this conversation with Henry already. She hadn't planned on it taking place for several more years yet. "She died when you were a baby, Henry."

His head lifted and he let out a frustrated sigh. "You always told me that. No one ever told me that Da didn't marry her."

"He was goin' to. She died before he had a chance. Henry, this has naught to do with you. You're my boy, and your da and I love you with our whole hearts." She was probably lying about Seamus, but Henry didn't need to suffer any more over her brother's stupidity. "God has a good plan bigger than our mistakes, and He chose you to be His before you were born. He created you out of His good purpose to be smart and gentle and brave and so I'd have reason to smile every day."

She ran her hand up and down his arm. "No one should know you simply based on your parents' choices. That's wrong, because you had naught to do with it."

The memory of her words with Cara in the school came back, and she felt her cheeks flush with anger again. "And it was wrong of me to call Miss Murphy the name I did."

A giggle burst out of Henry. "You did? What did you say?"

"It's not something that ought to be repeated. I'm so sorry she said that to you, my boy. I hope you always remember what I've taught you about how to speak to others." Hopefully after her conversation with Seamus, Cara would be gone from their lives for good, but the last thing Henry needed in the meantime was to pick up bad habits from the lowlifes Seamus fraternized with.

"Da should have married her first."

Oh, he was back to his mother. "I'm sorry their choices hurt you." She didn't know what else to say, because Henry was right, but she shouldn't say anything that might deepen the gulf between Seamus and his son.

"I'm sorry you never got to know your real ma." Another half-truth, because Betha hadn't approved of her either, but she couldn't imagine never knowing one's mother. It had to leave a hole, even to a child who had a committed aunt caring for him.

"Did you know her very well?"

"No, not very. The first time I saw you was after we found out that she was gone. You had come early and were just a wee thing then. As soon as we had you in our house, I took you under my care. I hardly let your da touch you when you were small. He didn't know anything about babies, and I was afraid he'd drop you on your head!"

Henry laughed, and the sound soothed Betha's emotions. She kept going with her diversion. "We all adored you though. Your daideo was so gentle with you and could always calm you down when you were in a fuss."

"I remember helping him weave."

Betha smiled and nodded at the memory of her father's affectionate, patient care of the infant. "I've thanked God for you every day I've known you, Henry Young. And I'm proud of your recitation tonight."

"Thanks, Ma. Are you ready to go home?"

Ah well, he must be done being sentimental for the night. Betha stood and offered him her hand, and she warmed inside when he took it. They passed the lighted, noisy door of the school, and she only briefly considered going in to get the lantern from Seamus. Only some of the streets were gaslit, but there was a bit of a moon and they should be able to pick their way home.

Through the doorway, Colm met her eye. "Excuse me." He gave a slight bow to whomever he'd been talking to and hurried down to the street. "Are you leaving already?"

Betha nodded.

"What happened?" He gave Henry a worried look. "Something upset you."

"It's nothing," Betha said firmly, begging him with her eyes to understand.

"But you haven't even had your cake yet, have you?" He looked back at Henry, confused.

"No, sir."

Colm hesitated only briefly. "I'll be right back, and then I'll walk you home."

"Colm, no." Betha reached out and touched his arm as he turned to go. "It's an important night for you. You need to be here."

The light pouring out of the school reflected in his irises as he studied her. "You don't even have a lantern."

"Seamus has it," Betha admitted.

Colm sighed and glanced back at the school, a torn look on his face. "Just don't go anywhere until I get back."

Betha finally acquiesced with a nod, but she moved herself and Henry into the shadows after he left. Only then did she realize how cold she was and pulled Henry closer to warm him up. A few minutes passed before Colm reappeared with a lit lantern and a wedge of something, which he placed in Henry's hand.

"Thank you, Mr. Gallagher," Henry said and took a ravenous bite.

"I'd rather go with you." Colm let his breath out as he extended the lantern to Betha.

"Methinks you don't actually want to spend another hour conversing with your students' relations," Betha teased.

Colm's guilty grin told her everything she needed to know. "You're escaping early yourself."

"We've had enough socializing for tonight. Is it too cold for Patterson Park yet, or are you otherwise engaged on Sunday?"

"Actually, I'll see you at church. I think I'll be attending there for now." He added under his breath, "Another thing I haven't told Patrick." A shadow crossed over his face, and Betha looked at him with concern.

"What does that have to do with Patrick?"

"My whole life has to do with Patrick these days," he said with an edge to his voice. "I'm sorry. I shouldn't keep you, and you're right that I ought to get back inside. We can talk about it some other time." Hope rose in his eyes with the last statement.

Betha didn't know what could be wrong with Patrick, but she'd hold Colm to his offer of conversation as soon as possible. "All right then. Good night."

"Good night, you two. Be safe on the streets."

The distraction had been a welcome one, but as soon as Betha turned the corner to head home, Patrick fled from her mind. In his place was Seamus and the confrontation Betha couldn't put off any longer.

As soon as Henry was in bed, Betha fixed herself a cup of tea and brought it out to the table in the front room. She dusted it of linen fuzz while she waited, but it wasn't long before Seamus came through the door.

"You really have to stop doing that." He closed the door behind him a touch too hard, and Betha hoped the bang hadn't woken Henry. "You keep goin' home without telling me you're leaving."

"Why do you care where we are?"

"It would be nice to know is all." Of course, he didn't actually miss *them*. He dropped his hat on the table and his coat on the chair closest to the door.

"Cara could have told you why we left."

"Oh, and what was the altercation about?"

"Did you ask her?"

"No."

Betha wasn't in the mood for a verbal dance. "She called Henry a bastard in front of his face."

Seamus stared at her for a moment, then let out his breath with a little shake of his head. Without a reply, he turned and headed into the kitchen. Betha pushed back from the table to follow him.

"Seamus, you can't keep her around here. You're responsible for Henry's needs, and she has no consideration for him."

Seamus didn't look up from the ale he was pouring. "He's just a child, Betha. Cara may be on the bold side, but she was right. And it's not like Henry doesn't know it."

Trembling with anger, Betha searched for a response that would get through to him. "He does now; he had to find out the hard way. We left New York to get away from this, and here Cara Murphy is blabbing it around town! And *in front of Henry*! That's not bold, Seamus; that's abominably rude."

Seamus lifted a brow. "You can't protect Henry from the truth forever. It is who he is; he's goin' to have to get used to it. Grow some tough skin."

"Not in this house," Betha said, her tone steely. "No one should have to grow tough skin to be protected from the people in their own house. And *your* mistake is certainly not who *he* is."

Seamus swallowed his swig of ale and wiped his cuff over his mouth. "Cara and Henry will get used to each other soon enough. And you should too."

"I have no intention of getting used to uncouth behavior," Betha snapped, fear rising with the fury.

"It would make everything smoother for you when I marry her."

Goosebumps crept over Betha's skin and she shivered from the chill. "*What* did you say?"

"I'm planning to marry her by the end of the year," Seamus said casually and took another drink.

"Seamus, you can't be serious." *Oh God, please no.* "Why?" Betha whispered. Tears threatened and she swallowed against them. Weeping would only bring her brother's disdain and would do nothing to help her position.

"I've a right to pick my own wife, I do. I've been waiting all these years, and Cara is who I've been looking for."

Betha fumbled for words, but Seamus continued. "It shouldn't affect you for long, since Colm Gallagher has his eye on you."

Betha choked. Things were still so early with Colm; who could say whether more would develop there? "Has he spoken to you?"

"Anyone can see it. I would approve, if he asked. If you're goin' to leave me and Henry anyway, then why should you care if I take a wife?"

"Because of Henry," Betha enunciated. How did she end up with such a thick-headed brother? "Because the last thing on Cara's mind is being a good caregiver or influence on Henry, and I wouldn't leave him without one." Her fists clenched tight in her skirt in an effort to move the tension away from her face. "And you're my brother, Seamus. I care a great deal about your own happiness."

Seamus's snort told her that he doubted that very much.

"Please take some time to think about it. There doesn't have to be any hurry." *Please let there not be any hurry.*

"Betha." Seamus held his mug aloft in an air of unconcern. "I can make my own decisions. I don't actually answer to you."

"No, sir, you don't," Betha said, drilling into him with all the fierceness one look could muster. "You answer to God. Read the Bible for once and then tell me this is the right decision."

Seamus answered by filling his ale mug again and retreating to the front room. Betha grabbed her shawl from the nail by the kitchen door and stepped out into the cool night. There was nowhere to go and no one to confide in. Colm may be the only friend she had in Baltimore that she'd ever shared with on a heart level, but he was also a gentleman, not someone whose doorstep she could show up on.

So she dropped to the back step, thankful that it was too cold for snakes, and drew her knees up to her chest. It would help so much to have a human to talk to who could wrap an arm around her shoulders and respond to her anxious fears. Twelve long years had passed since she'd had someone like that. A tear rolled down her cheek, and she used her shawl to wipe it away.

"Lord, I miss my mama." Another tear fell until they came too fast and hard to keep at bay. "I miss Seamus having someone he'll listen to. It just became much more tempting to try to convince Colm that I would make him a good wife, all for selfishly wanting to escape from Seamus and Cara. You call us out of fear, though, Lord, not to be driven by it. Please change Seamus's mind and block him from this foolish marriage. If he won't listen to You, will You help me set an example for Henry of how to live in courage and integrity even when our lives become difficult?"

She laid her wet cheek on her knee. "Please, Lord, change his mind, for all our sakes."

16

Colm watched Maisie tie her bonnet on while inside his chest, a wrestling match had him in knots.

"Where are you going?"

"Ava is coming in a minute, then we'll go see if Betha wants to go shopping with us."

Colm's eyes flitted from the door to where Mor sat wrapped in a blanket by the fire, a poultice on her inflamed throat. Would shopping with Maisie be better for whatever troubled Betha than his company? She did need female friends. But . . . did she need him more?

Maisie had paused with her gloves in her hand, her head cocked playfully. "Did you want to come with us, Colm?"

"I . . ." Of course he had no interest in shopping with his sister and her companions. If he were there, Betha would have neither a relaxing time with her friends nor the unburdening conversation with him; she wouldn't be helped at all. "Actually, I'm going over to see Betha now. I'll bring her to you in a little while. Which shops?"

Maisie didn't seem perturbed by his intrusion in the least. "Whitney's Stationery and Douglas's Books. We can start at Gaither's Dry Goods before she comes."

Colm nodded and turned to the stairs to retrieve his outerwear. Not two minutes later, he passed Ava on his way out the front door and tipped his hat to her. As he walked away, he could hear Maisie's amused whisper, probably telling Ava about his plan.

He took a chance and walked around to the Youngs' kitchen door and gave it a light tap. After only a brief wait, Betha swung it open.

"Colm! Are you making a delivery?" The pleasure on her face wasn't accompanied by the flustered movements she'd displayed on his early visits.

"Only delivering an invitation. Are you available for a walk uptown? I'm to take you to my sister eventually, although I have no plans to hurry."

"It would be just the thing. Sit down." Betha closed the door and shooed him to a chair. "I'm finishing up corn cakes." In short order, a mug of hot tea was set at the place she'd indicated to him. Spoonfuls of fried potatoes were deposited onto three plates, and Betha slid steaming cakes beside them.

"Is Seamus here?"

"He's about to leave for the pub. Henry!"

Henry traipsed into the kitchen with Seamus at his heels. "Hello, Mr. Gallagher."

"Good evening. I wasn't expecting supper."

"It's just a little nunch," Betha said, taking her seat.

Henry and Colm followed suit, but Seamus remained in the doorway, eying Colm. "Did you come in the back door?"

Coming out of Seamus's mouth, Colm's arrival choice sounded more clandestine than he'd meant it to be. "I came to ask Betha on a walk is all."

"You're welcome to come to the front door like a proper caller. She's not the servant that you need to come to the back."

"I didn't think of her as such; just thought this door would be more efficient."

"Are you goin' out then?" Seamus asked, addressing them both.

Betha took a drink of tea and swallowed down her bite. "In a bit. What are you doing this evening, Henry?"

"Little John invited me to a game of chess."

"All right then." Seamus put his hat on and gave it a tug. "I'm heading out."

At his departure, Colm picked up his fork and dug into Betha's cooking. "Do you think he really minds that I'm here?"

Betha gave a choked laugh. "Not as long as he doesn't want me to give him a hard time about his choices, no—he doesn't mind at'all."

Amused, Colm returned to his food. Henry was almost finished, and he needed to leave with Betha when Henry did so they wouldn't be in the house alone. After the quick meal, Colm kept Henry entertained with questions about his new schooner while Betha retrieved her things. When she was ready, he placed his dishes in the dishpan, grabbed an unlit lantern from its hook, and opened the door for her. With a wave goodbye, Henry raced to the neighbors', leaving Colm and Betha on the doorstep in the quiet.

"Are you ready?"

She nodded and closed the door, and Colm offered her his elbow. The evenings were getting chillier, so he was glad when she slipped her hand into his arm. Finally alone with her, he tried to think of what to start with, but a frenzy of thoughts about Patrick, school, and whatever had happened to her the night of the exhibition assaulted him. "I'm glad to have you to myself. It seems we have a lot to catch up on."

Betha had to tilt her head to look up at him, and Colm wished for a portraitist to capture her face. He liked her black hair, the curl in the strands that came loose from her braid, and the way the plait fell down her back. But the way this bonnet framed her face made her eyes look bigger and, if it were possible, even more alluring in the golden light before dusk.

She pressed her lips in agreement. "I want to know about Patrick, and you should know about Seamus."

"You start then." Colm took the first reluctant step down the stairs, setting a slow pace down the street.

"He intends to be married, sooner rather than later."

Colm took a moment to process the news before blurting out a response. "Is that what had you upset at the school last night?"

"No; he told me later, at home. At the exhibition, I found out about Henry's use of your dictionary."

A nervous sort of confusion came over Colm. He flexed his hand to relieve the tension in it. "Should I not have let him?"

"Seamus is right; he'd have found out soon enough. I didn't know he knew what the word meant when Cara used it to refer to him."

Colm halted on the street, prickles crawling over his skin. "Betha. Tell me she didn't."

"She did, with Henry and me both right there."

"No wonder—"

"It's why we left New York, Colm. I'm guessing you've figured that out. Henry has been bullied his whole life because of choices Seamus made eleven years ago. No one here was supposed to know, and Henry could just be Henry for once."

"It wasn't . . ." Colm cleared his throat. "It's not that uncommon for parents to, ah, marry after the . . . I know several people in such a situation."

"But he didn't," Betha said with a sigh. "The baby came early, and she died a few weeks later. Just a couple of days away from the planned wedding, and no way to redeem Henry from being branded forever."

Poor lad. He was such a good boy for all this to be laid on him.

"How did Seamus end up with the babe?"

"Well, the girl had no family left but an aging, half-senile father and a good-for-nothing single brother. Our mother was already in the grave. There was no one else to take him. I'm glad too."

"I can imagine you are." Colm smiled down at her before moving them forward again.

"But now Seamus intends to move a wife into the house who thinks nothing of calling Henry such things. She sees him more as a hindrance than a gift."

"Do you fear someone else taking your place in his life?"

Betha barked out a bitter laugh that didn't sound like her. "It's the least of my worries. Henry will never attach to someone who belittles him the way she does, and she doesn't appear to have a mothering bone in her body. Would that she were a real competition for his affection! Then I wouldn't be half so concerned. At least, I think I wouldn't."

"It doesn't seem to be a pleasant prospect for either of you. I am indeed sorry to hear it. You said you spoke to Seamus later?"

"He told me he doesn't answer to me, he did. The concerns I raised fell on his stony heart."

Colm reached his gloved hand over to cover hers on his arm. "And as he doesn't go to church, he has no authority to answer to in life except his own self."

"His own rotten self," Betha muttered, and sighed. "You know I fear for Henry anyway. How will this foundational change affect him for years to come?"

"The Lord knows, Betha, and he loves Henry more than you do," Colm said in a deep, soothing voice.

"I do wish He would do us all a favor and whack Seamus upside the head from time to time. When it's just the three of us, I can manage Seamus enough to keep life tolerable, but . . ."

Colm waited, but she didn't finish her sentence. The truth was, a man couldn't help but put the woman he was in love with ahead of the sister he'd lived with for thirty years. Where would that leave Betha but displaced in her own home, demoted from mistress to subordinate? Most young women went from being subordinates in their father's homes to married mistresses of their husband's, not the other way around. It would be a difficult transition indeed to give up the role of decision-maker. And to a woman like Cara Murphy, no less.

"I am sorry, Betha. I'm only beginning to grasp all the repercussions this will have on your life. I can see it could be most unpleasant."

"It could. I'm trying to have faith that God is in control and He will give strength where it is needed. Now let's please change the subject before it depresses me further. What did you mean last night about your whole life having to do with Patrick?"

As much as Colm didn't want to talk about Patrick, he could see how doing so would be a mercy to her.

"Oh, Patrick." Colm let out his breath slowly. It wasn't that long ago that they'd been best friends. When was it that the distance started growing? "I suppose you know he's an abolitionist."

Betha's head jerked slightly, revealing her surprise. "I didn't, truth be told. I never tried very hard to guess what it is he is involved with."

Colm nodded. "To be honest, I support abolition as well, although perhaps not in the sweeping, immediate way Patrick does. He's simply grown . . . unable to accept that." It was Patrick who changed, not him. He'd long held his position; Patrick was the one who grew more and more extreme in his views every year.

Betha gave him a questioning look. "Is he angry with you?"

"Worse. He's disappointed."

"Why? What did you do?"

"According to him, nothing. I'm not willing to rearrange my life to serve in the cause alongside him."

She gave a short laugh, startling him. "Why, that doesn't even make sense, Colm. Doesn't he know that we are all members of one body with different gifts and different roles in accomplishing God's work on earth?"

Colm stared at her, taken aback by her quick insight. "No, I don't think he does." How could he articulate how Patrick's accusations confused him when he knew and, to a degree, believed in the importance of the cause Patrick was willing to sacrifice everything for?

"What does God require of you," Betha went on, "but to do justice, love mercy, and walk humbly with your God? Do you not do that in your own arena?"

The familiar choking feeling rose in his throat, and he cleared it as if that would help. It didn't.

"I try," he said feebly. Besides his teaching, he attempted to do so with his charitable donations, his vote, even assisting Patrick when he was able, such as on Guy Fawkes night. He was soon to start the prayer meetings and the Sunday schools. So why did it always feel like however much he did wasn't enough?

Because of Patrick, that's why.

Because Patrick was doing more and believed Colm should do more, too, and deep down, Colm couldn't help but wonder if he was right. He sucked cold air into his lungs and tried to breathe normally again.

Betha seemed unconcerned beside him. Maybe she simply couldn't imagine what it would be like to have a brother who spurred her to be a better person. She was still talking in her soft way, saying something about the importance of serving where God placed him and how everyone was uniquely equipped for different tasks.

She suddenly broke off and looked up at him. "You really care, don't you?"

Colm lifted a shoulder weakly. "He's my brother." There was no need to repeat to her that Patrick was barely talking to him. It sounded childish, when it was in fact a real strain on his mental state. Something had broken between them, and Colm couldn't fix it.

"I'm sorry, Colm. Here I was going on as if Patrick's opinion shouldn't matter to you, when it obviously matters quite a bit."

But what if God was disappointed in him, too, because he didn't do enough justice or love mercy enough?

"We make quite the pair with our brother problems, don't we?"

"But that's just the thing, Colm," Betha said hesitatingly. She withdrew her hand from his arm. "I shouldn't be . . . shouldn't be making you think . . . well, I can't imagine leaving Henry alone with Seamus and Cara."

His heart protested against what she was trying to say, but he brought it into submission to his head. This was a time to be reasonable. "There's been no promises made," he reassured her. "I know that. You've only said that I'm allowed to care for you. Please don't be too hasty to withdraw that right when there are challenges looming for you. Not when the future is unknown and you may be in even greater need of a listening ear."

The concern on Betha's face morphed into relief, and just in time, because they'd reached the street for Whitney's. "Thank you, Colm. It means a great deal that you understand."

Colm gave her a wry look. "I suppose that is the one thing I have learned lately—one cannot judge another for doing the work they feel responsible for."

17

Colm removed his hat as he stepped into Second Presbyterian Church and lifted his eyes to take in the gleaming organ pipes and stained glass.

The large room was well lit, with six windows on the back wall opposite the pulpit and eight on each side, and a reverent quiet met his ears after the noise of the streets. Or maybe the quiet was due to the fact that the size of this congregation had dwindled in recent years, significantly fewer present than the thousand the building was built to hold. He smiled at a sibling set of his pupils and sank onto a wooden pew near the back since he didn't yet have a pew rental. It was the first Sunday in his life sitting anywhere besides the Gallagher pew at First Presbyterian.

He placed his hat and coat beside him and opened the Bible he'd carried in. He'd only bought it for himself a few years prior, finding that the family Bible was in high demand. It still brought a sense of wonder as he clutched the leather volume that he had a copy he didn't have to share, even though the family had added to their collection since then.

The book sat open in his hands while he took in the moment. It felt monumental to be here, across town from the church he'd grown up in and its familiar twin spires. Away from the pastor he'd always sat under and people he knew. But between the prayer meeting and Sunday school, it seemed like God was doing a new thing, not only with Second Presbyterian, but also with Colm. Like maybe all of it wasn't a coincidence and he was supposed to be here at this time.

Maybe it wasn't fully excitement yet that he felt, but it was interest—a curiosity to see what God was up to—and a hope that somewhere in the midst of it, he'd come to understand his own heart. The breaking away wasn't painless though. Sitting alone in a room with people largely unknown to him... well, maybe by going to the same church all the time, his understanding of unity in the body of Christ had been incorrectly configured. He'd never known what it was to be a stranger in church before.

More than that, however, was that breaking away on his own felt like one more nail in the coffin in his relationship with Patrick. Their paths were no longer parallel, but moving in two different directions. Patrick had made him choose, and he'd chosen . . . not Patrick. He didn't have to wonder if his brother felt the wrenching of it too. Although they still shared a bedroom, the gulf in the space gaped wide and bleeding. It was only a matter of time before Patrick figured out a way to move out, and then what would become of them?

Colm bowed his head and offered up a prayer for the severed bond. *Lord,* he added, *make me attentive in this service and always to Your voice so I can follow where You lead.*

He lifted his head in time to see Betha and Henry passing him on their way up the aisle. They were bundled in their coats, and Betha held a foot warmer with both hands. She was watching him and smiled when his eyes met hers.

"If Seamus were here, I'd invite you to sit with us," she said apologetically.

But without Seamus, his presence in a pew with her would make an announcement neither of them would be ready to make for quite some time yet. "I understand," he said.

"I'm glad you're here."

Her simple comment swept him away into his thoughts again, to the question of whether he could say he was glad to be there too. Finally, he came back to her with a blink of his eyes. "Thank you."

They moved on toward their pew, and Colm returned to the Bible in his hands. Only another minute passed before the organ belted out and the service began. When the singing was over, Colm reseated himself and pulled his Bible onto his lap. He'd had it open to Micah 6 earlier, poring again over God's simple and yet weighty explanation of man's duty. But now, his eyes inadvertently landed on the opposing page.

"A man's enemies are the men of his own house."

The jarring statement caught his attention. Even though Patrick was a long way from being his enemy, the words were unsettling. Was this passage speaking of when the people of Judah were facing their pending exile? Colm could only imagine the pain of considering a family member a true enemy. What would a person do under those circumstances?

"Therefore I will look unto the Lord; I will wait for the God of my salvation: my God will hear me."

He could stand to be better at remembering to look to the Lord and waiting for God to move and speak in his own timing. He wasn't on Colm's calendar. It was so easy to spend more time focusing on the broken relationship and what Colm was or wasn't doing for God instead of simply looking to the Lord and waiting for Him. Following Him.

The light in the church dimmed, and soon the sound of rain came, spattering against the windows.

Father, I don't know how good of a job I'm doing at living out what You said in Micah that You require of man. After all, I've hurt my own brother. As a result, I'm spending too much time looking at what I'm doing rather than at who You are and what You're doing.

He took an extra minute to pray for Patrick and his undoubtedly worthy work. Finally at peace, he turned to the passage the preacher was addressing and redirected his attention to the sermon.

When Betha reached the back of the church after the service, Colm was standing in his pew waiting for her with his Bible tucked under his arm.

"I'm sorry I didn't bring an umbrella. I ought to be able to escort you home, but I'm badly unprepared."

Betha gestured to Henry, who lifted the closed umbrella from his side. "We aren't. But I'm not sure that I can do much to save you from the rain."

His father's carriage was likely at First Presbyterian, and he was further than usual from home. She'd had other priorities for her afternoon that involved Cara and an awkward conversation, but it was pouring, and her house was close.

"However, if you come with us, we can give you shelter, a hot meal, and a warm fire to dry out while you wait for the rain to stop."

His eyes lit up and the little crease that had taken up residence on his forehead of late smoothed out as he picked up his hat. Yes, so this would be far more enjoyable than her planned Cara confrontation. At the door, Henry thrust the umbrella into Colm's hands, and flipping his collar up, shoved his hands into his coat pockets and took off down the street, dodging puddles as he ran. Colm and Betha watched him for a moment before Colm opened the umbrella and turned to her with both dimples blazing.

"Well then. I guess it's you and me."

He offered his elbow, tucked her into his side, and they started into the downpour.

Betha had held Colm's elbow on their walk through town just last night, but there was something intimate about an umbrella. She pressed against him, alone in their own little shelter, feeling very much like a couple. The shiver that ran up her spine had little to do with the autumn storm.

This was ridiculous. She had Henry, and Colm had . . . every other female in Baltimore.

But on her doorstep, Colm stopped under the overhang and didn't reach for the latch. In no particular hurry to end the moment, Betha didn't either, although the rain fell around them, soaking her skirts and his trouser legs.

His eyes latched onto hers, something dark and new in their intensity. For a moment, Betha wondered if he wanted to kiss her. Was it only last night that she told him that she couldn't consider an attachment? Surely there was some way to make one work and still take care of Henry, wasn't there? Because it would take a special kind of fool who would turn down the interest—and if looks were any indication, he was very interested—of Colm Gallagher.

Colm didn't move or speak, just held her gaze fiercely, chasing away any doubt of whether he wanted to kiss her.

"There are a lot of other girls," Betha said, her voice odd and high and unfamiliar in her ears.

"I don't see any others," Colm replied without moving.

Betha's breath caught in her throat. "Maybe you should," she croaked. "Maybe you should notice the ones who are educated and beautiful and established in society and don't come with complicated families."

Colm cracked a smile. "I'm trying very hard not to kiss you right now, and you're not helping."

Although he didn't make any sense and Betha knew better, something in her wanted to go on naming reasons why someone else would fit him better just to see if he would. She wrestled the desire to the ground.

"Colm, you assured me last night . . ."

"I know. That's the only reason I haven't. But you should know that there isn't any other girl. There never has been." Sticking the tips of his fingers under the hand holding the umbrella, Colm pulled his right glove off and lifted a bare finger to Betha's cheek. It was all she could do to keep the foot warmer clutched in her hands and not drop it on his feet. She couldn't help the noticeable shudder when his skin met hers and mentally kicked herself for not showing more decorum.

"I don't understand," Betha whispered as he turned his hand and ran his thumb along her jaw.

"Just this—I'll wait however long we need to wait, but I don't want anyone else but you. There are a lot of things in my life I'm not sure about right now, but you are not one of them."

The door clicked, and Betha's heart dropped when Colm pulled away just in time before Seamus opened it. She quickly stepped into the dry house, and Colm closed the umbrella and followed her.

"There you are," Seamus said as he moved around the table. "Henry came home a few minutes ago, but I thought you must have gotten lost."

Still untangling her mind from the previous moment, Betha wasn't ready to engage with her idiot brother. "Where is he?"

"Upstairs changing. Are you staying, Colm? I'm goin' out."

"I thought Cara was coming here," Betha interjected. "Colm is just here to dry out until the rain stops."

Seamus shook his head. "I needn't make her go out in this, and I don't think you exactly gave her the impression that she would be welcome. But with Henry around, you two should be fine being here." He gave Colm a commanding look that said it *would* be fine, or Colm would pay the consequences. "If my sister gets sick from staying out in the rain, I'll hold you responsible," he added.

"I'm not even wet!" Betha chose to ignore the comment about Cara being welcome and peeled her coat off, revealing her dry blouse underneath. "I'll put on a fresh skirt. Go dry by the fire."

She shooed Colm toward the hearth and passed Henry on her way up the stairs. He'd combed his wet hair and tied a dry muffler around his neck. "Go warm up with Mr. Gallagher," she whispered, patting his shoulder as he descended the stairs. After his run through the rain, Henry was in far more danger of catching cold than she was at the minute. One more minute under Colm's smoldering look, and she would have been in more danger of turning into a pile of ash.

She changed in a hurry, shivering in the chilly room. The rain had left a crown of wayward curls around her face, so she took her hair down, combed it into submission, and threw it into a quick braid. When she reached the kitchen, Seamus was gone, and Colm was pulling mugs off the shelf and handing them to Henry to place on the table. The kettle shrieked, and she stared at it in astonishment. The man had even put the kettle on?

"I'm afraid this is as far as I can go," he said sheepishly.

"The tea is here, unless you prefer coffee." She reached across him for the tin and at once regretted the move that brought his breath warming her neck and his gentle touch on her elbow.

"Tea would be good," he said in a low rumble.

Betha didn't dare look at him. She busied herself spooning tea into the pot. "I'll scare up a little dinner," she said in an effort to get Colm to leave her kitchen. She filled the pot with water from the kettle and carried it out to the front room table with Colm and Henry traipsing after her with the mugs. On a second trip, she brought a leftover tray of biscuits. The heat of Colm's gaze and his words on the front step followed every movement she made until she could escape back into the kitchen.

Was the man daft? She'd given him multiple reasons to find someone else to bestow his attention upon, and his response was that he didn't want anyone but her. The words and the way he said them sat in her chest, seeping into her bones.

"Has he gone mad?" she whispered to the Lord as she moved the pot of beans she'd left in the coals to the front of the hearth. No one had ever looked at her the way Colm Gallagher did. Somehow she'd always assumed that if she married, it would be to a Scotch-Irish laborer, or an artisan like her father. Not a worldly, educated man like Colm. And the match certainly would have been made because it was sensible, not because of romance.

"Here."

At the sound of Colm's voice behind her, she jerked upright, dropping the spoon on the floor.

He stood in the doorway, extending a steaming mug to her. "You didn't get your tea yet."

She nodded dumbly.

"I can't be responsible for allowing you to catch cold." His eyes danced, and Betha couldn't help but relax into a smile.

"Thank you," she said softly.

He placed it on the table and she looked back at her feet, where beans had splattered from the spoon across the hearth.

"No one . . ." She took a deep breath and met his eyes again. "No one treats me like you do, Colm. I'm not quite used to it." It had been twelve years since someone besides her had put on a kettle in her kitchen. It was such a small action, but an enormous gesture.

"I hope you do." Colm slid his fists into his pockets. His hat and the damp air had left his hair slightly tousled, giving him more of a boyish look than she'd seen on the proper teacher before. "Get used to being taken care of, I mean."

What was there to say in response to that? Betha used the hearth broom to sweep the spilled beans into the coals and then straightened and lifted the cup of tea. Looking up, she found Colm rocking on his heels.

"I, um . . . is Henry allowed to play chess with me?"

His change of demeanor seemed odd, and Betha could only guess that his declaration on the doorstep had left him feeling vulnerable. Especially since she hadn't had a chance to respond before Seamus interrupted them.

"Yes, of course." She inhaled. "I appreciate . . . you," she blurted out in an attempt to be helpful. "More than you know."

He gave her a small smile and turned back to where Henry waited.

Betha blew out her breath, wiped her hands on her apron, and attempted to slow her racing heart.

18

It stopped raining a long time before Colm stepped back through the Youngs' door into the street with his Bible in hand. Even the act of exchanging the cozy front room for the cold, wet street didn't quiet the song ringing in his heart. It had been a good Lord's day.

His first Sunday at Second Presbyterian had ended up being a positive experience. From his meeting with Reverend Breckinridge about the Sunday schools, he'd come to respect and appreciate the man and his heart for God and the people of Fell's Point. Hearing him preach for the first time not only solidified that but gave Colm a deeper appreciation for what was happening in his city beyond the walls of his own church.

But then that walk in the rain with Betha—Colm warmed all over just at the memory. Something had changed between them in that walk, and he didn't believe for a minute that it was one-sided. He'd been interested in Betha lately, intrigued by her, and enjoyed her company . . . but fitting her into his side as if he were her protector and walking home together as if it was something they did every week? That had set every part of his brain on fire. What had started out as an innocent escort home had left him breathless on her front step, wondering what it would be like to promise his entire future to her.

It broke his heart a little, the way she'd looked at him and suggested that he really ought to consider other women before her. It was clear that it had been far too long, if ever, since anyone saw Betha for herself and not for what she did for them.

The afternoon playing with Henry while she curled up in a chair in the corner with a book of poetry had done nothing to douse the fires. Especially since she didn't turn a single page the whole hour, revealing that she was as impacted by his presence as he was by hers. After he beat Henry at chess, they'd read the Bible with him and reviewed his catechism questions. By the end of it, Colm was ready to walk her down the aisle if it only meant that every Sunday could be like this one.

When only yesterday, she'd trounced on the suggestion of the two of them being a couple. *Slow down, Colm.* This wasn't what she needed from him right now. Only a cad would promise a girl that they could stay friends one day, and the next, show such disrespect to her request.

Colm slid inside the door of his father's house, hoping to escape upstairs unnoticed. Before he could even shut the door, he was met with the household in an uproar.

Maisie stood in front of the stove, crying, her arms crossed angrily across her chest. Father paced in front of her, rubbing his forehead with his fingers. Mor seemed to be trying to explain something to him, her voice rising in frustration that she wasn't being heard. Ben and Lyla sat at the table, their heads bent together in low whispers as they kept their eyes on the unfolding situation, and Bridget snapped her towel at the youngsters gaping around the room, ordering them to go find something else to do.

They scurried off, and Colm took a seat beside Lyla. "What's going on?"

Bridget spied him and crossed the floor, her hands worrying the towel. "Where's Patrick?"

Colm leaned back, turning to her in confusion. "Patrick?"

"He hasn't been around all day. Since he didn't go to church with us, we assumed he must have gone with you."

"No. I went to church alone and then was at the Youngs' until the rain stopped."

Lyla giggled. "It stopped two hours ago, Colm."

He sent her a wink. "I had to make sure it wasn't going to start again. But no, he's not been with me. What happened?"

"Oh, this has nothing to do with Patrick." Lyla gestured at Maisie and Father. "His absence is a separate issue."

Oh. Colm turned a questioning look on Bridget. Father came over, weariness lining his face. "Did you know about this business with Ezra Wright?"

"Nooo." Colm drew the word out. "Is he back?" Ezra had been in school with Maisie and Mor years ago, but best Colm remembered, his family had moved away at some point.

"I forgot you're barely around these days. Apparently he was given the wrong idea about Maisie's interest in him."

Colm bristled at the suggestion that he hadn't given his family any of his time lately, and then at the realization that if he didn't know about Ezra, he hadn't. "What did he do?"

"He proposed," Father said tightly.

Colm came to his feet. "Did he ask you?"

"He did, and I gave him my blessing. Neither of us knew that my daughter had merely toyed with his affections."

A sob burst out of Maisie and she buried her face in her handkerchief.

Colm stared at her. "Maisie?" This didn't seem like her. Maisie was friendly to everyone; shouldn't Ezra have picked up on that?

"She broke his heart," Lyla added in a whisper loud enough for the room to hear.

From the looks of things, Maisie had broken her own heart. Colm moved toward her and placed his hands gently on her shoulders. "What happened?" he asked softly.

"I didn't mean to do it," she quavered. "I thought he knew I only saw him as a sort of brother. Why did he have to be stupid and fall in love?" Tears trickled down her swollen face.

Because men did stupid things and let their hearts get entangled against their better judgment, that's why.

"Did you flirt with him?"

Maisie lifted her shoulders and huffed. "I might have done. I didn't treat him any differently than I treat anyone else, and he should have known that."

Colm had seen it more times than he could count—Maisie, vivacious Maisie, teasing the boys gathered around her, not unkindly. Throwing them smiles, accepting flowers, hanging on their arms. It was more than that, though; she cared about her friends, showed concern over what was going on in their lives, and offered comfort. Things that would make any young bloke fall in love.

"That's not quite true," Mor cut in. "You don't treat him like anyone else, Maisie."

"He's my friend," Maisie admitted with a sniff. "I would never want to hurt him."

Ah, so Maisie really cared for him but wasn't yet willing to face the natural morphing of a platonic friendship between young people into one of deep love. And poor Ezra must have been too dense or enamored or something to have missed the signs.

"That's what I thought. You and he used to be close chums when you were younger."

"Why couldn't it stay like that, Colm?" Maisie whimpered, leaning into his chest. "Why did he have to go and ruin everything?"

"Have you ever considered that at a different time, he might be the one for you?"

Maisie shook her head against his lapel. "Not Ezra. He has freckles and a pointy chin, and he stutters when he gets nervous. He could barely get the proposal out. I need to be swept off my feet."

"There are more important things than being swept off one's feet," Colm said gently.

Maisie wrapped her arms around his middle and sighed. "I just can't think of him that way."

"And now you've lost your friend." And ruined her reputation and shamed her family and . . . Colm couldn't keep going down that path.

"You didn't know he was falling in love with you?"

Mor gave a *hmph*, and Maisie separated from Colm to glare at her. "I might have wondered a little, but I tried to divert him."

Colm nodded. "Because you wanted to keep him, on your own terms."

"I already know everyone thinks I'm horrible." She pouted at him and looked around at the rest of the family watching the scene. "I have a headache. Can I go lie down?" she asked Father.

He nodded with a sigh, dropping his hands that had been resting on his hips. Without another glance, Maisie swept from the room. In the quiet that followed, Colm slumped into a chair and exhaled. He ran his palms up and down his thighs, suddenly exhausted.

"Do you think Ezra will mend?" he asked Mor.

"Not for a long while yet, if I had to guess based on how he looked today."

Poor kid. Colm had always thought he was a decent boy, and he didn't deserve this.

"And no one knows where Patrick is?"

Several heads shook in the negative.

He'd been off all day in his own dreamworld while his family faced multiple crises. He was no better than Ezra, living in a reality of his own imagination instead of keeping an objective outlook. Colm could only begin to imagine what the fellow was feeling right now, and the sympathy alone was more of a heartbreak than he wanted to experience. It would be best if he took Betha's words deeper to heart than whatever shivers she gave when he touched her. It was completely unfair to her that he had done so after what she'd said last night. *I'm sorry, Betha.*

Leaving his family mellowed downstairs, Colm picked up his hat and Bible from the table and retreated to his room. His eyes fell on Patrick's bed and the ache returned. Would this room ever feel like a safe retreat again, or would it always hurt a little whenever he stepped inside? *I'm sorry, Patrick.*

He dropped onto the edge of his bed, wondering what had happened to the song that had played in his heart when he left Betha's. Reality had shown up and gotten in his face with a reminder not to get ahead of himself. *I will look unto the Lord; I will wait for the God of my salvation.* That would be a really good place to get back to right about now.

Complete silence.

Colm rolled over, balled his pillow up, and stuffed it under his aching neck. Hours had passed since the household and the city around it had stopped moving and creaking. The constant strain to hear the click of the door latch prevented his body from relaxing into sleep. It didn't click, though, and at this point, it was foolish to keep thinking it might.

Wherever Patrick was, he wasn't coming home tonight. Colm should accept the fact for what it was.

He pushed himself out of bed and lit a candle. Careful to avoid the floorboards that squeaked, he gently nudged the bedroom door open. The kitchen was empty when he reached it, slightly disappointed. No one else was kept up out of concern for Patrick, which meant he was probably overly worried himself.

The wind blew, rattling the glass panes and drawing his eyes to the darkness outside, and then everything was quiet again. Colm filled a cup with water and sank onto a chair at the table. Leaning forward, he rested his cheek on his fist, stared at the flickering candle, and waited.

19

After seeing Colm three days in a row, the following week dragged slowly by in the monotony of Betha's daily responsibilities.

The bulk of her days were spent spinning in the middle room, with only the clack of Seamus's loom and whirr of her wheel to keep her company. Whenever she paused from her ongoing conversation with the Lord about the need for Him to do something to stop Seamus's marriage, Colm's blazing gaze on her doorstep quickly stepped into the void.

Is this thing with Colm from You, Lord? she would ask, but as often as she thought about it, she never once felt guilty for the affection growing in her heart for the man. So maybe it was, but it was too early yet to be sure.

She was preparing for her Saturday evening out with Maisie and Ava, hoping that Colm would be the one to pick her up again, when the front door clicked open. It would be neither of them, since any of the Gallaghers would have knocked. When the sound of voices met her ears, her heart sped up with apprehension.

Betha picked up her lace cap, smoothed her hands down her skirts, and descended the stairs to find Seamus and Cara in the front room. Cara glanced up at her and then away.

"Are ye staying here? I'm goin' out," Betha said to Seamus. Henry had left earlier to sail model boats with his friends in the stream.

"We might go to McColgan's after a while," Seamus replied. He had shed his coat and settled into a chair by the fire while Cara stood waiting uncertainly during the exchange.

Betha gave him a look. She had no interest in giving up part of her evening to chaperone Seamus, but could she in good conscience leave the two of them alone in the house?

"I'll bring in drinks," Betha said after a moment's consideration.

It was the polite thing to do for a guest, but as Betha put the kettle on, she couldn't help the thought that the more provisions she gave them, the less incentive they'd have to go anywhere else for sustenance.

They had been talking but broke off when Betha returned. She poured out the tea in complete silence. Taking a fortifying breath, she clutched the handle of the teapot and asked for strength from the Lord.

"Cara, I owe you an apology for the name I called you at the exhibition last week. I'm sorry."

It was as much as she could apologize for; losing her temper still didn't seem at all wrong, under the circumstances.

Cara only pressed her lips together and nodded, accepting the mug Betha handed her. Betha couldn't stop the words that came next from spilling out.

"The details of Henry's birth have no bearing on who he is, and as they are no fault of his own, we've worked hard to keep them out of public knowledge. The most anyone outside of the family needs to know at this late date is that Henry is Seamus's son and his mother is dead."

Please understand, she silently begged.

Cara shifted her eyes to Seamus. "I had no idea it was supposed to be a secret." She gave a little laugh, toying nervously with the handle of her mug.

"What's done is done," Seamus said, hitting his thighs with his palms. "They know now."

Even though Betha hadn't expected more from either of them, their responses still sent indignation through her veins. Why must adults be so inconsiderate of children? Shouldn't those who knew better do more to protect the little ones under their responsibility?

Turning away, she collected her work basket from the middle room. The seat she selected was at the other end of the table, away from where Seamus and Cara had claimed the seats by the fire. Neither paid any more mind to her but were soon speaking in low voices to each other.

The room grew darker and Betha lit a lantern, but still no Gallaghers arrived. Seamus and Cara didn't make any move to leave, or else Betha might have ventured out to see what was keeping her friends.

When her stomach finally grumbled, she addressed Seamus. "Are you goin' out, or should I serve supper?"

Seamus grinned at Cara. "Might as well. We're comfortable here."

Betha was too concerned about the Gallaghers to be annoyed. Having a reason to be in the kitchen was preferable to the present company, anyway. It didn't take long to cut up the leftover fish from dinner and throw it into soup, but it gave her mind opportunity to create several explanations for Colm's absence.

It was tempting to think that he'd wisened up and taken to heart her advice to find a woman better suited for him. Yet that just didn't seem like him, especially considering the way he'd looked at her. More likely, he was serious about being willing to wait for her and was doing just that. As for Maisie . . . she could have contracted Mor's sore throat. Chances were, there was no need to exaggerate either absence in her mind.

When the food was almost ready, Betha headed into the front room to set the table. She hadn't noticed how quiet the front room had grown, being distracted in her own thoughts in the kitchen. There was a flurry of movement and a thump as Seamus and Cara both leapt to their feet from Seamus's chair, red-cheeked and hair slightly askew. *Oh, for heaven's sake.* Ignoring them, Betha pulled bowls from the sideboard.

Seamus coughed and ran his fingers through his hair to right it while Betha pretended not to notice. There was no use in saying anything; both of them had proved that they cared neither for Betha's opinion nor moral behavior. At least they had the decency to pull apart when she came in.

When supper was served, they sat at the table and Betha spoke the prayer aloud. She lifted her head and glanced to the window. It was fully dark now, and Henry should be returning any minute. She'd had enough of the awkward silence in the meantime.

"Would you tell me about your family, Cara?"

"Oh." Cara wiped her mouth with her napkin. "There isn't much to tell. I've no living brothers or sisters, and my mother died of yellow fever when I was ten."

"I'm sorry to hear that." Yellow fever broke up far too many families and had been one of Betha's greatest concerns when Seamus raised the idea of moving south. "And your father?"

Cara focused on the soup she was slowly stirring. "I don't know where he is. It's been several years since I've seen him." She gave a harsh laugh. "He could be dead, too, for all I know."

Although it wasn't an excuse, it did explain some of Cara's lack of propriety. Betha ate slowly, wondering if Cara would ever view her as a sister and desire to follow the example she set of respectable womanhood. She would have to work hard to be someone worth emulating. *May it be, Lord. By Your help and grace.*

"You live with an aunt and uncle now?" she asked.

"Yes, my mother's brother and his wife and my two cousins."

She didn't offer anything more, leaving Betha uncertain of the closeness of the relationship. Were they unkind people? Was this why Cara had latched so fiercely on to Seamus, because she was desperate for an escape? Or was she looking for a way out because they were pious and Seamus allowed her to shed all restraints of religious conduct?

Betha was going to ask about her uncle's occupation when the door opened and Henry came in with his schooner tucked under his arm, lantern swinging. Betha rose to welcome him and serve up his food. The conversation shifted with his entrance, and Betha tucked the remainder of her questions away for another time.

The sight of Colm's brown head in the back pew brought shyness over Betha when she entered the church on Sunday with Henry and their foot warmer. How should she approach him when she didn't know the reason for his distance from her this week? If it was for unrelated reasons and his ardor for her still burned as brightly, she didn't want to come across as cold in her greeting, but if he had made a deliberate choice to create more space between them, it would be indecorous of her to address him too warmly.

Henry halted by his pew first. "Good morning, Mr. Gallagher."

"Ah, good Lord's day, Henry." Colm lifted his head, which had been bent over his Bible, and Betha saw the dark circles under his eyes. The man had noticeably aged. "Hello, Betha."

"Colm." Betha inclined her head in concern. "Are you quite well?" His distant gaze stood in a stark contrast to his demeanor of the previous Sunday.

He hesitated before glancing briefly at Henry. "I am well, thank you."

He seemed intent to leave it at that, so Betha nodded and ushered Henry on to their seat. Hopefully he would be willing to offer more of an explanation in private.

Henry stayed by her side when Colm escorted her home after the service ended. Colm didn't speak as they walked, so Betha didn't either.

"Go on, Henry; I'll be right in," she said on the street in front of the house.

He said goodbye to Colm, took the foot warmer from her, and obediently tromped up the stairs.

"Are you goin' home?" She tilted her face up to see Colm's, lifting her hand to shield her eyes from the sun.

He nodded, and the movement looked reluctant. "I don't think I can take a walk today. But I received the books from the Sunday School Union, so we should review them together sometime."

"I'm available anytime you need me to be. Perhaps I should come to the school one day after class?"

"Yes. I'll have them there. Maybe Tuesday?"

"I'll see you Tuesday."

She waited, but the Colm of the previous week still didn't reappear. "You look knackered today, and I missed seeing Maisie last night. Is there trouble?"

Colm pursed his lips before nodding again. "My family faced some difficulties this week."

"Oh, I'm sorry, Colm." Even though she wasn't the oldest in her family, she understood the way the lines deepened on his face. She felt a similar weight of responsibility for hers. "I wish I'd known. Is there anything I can do?"

"There's not even anything I can do," he said, and Betha felt the helplessness emanating from him. He glanced around the street before lowering his voice. "Patrick was arrested."

Betha started. "Patrick was—?" What on earth?

"He was caught . . ." Colm shifted on his feet. "He was helping runaway slaves. The slaves were recaptured, and he was arrested. He was fined and released."

So when Colm said Patrick was an abolitionist, he didn't mean in name only. Patrick was actually risking himself, breaking the law, to help fugitives. The news made Betha's head spin.

"Oh my. Was the fine very much?"

"More than Patrick had."

The pieces clicked into place, and Betha understood. "You paid it."

Colm didn't deny it. "He's been quite out of sorts since he got home. What became of the runaways haunts him all day, and he can hardly take it. He's a bear to live with."

It didn't take much to hear between the lines and see that despite the words he spoke, Colm's greatest concern wasn't annoyance at his brother's moods.

"I can imagine the effect this must have on the whole family," Betha said softly. "I hadn't heard anything about it." Her fingers had grown cold through her mittens, so she stuffed her hands into her pockets.

"It will make its way around town soon enough. I—" Colm stared down the street with a pensive look on his face. "He wanted to have his own house so he could harbor travelers coming through the city. I suppose there's no harm in telling you that. But now that he's been arrested, he'll be watched. He can't help anymore without being a liability to those he's helping. It would have all been a waste if he'd already bought the house."

"Maybe. Or maybe the house would have been what he needed to escape detection."

Heat entered Colm's eyes of a different variety altogether.

"You're probably right, though," Betha said to extinguish the fire. "It's a dangerous business he's in."

Colm let out a frustrated breath, his jaw still clenched tight. "I'd better get home. They'll likely be needing me."

"I do understand, Colm. And you look like there's a lot more you'd like to say."

Finally his face softened, as if he just then saw Betha for the first time instead of Patrick. "I'm sorry I'm not good company today."

"You don't need to be," Betha said simply. "But it's better to talk about it with me than try to make him understand right now when you're both upset about it. I'm happy to listen."

It was forward, but she'd said it anyway, because it seemed like Colm needed to know it more than he needed propriety. He reached out to squeeze her hand. "I appreciate it, but I'm sure I needn't make you hear all of it. Thank you, Betha."

She pressed his hand in return. "I know you're praying about it, but I'll be praying for you, too, to be what your brother needs right now." The words coming out of her mouth brought a twinge of guilt. Why had she never considered such a prayer for herself?

He gave her a halfhearted smile and then he was gone.

Betha hugged herself against the cold as she turned to the house. Arrested, indeed. Ava had said Patrick's big heart got ahead of his head. Betha hadn't imagined before just how much it was true.

20

Colm opened the schoolhouse door to a gloomy gray afternoon and a chilly burst of air. Boys rushed past him into their freedom, still pulling jackets on and slapping caps on their heads.

"See you tomorrow, Mr. Gallagher!" they called one after another as they tumbled out of the door and disappeared into the mist. The clatter of girls' footsteps on the stairs began, their voices mingling with the boys' as they met up with brothers and neighbors for the walk home.

Colm frowned at the sky. Betha shouldn't have to come out in this kind of weather for their meeting when he was capable of bringing the books to her house. By the time the boys were gone and the schoolhouse tidy, she'd already be on her way. He'd risk missing her if he walked to her house at the same time she was coming to the school.

"Goodbye, Mr. Gallagher."

"See you, Henry."

Colm stood watching his receding head until a long blue hooded cloak appeared from around the corner, stopping to greet Henry before continuing toward him. The last of the boys flew out the door, and Colm straightened to greet his visitor.

"Maisie."

She stepped into the schoolhouse and lifted the hood off her lace day cap. "Do you have some time to spare? I needed someone to talk to without the whole family eavesdropping."

Colm hesitated, glancing out into the street before closing the door. "I have a meeting, actually. I'm sorry." He hated to turn her away when she looked so unhappy and had chosen him out of everyone to be her confidante.

Her face fell, and he felt like a lout.

"If you're willing to wait . . . you could stay. Maybe you could even be of assistance, if you wanted."

"For what?"

The door opened, and this time, it was Betha. "Good afternoon," she said with a demure smile for Colm. She untied her warm cloak and took the liberty of hanging it on a hook by the door. She wore an apron pinned over her mulberry-colored dress and a cream linen fichu at her neck, and she, too, had a day cap over her hair. "Maisie, I'm glad you're here. I didn't know you were to help." She brightened as she spoke, her pleasure at seeing both of them unconcealed.

"Help with what?" Maisie turned curious eyes on Colm.

"Sunday school. It's starting the Sunday after next," he explained, stepping behind his desk to retrieve the books. "Now that harvest is over and winter is upon us, children have more time to attend. I don't want to keep delaying the start of it. You should join us, Maisie, if you can."

Betha pursed her lips at Colm thoughtfully. "Not *should*, but we would be glad to have your help."

Her correction sank in. He'd just done to Maisie what he'd always chafed against Patrick doing to him, assuming what would be good for her. He tipped his head in concession. "Quite so."

Maisie gave a sort of smile, but she lifted both hands in agitation. "I didn't mean to interrupt your meeting. I can wait to talk to Colm."

"Oh no, this seems more important." Betha backed up, turning questioning eyes to Colm. "Is it about Patrick? I can come another day."

Colm didn't know what to do, when he still didn't know what Maisie wanted to say to him. He hated the thought of sending Betha back out into the weather alone without even accomplishing the meeting.

"Not Patrick." Maisie pushed her eyebrows together in confusion.

"What is it?" Betha asked, wrapping an arm around Maisie's shoulders. "You look troubled. If you need to talk to Colm, I can go."

"Or you can talk to both of us." Colm finally stated the obvious, frustration rising.

Maisie groaned and plopped onto a bench. "Did he tell you about Ezra?"

"No, of course not." Betha managed to answer without the offense Colm would have taken. She took a seat beside Maisie and leaned forward.

"Ezra was an old friend of mine since we were small, and recently he decided to become an imbecile and fall in love with me."

Colm left his books, coming around the desk to lean back against it with his arms crossed over his chest. "Was it really only recently though?" he asked carefully.

"Colm is the only person in the family who hasn't judged me for how it all happened," Maisie said with a flash in her eye.

Taking the hint, Colm rubbed his fingers across his forehead. His sister was in fine form since the Ezra fiasco. Her sarcasm combined with Patrick's anger had made the Gallagher home a lovely place to be the last few days.

"Oh, I'm sorry." Betha took Maisie's hand and clutched it in her lap. "It's not an easy thing for either one when such deep feelings run only one direction," she added.

"He's making me miserable." Maisie melted into Betha's side.

Colm straightened, lowering his hand. "Has he spoken to you again?"

"No. He seems to have taken my refusal seriously, as he should. But the Wrights sit two rows in front of us in church, and he sits there looking pathetic and dejected, with his head bowed and shoulders slumped. I can't stand it."

Somehow Colm managed not to snort a laugh, and inwardly applauded his own self-control. Maisie could hardly be the most miserable of the pair.

"I can see you still care a great deal about how he is doing," Betha said soothingly.

"Of course I care! He's my friend."

"Have you thought about speaking to him?" Colm asked. Because honestly, anyone could see that Maisie was in love with the fellow. Everyone except Maisie.

"I can't imagine that he would want to hear from me, after how I treated him."

She was exactly who Ezra probably did want to hear from. Colm shook his head.

"I rejected him, and he's hurt. There's nothing I can say to change the situation, so what else would help?"

Her words niggled in Colm's mind, sounding eerily similar to what he could say about Patrick. What would help Patrick and mend their relationship, when his mind hadn't changed about the choice he'd made?

"I'm sure that it would mean a great deal to him to know that you're sorry for how things went between you and that you care for him as a person," Betha said. "He might now be wondering if you hate him, and it would set those fears at ease."

Was she speaking to Colm or to Maisie?

"It wouldn't give him false hope, do you think?" Maisie asked in a small voice. "Or make him even more bitter to discover that after saying such things, I still uphold my decision?"

"I can't promise that it won't, but in my opinion, it's always best to do everything we can to pursue reconciliation and honest communication.

If your motives are true and you consider how he typically responds before choosing your words, he should be able to receive it in the spirit that you approach him in. But if he can't and you said what the Lord directed you to, then his response is his responsibility, not yours."

Colm caught himself tugging at the hair at the back of his neck and slowly lowered his hand, hoping no one had noticed. Where did Betha get this kind of wisdom from? He cringed to think of what he might have said if Betha hadn't been there.

Maisie lifted questioning eyes to Colm. "Do you think this would help Ezra recover?" His little sister, always looking to him for direction. Even though the mess she was in was largely her own fault, he'd always felt protective of her and would do what he could to help.

Colm cleared his throat. "Forgiveness and being assured someone cares for you are both excellent healing remedies for the human spirit." But would they restore Ezra's—or Patrick's—broken heart? Not likely.

From the looks of things, Maisie still had a long way to go before she could admit to herself that she was in love with Ezra, and no one else could convince her of it. Opening communication between the two of them would at least be a good first step in that direction.

"So you mean I should forgive him too," Maisie said with a sigh.

Colm hadn't thought of that, but she wasn't wrong. "Forgive a fellow for falling in love with you?" he said and quirked a grin.

"It isn't funny, Colm. He was supposed to know better."

There was no point in arguing with her. "It would do you good to work toward that and ask the Lord for help."

Maisie blew out her breath and removed her hand from Betha's lap. "I suppose I will. Mor said much the same thing." She rubbed her hands up and down her apron. "I shouldn't keep delaying your meeting, and I am interested in hearing about the Sunday school."

Colm pushed off the desk. "Don't stay away if you ever have more questions. We don't mind." He looked to Betha for confirmation, since he was speaking for her as well, and she smiled and shook her head in agreement.

Maisie thanked them as Colm turned around and picked up his books. "As for the Sunday school—its purpose is to teach students how to read using the Bible and also focuses on learning the catechism and memorizing scripture. I will teach the boys"—he handed Betha several small books and pamphlets—"and Betha will teach the girls."

Betha sifted through her materials while Maisie leaned on her shoulder, looking them over together.

Colm gave them a moment before continuing. "We have two hours after the morning service at Second Presbyterian. The Sunday School Union sent alphabet cards and there are readers that start with simple Bible stories and moral lessons. We have memory verses listed by difficulty, and here are the catechisms and hymnals. Oh, and cards with the Ten Commandments." He picked them up and waved them.

"The lessons won't be divided. We'll just start at the lower level and work our way up together as a class. Then we'll study one catechism question each week, and everyone will start with the same memory verses, although the older children will be assigned more of them every week than the little ones. They'll get these tickets for each verse they memorize."

Maisie sat up. "If it's after the morning service, the children will be hungry. And if you send them home for dinner after the service before class, it will be less likely that they'll come back."

"Many of the students might not go to church at all," Colm said.

Betha closed the book, pondering. "Do you think we should feed them?"

Colm and Betha looked to Maisie, who chewed on her lip. "Maybe that's how I could help. It would have to be a cold meal, though, since I'll be at church beforehand."

"Or something simple like beans that can be left sitting in coals while you're away."

Colm remembered that Betha had done that at her own house. It was a smart way to have a hot meal on a cold winter Sunday, and he knew many of his students weren't guaranteed more than one meal a day.

Maisie was nodding, her earlier despondency gone. "I can do that. Let me provide dinner for the children every week, Colm. You may even get more students who are interested in coming if they know there will be food."

"You're hired." It was good to see a grin on Maisie's face in response to the one he gave her.

"This is wonderful." Betha ran her hand over the reader in her lap. "Just think of how God's Word will be within reach for all these children now. Even if they don't have parents who go to church, they can come and learn how to love and worship God."

She lifted awe-filled eyes to Colm, and his heart pricked. The materials had made him excited, but they hadn't brought tears to his eyes. Excited, but also apprehensive. After all these years, he was really going to do what he'd always hesitated to do—teach the Bible to children.

Betha must have read the uncertainty in his carriage. "You aren't your old teacher, Colm. What was his name?"

"MacMurrough." The name still tasted sour in Colm's mouth.

"It was wrong of him to use God's Word to instill fear in his students. But that's not what we're doing at all. We're here to instill . . . God. So children can know *Him*, not so they will obey the whims of their masters."

"'God is love; perfect love casteth out fear,'" Maisie quoted, studying her with fresh respect. It was just like Betha to get straight to the heart of the matter.

"I wish that all teachers remembered to teach those parts of the Bible," Colm said quietly. He heard a rustle and looked up to see Betha approach with her finger still stuck in the book tucked against her chest.

She stopped in front of him, waiting until he locked his gaze with hers, as if she needed to be sure he heard her. "We will. The children already know that you love them, and that's already a weighty difference from your own experience as a student. When you stand up and tell them that the confession of our faith teaches that God is 'most loving, gracious, merciful, longsuffering, abundant in goodness and truth, forgiving iniquity, transgression, and sin, and the rewarder of them that diligently seek Him,' they'll believe you. Because you are gracious and longsuffering and forgiving with them the rest of the week."

Colm rubbed his chin, still trying to catch up. The students knew he loved them? He hadn't known he did; it wasn't a thought he'd ever put together. But he supposed it was true, though he still reeled from the idea that his students, also without words, could already believe such a thing.

"And we will teach them to sing"—Betha opened the hymnbook in her hand—"'O children, come, and taste his love; Come, learn his pleasant ways, And let your own experience prove The riches of his grace.' We'll teach them that this is who God is, Colm. We can't make them believe, but they won't walk away thinking that God is short-tempered and unforgiving."

Maisie was sitting with her palms pressed into the bench on either side of her, listening raptly. "I think I want to be a child in Betha's class," she said with a laugh. "Who wouldn't want to listen to her teach such things?"

The joy that was on Betha's face faded at Maisie's question, and Colm knew the unspoken answer to it: Seamus didn't listen. He reached out and covered her hand on the book. "Thank you."

He didn't know if he was thanking her for the reminder that his God loved him, for recognizing the seeds he'd already sown into his students, or for believing that he was capable of teaching the Bible in a way other than the one he'd been taught. Or maybe he was thanking God for bringing her into his life for all those reasons.

Knowing they couldn't make anyone else believe wouldn't take away the pain it caused her though. The inability to be truly helpful chafed like an itch Colm couldn't reach. He shifted his stance in an effort to ease his discomfort. "Do you have any questions about the materials?"

"Not yet. I'll take them home and let you know if I think of any."

Something he'd learned from his years in the classroom came to mind. "Just remember that you're the teacher; the materials are just a tool.

If you want to alter the lesson, you can do so. For example, since it's Thanksgiving, you can make the choice to teach about thankfulness."

"Do people celebrate Thanksgiving here?" Eyes wide, Betha looked from Colm to Maisie and set the book aside.

Colm answered first. "We do, though not everyone does."

"I'm glad. I thought it was only a holiday up north, but I was still goin' to try to make a Thanksgiving dinner since we've always celebrated it."

"Oh, come have Thanksgiving with us." Maisie stood and reached out for Betha's arm. "You needn't do all that work yourself."

"Truly?" Betha twisted her fingers uncertainly.

"Of course," Colm put in. "There will be plenty for your family too."

"This Thursday," Maisie added.

"It would be nice," Betha admitted. "Thank you."

Colm's heart lifted at the thought of Betha in his house, meeting the rest of his family. He wasn't impressed by girls who weren't sensible enough to accept invitations or were too proud to own their limitations. There were a lot of reasons that Betha had caught his eye and was starting to consume his heart. She never made much of herself, but she didn't make too little of herself to accept help.

When she had wrapped up her books and departed, Colm stood in the silence with Maisie, lost in thought as he ran a finger over the embossing on the catechism on his desk.

"I like her," Maisie announced with a cheerful sigh.

Colm did, too, but his mind was elsewhere. His attitude toward teaching the Bible had been gradually changing over the last months. And now in just one meeting, he'd somehow gone further, from being willing to teach it for the sake of the children and service to God, to looking forward to it in anticipation. All because of what Betha had said. Because of who she was through and through.

"She is something special," Colm murmured, more to the book than to Maisie.

And he was becoming a different person as a result.

21

The sharp scent of tallow mixed with pipe smoke and the occasional shuffle of Seamus's feet took Betha back to her childhood, watching Da rub the warp threads. Her spinning wheel was strategically placed in the middle room so she couldn't see Seamus and could work in peace, and it was easy to picture the movements she heard as Da's. Seamus had Ma's black hair, but the way he stumped about was very much like his father.

It seemed a lifetime ago when it had been the four of them building a livelihood together, eating together, going to church together. Betha caught herself getting lost in the memories. There had been no Henry then, so the old days could never be more perfect to her mind than today was.

There was a clank of metal meeting metal as Seamus pressed the lid back on the can. He banged around the room for a few more minutes, and soon he appeared in the doorway with his arms crossed over his chest and his mug in hand. From his position against the doorjamb, he watched Betha work. When he cleared his throat, she looked up.

"I proposed to Cara."

Betha's foot stilled and she dropped her hands to her lap as dread ate its way up her chest.

"Last night," Seamus continued. "She accepted."

Was she expected to offer congratulations to such news? Betha couldn't get the word past her lips when her stomach felt like it had received a death blow.

"When will you marry?" she managed.

"New Year's Eve."

Betha nodded. It was fear that clutched her stomach, she realized, and offered up a prayer to release it to God. Her stomach didn't unclench, but the prayer reminded her of existence beyond herself. God was on His throne in the heavens. *You see, Lord. You know. Please send help.*

"What do you want me to do?" she asked in a small voice.

Seamus gave her a questioning look.

"I suppose I'll spin for you still and she will too? Do you want me to keep house or let her do it how she likes?"

Seamus lifted his chin in understanding before taking a sip from his cup. "I'll ask what she wants. I guess you'll have someone to split the work with now."

Betha worked a piece of flax through her fingers. "It will help with income, having two spinners in the house." They'd need it if they were to add another to clothe and feed. She could only hope Seamus had done all the figuring before he proposed.

"When will you tell Henry?" A spasm rolled through her stomach at the thought of Henry having to live with Cara. As much as she didn't want to share her space with the woman, she was an adult and would learn to live with it. But Henry needed to be protected from his new stepmother as much as possible if she couldn't learn to respect him. Thankfully, he already slept near Betha and had since he was a baby. At least that wouldn't change for him.

"I don't suppose you want to do it?" The wry grin on Seamus's face could mean he was joking, but Betha couldn't be sure.

"No chance of that. And we're goin' to the Gallaghers' for Thanksgiving tomorrow, so it should probably be tonight."

Seamus sucked in his breath, pushed off the wall, and took another drink. "You shouldn't have accepted the invitation without asking me first. What if I wanted to go to Cara's tomorrow?"

"Maybe you shouldn't have proposed without asking me first," Betha said with a lift of her nose. "You can manage to have one dinner with my friends."

He walked away, and Betha shook her head at his back. He knew he couldn't win that one, after what he'd done by proposing against her advice.

She sat idly while her eyes traveled around the room and then into the kitchen. Bags of flax—enough to keep her wheel busy through the winter—leaned against the corner closest to her, next to her tailoring and mending workbasket. Seamus's bed was in the other corner, under the linen-curtained window. A crate beside it doubled as storage for his best suit and a bedside table for a candlestick. Currently, Henry's piece of ashwood leaned up against it, since he'd been whittling on Seamus's bed the previous evening.

Through the doorway, the kitchen table stood in the center of the room in front of the shelf where her mugs were lined. From her vantage point, she could just see the edge of the pots and cooking utensils that hung on hooks beside the fireplace on the adjoining wall.

Their belongings weren't much, but they were arranged how she liked them. Somehow she'd have to make room for Cara's things and her wheel in just a few weeks. How much of her comfortable existence would change when Cara came in? Would she take over, or expect Betha to keep doing everything for her? How would it all affect Henry, and what could Betha possibly do to help him through his life being upended?

Betha inhaled sharply at a new thought. What would happen when Seamus gave Henry siblings? That was something in the whole mess that would probably be good for Henry, something he'd find joy in. More was changing in the coming days than she had thought of before.

She pushed back her chair and stood, wiping her sweaty palms down her apron front. One day at a time; and now she needed to start the bread for the pudding she'd promised to bring to Thanksgiving dinner.

Nerves assaulted Betha as she stared at the two-storied, double-chimney brick house before her. She had assumed that Colm's house would be unlike hers, with his father in the government and so many family members living together. To see it with her own eyes, however, confirmed the suspicion she'd long carried that Colm was not like her.

Seamus and Henry were moving forward, with or without her, so she forced her legs to keep up. If Colm Gallagher belonged to such a respected family, his father could surely find him a job in the government with little effort, yet he'd chosen to be a schoolteacher in a poor neighborhood. With Patrick in the newspaper, it was clear that Mr. Gallagher had allowed his sons choice in their careers rather than expecting them to follow in his footsteps.

That thought prevailed in her mind when Seamus knocked on the door and Colm himself opened it. His hair was neatly arranged, and he wore the suit he wore to church, the black-tailed coat with a black waistcoat, long trousers, and a white cravat tied in a bow.

His smile lit up his face. "Welcome." He moved aside to allow them entrance, and another thought struck Betha: the Gallaghers, though seemingly on the upper edge of middle class and in a slave state, did not keep a butler or housekeeper, even paid ones.

The house was warm and aromatic after the cold walk. Betha pulled her hood back from her lace cap, her face beginning its thaw as Colm shook hands with Seamus.

"Leave your wraps here, and we can meet everyone in the kitchen," Colm said, taking the bread pudding from her hands so she could unbundle herself.

Two faces around Henry's age appeared in a doorway to their left. Noticing his guests' diverted attention, Colm turned and spotted them.

"Finn and Hanna, come meet our guests."

The pair stepped mutely into the hall, their dress clean and tidy, not one of their russet hairs out of place. Colm addressed Henry. "My youngest brother and sister. Finn is eleven and Hanna is nine."

"I didn't know you have siblings my age," Henry said, still staring at them.

"We met them at the picnic that one time," Betha prodded. "Before we knew they were Colm's siblings. Good day, Finn and Hanna."

"They're my half-siblings, but siblings just the same." Colm took a step toward the door on the other side of the hall. "Henry's a student and a friend of mine," he said to the children over his shoulder. "Come join us."

He placed his hand on the door latch but paused. Betha lifted her eyes to his and he smiled. "Happy Thanksgiving. Thank you for coming."

Betha pressed a hand over the stomach of her pearl-gray linen lawn dress in an attempt to calm herself, from nerves or from the well-dressed man paying her compliments, she wasn't sure which.

"You've a lovely house," she blurted, feeling like a muttonhead for her less than intelligent reply.

His eyes crinkled into laugh lines as he looked around at the crown molding and the staircase. "We've lived here since Father's marriage, and it's served us well. I'm afraid when I buy my own house, I will start out smaller, as he did."

He opened the door and led Betha into a room that extended the legnth of the house. A long, bare wooden table reached from the front wall to the middle of the room, where a large black stove stood in the place the hearth would have been. Betha spotted Maisie in the cluster of females chopping, stirring, and opening stove doors to adjust coals.

Colm set Betha's dish on the table next to a scruffy character wearing an everyday work coat, informal compared to Colm's brushed suit.

"Patrick!" Betha opened her mouth to say more to him, but she'd commanded the attention of the room by her exclamation. Maisie dropped her knife and came her way, arms open.

"Hello, Betha," Patrick said, shifting around. A new beard crept over his face, and his usually unruly curls looked like they hadn't seen a comb recently. While Maisie hugged Betha, Colm introduced Seamus to Patrick and then the three guests to everyone else. Betha recognized Mor and had seen Lyla at their one shared picnic.

"Is this everyone?" she asked Colm.

"I have two more brothers. Ben and Reuben must be in the other room."

Betha looked around at everyone, repeating their names silently to herself. *Colm, Patrick, Maisie, Mor, Lyla, Finn, Hanna; and Ben and Reuben.* Once they were cemented in her mind, she addressed Bridget. "Can I help?"

"Oh no, we're almost done," Maisie cut in. "Besides, you already brought a dish. Hanna, can you lay the table?"

"I'll show you the other rooms," Colm offered. Patrick and Seamus were blocking the doorway with their conversation, so Betha followed Colm with Henry and Finn through another doorway at the opposite end of the room. It took them back into the main hall on the back side of the staircase from the front door. Colm led them to a matching doorway across the hall and into a room papered in lavender.

"The older girls sleep here, and it's the parlor for the women to receive company," he explained, giving Betha a moment to admire the attractive four-poster bed, the plush chairs, and the embroidery frames. "Did you make it to church this morning?"

"Henry and I did. Were you with your family?"

"We went to the Thanksgiving prayer meeting at First Presbyterian. Not many people were there."

"It was a small meeting at Second as well."

The doorway across from Patrick and Seamus, where Finn and Hanna had appeared from earlier, led to the master bedroom. Besides the bed and washstand, it also harbored a desk and a small round table, clearly the place where Mr. Gallagher hosted his guests and conducted business. He was in there, as were Ben and Reuben, who were engaged in a board game Betha didn't recognize. Betha noted how very much Colm looked like his father and what he himself would probably look like in another twenty years. Mr. Gallagher greeted her politely in response to Colm's introduction, and when Finn and Henry stopped to watch the game, Colm led her back into the hall.

"There are three bedrooms upstairs. One was the nursery, but Hanna was the only one left in it, so we decided last year that it's not the nursery anymore. When Finn moved in with Ben and Reuben, Lyla moved back in with Hanna."

Seamus broke away from Patrick, meandering into the study. The hall was quiet, so Betha took the chance to apprehend Patrick while she could. With the dark circles under his eyes and the new beard taking over his face, he didn't look anything like the bright-eyed youth she'd met in front of her house a few months ago. Her heart ached to think of all that Colm had shared about him over the past weeks.

"I was sorry to hear of your recent trials from Colm," she said, peering up at him with compassion. "You're brave for what you did."

"Brave or foolish?" He looked weary, but the bitterness in his tone was new to Betha. Colm had tried to warn her, but it was jarring to see the change in person.

"Brave, I think. It's never foolish to take risks in an attempt to stop suffering and help people."

Patrick crossed his arms. "It doesn't feel brave when they're suffering worse as a result of your interference than they were before you tried to help. That seems very, very foolish."

Betha studied him for a long moment while he cocked an eye back at her as if he thought he'd silenced her.

"The only foolish thing that I see in the situation is the fact that it's legal to capture people and send them back into bondage and not to assist desperate people in need. It's brave to stand up against unjust laws and to keep going after difficult setbacks. It's brave to think through and figure out better, safer methods so you can be successful in bringing even more people to freedom in the future."

The look on Colm's face suggested that she might be crazy for encouraging his brother to continue doing what had gotten him arrested before—something which had cost Colm a lot of money—but Patrick looked downright ragged. He needed to be able to do something about the passion that was clearly burning a hole through his chest even still.

"What are you goin' to do now?" Betha asked, not backing down.

Patrick opened his mouth but nothing came out.

"If the way you were operating before is no longer possible, what can you do instead?" The sound of Colm's voice behind her swelled pride in Betha. Colm was laying aside his own misgivings because even he could see that in order to mend, Patrick's wounded soul needed a way forward. A way out of the pit he was in.

"I honestly don't know." Patrick lifted his hands in defeat, but at least he and Colm were speaking to each other.

Betha would have said more, but a knock sounded at the door behind her. She stepped out of the way, and Colm opened the door to a freckled young man with a thin face, wearing a black suit like Colm and carrying a black hat.

"Ezra!" Colm hesitated, as if unsure what to do with this particular visitor.

"Hello, Ezra." Patrick leaned around the door frame, reaching across Colm to push the door open. "Come in."

Ezra took a cautious step inside and Colm backed up. "Did Maisie invite you?"

"I did," Patrick said nonchalantly, closing the door. Betha and Colm stared at him, confused and not a little dismayed.

"I mean to ask Maisie if she minds," Ezra said slowly, looking between the brothers.

"Why would she mind? She's friends with you just the same as I am." Patrick frowned, and Betha covered her mouth as the awareness of the situation hit her. Had Patrick been in jail when Ezra proposed to Maisie? And had no one in the family talked about it in the house since then?

Maisie appeared in the doorway, wiping her hands on her apron, her cheeks flushed and panic in her eyes. "Hello, Ezra."

Ezra twisted his hat in his hands. "Hello, Maisie. Patrick invited me today, and I didn't get a chance to ask if you would rather I didn't . . ."

"What's all this?" Patrick exclaimed, throwing his hands in the air.

"I can tell you later," Colm muttered.

"You can stay," Maisie said in a soft voice. She took a deep breath and chanced a glance at her older brothers before peeking back at Ezra. "We should probably talk anyway."

Ezra nodded without a sign of relief on his clenched jaw, but Betha knew what it had cost Maisie to offer the conversation. It was no small thing for Ezra to have shown up either.

"Well, come on in then," Colm said, gesturing to the study as Maisie took Ezra's hat.

Colm made to follow Ezra, but Patrick stopped him with a demanding "What's going on?"

Thankfully, Maisie removed herself back into the kitchen, and Ezra was swallowed up in the activity in the study. Betha stood uncertainly in the hall, feeling that she ought to return to the kitchen but too caught up in the scene to leave.

"He proposed to her, you blockhead," Colm hissed.

"And?"

"She turned him down."

"You can't be serious."

Colm tilted his head, indicating that he was quite serious.

"I suppose I can't do anything right these days." Patrick jammed his hands onto his hips. "I can't believe he accepted my invitation and didn't say anything."

"He probably thought you knew, and I can't imagine he wanted to talk to anyone about it. But Maisie is right; they needed to face each other sometime."

"I'll see what I can do in the kitchen," Betha interjected in a timid voice.

Colm blew out his breath with a nod, and she and he separated into the opposite rooms, leaving Patrick alone in the hall.

22

Colm and Maisie were not wrong about the Gallagher Thanksgiving. The table was laden with plenty of food for the family and guests, with more to spare.

Betha savored the roast goose that melted in her mouth and could only imagine what it would be like to share a kitchen with so many pairs of hands on a daily basis or eat at a table hosting multiple conversations like this one. She sat between Colm and Seamus, across from Patrick and Ezra and within hearing range of Mr. Gallagher and Bridget on the other side of Colm.

She caught Henry's eye from his place at the other end of the table, and they exchanged grins. It was unfortunate that Colm's brothers didn't go to his school, because they seemed like good people that Henry could look up to and whose company he would benefit from.

The conversation ranged from General Jackson—whose presidential bid Patrick stood strongly against but Seamus was intrigued by—and the New York election to the Sunday's sermon—which Colm hadn't heard—to recent ship commissions and the Lowell cotton mills. It did not touch on the way Maisie picked at her food by the side of Ezra, who looked almost as miserable as she, or when Seamus planned to tell his son that he was gaining a stepmother, or whether the Baltimore Gazette was inclined to keep Patrick on at their printing press after his arrest. Apparently topics were safe as long as they didn't actually pertain to anyone in the room. Mr. Gallagher added only occasional comments to the conversation, striking Betha as a more reserved than active leader of his family.

During a pause, Colm asked Betha if she'd had a chance to study the Sunday school materials any further.

"She pored over them nearly all day," Seamus said, which was a lie. She'd still produced the usual number of spools of linen thread for him that week, but she did want to do her reading while the light was good.

"What brought all this on?" Patrick waved an empty fork between Colm and Betha. "Did Breckinridge ask you to start one?"

"We asked him, actually." Colm sat rigid, carefully placing his knife on his plate. "Since Oliver Hibernian only offers a lay education, we wanted to offer a religious one to the children in Fell's Point."

"Even lay educations are religious," Patrick said with a snort. "All education comes from some philosophy or other. If it's not the Bible, then it's something else."

"The Bible has no bearing on arithmetic," Seamus interjected, "or learning letters."

Patrick straightened. "The mathematical order of the earth comes from the God of order. Noah Webster said that education is useless without the Bible. Nothing we do or study has any meaning apart from God, so we'd do well to know what He has to say on the matter."

Seamus snapped his jaw shut like he had no intention of continuing an argument as a guest in someone's home. Colm sighed audibly. "All things I try to teach, but without the use of the Bible, it's failing to take root with the children. With the Sunday school, we can give them that foundation outside of Oliver."

"Do you think they'll come?" Patrick asked next.

"I do," Betha said, because surely the students would be at least curious to see what else their beloved teacher was offering them.

Colm answered at the same moment. "Maisie is taking care of that for us. She's agreed to provide dinners for the children."

Ezra's eyes widened. "You are?" he asked in a low voice, dipping his ear toward Maisie.

"I didn't like the thought of them being hungry," Maisie replied, studying her plate.

"We haven't had our first class yet, but Betha and I are the lone teachers," Colm said to Ezra. "We'll take all the help we can get, if you're interested."

Bridget smiled across the table at Colm and Betha. "I think it's a wonderful thing and am grateful that you two are taking initiative."

"I'll think about it," Ezra said, remaining turned away from Maisie. "I do miss being around children."

The way Patrick suddenly bent over his food made Betha wonder how he felt about everyone's willingness to jump into Colm's project when his own had brought so much disappointment. Since no one else was mentioning his work, it seemed best to save her comments for a private conversation. Even if she didn't get a chance to talk to him again, she'd pray for the confusion he must be experiencing after his arrest.

When dinner was over, the men returned to the study and the boys ran outside to play. Only Ezra lingered until Maisie led him to the ladies' parlor, looking rather like she was on trial in a courtroom. Betha slowed her movements as she stacked dishes and watched Bridget peer out into the hall to check on the open parlor door before shutting the kitchen door with the other girls inside. Betha brought the plates to the dishpan, but Mor and Lyla waved away her offer to wash.

"Let's sit and have a cuppa," Bridget invited, using her apron to pull a bubbling kettle from the stove. Betha felt guilty relaxing while Hanna swept the floor around them and Mor filled the dishpan with steaming water. Bridget had done far more to earn a rest than she had, but she obeyed and accepted the tea from her hostess.

"Now that Colm has finally brought you over and had you properly introduced, you can come calling anytime," Bridget said warmly, settling into a chair across from Betha at the empty table. "He doesn't share much with the family, but we keep hearing excuses for why he's at your house and not ours, so the introduction was overdue."

Betha focused on the steam rising from her cup, hoping the heat in her face wouldn't be noticeable. "Henry loves learning under him," she said to divert the conversation from Colm's attentions on her. "Colm is markedly kinder than his old teachers. Not many men lead so many rowdy young boys as well as Colm does day after day."

"And that's the truth." Bridget gave an emphatic nod. "He was nearly grown when our families joined together and had already decided to become a teacher. When that man sets his mind to something, he does it and does it well."

The compliments to Colm made an ache rise in Betha's heart. If it weren't for Seamus and his infatuation with a woman who was no good for him, Betha could be free to receive the attention of such a good man. But as long as things continued as they were at home, Colm couldn't be hers, no matter how much she liked him. Seamus's proposal had all but put an end to any hopes she'd entertained of a future with Colm.

It was all made worse by the fact that he now attended her church, and the Sunday school would throw them together every week. It was for a good purpose, though, which was for the sake of the children of Fell's Point and the glory of God, not for her own selfish desires. But, oh, what she wouldn't do to be able to marry into a family like this one.

Anything except abandon Henry to Cara Murphy.

"You look troubled." Bridget set her cup down and extended her hand across the table. "Is it about Colm?"

At the other end of the room, Mor's hands were deep in dishwater and Lyla stood close beside her with a towel in hand, whispering and giggling. Most likely about Maisie and Ezra, Betha guessed. Hanna had a cloth doll propped on her lap on a chair near the stove while she stitched what appeared to be a doll-sized quilt.

"My brother's recently engaged." Betha felt safe admitting it with no one else within hearing range. "I've not even told Colm yet. She's not someone I would have picked as a good influence for Seamus or Henry, but there's naught I can do to avert the situation."

"A heavy burden indeed," Bridget breathed.

Tears pricked Betha's eyes at Bridget's response. She never cried in front of anyone else, but how long had it been since she had a mothering figure offer a listening ear and compassion—to her? She blinked rapidly. "I simply want to do my best to obey the Lord and be an example to my nephew of how to stay faithful to God when others aren't, even those in our home. But he's young still and quite as impressionable by Seamus's actions as my own."

"Oh, my dear." Bridget clutched Betha's hand, and she squeezed back as if that touch was her only lifeline. "That's all you can do. You can't give your nephew more of the Holy Spirit by striving more." Her eyes swept around the empty chairs, each one a representation of a young person in her charge. "The only thing that will do is break your heart more and burden you with more guilt if he does turn from the Lord. The Lord doesn't give us control over each other's outcomes."

Betha pulled out her handkerchief, because holding back the tears had become a hopeless cause. "But I can do something," she whispered. "I can expose him to God's Word daily and pray with him."

Bridget nodded. "And create routines around the spiritual disciplines that will guide him to truth long after you're gone, and love him no matter what choices he makes. Yes, there are things we can do, but for all our efforts, we can never change hearts. He just didn't give us that power."

She leaned forward across the table. "The burden is heavy, though, and as much as I ought to say it's best to leave it with the Lord, it's a message I haven't completely learned myself. We are, after all, told to bear with one another's burdens, but we're also told that the heavy laden who come to Jesus will be given rest. So even though we walk with the Lord, our journey is never completely burdenless."

The door clicked open behind Bridget, causing Betha to pull her hand back and furiously swipe at her eyes.

"Go away, Colm," Bridget said in a dry tone without turning around to see who it was.

Colm walked around the table, though, and seated himself on the bench beside Betha. His unique Colm scent settled over her, a mixture of ink, woodsmoke, and a hint of clove, which must come from his shaving oil, tempting her to lean into him and the kind strength her unruly mind associated with the smell. Despite her embarrassment at his witnessing her tears, she couldn't echo Bridget's command to him when his very presence was always so comforting.

"Thanksgiving dinner wasn't supposed to be so upsetting."

Betha giggled, drying the last of her tears. "Dinner was lovely, Colm, and so is your stepmother. It was enough to bring tears to one's eyes."

"I know it's risky to leave our brothers together without a dedicated intermediary, but it's still light enough for a walk, and I was hoping you'd join me."

"Is Maisie done?" Bridget asked.

"I haven't seen her yet."

At that, Bridget took a final sip of her tea and pushed back from the table. "I'd best go check on things then."

"Is Seamus being polite?" Betha asked, a warning in her voice.

"Considering how hotheaded Patrick is being, yes, quite." Colm came to his feet and extended his hand. "Walk with me?"

Betha stood without taking it, hoping that remaining physically distant from him would help keep her heart in line.

"You can tell me what made you cry if you want, or we can talk about something else."

"We'll see." Betha offered him a small smile before following him out to the coat pegs.

The boys were playing kickball in the street when Betha preceded Colm onto the front step. Henry paused, looking expectantly at her from under his worn cap, but when he saw Seamus wasn't with her, reared back and gave the ball a powerful kick toward Ben.

Colm darted forward, halting the ball with his shins, and sent it skittering across the dirt in a straight shot to Reuben. Betha walked ahead, affection rising in her chest as she watched him. Maybe it was wrong to keep agreeing to walks and meetings with him, because the growing attraction would only make things harder on both of them as time passed. She already liked him far more than she should for someone who wasn't free to receive a suitor.

He jogged to catch up with her, his cheeks now rosy and hair less under control. Betha's heart skipped at the sight of his boyish grin aimed solely at her. Whether it made any sense or not, he already liked her far more than he should too.

Betha's tongue stuck to the roof of her mouth, refusing to allow her to suggest that maybe the walk wasn't such a good idea after all. Heaven help her, this wasn't just about the pain she was building up for herself against a later date. It was about him too.

She stopped walking as soon as they were out of earshot of Henry. "Colm—"

The light in his eyes dimmed as he rounded toward her, his face suddenly serious. "I know."

"What?"

"Seamus told me, and I know what you're going to say. Please don't." The pleading in his eyes was entirely new to her, throwing her further off balance. "Not today. Just let us have this walk. Just this one?"

No, Betha did not want to agree to no more walks. How could she accept this being the last one? What would she do when he finally gave her the distance she'd insisted upon and they passed each other at church and school as mere acquaintances? The war raging within her nearly shredded her resolution while Colm stood begging her with his eyes to not leave without a proper goodbye.

She wanted to hate Seamus for forcing her to make this choice, but harboring unforgiveness was exactly contrary to her commitment to display Christ to Henry and Cara.

When I am afraid, I will trust in You.

Truly, the anger she felt against Seamus was but a product of fear that had rooted itself deep in her heart. Fear for Henry, fear of a broken heart, fear of difficult days ahead. She could not let any of it keep her from doing what she knew was right. After all, God knew every angle of the situation. *I will trust in You.*

"Just this one," she whispered, commanding the threatening tears to flee.

Colm extended his hand to her again, and this time, she took it. He brought it to his elbow without breaking eye contact, and she curled her fingers around his arm, the action shooting a new pang into her heart. With a sad sort of acceptance in his brown eyes, he pivoted around until he was once more by her side, and led her down the street.

23

December 1827

Betha clutched a stack of quilts, sheets, and Seamus's pillow to her chest as she bid good day to the departing chimney sweep. Returning to the middle room, she found the carpenter and his apprentice assembling the new four-poster bed.

Through the doorway, the sounds of bumps and muttered oaths communicated that Seamus and Mr. Oliver were having a time getting his old single bed up the stairs, where it would take the place of Henry's trundle. That would be a good thing, all things considered. Henry was growing, and it was time for him to have a proper bed of his own. But in the meantime, Betha stared at the shrinking middle room, wondering how she'd fit Cara's wheel and personal belongings into it.

The carpenter hammered the last peg into place and stood, dusting his hands and examining the finished product. "Do you want us to string the ropes?"

Betha's face brightened at the offer. "Would you?" She could do it, but if they were offering, it would save a significant effort.

"'Twould be no bother." He reached for the rope pile, and with the help of his apprentice, the bed was soon strung. They even lifted the flax-stuffed mattress Betha had finished the day before onto the bed without being asked. By the time they finished, she could hear Seamus trudging down the stairs. She thanked them, and they left her to work out their payment with him.

Betha didn't want to think about how much was being spent on this marriage. At least she didn't need new dresses every year, and she could let out Henry's pants and coat once more. She'd already cut out two shirts for him, bigger than they needed to be so they would last longer. If only they had a stove like the Gallaghers; they were so much cheaper to keep burning than hearths. As it was, she'd already quit keeping a fire in the middle room even though the weather had turned frigid, relying on the ones in the front room and the kitchen to keep her warm during the day. They didn't.

Betha set to work making up the monstrosity of a bed. When the sheets and quilt were tightly tucked over the mattress, she stood on Seamus's crate to hang a canopy from the bed posts. Bed curtains were no longer expected these days, but she'd made them for Seamus and Cara because—well, because she had.

"Hello, Ma."

Henry's voice startled her, and she teetered on the crate, grabbing a post to keep her upright.

"Henry! Welcome home. How was school?"

"About the same. That's a really nice bed!"

She supposed to a youngster, anything new and big was exciting. "'Tis. What do you mean, about the same?"

Henry climbed to sit on the new mattress before Betha could stop him, stretching out his hands on either side of his body. "I don't mind learnin' the lessons, but the boys in my level were acting the maggot."

Holding onto the post with one hand, Betha lifted her skirts and stepped to the ground. "I'm sorry. We were hoping that you could find friends at this school."

"Aw, don't feel bad. There's some good ones, but a lot of them don't care about school at all and are always trying to pull pranks and fool around. They don't ever want to be serious. And some of 'em have to go to work after school and can hardly stay awake during the lessons."

Colm entered her mind, as all of the problems Henry listed would be his as well. He had such a gift for taking the challenges as they came without getting rattled by them. The image of his face and knowledge of his character caused her heart to twist, and she quickly returned to the present and Henry. There was no use in pining over him. One of these days, he would realize she was right about all the other eligible females in Baltimore and find someone else to walk out with. The sooner the better, because then maybe she could truly let him go in her heart. Thankfully, he had been gracious to give her a wide berth since Thanksgiving. When they were forced into the same vicinity at church and Sunday school, he was his usual kind self, but with a marked boundary in the way he interacted with her. Betha hated it.

"Off the bed, Henry," she said, gesturing for him to vacate it. "Once Miss Murphy joins us, you can't be so informal about things that are your da's and hers."

He sighed but obediently scrambled to the floor and picked up his half-finished French schooner. Turning it over in his hands, he scowled at it.

"You're still stuck on it?"

"I need Da to help drill the holes for the rigging. He won't let me try it by myself."

"But he doesn't have time right now," Betha finished with a sigh. "Give him some time after the wedding before you ask him again. If he said he'll help, surely he'll keep his word. You must needs be patient."

"Yes, ma'am," Henry said, but he didn't smile. Betha watched him with concern. He had the same gloominess about him that he'd carried since Thanksgiving night, when Seamus had pulled him aside after they returned home to tell him of his engagement. Henry had responded better than Betha had hoped, even though it merely reflected that familiar resoluteness she'd seen him wear a hundred times. But ever since that night, he hadn't been happy.

It was everything Betha could do to keep from giving Seamus her mind daily. She could take almost everything except the glum resignation that Henry carried around these days. But how could she convince Henry to trust Seamus and give Cara a chance when she wasn't doing so herself?

Stepping up to him, she wrapped him and his schooner in her arms and kissed his head. "I'm glad you're home. I need to get back to work, but I left you some cornbread in the kitchen, and you can have molasses on it before doing your chores and studies."

He set down the schooner and bounded off. Just two more days—one, really—of him to herself before everything changed. She could hardly think on that now. After examining the canopy to make sure it was even, Betha moved her pile of books back onto Seamus's crate and pushed it into its spot in the corner.

Picking up the catechism from the top of the stack, she turned it over in her hands. She'd taught the children the fourth question on Sunday, and now the words came back to her: *What is God? God is a Spirit, infinite, eternal, and unchangeable, in his being, wisdom, power, holiness, justice, goodness, and truth.*

Even when the future looked bleak. Even when as the girls repeated the lines back to her, she could hear Colm's voice in the next room, reading the same question to his boys. The same voice that had leaned toward her, strangely husky, and said, *I don't see any others.* God was infinite, eternal, unchangeable, and wise, even when it was almost Saturday evening and no Gallaghers would come for her for the fourth Saturday in a row. Betha assumed Ezra's presence was the reason Maisie didn't invite her to shop these days; she hoped it wasn't because of her distance from Colm.

God was power, holiness, and justice even when her brother didn't have time for his son, and He was goodness and truth even when she was back at the beginning, a stranger in the city looking for friends again. Betha lowered to her chair at the wheel with the book still in her hands. Opening it, she flipped to the next question she would be sharing with her small class.

Are there more Gods than one? There is but one only, the living and true God.

Only one God, and He, her only hope. He was not only true, but alive. *Thank You, Father.* With the question and its answer repeating in her mind, she set the book aside and reached for her sack of flax.

Betha fed Henry an early supper on Monday. She knew she should probably eat something, too, but her stomach was clenched too tightly to hold anything.

"You ought to comb your hair and put on your church suit," she said even though she was wearing the same dress she'd spun in all day and had no intention of changing. Henry didn't even argue. Betha wished he would shed tears or have an angry outburst or something that showed how deeply he cared. The detached set of his eyes was more frightening than anything else.

Seamus had left to rent a carriage, leaving them alone in the house. If she wanted a chance to speak openly with Henry, this was it. Betha pulled out a chair and took a seat beside him. "Henry, my boy."

She waited until he lifted his head at her gentle tone, displaying the thin line of his lips as they pressed together. "You can tell me what you're thinking and feeling."

The room remained silent until his plate scraped against the table as he pushed it away. He kicked the table leg, causing the dishes to rattle and Betha to retreat into her chair. "I don't like her."

Lord, give me wisdom. He has every reason not to like her.

"I suppose it will do us good to remember that your da likes her enough to want her to live with him. She makes him happy at least, and don't we want that?"

Sullen silence met Betha. She released a deep sigh.

"Henry, our Heavenly Father knows the burdens of our hearts and will give us grace to carry them if we give them to Him. We don't truly know what the future will be like, but we do know how God enables us to live before Him. To esteem others as better than ourselves. To love one another, because love is of God."

Extending her hand, she rested it over his on the table. She didn't want to preach at him, just offer whatever truth might help. He didn't move or look at her.

"These aren't heavy burdens given by a cruel taskmaster. They are God's good guidelines for his people to live in harmony and understanding with one another. They protect us from bitterness and resentment that steal our joy and erode our souls."

She squeezed his hand lightly and produced a smile with effort. "I'm not goin' anywhere, and neither is Mr. Gallagher. Your school days will be the same, and after your studies, you can run out and play with your friends. We can read together as we always do, and go to church and Sunday school. Much may be changing, my boy, but not everything. God and His love for you never change, and mine doesn't either."

Pushing back from the table, she moved around it to wrap her arms around his shoulders and press her cheek against his hair. Ah, but he was growing so fast. Not that long ago, she would have pulled him onto her lap and chased away his fears with tickles.

"We will be just fine if we remember these things," she whispered. "I love you."

"I love you, too, Ma." His voice had lost its steadiness. "You think Da is happy?"

Mercy, did he have to ask such probing questions? Seamus thought he was happy, but that didn't mean that Betha truly believed it. As joyful as marriage could be, without the Lord in his life, he would only have a portion of the happiness available to him.

"He truly loves Miss Murphy. With God's help, don't you think in time we could come to love her too?"

"Anything is possible with God," Henry mumbled.

"Exactly." Straightening, Betha patted his shoulders and reached for his dishes, removing them to the dishpan. "Your da will be back soon, and we should be ready to go."

Without another word, Henry rose and left the room. Betha eyed the monstrous bed in the next room with a critical eye to ensure everything hung straight and in order. She may not know what to expect when Cara moved in tonight, but she'd do the last few dishes and glance over the already sparkling house one more time for any stray speck of dirt. It would be as welcoming a home tonight as Betha could make it for the newest member of the family.

24

Colm stopped at the bottom step of Cara Murphy's house and glanced around the street, but all was quiet. It was still a couple of minutes before five by his pocketwatch, so he took his time mounting the stairs, wondering if the Youngs were already inside.

His question was answered by the sound of harnesses jangling and the appearance of a carriage turning the corner with Seamus at the reins. The stocky Irishman jumped to the day-old packed snow on the street and tied the reins to the hitching post before opening the carriage door. Henry clambered out and ran straight to Colm like a baby chick to the protection of its mother.

"Hello, Henry. An important day, this is." He didn't miss all of his students over the holiday break, but he had missed Henry and wondered often how he and Betha were doing.

"I guess so." Henry sounded uncertain.

Together they watched as Betha stopped Seamus by the open carriage door and calmly spoke to him. She must have wanted to communicate one last important message to her brother before his marriage. From his spot on the doorstep, Colm couldn't hear her short speech. Seamus showed no emotion, and they didn't touch when she finished. Colm couldn't imagine one of his sisters speaking to him at such a momentous occasion without wanting an embrace at the end of it.

Seamus reached Colm first, shaking his hand and thanking him for coming. The front door behind him opened, and Seamus ushered Henry through it, leaving Colm to wait for Betha. She stopped before him as he removed his hat, any emotion she must be feeling neatly tucked away.

Her face was fresh and clean, her hair pinned up under a beribboned winter bonnet.

"I didn't know you were coming."

She sounded glad to see him, and Colm felt relief to know he'd made the right choice. "Seamus invited me." He was tempted to add that he'd come for her, not Seamus, but maybe she knew that. As hard as he'd tried to give her the requested distance lately, he just couldn't do it for this occasion. He had more than a sense that she'd need a friend, and Seamus must have understood that too. "Are you ready for this?"

Betha produced an unconvincing smile, an obvious wall behind her eyes. "Ready enough, thank you."

At least she knew he cared, that it hadn't changed just because a romantic relationship wasn't available to him. With a gesture toward the house, he followed her inside.

Voices came from a yellow-papered parlor to the left of the front hall, luring them in. Colm recognized Cara's uncle and aunt speaking to Seamus and Cara but didn't know them, and he wasn't familiar with figures who appeared to be the cousins and hired minister at all. Betha must not either, because she sat on a settee next to Henry without speaking to anyone. Colm considered the seating options arranged facing the flower-laden hearth. There was only one obvious choice. A moment later, he was settling onto the end of the settee beside Betha.

The minister lifted the large Bible in his fleshy hands. "Shall we get started?"

Seamus nodded, his hand clasped with Cara's, and her uncle showed his wife to an embroidered chair. The room was silent for a moment, then the minister lifted his hands and uttered a thundering invocation. It went on for several minutes, his voice rising and falling with the performance. When that finished, he paged through his Bible and read passages instructing husbands and wives on their responsibilities to one another. Seamus and Cara stood motionless together, facing him. Colm prayed that some portion of the Word of God that was being shared would trickle into their hearts, if not today, then at some point down the road.

He listened attentively, but the way Betha's skirts pressed against his leg colored how he was able to receive the biblical mandate "Husbands, love your wives." Truly, a month's time plus one fiery wedding sermon did nothing to lessen his determination to one day give that role to the woman sitting by his side. *Let it be, Lord.* Perhaps she didn't consider herself free to entertain suitors for the foreseeable future, but he couldn't bring himself to turn his affections elsewhere. Not when he felt so completely at home sitting on a bench with her and Henry, listening to a man of God preach.

With the sermon finally ended, the time for the vows arrived. Seamus and Cara repeated them confidently, a measure of excitement in their tones. Colm had to stop his hand from clutching Betha's for the duration. He was here to help her, not cause her distress, but the temptation to give her something solid to cling to was strong.

A wedding dinner had been spread in the next room that smelled exquisite, but seated before it thirty minutes later, Colm took little interest in the delicacies. Betha and Henry seemed equally disinterested in what was on their plates, but both made a brave effort to appear merry. Whether or not they benefited from Colm's presence, he was beginning to feel that it had been detrimental to himself to have come. The last thing he needed while trying to lessen the desire his heart stubbornly held for Betha was to attend a wedding with her. All it had done was bring to the forefront of his mind just exactly what he wanted with her.

"How is Maisie these days?"

Betha's voice shook him out of himself and the pit he'd been sliding into.

"I've not seen her much lately," Betha continued, "except for Sundays, when we're working, not chatting."

Colm pushed a beet across his plate with his fork. "I think she's doing well. The Sunday dinners seem to have given her a renewed purpose and something to focus on. She seems to recognize the mistake she made with Ezra, and he's coming around the house again."

"Do you think—" Betha left her sentence hanging.

"Not yet, but if he keeps being patient, she'll get there." Colm had a lot of unspoken respect for the man and what he was willing to undergo in his attempt to woo Maisie. "Almost having lost him has made her appreciate him more, I can tell."

"He's been invaluable on Sundays. The work he does to set up for the classes and keep the children in order has made everything run smoother."

"Indeed." Finally spearing the beet, Colm moved it to his mouth. At the head of the table, Seamus was enjoying his wine, and the others roared at a joke he told. Colm wished Henry was between him and Betha so he could spend time with him, but it was everything Betha could do earlier to keep the child from getting sent to the kitchen to eat alone. Having him on the end beside her had been a victory hard-won.

"Are you going to McColgan's after this?"

Betha's head jerked up. "Why would I do that?"

Clearing his throat, Colm lowered his fork. "Seamus said that he and Cara are heading there to celebrate with their friends with dancing and so on. I wondered if you were joining in the festivities."

"I haven't heard of it, but I assumed I'd take Henry home to bed." Betha set her brow in concentration, probably weighing whether she ought to lay aside her desire to go home in order to support her brother on such a notable occasion.

"He must not be expecting you," Colm said to reassure her. "I can walk you both home if that's what you'd rather."

"You weren't goin', were you?"

"Why, did you want to dance with me?" Colm knew he would be in trouble for the question, but he couldn't stop the teasing grin. "No," he said before Betha could form a reply. "I wasn't going to." It seemed best to allow Seamus and Cara to celebrate with their neighborhood friends without intrusion. "You look relieved."

Betha dipped her head, focused on her plate. "Just at the thought that I can get myself and Henry squirreled away upstairs before they get home."

He couldn't blame her for that.

It was dark when Seamus helped Cara and the cousins into the carriage and they left for McColgan's, accepting Colm's offer to get Betha and Henry safely home. Colm watched them drive away, feeling like a beast for not having brought a conveyance that would keep Betha out of the wind on the bitterly cold night.

"It is icy in spots," he said apologetically, and she took his arm without argument. Colm tried to engage Henry in conversation as they crunched through the frozen streets. When he only received short answers, he didn't push further. The cold alone was enough to chase communication away. By the time they reached the Youngs', his face and toes were in pain, but he released Betha at the bottom of the stairs and backed away before she had to decide whether or not to invite him in. She'd been through enough today already, and he knew how much she needed the quiet evening.

"Thank you," she called after him.

Colm was already a house away when he turned back to watch the door close on them. Nothing in him wondered whether Betha should be with Henry tonight instead of him. Still, he almost ran, sliding down the street to get away from the memories of the wedding, the doorstep where he'd almost kissed her, and the thought of her retreating into the empty house without him.

25

The creaking stair echoed loudly through the quiet house and Betha froze, lifting her foot from it. Nothing stirred, so she tiptoed the rest of the way downstairs and halted outside the middle room.

At the sound of Seamus snoring, she dared to peek inside and was relieved to see the canopy drawn around the bed. She tiptoed through and quietly shut the kitchen door before leaning back with a sign of relief.

Would making breakfast be this stressful every day? She had prayed for herself and Henry to sleep the night before, desperate to be oblivious when Seamus and Cara returned. But she'd been awakened by their arrival anyway and forced to endure the sound of drunken voices and laughter for an undeterminable amount of time. They'd be in need of some strong coffee this morning, and she'd need something to purge the night from her brain. Before falling asleep the first time, she'd instructed Henry to not come down under any circumstances until she banged a pot at the bottom of the stairs, her usual method for waking him up. The chamber pot was up there if he needed it.

It was too cold in the kitchen to linger, so she pushed off from the door and coaxed the fire to life. Retrieving her coat and gloves from the hook by the door, she grabbed a pail and went out for water. Fresh frost sparkled on the rooftops and the handle of the well in the gray dawn. It took several pumps to get the water moving, but the kitchen was welcoming and cozy when she returned to it.

The coffee was steeping and eggs nearly set when Betha remembered that it was New Years' Day, and 1828 had arrived.

She'd always liked attending church on such days. Would this one allow her the pleasure? Once the frying pan was pulled off the fire, she settled into a chair with her coffee to begin her day with the Lord and wait for the rest of the family to rise.

Seamus came in first, about thirty minutes behind his normal schedule and rubbing his temples. His hair was as haphazard as ever, his top button unbuttoned beneath the scruff of his chin. He did usually take time to look more presentable, but never until after breakfast.

"Good morning." Betha rose and poured his coffee. "And happy new year." She didn't know what else to say. *How are you?* He looked like he needed food in his stomach and a bit more time before the world stopped tilting. *Did you sleep well?* She didn't want to know.

She waited until he'd dropped into a chair and had drunk half the coffee before she pushed a plate of eggs his way. "What are your plans today?"

Seamus coughed and blinked his eyes fully open. "Figured we would make the rounds and visit Cara's friends and relatives." It would be expected both for their marriage and the holiday. "Did you want to come with us?"

"I was hoping to go to church. Are you taking Henry?" She knew he wasn't, but maybe if she asked him often enough, he'd remember his other responsibilities.

Seamus scooped eggs onto his fork. "I think we'd best not for this."

Betha wasn't going to complain about her good fortune. "He can come with me then. When are you goin' to get Cara's wheel?" Only a single trunk and a gilt-edged mirror had arrived from her uncle's house the previous morning.

Seamus chewed far longer than was necessary before swallowing. "She doesn't have one."

Betha nearly dropped her mug. "What do you mean?"

"Cara doesn't spin," Seamus said, enunciating each word.

She heard him, but the words didn't register. Every woman spun. Betha didn't know any who didn't, even though most only did it for their own households, not for income like her. "Did you know?"

"Only recently."

She shook her head, trying to understand, but couldn't. "She will, though, right? She married into weavers."

Seamus lifted a shoulder, looking doubtful as he worked on another bite. "If she takes care of the kitchen and such, you'll be freed up to spin more."

Betha's fingers curled around her mug in a concentrated effort to not throw it at him. Who wanted to spend ten or twelve hours a day sitting at a spinning wheel? If she wanted such a painful, tedious life, she'd go work at the Lowell Mills.

"Can we afford this?" she asked in a low voice, in case Cara was on the other side of the door. "I know the linen you sold last week was down five cents a yard, and now we have another mouth to feed. We should be thinking ahead to what we should do, because it's bound to drop again." She leaned forward. "I can teach her to spin."

"I'll suggest it to her. For now, we have her dowry, and you and I will have to increase our output while I make a plan. I'll think of something."

Betha tried to take another drink, but her jaw was clenched too tight. Could this match possibly be any more ill-suited? "I need to let Henry know when he can come down to breakfast. Is she up?"

"We got in pretty late last night," Seamus said, as if Cara was merely overtired and not sleeping off whatever she'd consumed. "I'll go make sure the bed is closed."

"I don't want to have to worry about Henry coming through while she's dressing. I don't just mean today."

Pushing back from the table, Seamus came to his feet. "If the middle room doors are closed, he can go around the house and come in the kitchen door. We'll leave the doors cracked open anytime it's safe to come through."

He left, and Betha could hear him and Cara speaking to each other in low voices. The house fell quiet again, but he didn't return. Betha finally chanced poking her head in the room and found Seamus shaving by his washstand. Cara was partially visible through the canopy, watching him.

"I'm goin' to get Henry up," Betha warned as she pushed through the room. At the bottom of the stairs, she banged on the pot, and Henry appeared immediately, already dressed. It was a good thing it wasn't a school day, because he'd probably have been late, although he was surely starving as it was. When she marched him back through to the kitchen, the canopy was closed again and Seamus was combing his hair.

Betha sat Henry before his breakfast a moment before Seamus came back into the kitchen for a new plate of eggs and cup of coffee, which he took into the middle room before clicking the door shut. She had to remind herself that it was a holiday and he was on his honeymoon; work days wouldn't be like this one. Their financial troubles could also wait another day. For today, she was going to thank God for the new year, for His daily morning mercies, and for the good excuse to whisk Henry and herself out of the house.

It was late afternoon before Betha brought Henry back home, having kept him out as long as she could. She had missed seeing Colm at church, but he'd probably gone to First Presbyterian with his family for the holiday. In an attempt to do something jolly and yet avoid the pull to the Gallaghers' house, she'd taken Henry calling at Ava's after the service. They'd been fed well there and treated warmly by Ava's family, and Betha had determined to do more to invest in the friendship in the coming year. Maybe she would even use her last bit of spending money on a subscription to the Bible Society Ava belonged to, since their activities would give her an opportunity to get out of the house every week.

When they were rising to leave, Maisie arrived with Ezra and Mor. The visit was thus prolonged, and like the church service, did much to lift Betha's spirits. Once everyone was settled into the parlor again with cups of wassail, Betha was pleased to find herself in a quiet corner with Mor. She liked the girl, who reminded her of Colm in more ways than her trim build and the strong facial resemblance. Betha figured her to not be over twenty, but even though there was much girlishness still about her, she was bright and keen, with the manners of a lady.

"Mother's been asking after you. She was hoping you'd visit us again after Thanksgiving." Mor peered at Betha over her cup, the hesitancy in her demeanor telling Betha that she knew her reasons for holding back.

"I was hoping to as well," Betha replied truthfully. "My brother's marriage has affected many things."

"We have tea at two every day. We don't need to know ahead of time if you are ever able to drop over, and I'm sure we would all be glad to have you."

Betha thanked her, appreciative of her circumspection. School wasn't yet out at two, and only the older Gallagher females would be home. Still, even if she could get away from her wheel, it would be impossible to be in Colm's home without sensing his presence every second. It was bad enough at her own table, where he'd studied her so thoughtfully, flashed his dimples, answered every one of her hard questions.

Betha's gaze trailed to Henry, the reason for the ache in her chest. He was worth all the sacrifices. She watched as Ezra used a string from his pocket to demonstrate sailing knots for him. Apparently such everyday treasures were so universally intriguing that even overgrown boys filled their pockets with them. Henry's eyes sparkled as he studied the moves intently and then took a turn attempting to recreate the knot. Ezra smiled, praised him, and repeated the process.

Maisie suggested music after several minutes of conversation, Ava taking the piano as they all joined in singing several familiar songs. Henry had brightened by the time they bid their last farewell and finally started out the door.

Between their own feasting and Seamus and Cara's visiting, Betha wouldn't have to make a full supper, nor did she have any intention of spinning on the holiday.

"Let's just light the fire in the middle room," she told Henry, hoping that it would be enough to warm the house and save firewood.

He worked to get the fire going while she pulled out her sewing basket. Before long her fingers were busily basting together the new shirt for him, and she let him continue poking at the fire. His eyes had landed on the half-finished schooner and darkened more than once, and without his whittling, there wasn't much else to busy his hands on a long winter afternoon.

Presently he stood, wiping his hands down his trousers. "Perhaps I'll run over to the Olivers' for a bit."

"That sounds nice. Be back by bedtime, because you have school tomorrow."

He'd only been gone a few minutes when Seamus and Cara returned, flushed from the cold, their faces wreathed in smiles. Betha met them with a smile of her own despite herself. How long had it been since she'd seen Seamus like this? Even though he refused to look for the lasting joy promised in eternal things, he was more cheerful than he'd been in a long time, and it was a nice change. It likely wouldn't last once the soirees were over and reality set in, but no loving sister would wish to see a grin like this one leave her brother's face.

With her coat still on, Cara collapsed, breathless, into a chair. "It's so snug and cozy in here," she said, looking around. "I've always thought that about this house. My mother always insisted on keeping a fire goin' in every room, she so hated being cold, and this coziness reminds me of her."

Betha decided to take it as a compliment.

"It's your house now." Seamus peeled his gloves off and stuffed them into his coat pockets.

"You wouldn't mind if I changed a few things?" Cara looked to him, not Betha.

"Of course not," Seamus said, and Betha was invisible.

"Well, I've been thinking about it." Cara's eyes traveled around the room. "It would make more sense to separate the living quarters from the workroom. I'd move the wheel and flax out to the front room with the loom and move the table in here, where I can receive guests."

Betha clamped down on her lip to keep her mouth shut. What Cara proposed wasn't at all unusual, but when Betha was in charge of her own life, she'd taken advantage of the fact that she didn't have to have Seamus watching her work and fussing at her all day if she didn't want to. Not to mention the fact that Cara made it sound like she would be receiving guests while Betha spent her time out front keeping the family fed.

"That does make sense," Seamus agreed. "That way we can keep all business relegated to the front room."

Cara untied her bonnet and carefully removed it. "Then this room shall be called the parlor henceforth."

Betha cleared her throat. "Seamus suggested that you may be interested in doing most of the cooking and so on. I can show you around the kitchen if you'd like." She was tempted to add the offer to teach spinning, but Seamus had said he would handle that, so she ended by giving Cara as friendly a smile as she could muster.

"And let me know if you need anything from the market," Seamus added. "I usually go on Tuesdays and Fridays."

Cara made a noncommittal noise, leaving Betha to wonder what she was thinking. She stood, slipped her heavy beige coat off, and tossed it onto the bed. "What are you making?"

Betha turned the garment over in her hands. "A shirt for Henry. He's growing so fast these days."

She looked up when Cara didn't reply and saw her sidle up to Seamus, wrapping her arms around him. "What was that song you sang last night at McColgan's? I didn't recognize it, but it was a screamer."

Seamus pulled her into his side, planting a kiss on her nut-brown curls. "'Reilly's Daughter.'"

"Oh, do sing it for me."

Seamus had the good sense to turn red under Betha's scathing glare. "I don't think Betha would appreciate it."

"Why not?" Cara pouted at Betha. "It was enough to make a dog laugh. It's just a joke, Betha."

Seamus started humming the tune, and Betha felt caged in. She had nowhere else to go if he did start singing the tawdry ballad; this was the only room of the house that was heated. But she couldn't tolerate listening to it either. "Perhaps you can share the song after I go to bed. Do you have anything else you could sing now?"

"You can't be serious, Seamus," Cara huffed.

Betha bent over her seam to avoid Cara's annoyed look, even though she was as interested as Cara to see whose side Seamus would pick.

"Have you heard 'Peggy Bawn'?" Seamus launched into the song before Cara could reply. Betha had always loved his singing voice, which carried more of a brogue than his speaking accent. It was a rare day that she could have gotten him to sing for her before. Maybe having Cara around did come with advantages.

The song choice was a clever one, being deeply romantic. After Seamus finished belting out how much he loved her, Cara kissed him, hopefully forgetting that just this once, Betha had been given a small victory. Betha tied off her thread and snipped it, carefully schooling her features even as she counted her blessings. As deliberately unaware as Cara chose to be, she probably had no idea how very much Betha had already given up for her.

26

Betha tiptoed into the kitchen on Wednesday morning as the sun was rising and latched the door behind her. Lacy frost patterns decorated the windows on the west side of the house, including the one in the kitchen.

The door had been cracked, so she'd gone through the ... *parlor* ... even though low giggles came from behind the bed curtains. When exactly was Cara supposed to start taking over cooking breakfast? Until Betha actually had a chance to taste the woman's cooking and ascertain its quality, she was perfectly happy to fry up bacon and make coffee herself. Hopefully, no one else minded that she continued to make herself at home in the kitchen.

Seamus eventually stumbled out, Betha banged the pot for Henry, and the day began. When Henry raced out the door for school after breakfast, Seamus followed with his market basket in hand and a list from Betha to do the shopping that the holiday had delayed. Cara sat at the kitchen table with a cup of tea—apparently she hated even the smell of coffee—while Betha looked from her to the pile of dishes, wondering whether she dared leave them. At the thought of her spinning wheel now in the front room where a fire had yet to be lit, she deliberately poured tea for herself and pulled out the chair across from Cara.

"I like to read a chapter of the Bible aloud over breakfast," she announced lightly as she sat. "We can get back to it tomorrow, I suppose, since we're all still settling in. I've decided to join the Female Bible Society with Ava, and we would be happy to have you join us, if you're interested."

Cara's cup lowered slowly. "I don't know how I shall have time for societies now that I've a husband and home to care for. It seems they're mostly filled with single young ladies, anyway." Her hair was pinned up loosely as if she hadn't taken the time to fix it yet, but she was dressed in a black calico dress Betha had seen her wear often.

"I don't know about that," Betha said truthfully. The only members she knew were single, but she'd never been to a meeting yet to find out more. Cara's excuse was expected, however. "If you have any questions about keeping the house, I'm here to answer them, though I'm sure you will manage it in your own way."

"Have you any receipt books?"

Betha opened her mouth and shut it with a quizzical look.

"Such as *The Virginia Housewife*," Cara clarified. "Mrs. McColgan mentioned it to me and said it has receipts for cooking?"

"Oh, no, I haven't. I cook the way my mother taught me. It's not fancy enough to need receipts."

"My mother tried to teach me too." Cara gave a light snort to her teacup. "It was long ago, of course, but even then I tried to add my own flair to the dishes. She didn't like the peppercorn I added to the rye bread or the sage in the gingerbeer. Now I'm not sure that I could remember much of her methods."

Betha ignored the dread rising at the mountain of responsibilities accumulating before her very eyes. There was no way to get out of it but to plow through. "I could teach you what I know as I'm able around the spinnin' Seamus expects me to produce. Do you know where to get the book?"

"Gaither's would have it, I'm sure. I can ask Seamus to buy it for me so I don't bother you—"

A wide smile split Betha's face as she pushed her chair back from the table. "I'm interested in it as well. I told you my cooking is simple. Perhaps we could go through it and learn together."

Cara lifted hope-filled eyes under her dark brows. "He would like that, wouldn't he? Trying new dishes?"

"Seamus would be happy eating old Hibernia fare his entire life. Colcannon, brown bread, beef stew, and a hearty ale. I think it would be interesting, though, and give us both the chance to broaden our skills." And while Seamus might not have given Betha money for the book, he'd surely find it in his budget for Cara.

"Have you considered marriage?"

Betha's cheeks heated even before she turned gaping to Cara and saw the intent look on her broad face. "I . . . I suppose like most, I imagined it would happen sometime." *But not anymore.*

"It was a silly question." Cara gave a nervous laugh. "Of course you have, with the attention Colm Gallagher gives you."

"It's not like that," Betha lied, her face burning. It *had* been like that, not too long ago.

Cara's laugh turned to a brashness Betha didn't like. "Once we have you graduated from the school of *The Virginia Housewife*, he'll be whisking you away from here. You'll see."

By the time Betha had shown Cara the stores in the kitchen and cellar, talked her into a simple barley soup for dinner, and showed her how to start the mutton and vegetables on a slow boil in the hearth, Seamus barreled in with his arms full of packages. He beamed proudly when he saw Cara chopping carrots with Betha, and dropped his purchases on the table. Coming up behind Cara, he wrapped his arms around her and applied a loud kiss on her neck.

"There was a nice leftover Christmas ham that I got on sale." He indicated the large brown paper package. "And there's eggs here, and flour . . ."

Betha busied herself putting everything away once he'd shown them off. She was about to slip out to her spinning wheel when Cara turned her dark, beseeching eyes on Seamus. "I think a stove would serve the kitchen so much better; it'll be ever so much less strain on the back."

"I think so too," Seamus returned without hesitation, running his hands down her arms. "Do you want to come with me to pick it out?"

Betha backed out of the room before they heard the choking sound her throat was threatening to make. Her wheel ought to get going if Seamus was going to spend Cara's dowry on a stove. She couldn't even encourage caution about the purchase, when she had pushed Seamus to the same thing a dozen times already, to no avail. Excitement coursed through her as she settled into her chair in the front room. A new stove indeed! Her days of backbreaking hours over the hearth were finally coming to an end.

Soon her foot was tapping at its usual pace, the wheel whirring to life as the flax flew through her careful fingers. She liked spinning, she did; she'd always loved being in a weaving family and viewed her birth into one as a gift. Soon she could teach this to Cara, whom she hoped would grow to love the trade too. Sooner rather than later, before they were bankrupted due to the speed money was currently flowing out of this house.

After more time than was necessary, Seamus clomped whistling into the room, stopping to examine his current piece on the loom before taking his seat.

"You didn't have to arrange your wheel so your back is to the room."

"It's facing the window," Betha corrected. "For better light. Since I'll be spinnin' until dusk now."

Which also so happened to mean that she didn't have to face him all day, but what of it? Betha returned to her silent prayers, but Seamus resumed his song at the same time as his loom began thumping behind her. *Oh dear Lord—help me through this long day.*

The day the stove was delivered, Betha couldn't stay at her wheel. She stood with hands folded beside Cara, watching as the black beast with all of its gleaming knobs, doors, and trays was assembled in the kitchen and its pipe fitted into a hole cut in the chimney. Cara clasped her brand new copy of *The Virginia Housewife* to her chest as she watched the men work, her bushy eyebrows drawn tight together.

"Mrs. Randolph didn't say anything about how to use it in the book," she whispered to Betha. "Do you know?"

Betha shook her head. "I know who does though." But that would involve a trip to the Gallaghers'. Only a week had passed since Mor's earnest invitation, which Betha had made a valiant effort to put from her mind without success. "I'll go ask Colm's sisters. You won't forget to stir the meat and add water if it starts to stick?"

"Of course not," Cara sniffed, even though she'd burned two dinners this week already.

"I'll be back as soon as I can." Betha slipped into her coat and left through the back door before Seamus realized she wasn't returning to work. For the first time, she allowed the pull of the large brick house to draw her through the slushy streets. Anticipation built inside her chest until she stood before the double smoking chimneys and tried not to think about the ache in Colm's eyes as he stood in the street and told her, *I know.*

Mor answered her knock and engulfed her in a hug before tugging her into the kitchen. Betha had been hugged by every Gallagher female and had a cup of coffee pressed into her hand before she had a chance to catch her breath and explain her errand. The warm welcome she'd received left her feeling unexpectedly choked up, and she had to work to keep her voice steady.

"I'd be glad to come teach you," Maisie exclaimed, coming to her feet. "Which stove did you get?"

"It says Freedom on it." Betha eyed the pile of basted shirts lying on the table before the window. "I don't want to take you from your work."

"It'll still be there when I get back. My legs need a stretch anyway. Are you coming?" She handed a coat to Mor while Betha took a sip of the coffee. Mor responded by shoving her arms into the coatsleeves.

"Come back and see us sometime," Bridget interjected with a gentle staying hand on Betha's arm.

Looking into her kind eyes, Betha's breath caught in her throat. Could she build relationships in this house without causing terminal damage to her heart? She'd lived with joy and sadness as constant companions for so long that she didn't question whether they could coexist; only whether being reminded of the loss of Colm was worth the joy that friendship with Bridget and her daughters would bring. In some cases it was; today seemed like it wasn't.

Betha nodded, swallowing over a lump, and then managed, "I don't know."

Bridget's smile turned sad. "The door's always open to you, lass."

Betha turned away from the table where she'd eaten Thanksgiving dinner across from Colm's brown eyes and focused on the door. "I told Cara I wouldn't be gone long."

A moment later, she was swept out into the street between Maisie and Mor. "Our aunt has the Freedom stove, so I've used it before," Maisie reassured her. "I know you'll love having it."

Betha heard without listening. Why had she already categorized the loss of Colm as grief? Why did her heart fill with sadness just to step inside his home? She'd only known him for a few months; it shouldn't hurt this much. Was it merely his presence that she'd lost, or was it the death of the hope he'd brought into her life that caused the ache? She'd never had hope for love, a home of her own, or babies before him, and now it was gone again.

A hand slipped into hers, and she turned her pensive gaze to find Mor peering at her in concern. "You look unhappy."

Betha opened her mouth. "I love him." The words almost slipped out before she snapped her lips shut, eyes widening at Mor. She *loved* him? "I'm sorry," she said instead. "I was feeding on discouragement instead of being grateful to you for coming to help."

Mor glanced to Maisie a step ahead of them and quickly back. "I don't know what happened," she whispered hurriedly, "but I'd counted on you being my sister one day. I still hope things will work out."

Maisie slowed to come alongside them again, so Betha didn't have to concoct a response. She'd never spoken of Colm to Mor before, but now her mind was reeling. *I love him? Truly?* Only one answer thrummed through her heart with every step she took: *I do . . . I do . . . I do.*

It fit. It didn't make the distance from him any easier to bear, but it explained why she hadn't snapped back to her normal self since parting ways with him as quickly as she had hoped.

So why couldn't they figure out a way to make things work out, like Mor suggested? *Lord, You can make a way, couldn't You?*

Unless Cara started meeting Henry's basic needs, the job was hers until he was old enough to do so himself. It would indeed take a miracle for the situation to change enough for her to be free to accept Colm's advances.

It was all made worse by the fact that by the way the man cared for her—becoming her rock when she needed one, considering honest change when challenged, being willing to walk away when she asked him to—Betha knew that Colm Gallagher, with all his lack of curmudgeonliness . . . loved her too.

27

February 1828

Colm flipped the Ten Commandments cards through his fingers mindlessly in the empty church classroom. With nearly twenty boys in class today, it was time to think about finding additional teachers. But instead of concentrating on the possibilities of who he should ask, he was distracted by the sound of Betha softly singing in the next room.

She probably had no idea that he was always acutely aware of her movements and the cadence of her voice next door as he taught. He'd barely talked to her in the last couple of months, even though he was tempted every week when the church was quiet and he knew she was alone. Today he had reason to and only hoped that he could carry on a conversation like a normal person.

He tapped the edge of the cards against the table, straightening them into a stack, and placed them on his pile of books. With a slow exhale that did nothing to calm his nerves, he poked his head into the other classroom.

Betha froze from her tidying as soon as he appeared.

"How did it go today?"

Her head dipped a slight degree. "It was noisy. Did we disturb you?"

Colm shook his head. His class had been noisy too. "How many did you have?"

"Nearly thirty, but Mor was here to help."

"She already left?"

"She's helping Maisie pack the dishes away."

"Ah. I think it's time to add teachers and divide the classes up. They're getting too big now, and we could benefit from separating out the smaller children from the older ones."

Betha curled her lips in thought and nodded. "I think so too. I'd rather teach the small ones, if you know of a fitting teacher for the older ones."

"I'll ask around this week. I know Mor would rather work in the background than teach." It was time for Ezra to start teaching the boys though. He'd been helping for months, and whether he knew it or not, he was ready.

"Oh no, I don't want to lose her help in my classroom if possible."

"All right." See? He could be normal around Betha. He could talk to her like any other person and not get lost in her sparkling blue eyes. Well, maybe not. She wasn't meeting his eyes, and the fingers of her clasped hands were fiddling with each other. She was as out of sorts from this conversation as he was.

Colm cleared his throat, recentering himself. "I would like for the teachers to come a few minutes early every week and spend some time in prayer together before class. Do you think you could?"

"Absolutely. We need to pray for the students. One of my girls just lost the grandmother she was living with and was sent to live with an uncle. I didn't hear about it until today, after she was gone."

"That's sad." Colm frowned. "I'm sorry to hear it. Yes, then I'll see you at one-thirty next week?"

Betha donned her coat and picked up her hat. "I'll see you at the evening service tonight," she said, sliding the hatpin into place. "But I can be here at one-thirty on Sundays."

She scooped up her books, but the top booklet slid off to the floor. Before he could stop himself, Colm had lunged forward to grab it, but in one deft dip, Betha retrieved it herself. Now he just stood there awkwardly and in her way, like an unnecessary hero in a story. He really should let her go, but another topic came to his mind that would allow him to prolong the conversation.

"Henry. He's growing as a monitor and has more confidence. But some of his marks are suffering these days."

Betha stilled, her face growing somber, but she was looking at Colm now. "How bad is it?"

"Not very bad," Colm hurried to add, "but it's not at the level I'm used to from him. This time of year always sees a dip when the students are tired of being cooped up and spring is almost here. But I knew you'd want to know."

"Yes, thank you. I'm not sure I'll say aught about it to him."

Colm cocked his head. "Do you think it's related to other things going on in his life?"

"I do," Betha replied softly, without hesitation. "It's been a fierce hard year for him. I'll see what I can do to help him improve without making him think he's in trouble with you."

"He's not, so that would be helpful." He briefly hoped that Betha would invite him to come call on Henry sometime and then quickly decided that he hoped she wouldn't. "I'm sorry to hear it's been difficult."

"Me too." Betha hugged her books against her chest. "I keep praying the Lord would use these things to grow Henry into the person He wants him to be. If I didn't know that God doesn't waste the difficulties in our lives, I would—" She stopped, closing her mouth as if realizing that she was crossing into territory that she didn't want to go with Colm.

Maisie, Mor, and Ezra appeared at the end of the hall, holding crates of wooden dishes and saving Betha from the unfinished sentence. Maisie was talking about Patterson Park, and Colm heard enough to gather that she was comparing their current Sunday activities with the old picnics. These days, Sundays were both far more challenging and far more rewarding.

"Let us give you a ride home," Colm said, backing out of the classroom. "It's too cold to walk."

"I ride with Ezra because he goes that way."

Of course. Colm knew that. He couldn't do anything to help her, and he should stop trying. Henry's school performance alone was evidence that Betha was needed to be committed to his well-being and keeping at least one part of his life stable and nurturing.

Outside, Colm helped his sisters pack their supplies away in the carriage. When the job was done, he straightened up in time to see the back of Betha's coat as she walked with Ezra to his buggy. Maisie had stilled next to him, and he glanced over to see her watching them also.

They were almost home when the horses clip-clopped past Patrick walking purposefully up the street in the direction of the house. Colm descended from his seat on the front walk, reaching the hitching post as Patrick broke into a jog toward him.

"Can I use the carriage?"

Colm tugged the reins through the hitching ring and looked him up and down. Patrick was still dressed in his church clothes, a fierce concentration in his eyes. His usually rakishly set cap was tugged on straight over his forehead with rogue curls peeking out at the sides.

"What do you need it for?"

Patrick's chin rose slightly and his jaw spasmed. "There's someone who needs help."

Colm leaned his hand on the open carriage door and returned his brother's serious look. Behind him, the girls had exited and were walking toward the house with crates in their hands. It wasn't his carriage to lend out or withhold, but it had been too long since he'd seen this version of Patrick. In fact, this one was more determined, more authoritative than Colm had ever seen him. He didn't doubt that Patrick would be taking the carriage, regardless of what he said. He had the appearance of a man who had counted the cost and concluded that he had no more room in his life for half measures.

"Help us carry in the supplies first," Colm said, instead of the *I'm glad you're back* or *I'm proud of you* that he would have spoken had it been Maisie or Mor. He turned, hefting a crate into his arms, and started up the path. Stopping midstride, he paused until Patrick's head backed out of the carriage. "Do you want me to come with you?"

"No." Patrick shifted the crate in his arms so he could shut the carriage door. His tone was unreadable.

Colm didn't move. "I'm available if you need a second person."

"I don't today. Maybe another day."

It was an olive branch, and Colm took it with a short nod. He headed to the door, throwing his own olive branch behind him as he walked—"Be careful."

28

April 1828

"Here you are." Betha overturned the bowl of kitchen scraps into the sunlit yard for her new brood of chicks, pausing to smile at her little friends as they reacted to her presence and waddled over. By the end of the summer, she should have eggs of their own again. It had been painful to sell her flock in New York, but Seamus had refused to travel with live animals, promising her a new brood come spring. Chicks never failed to bring a smile to her face, and she could hardly wait to stop giving some of her weekly budget to the egg lady.

Wiping her hands on her apron, she wandered over to the fenced garden square and knelt to pull a weed. Cara stopped behind her with a basket of wet laundry hoisted on her hip and peered over her shoulder.

"Is the asparagus ready?"

"Almost."

"They look so funny, like little people pushing up out of the ground."

Betha had to agree. The bright green stalks were about a half foot tall, but she had hope she could wait until tomorrow before they made an appearance in the asparagus soup from Mrs. Randolph's book.

"I can almost taste the asparagus soup," Cara said, as if she could read Betha's thoughts. When they'd first opened *The Virginia Housewife* together, Cara had suggested going through it in order, starting with the asparagus soup on the first page. The reality of seasonal crop availability had dashed her hopes until they discovered asparagus growing in the weed-infested garden bed. Now Betha was afraid that the asparagus soup had become so highly anticipated that they would all be disappointed when they actually experienced it.

"I think it's almost warm enough to plant the peppers and cucumbers." Betha leaned forward, tugging another weed up.

Already the peas and green beans were winding their way up Betha's poles, something she never could have seen this early in New York springs. It was risky to plant the summer crops in April, though, when the danger of frost was unlikely but still possible. Cara moved away to hang the wet clothes on the line. That too was new, since Betha had dug up all the grass they used to spread the laundry out on to make room for the chicken pen and expand the garden.

By the time the last weed was pulled, Cara had half the laundry hung. Betha stood, wiping her hands on her apron. "Should I start chopping the cabbage for dinner?"

"Oh, do. I was goin' to start that next."

Betha was sure she was, but she'd never seen a woman who worked as slowly as Cara did. At least she was willing to work, even though she took little initiative. She'd helped with spring cleaning when Betha started it the day after emptying her last bag of flax. Since it was unlikely that Seamus could find affordable flax this time of year, it would probably be after the first crops of the year came in that her wheel would be back to work. In the meantime, there was plenty of work for two industrious women to stay busy—or at least, one and Cara. It was nice to be out in the fresh air for most of the day again, even if it was spent restuffing mattresses and wringing out heavy, wet quilts.

Betha lifted the cabbage out of the bowl, where it was submerged in water to remove the dirt, and patted it dry with a towel. At this rate, dinner wouldn't be ready when Henry came home for it. It often wasn't, because Cara didn't seem to care whether Henry was inconvenienced or forced to miss a meal. As often as possible, she ignored his presence in their lives altogether. Betha had started keeping a loaf of yeast bread in the house all the time so there was always something Henry could grab quickly if needed. Which reminded her; she had only the heel left and needed to start the yeast proofing right after dinner instead of making it to the Bible Society meeting.

Slicing the cabbage into neat ribbons, she fought disappointment at having to miss her friends and the Bible distribution. *And whatsoever ye do, do it heartily, as to the Lord, and not unto men—whether baking bread or handing out Bibles.*

Her mind trailed back to a conversation with Colm near the beginning of their friendship, when he'd been struggling with Patrick pushing him to other, seemingly more worthy work. It was a struggle Betha didn't share. She'd never wondered if she was needed in the work before her or whether it was what God had given her to do. Did Colm still have doubts, or had spearheading the Sunday school changed that for him? Hopefully, God had helped him to see his teaching as important as Betha did. Even if he couldn't read the Bible openly in class, his wise, patient presence in the children's lives would leave a mark on them and give him opportunity to share more outside of school. She understood that now.

The back door opened and Cara shuffled in. "Oh, you're almost done! That was quick."

It had to be, because there weren't enough hours in the day for the amount of work necessary to keep them out of debt. The garden needed to start producing soon, because linen was down to forty-seven cents a yard and the root cellar was almost empty. The smile Betha produced was more wry than friendly. "Mrs. Randolph says to boil the cabbage and onions separately and then either stew them or fry them into cakes. I was thinking about frying."

Cara leaned against the counter and wrinkled her nose. "Frying has such a strong smell. Can we stew this time?"

Betha paused, her hands full of chopped cabbage, and looked at Cara. There had been several little signs lately, but now she was almost completely convinced that she would be an aunt again soon. If that was the case, she didn't need to make things more difficult by insisting on her own way needlessly. "Stewing is fine." Cabbage and onions smelled strongly any which way they were cooked.

Releasing the cabbage into a pot of boiling water, she returned for a second trip, pressing down the questions rising in her chest. Cara would tell her the news in her own time—if she even realized herself what was happening yet.

Betha gave the cabbage a stir with a wooden spoon—the novelty of standing at the stove hadn't worn off yet—before backing up to the table and reaching for an onion and her knife. Cara hadn't made a move to help, but if she had morning sickness, just standing there could be more than was comfortable.

"I can handle this," Betha told her. "The instructions are simple. Why don't you go off and lay the table?"

Cara didn't even argue about the uncharacteristic way Betha took command; she picked up the stack of plates that had been wiped down after breakfast and headed into the parlor with them.

The onions had just been set to boil when Henry arrived. Betha didn't hear his voice until he appeared in the kitchen doorway, even though he'd passed both Seamus and Cara on his way in. He'd come to find her first thing, as usual. All of Betha's encouragement for both sides to make more of an effort for the other continually fell on deaf ears.

"I'm sorry I'm a bit behind. Dinner will be ready soon." Betha handed him the last bread crust and moved the cutting board and knife to the dishpan.

"Can I have some butter on this?"

"Just a wee bit." Betha eyed him cautiously as he reached for the butter crock. That was another thing that needed to be replenished sooner rather than later. She didn't know when she'd have time to make more, but it should probably be before the end of the week.

"We did laundry this morning, then I fed the chickens and worked in the garden. It all took longer than I expected."

Henry chewed his bite and didn't reply. It wasn't just her imagination that he was even withdrawing from her. He was eleven now, though, and she'd observed enough youngsters to know that his behavior wasn't that uncommon at an age when boys became more responsible and independent. It didn't mean she didn't miss her sweet little boy or worry about what Seamus's marriage was doing to his heart.

"How is your day?"

"Jolly," Henry replied without feeling.

Betha lifted an eyebrow, giving him a pointed look. "Anything you want to talk to me about?"

"What's for dinner?" He shoved the rest of his bread in his mouth.

Truth be told, that probably was the only thing on his mind, she'd give him that. "Cabbage and onions."

Henry hadn't finished swallowing when he asked, "Can't we have some meat?"

Betha couldn't help the sigh that escaped as she studied him. He didn't used to challenge everything like this, let alone let go of his manners. "We don't have enough unless I put in the bacon I was saving for your breakfast."

His frown told her how he felt about it, but he didn't push further. There was no point in pretending things weren't the way they should be, since there was nothing Betha could do to change the situation. She thought about the new baby and panic tightened her belly. How in the world would they afford another family member? She was exhausted as it was. Seamus was still holding out misplaced hope that things would turn around for linen and didn't answer when she asked about teaching Cara to spin. Betha had considered talking to Maisie about spending her summer plying a needle for her employer, even though the thought started a dull headache in the back of her head. Summers were usually spent putting up stores for the winter—making soap, cheese, and ale, drying fruit and meat, pickling vegetables, and doing a hundred other chores. She couldn't imagine when she would fit in becoming a seamstress.

Henry sat silent behind her as she stirred the vegetables one more time. They were soft now, so she strained the onions and added them to the cabbage, liberally adding salt and pepper, and butter much more sparingly. "It's supposed to stew longer, but I suppose you ought to go ahead and eat so you're not late for the school bell."

"Some of the boys bring a bit of dinner with them to school so they don't have to go home between times."

"Is that what you want to do?" Betha asked as she spooned the vegetables into her mother's blue serving bowl.

Henry only shrugged in response, which meant he did but probably also didn't want to give up having a hot meal midday. Funny how he'd never asked about staying at school all day before Seamus got married and changed the atmosphere of their home. Betha hefted the bowl into the crook of her arm and he followed her into the parlor in ignorance of all the troubles swirling in her heart.

Betha served up dinner, but her thoughts were on what she'd give to have a long conversation with Bridget. The time with Colm's stepmother at Thanksgiving had been short, but long enough to appreciate the value of it. Bridget wouldn't bat an eye at Betha spilling all her fears to her. But someone who didn't have time to make it to Bible Society meetings didn't have the leisure for long conversations with friends either.

Cara wore a brave look as Betha filled the last plate with the very aromatic entrée and took her seat across from Seamus. He was waiting for her to say the blessing, as usual. Bowing her head, she spoke the prayer aloud, silently inviting the Holy Spirit's peace into her heart. Long conversations with Bridget might be a luxury, but she had all-day access to prayer and a Savior who beckoned her to surrender her burdens to Him.

By the time she said "Amen," Betha had committed to spending her kneading time that afternoon the way she should have all along—in prayer.

Something has to change, Lord, because I'm doing everything I can, and I can't keep up.

Perhaps it wasn't the most reverent way to start her prayer time, but it was what spilled out of Betha's heart. At once, she remembered what Jesus said in Matthew 11: *"Come unto Me, all ye that labor and are heavy laden, and I will give you rest."*

Yes, she'd been trying to carry the burdens of the household alone, as if their survival rested on her shoulders instead of the Lord's. His hands were much more capable, and the worry and anxiety she carried did not come from a place of trust in Him.

Folding the dough over, Betha punched it down, stopping to use the back of her hand to rub at an itch on her cheek. But what had Benjamin Franklin said quoting the ancient Greeks? That God helped those who help themselves? God's loving care didn't come with conditions. That didn't mean she could be idle while expecting God to miraculously provide for the family's needs. He'd outfitted their family with healthy, capable members who could work diligently and accomplish that purpose. She wasn't wrong to work hard.

It's my heart though. I've not just been doing my part to help keep food on the table, but running myself ragged and allowing the strain to wear down my heart.

So Lord, I give control of the household to You. Seamus has been doing a terrible job at it, and I suppose I thought that meant it fell on me. Because she didn't want the discomfort of being poor if there was something she could do about it. That fear had her working herself to an early grave.

If she'd accepted Colm's suit and married him like Seamus and Cara suggested, would she be finding ways to be unhappy with his choices too? He wasn't perfect either, but he was always willing to consider another perspective. Unlike Seamus. Colm would have been a much more intentional household manager. Even so, if fear of poverty was something to release to God under a different man's roof, it was God's to carry now too.

Lost in her thoughts and prayers, Betha didn't notice how quiet the house had become until she dropped the shaped loaves into bread pans to rise. Wiping down the table and washing her hands was the work of a minute. She took off her floury apron, shook it out on the back step, and hung it up before peeking into the parlor and finding the bed curtains closed. Cara was napping in the middle of the day, and Henry definitely was getting a younger sibling before the end of the year.

Tiptoeing through to the front room, Betha clicked the door quietly behind her, closing her in with Seamus and his silent loom. He was on a stool at the back of the loom, concentrating on threading the heddles. It was one of the most tedious parts of his job, so Betha didn't speak until he saw her, acknowledging her presence with a "Hello."

"Hello." Betha leaned against the wall and stifled a yawn, envying Cara and her nap. "Looks like you have a couple weeks' worth of thread left?"

"Yes, and Mrs. Gallagher has a few more spools for me after that."

It was nice of her to use Seamus for her weaving.

"Have you thought about what you're goin' to do this summer?"

"Figured I'd help with haying season." Seamus slid the metal pin over and reached for the next one to thread. "There are some farms I could probably work at before that."

He had been thinking ahead, but his answers alone weren't enough to keep Betha as peace filled as prayer did. His summer work never paid better than weaving.

"I've been thinking about our options. Since we don't grow our own flax, it's hard to keep afloat with just one loom. I could see if a bank would give us a loan for property outside the city for planting flax. I could start Henry on the other loom. Or"—Seamus pulled the thread through the heddle and tied it off—"I could admit linen weaving can't compete with the cotton mills and pursue something different. Maybe sailmaking."

Betha didn't move. Each idea was worse than the one before it. Become farmers—by taking out a loan that they'd never make enough to pay back? The thought interested her not at all. Take Henry out of school? Absolutely not. But for Seamus to become a sailmaker, he'd have to be gone from home for months at a time. Betha would never wish such a thing for Cara. Although from the look in Seamus's eye, sailmaking had been the industry he'd mentioned simply because it was the one that interested him the most.

He worked steadily on, avoiding looking at her.

"Which choice would be your first?" Betha asked quietly, the dread in her stomach already providing the answer.

"I've no inclination to be a farmer or guarantee that it would be a successful venture. Henry will be out of school soon. I could spend time this summer workin' with him on the loom."

Henry did need something to keep him busy over the summer months; even Betha could admit he was too old to spend the summer running the streets anymore. But—

"Linen won't support him by the time he's grown though. It might help us for a time, but it's not an industry he'll be able to stay in."

As soon as the words were out, Betha wished them back. What other option was there but to indenture him to someone else? At least with weaving, he'd be with her all day and she could be sure he was not mistreated or underfed.

"I don't know what else to do, Betha." Seamus's fingers stilled and he sat hunched over his loom as if the weight of the world pressed on him. "You're already workin' as much as one person can, and I am too. He's old enough to contribute."

So was Cara. Betha bit her tongue. Seamus had noticed her efforts, at least. "I'll start wiping down the other loom by the time school ends. On one condition."

Seamus fiddled with the thread in his fingers, waiting.

"You help Henry finish his French schooner before you fit together a single peg of that loom."

29

"Colm."

The prayer meeting had just ended, handfuls of men still milling about the sanctuary in clusters. Colm had made it three steps toward the door when he recognized his name in Stewart Brown's penetrating voice. He halted and turned with a smile for his friend.

"I wanted to say how much I appreciate you coming to these." Stewart was well-dressed despite the informality of the event and the late hour; he must have come straight from working late at one of his shipping offices. "Your prayers for the Sunday school are poignant and heartfelt. I can see how much it's come to mean to you. How are the classes these days?"

"Better than I expected," Colm admitted. It still felt a heavy responsibility, teaching children about God, but the classes themselves had been proceeding without much opposition.

"One of the Sunday school families came to church for the first time on Sunday, including the parents." Reverend Breckinridge broke off from his nearby conversation, stepping forward to join Stewart. "You're a gifted teacher, Mr. Gallagher. I can't help but praise God when I see you exercising your spiritual gift. He's obviously equipped you well for this work."

"What makes you think teaching is my spiritual gift?" Colm had often viewed teaching as the work God gave him to do, but for some reason he'd always thought of his bent toward it being natural ability, not the result of spiritual endowment.

"Isn't it?" The pastor looked surprised. "I've always seen it that way because of how the hearers are edified by it. You have an ability to open God's Word and connect it to the children, and there's good fruit from it."

"Another way to know is if *you're* edified by it. Have you seen growth in yourself as a result?" Stewart asked.

"Well... yes." Wouldn't growth be expected with any job that stretched a person beyond their comfort level?

"The exercise of one's gift leads to others being stirred up to exercise theirs. It's obviously not a source of pride for you. I believe it is a gift of grace, and God is honored by the way you teach." Reverend Breckinridge reached out and gently squeezed Colm's upper arm. "Let me know how the church can continue to support your classes beyond our prayers."

"Thank you. I'll organize the thoughts I've had on our needs this week."

Together they migrated toward the door. Colm picked up his lantern from the back table and lit it, and Stewart did the same with his.

"Are the Sunday schools ceasing for the summer?"

"I wasn't planning to do so. For some of the children, summer gives them greater availability to come. For the rest, they still need to consistently be fed, spiritually and physically."

"Very true." Stewart put on his hat. "How will you be spending your summer when school is out?"

Colm bid the reverend good night, holding the door open for Stewart to precede him into the night. "I always work on the Comptons' farm. I'm open to less strenuous options, if you have any in mind," he added, half-facetiously.

Stewart stopped on the bottom step, a thoughtful look on his face. "I could probably come up with something for you to do."

"Truly? I didn't actually expect..."

"Truly. Let me work on that, and I'll let you know."

Stewart tipped his hat, leaving Colm on the dark step, grinning at his retreating form.

The day before school let out in May, Henry came home to find Seamus waiting for him with the schooner in hand, the holes he needed already drilled. Betha was sweeping out the fireplaces, trying to be as quiet as she could so as to not disturb Cara's nap. Stacked against the wall were the spools of linen thread from overpriced flax Seamus had bought for Henry to practice on and which Betha had spent the last week spinning up for him.

Bent over the schooner in the front room, Seamus worked patiently with Henry, and it almost felt like the old days again. But the next day, when he started Henry on the loom, Betha could have cried. She didn't dare ask Seamus yet if he had plans to allow Henry to return to school in the fall.

Henry had a lifetime of experience with weaving and had learned how over the years, though not as formally as Seamus taught him now. The patience of the previous day was a thing of the past as well. Betha escaped to the garden to avoid listening to Seamus's frustrated mutterings and prayed for Henry to withstand it.

A few days later, Seamus started summer work at a local vegetable farm. When he came home in the evenings, he was dirty, exhausted, and critical of Henry's progress. Some evenings, he took out everything Henry had done that day, accompanied by a gruff, "It's how you learn, Son. My father used to do the same to me. It's better to go slow and get a little bit right than try to do too much and need to redo it. Our linen has a reputation to uphold."

Betha still worked long hours on the house, garden, food preservation, and sewing, but with less fear and panic than the spring. When they surfaced now, she was quicker to surrender them to the Lord and choose trust. She was doing everything she could, and worry would not help her accomplish more. It was harder to remember that when it came to parenting Henry, even with Bridget's words in the back of her mind.

She wondered about that one day early in July, when Henry was surlier than normal. Cara was in the kitchen, because she avoided whatever room Henry was in as much as possible, so Betha took the opportunity to stop by his tense form at the loom and lay a soothing hand on his shoulder. There was purpose in work, she reminded him; they did it heartily, as unto the Lord, not for man. "No wonder we want it to be its very best," she finished with a smile.

"That's not why Da wants me to weave," Henry growled. "He wants me to do this because he can't afford to keep his own wife."

Betha stopped herself before she smacked him across the mouth for his disrespect. "He's your father, Henry, and she's part of our family now. You'd do better the sooner you accept that and remember the second commandment: to love your neighbor as yourself. Regardless of your da's reasons, as a follower of Jesus, you have different ones."

Henry threw the shuttle harder than necessary through the threads. Betha reached for it, pulled it back, and handed it to him again. "You'll mess up your tension doing that. Do you need to take a break and cool your head?" It was stifling in the room, even with the front door open. There was a good chance being overheated was contributing to his moodiness.

Crossing his arms over his chest, Henry scowled at the loom. "I'd like to take a break and not come back."

"Oh, Henry." Betha sighed, wrapping an arm around his shoulders. She'd been here before once, but Seamus was twenty then, not a mere lad when he'd started down this path, unwilling to heed the truth. "God loves you, Henry, even though we're in a situation we wouldn't choose and can't control. He's here to help us through it, if we'll let Him."

"She doesn't even want me here, Ma. I have to do all this because of her, and she doesn't even want me."

He was right, of course. He wasn't stupid.

"And what have you done to show you want her here? She doesn't know Jesus like you do, my boy. How have you shown Him to her?"

Henry slid off the stool. "Maybe I'll go take a walk. Clear my head, like you said."

When he was gone, Betha sat on the stool in his place with tears in her eyes, pleading in prayer for him. Had she allowed worry over Henry into her heart for so long that feeding it had become more habit than prayer? Seamus's choice to walk away from God had haunted her for years before she was able to surrender him to God. Look at him now—as far from God as he had ever been. What had surrendering accomplished? Should she have fought harder for his soul? Still fight harder? How could she give up on either of them?

"How do you release someone to God without slacking on faithfully doing the work God has called you to?" she whispered to the loom. "When do you surrender and when do you fight, or can you do both at once?"

Cara's boots clomped through the parlor, so Betha straightened, wiping her sleeve across her face.

"I was wondering about the nasturtiums," Cara said, poking her head into the room. "They've been sitting in the saltwater for three days. Is it time to add vinegar?"

"I suppose so. Mrs. Randolph said three to four days."

"I don't know what they're supposed to look like."

"Me neither. I've never had pickled nasturtiums before." She'd never had chicken pudding or bologna sausages before this summer either. Some of their experiments were tasty; other times, Cara tore out the entire page of the book and fed it to the stove.

Betha got up, hesitating. "Henry thinks you don't want him here."

Cara's face remained unchanged as she gave a muted *hmph*. "Of course he can live here. He's Seamus's son."

Betha proceeded cautiously. "But do you wish he hadn't had any other children before you married?" Cara's round middle was obvious these days, and rather than being sensitive around smells, she now ate anything she laid eyes on. From all appearances, the baby was growing as it should.

"There's naught anyone can do to change the past," Cara said in her matter-of-fact way, turning back to the kitchen. "I accepted that he had a son before I married him."

Betha gave a frustrated snort to the empty room. She was halfway across the floor when a knock sounded on the open front door. "I'll be coming," she called to Cara as she turned back to answer it.

Colm was on the front step, hat in hand, sweat already causing the ends of his hair to cling to his forehead. He hesitated when he saw Betha, giving her a moment to collect her own self at his unexpected presence.

"Good day." Her heart fluttered despite her efforts to calm it.

He blinked, shaking himself out of the momentary lapse. "Is Henry in?"

Of course he wasn't there to see her. "He's on a walk."

"I came to invite him to the parade tomorrow." He flung more than handed the *Baltimore Gazette* to her. "It's to celebrate the groundbreaking for the railroad. I hoped he could walk with us."

Betha glanced at the headline advertising the event, a smile curling at the edges of her mouth. It would have been impossible to not know about it, with the entire city talking of little else in recent weeks. The first railroad track between American cities was to be built, starting in Baltimore, of all places. The celebration parade on the Fourth of July would be no small display. She'd wanted to take Henry herself, but time with Colm and his brothers would be good for him.

"Of course. He'd like that."

"Dunkin is christening his new schooner, too, the *Fourth of July*. Do you want to come as well?" he added, uncertainty clouding his excitement.

Betha pursed her lips and shook her head. "I might walk out with Seamus and Cara to see some of the sights. Thank you though."

"Maybe I'll see you out there then. I'll come for Henry by nine so we can find a good spot."

"Thank you."

Distracting herself with a reminder of the nasturtiums she needed to return to, Betha backed away from the doorway and the magnetic pull to the man on the other side of it.

30

September 1828

Seamus was in the middle of haying season when school restarted. He was either too tired to argue or too unimpressed with Henry's weaving progress to prevent his son's return to school. Betha had fresh new bags of flax from the Delaware Valley, and for the time was able to work in solitude again.

The distant clanging of Cara puttering around in the kitchen gave a muted accompaniment to the whirring of her wheel. Through the open windows, children's voices arrived in the street, marking the end of the school day. A whistled tune met Betha's ears, and she smiled. Colm's presence must be good for Henry, if now that he was back in school, he was happy enough to whistle again.

It had been over a year now since she stood quivering in front of Oliver Hibenian for the first time, wondering if the changes they'd made for Henry's sake would pay off. She never would have imagined then everything that would happen over the course of the year. Ah, blessed naivety.

He came in and wove for an hour. They talked about his friends, the measurements of the latest merchant schooners launched from Baltimore shipyards, and a joke Colm told his class about a boy named Two-faced Tom. She could see the schoolmaster's dimpled grin in her mind, listening to Henry retell the joke but hearing it in Colm's deep voice.

"You can go play for a bit," Betha said after a while, lifting her foot from her treadle and stretching her fingers. He didn't need a second invitation. Stopping to grab his fishing pole, he ran out the door to enjoy the last hours of daylight.

For all its challenges, she enjoyed this age, when he was half boy and half young man, both working hard and playing hard. She could see in him not only the child he had been but the man he would become. Some days, what she saw was concerning, but she shouldn't lose track of the days like today, when he reminded her of the goodness he still had inside. Maybe she shouldn't be so overworried.

Seamus returned before the catfish Henry caught was done cooking. Cara had curry on hand already, waiting for a good catch to attempt Mrs. Randolph's catfish curry.

"It's not bad," Seamus offered helpfully when Cara frowned at her half-finished bowl. "I wouldn't burn the receipt yet."

"Perhaps we can improve upon it." Betha nibbled at the bite on her spoon. It wasn't the curry that was the problem, she decided; just the combination of it with the catfish. The asparagus soup was still the best dish they'd tried from the book. The whole family remained in agreement that she should plant more asparagus.

"I think I'll go back to baked catfish after this," Cara said with a shake of her head. She stood, smoothing a hand over her round middle, and picked up her bowl.

Betha had her next spoonful halfway to her mouth when she noticed the way Henry stilled, watching Cara. His brow flickered, and a minute later, he returned to his meal, devouring the remainder of the dish.

Betha made quick work of washing the dishes while Cara wiped them and tidied the kitchen. When they returned to the parlor, they found Seamus with his pipe lit, catching up on all the Irish-American news in the latest issue of *The Truth Teller*. Henry had out the poetry book he was supposed to be memorizing from, but his eyes followed Cara as the women entered the room and took up their sewing. He made no effort in subtlety, his gaze trailing from the jacket Betha was letting out for him to the tiny white linen dress Cara labored over.

He opened his mouth, coughed, hesitated, and bent over his book. A minute later, he was peering at Cara from under dark bangs that were due for a trim. From the corner of her eye, Betha watched him grow more agitated; first fidgeting his fingers, then shifting in his seat, and finally closing his book.

"Ma, are you almost ready to head to bed? It's getting late."

"Not quite," Betha said calmly. "Are you tired?"

"Rather." The word came out in a *whoosh* under his breath. "Maybe I'll head up now. Will you be up soon?" He was on his feet now, the book forgotten on his seat.

"Did you need to talk about something?"

"Well, I had a question . . ."

"I believe it's a question for your father." Betha knew he'd rather talk to her, and maybe that was the problem. Maybe he and Seamus both needed to act like Seamus was his parent for this. "Seamus, go talk to him."

"What is it?" Seamus asked without moving.

"Go talk to him."

"I can ask you later, Ma." Henry backed toward the door.

"You can ask your da. He won't bite. Seamus, don't bite. Just go answer his question."

"He can ask his question in here."

Cara stood up. "I think I'll make myself some tea. Do any of you want any?"

"I'd like some ale." Seamus crossed his arms, and Cara scurried into the kitchen, closing the door behind her.

"All right then," Seamus said when she'd gone. "What is all this about?"

Henry looked like he'd prefer to sink into the cellar. He stuffed his fists into his pockets, then took them out and clasped them behind his back.

"Go on," Betha said gently.

Henry licked his lips. "Well my friend Paddy, he just got a new little brother. His mother had a little baby. And I wondered . . . it seemed like . . . well, I guess it's true, isn't it?"

"What's true?"

Betha lowered her sewing to her lap. "Seamus, don't be obtuse. You know what he's asking."

"If the same thing will happen in this house? Seems likely to occur by the end of the year."

Henry's fidgeting ceased as the information sank in, took root, and was mulled over. Betha had watched him convince himself of the truth of it over the course of the evening, but having his father confirm it seemed to have a different effect on him.

"You didn't tell me," he almost whispered.

"Henry—" She reached a hand toward him but he just stood, staring at Seamus.

Seamus snorted. "That's not how these things work. When there's a baby in the house, you'd know then." Maybe it wasn't a brilliant idea to make Seamus talk to Henry about it after all.

"I didn't hear you mention that when you were talking to Cara about indenturing me. Is it because you can't afford another child yourself, or because you want me out of the way?" Henry's nose was red now, his voice growing louder and shakier, and Betha prayed for his own sake that he wouldn't lose his composure in front of Seamus.

Seamus turned red as well, revealing that Henry's words had hit their mark. He opened his mouth, but Henry rushed on.

"You don't want me unless you're using me to pay for what you do want." Henry paused to take an audible breath and swipe his hair away from his eyes. "Well, Da, *I* don't want any of this."

Before Betha or Seamus could react, he was through the door, pulling it shut behind him with a decided thump. They sat frozen, listening to him stomp up the stairs.

"What gave his ungrateful self the idea—"

"You hardly have to wonder, Seamus." Betha sighed. "You and Cara don't do very much to make sure he knows he's loved."

Seamus frowned, crossing his arms over his chest. "I don't know what you're talking about. Who told him he wasn't, and why does it make that kind of disrespect acceptable?"

Betha tossed the jacket into her basket and stood up. "It's not what anyone said to him but all the things you don't say to him. I'll talk to him about his disrespect, but he's upset for a reason, Seamus, and you'd do well to pay attention to what he's trying to tell you."

A headache pulsed across her forehead as she trod up the stairs, lantern in hand. Henry was sprawled facedown on top of his bed with his shoes still on. Betha went straight to him and sat on the edge of his mattress. Turning away from her, he wiped his eyes on his pillowcase.

"Ah, Henry," she whispered, tears coming to her own eyes. She wanted to lie down next to him, wrap an arm around his middle, and cry together. Instead she just rubbed his shoulder and then combed her fingers through his hair. "I'm sorry, my boy. I don't think your da isn't making mistakes, but I do know he doesn't mean to hurt you. He truly doesn't."

"Can you please leave me alone?" Henry hiccuped into his pillow.

Disappointment sagged her shoulders. "I will. But do you think the way you spoke to him was right?"

"I don't care," Henry mumbled, and his body shuddered.

A lecture would be pointless right now, no matter how compassionately given. Betha leaned over and kissed his head before standing up. "You always wanted to be a brother."

He didn't reply again.

When Betha had readied for the night, she returned from behind the screen to find him still sniffling. She climbed into her own bed and turned down the lantern.

"I love you, Henry," she whispered to the blackness, but only silence met her words.

31

Daylight still glimmered golden through the window when Betha halted her wheel, her stiff fingers unable to spin another inch. Henry should have been home hours ago; he always stopped in the house to greet her and weave before running back out. His response the previous night sat heavy in Betha's stomach all day, and several times she offered his heart up to the Lord as she worked.

He hadn't spoken at all that morning, coming down in his school clothes and swiping a biscuit and piece of bacon from the table on his way out the back door. It didn't bode well that he would stay out with his friends after school without letting her know where he was.

Coming to her feet, she followed the smell of baked veal to the kitchen and found Seamus leaning against the table, watching Cara slice the meat onto a serving tray.

"You've not heard from Henry?"

Seamus lifted his head and shook it. "I suppose he'll come in when he's hungry."

"He didn't come in for his nunch after school. 'Tisn't like him."

Cara handed Seamus the finished tray, and he pushed off from the table to carry it to the parlor.

"I'm running over to the Olivers' to see if Little John is home," Betha decided aloud, attempting to push the worry from her mind. Maybe Henry needed time to get used to another significant change and think it through. She had to believe he would come out stronger from all the upheaval. Surely he would enjoy having a younger sibling; he wasn't an uncaring person, and he did like babies.

She knocked on the Olivers' door, rubbing her arms nervously as she glanced down the street, but the boys out at play weren't Henry's age. The door opened, revealing Little John himself in his too-short knickers and threadbare shirt.

"Hello." Betha pressed her palms together. "Have you seen Henry since school? He hasn't come home."

Mrs. Oliver came up behind him, laying a hand on his shoulder. Little John wrinkled his brow at Betha. "Henry wasn't at school today."

Betha felt the blood drain from her head and grasped the doorframe with a hand that had gone suddenly clammy. "What?" she gasped. Her knees threatened to buckle, the pit in her stomach now a gaping hole.

"I haven't seen him all day." Little John scratched his head.

"He's-he's missing."

Mrs. Oliver pushed past her son, wrapping a steadying arm around Betha. "Where might he have gone?"

"I don't know." Betha shook her head wildly. "I need to get Seamus."

"We'll send for the constables," Mrs. Oliver said, supporting Betha even as she propelled her down the stairs and toward her own house. "Run and fetch Seamus now." Leaving Betha on her front step, she hurried back home, calling for Mr. Oliver.

Betha burst into the house. "Seamus! Henry's gone. He wasn't at school today." Repeating the words made them feel more real, and nausea rolled over her. Where would he have possibly gone, and why hadn't he returned? He didn't have any other family he could have gone to. They were everything to him. She was everything.

Seamus had the good sense to look panicked as he rushed into the front room with Cara behind him. Bolting past Betha through the open door, he found Mr. Oliver running out of his house.

"I'll find the constables!" Mr. Oliver called without stopping, and Seamus nodded in response, his eyes traveling frantically around the street.

"Let's run down to the school to see if we can find anything," he said to nobody.

"I'm goin' for Colm," Betha said and turned, lifting her skirts and taking off down the street before he could reply. Colm had to know something, had to have seen him. Little John could have been wrong about Henry being at school, right? Henry wouldn't have skipped school. But even if Colm didn't have answers, his was the only house she'd be running to right now. It was the man himself that she needed so desperately, even though he deserved better than to only be the person she turned to when in trouble. She couldn't face this night without him by her side.

She arrived on the doorstep, trembling and gasping for breath, and pounded on the door with her fist. During the brief pause while she waited, she tried to take deep breaths, but her mind wouldn't stop its racing. The latch clicked, and Patrick stood on the other side of the door.

"Betha?"

"Please, is Colm in?"

Instantly, a crowd of Gallaghers pressed behind Patrick, and Colm wove through the bodies, concern carving furrows in his brow. As soon as Betha spied him, her body began shaking involuntarily, a sob working its way up her chest.

"Have you seen Henry? Was he at school today?"

"No, he wasn't. I was afraid he was sick." Colm stopped in front of her, reaching out and then dropping his hands back to his sides before they touched her.

Betha wanted to scream at him, pound her fists on his chest, kick at his legs. *And you didn't come after school to check on him?* She'd done nothing to give Colm a reason to show special favor to Henry. Of course he wouldn't stop in at the home of every student who missed one day of class. But he'd done it before, for Henry.

A whimper was all that came out before Betha could swallow it away. "He left at the normal time this mornin', and no one has seen him since."

The Gallagher sisters gasped in unison from behind Colm. "Ye've not seen him at all?" Betha asked one more time, desperate for the answer to change.

"No."

"We have to find him. Seamus went to the school to look around."

Colm barely caught himself from stumbling into Betha as Patrick pushed past him and bolted down the street toward the livery.

"We'll check at the Shot Tower," Ben said, grabbing Reuben.

"Finn, come with me to Patterson Park." Maisie ran down the stairs with Finn on her heels.

"Take a lantern!" Bridget called, and Maisie swung around to grab it from her.

Betha felt the tears streaking down her face, everything a blur of movement around her as she gave Colm an anguished look. "Can you come?" she whispered.

Breaking away from him, she moved down the stairs and into the street, trusting that he wouldn't need to be asked twice.

"I'm not going anywhere with you."

Colm's low voice behind her stopped her retreat. Fear and despair jolted from her heart down to her fingertips, and she gasped for breath, unable to look at him.

"Not until we pray first."

He stepped forward, meeting her in the middle of the street. Betha forced air into her lungs and gave a tremulous nod. Of course he was right, and this was exactly what made him the person she came to first. Colm lifted his hands cautiously, and when he rested them on her upper arms, her trembling slowed. She took a deep breath and then another one, clinging to his liquid brown eyes as if they were her lifeline. It had been months since she had been this close to him, held his gaze for more than the briefest second at a time, felt his comforting touch. The effect was like opium, and she knew it would never be enough.

Colm lowered his head, and her heart stuttered. His forehead met hers, his gentle hands holding her steady as her breath became his. Betha closed her eyes. Colm began to speak, his deep voice calming, just above a whisper.

"Our God who sees. We know you see Henry, wherever he is. Protect him from harm, Lord, and heal the hurts in his heart. Direct our steps, we ask, that we might find him now. We entrust him to You and ask that You replace the fear in our hearts with trust in Your mighty hand and merciful heart."

"Amen," Betha whispered, unwilling to let him go.

He slowly straightened anyway until he stood tall and gazed unseeing down the street, still holding her against him. "The wharves." Releasing her shoulders, he took her hand in his, intertwining their fingers. "The shipyards."

They began to move east as one. Betha clutched her skirts up with her other hand so she could keep up with his confident strides. Her mind had trouble catching up, however.

"Why would he have gone to the wharves? Did he say something to you?"

"Not recently. He loves ships though."

This was true. Maybe Henry just found a quiet place where he could think and watch the ships and lost track of time. Right? But there were any number of dangers at the wharves, most of them related to the unsavory characters who frequented the area.

"He realized last night that he's soon to be a brother. I fear that's what drove him away. You don't think . . ." Betha double-stepped ahead, pivoting to look back at Colm. "He doesn't mean to get *on* a ship, does he?"

Colm didn't answer, merely setting his jaw as he strode through the streets.

"Colm, he . . . he wouldn't." More tears dripped from her chin, evidence that she believed it entirely possible. The scent of fish and seawater grew increasingly stronger as they approached the boardwalk.

The Fells Point wharves covered a length of nearly two miles. Colm didn't turn aside to the inns and warehouses that stood opposite the harbor, instead sticking to the shoreline as dusk fell. Without pausing or slowing his pace, he peered down the docks and around ship after ship standing at anchor. Mosquitos swarmed around them from the time they reached the water, and Colm slapped one on his neck. He inquired of every crewman walking past or at work on a boat, but none admitted to seeing a black-haired, landlubbing youth.

"Don't lose heart," Colm murmured even as the light slipped away from them. He unhooked a lantern from a light pole on the dock and lit it with a match from his pocket before continuing down the boardwalk. Betha started to lag behind, still clutching his hand but feeling the weariness of the fruitless search. Her heart had bled out an hour ago at the thought of Henry purposefully abandoning them—her—to take a position on a ship. Henry could be gone tomorrow, boarding a ship at high tide. What would they do if they found him and he was unwilling to return home? Was he that far gone from her?

No sensible captain would take him, though, would they? A child who was obviously fed and well-clothed without an indenture from his guardian? Betha couldn't trust them not to, but the thought made her feel physically sick.

"What made you think we should look down here?"

Colm shook his head, still craning to see every direction, still not breaking his stride or letting go of her hand. "I don't know. After I finished praying, something in my heart said he was here."

Betha tripped after him, wanting to collapse on a crate and succumb to her fear and sorrow, but forced herself to keep going. "What if we don't find him?"

Colm slowed, glancing quickly back at her and then away. "I should have come by after school when he didn't show up."

Betha pressed her lips against a biting agreement. "You wouldn't have done so for anyone else."

Colm pushed ahead. "Henry's not anyone else."

After a few minutes of silence, Betha wrenched her hand from his. "Colm, I can't keep up."

He stopped, as if realizing what he was doing for the first time. "You're right. You're right. We prayed, and we should be trusting that God will lead us to him."

"Where is he, Lord?" Betha whispered, turning in a circle to take in the barrels, rope coils, nets, and crates along the shore.

A fisherman hopped out of his boat and headed toward the street. Colm stepped forward, asked him about Henry, and returned to Betha with a shake of his head. She shook a mosquito off her hand.

They stood in silence, listening and praying as the water lapped against the fishing boats.

"I lost him." Tears choked Betha's words. "I was afraid I would lose him when he was grown, but I lost him before that. He's only eleven."

Colm let out a heavy breath. His mouth clicked as he opened it, and then he shut it again. Another minute passed.

"You've done everything you could, Betha. It's between him and the Lord, and it's not too late." He cleared his throat before adding, "We don't even know if he ran."

"Are you saying someone could have taken him?"

"I'm saying that God knows a lot more than we do right now."

A carriage rolled by on the street. A door closed nearby.

Where is he, Lord?

"Thank you for coming." She couldn't put into words anything more. A hundred raw emotions simmered below the surface, each fighting for an opportunity to erupt. She shoved them away.

Colm didn't answer. Betha wrapped her arms around herself and slowly turned. With a resigned inhale and the last weak prayer her bruised heart had to offer, she started back in the direction they came. A moment later, she heard Colm's footsteps join hers, the lantern casting shadows as he followed her.

Her legs, back, and head were aching by the time she reached the end of the docks and stepped into the street. None of the other pain compared to the ache in her heart, but it seemed an appropriate companion. Colm had returned his lantern to its pole, leaving them at the mercy of streetlamps and the stars to find their way home.

"Colm! Betha!"

Betha's head snapped up at the sound of Mor's breathless voice coming toward them. She held a swinging lantern aloft, illuminating her face and Hanna by her side.

"Patrick has him. He's safe."

"He's safe?" Betha cried out, her knees giving way. A strong arm came around her waist, and she found herself held upright against Colm's coat. "He's safe."

32

"He's taking him home now," Mor said. "I just passed them and came to find you."

All of Betha's weight sagged against Colm, and he wrapped his other arm under hers to keep her from collapsing to the ground.

"We're coming," he told Mor with a tilt of his head. Thankfully she took heed and continued on her way with Hanna. He didn't want to worry about attention drawing to Betha while he worked to stabilize her.

As soon as his sisters' backs were turned, great, wrenching sobs overtook Betha's body. Colm shifted her in his arms until she was against his chest, held in place by a firm, careful hand on her head and another on her waist. She wept like her heart had been rent down the middle.

"He's safe," Colm whispered to her, over and over.

At first he thought her tears were from relief, but then he began to wonder if all the emotions from the evening were finding their way out onto the front of his waistcoat. For several minutes, he didn't dare move his hands, unwilling to risk either dropping her or finding too much pleasure in the feel of her in his arms at the expense of her grief.

"Do you want to go to him?" he asked.

"Not like this," Betha said, sniffing. She must have found a handkerchief, because she wiped her nose on it without moving from his chest. "I don't want him to see this."

He felt her weight slowly ease from his hurting arms. He couldn't help himself. With one hand still gently cradling her head against him, he lifted the other to her face, tenderly curling his fingers around the back of her neck. With a deliberate movement, he slid his thumb up her jaw to the place behind her ear where he wanted to kiss her, and for a moment he saw stars. "What are you going to do?"

Betha swallowed—he felt it in every fingertip—before she said, "Hug him tight and then put him to bed. We can talk about it tomorrow."

Hopefully Seamus wasn't at home berating his son in Betha's absence.

Colm realized his thumb was stroking Betha's soft jaw again. This had to stop. He wasn't the type of man to take advantage of a female in a fragile condition. After one more sweep that included her cheek, he released her head, dropped both hands, and took a step back. After tonight, she'd go back to how things were before, taking this closeness with her. He missed her already.

Surrounded by darkness with the barest of scattered light falling over them, Colm could see the look of utter depletion on her face as she wiped the last of the tears from her swollen eyes. Without a buggy or horse, he had nothing to offer but his hand, which she took one more time.

They didn't speak again until they arrived back at her house. Unwilling to leave until he'd seen Henry for himself, Colm followed Betha through the door. Or maybe it was that he wanted Henry to see him, his schoolmaster and friend who cared enough to be out at ten at night searching for him.

Henry was seated at the table—which was in the middle room now—but he stood and rushed toward them, throwing his arms around Betha. Colm was glad to see that he wasn't as far gone as she'd feared. His black hair was tousled and his clothes rumpled, but he didn't look any worse the wear from whatever adventure he'd been on.

Seamus and Cara sat silently by the fire; Patrick was nowhere in sight.

"I'm sorry, Ma." Henry's voice came muffled from where his face was buried in her shoulder.

"I'm glad to see you safe, my boy. We'll talk about it later. Come and see Mr. Gallagher now." She spoke in a soft, even tone, the earlier storm smoothed away. This woman was as tough as they came.

Henry pulled back to stand in front of Colm, his head bowed, shoulders pulled up around his ears. His fists were buried deep in his pockets, and two bright red spots glowed on his cheeks.

"I missed you today in school," Colm said. "I was afraid you were unwell."

"No, sir."

"The Lord God has given you grownups to care for you, Henry. I'm thankful to say that they love you as well. You can be sure that the sight of you well right now is an answer to many prayers."

"Yes, sir."

"Will I see you in school tomorrow?"

"Yes, sir."

"I expect you to be late," Colm said, and Henry lifted his watery eyes for the first time. "You owe your mother a conversation in the morning, and I'll see you when she's done with you."

"Yes, sir."

"All right." Colm moved to put his hat on and realized he'd left home without it hours prior. "Good night."

He backed out of the silent house, closing the door softly behind him.

When Colm stepped into the foyer, Patrick's voice could be heard coming from the direction of the gentlemen's parlor. Although he wanted to know more about how and where Patrick had found Henry, he couldn't muster up the mental fortitude for conversation.

"How's Betha?" Mor stood in the shadows of her doorway down the hall.

"She'll be fine." Colm ran his fingers through his hair and crossed to the stairs before adding, "Good night."

"Good night, Colm."

Safely in his room, he dropped heavily onto his bed to remove his shoes before leaning back on his pillow, throwing his arm over his eyes. He couldn't get Betha's anguished face out of his mind, how it felt when she collapsed against him, or the way she suddenly pulled herself together for Henry. There was no way to imagine what the aftereffects of all this would be, especially since all signs pointed to the fact that Henry had intentionally run away.

Footsteps sounded on the stairs, and soon the bedroom door opened and then closed.

"How are you faring?"

Colm grunted in response. The moment of quiet had not lasted long enough.

"I bet you're wishing that the first time you spent time with her all year wasn't like this."

That was true, but not the primary thought in Colm's mind. Betha was hurting, and there was nothing he could do about it. "I just hated to see her suffering."

"She looked pretty rough when she showed up."

Colm moved the arm from his face. "How did you find him?"

"I asked around my friends that work at the shipyards. He'd found a captain in need of a cabin boy."

"So he did intend to leave then."

Patrick tossed his coat over a chair and unbuttoned his waistcoat. "He was scared enough by the time I found him that he was already having doubts about his choices. I gave the captain a piece of my mind. Maybe a bit of my fist too."

Colm watched Patrick ready for bed and then turned his head, blinking at the ceiling. Not that long ago, he'd wondered if he'd ever have his relationship with his brother back. If not for the somberness of the evening, having a conversation like this one with Patrick would feel almost normal. He thanked the Lord silently for the gift while Patrick continued talking.

"You took a horse?" Colm interrupted.

"I did. Henry came right with me when I asked, and I put him up front. It gave me a chance to talk to him on the way back."

"What did you say?"

Patrick stood facing the window, the candle casting a giant shadow of him on the wall and ceiling. "I told him that I wanted to run away too."

What? So much for pretending that things were normal between him and Patrick again.

"Patrick—"

"I don't know where God wants me. I get the sense I'm not doing everything that I'm supposed to be here. I'm just wasting my life when there is so much need out there."

Frankly, Colm's body still buzzed from the emotional evening with Betha, and he wasn't sure he could do more of the same with Patrick right now.

"And when you pray about it . . .?" It was everything he could do to not sound impatient and bite the words out. He'd waited all year for this conversation, but why did it have to be right now?

"Betha's right. I believe it's a burden God has given me to do something about. I need to figure out how. When I was with Henry tonight, I . . . I understood how he felt, wanting to help and having limited options and control."

"Help with what? What do you mean?" Colm was fully alert now.

"Supporting the family. Pardon me, but he told me his father was adding to the family, and linen prices have plummeted, and Seamus has talked about indenturing him. He went to look for a job himself."

Colm's heart broke a little more. Every year, he lost students to indentures and their family businesses. Boys Henry's age in Fell's Point were lucky to be allowed an education. Betha blamed herself, but he hadn't been able to protect Henry from such a future either.

"You were supposed to encourage him to stay home and keep going to school while he could, not validate his running."

Patrick turned sharply, picked up his pillow, and threw it at Colm's head. "I did, you dolt. What kind of person do you think I am?"

Colm grabbed the pillow and tossed it back to Patrick's bed. "He didn't run because he was upset about the changes to his family?"

A thoughtful look passed Patrick's face. "I gathered that things haven't been easy with his father and Cara lately and he doesn't know his place anymore, but he sounded . . . proud about being a brother. So I just talked to him about waiting on God, and in the meantime, not doing things to harm the people who love him."

Patrick saw the look on Colm's face and crossed his arms, scratching at a red bite on his forearm. "I know, I haven't been doing a good job at that. I suppose I just told him everything I've been telling myself all year. Maybe it'll help one of us."

It wasn't quite an apology. But then, Colm hadn't apologized for his part in their quarrel either. He wasn't expecting the opportunity to come tonight. It would be easier if it wasn't on an evening when he'd already dealt with so much—and had school to be up for in the morning—but too much time had passed not to take the open door.

Colm pushed up on his elbow and swallowed. He allowed his eyes to fix on the flickering candle instead of Patrick's face before he lost his courage again.

"You were right about my lack of faith. I don't . . . God hasn't given me the passion for abolition that He's given you. I believe in it, and I'll fight for it where I can, but my job, my calling, and my gifts are elsewhere. But I'm sorry for the way that I communicated that we always have to count the cost and know the end before we follow God."

Patrick had stilled, falling strangely silent.

"I don't really believe that," Colm added. "But I also can't be reckless. God is orderly, too, and that's one way I reflect Him. It's . . . I know it's right when I do. I don't think He wants me to become reckless."

He risked a glance at Patrick, whose head was now hanging and was scuffing at the floor plank with his stockinged foot. "I know," Patrick mumbled. "I don't want you to be either."

"Were your friends that helped you find Henry tonight—they were Black?"

"Yes."

"I'm thankful to them." Colm fell back on his pillows. "And you."

Patrick lifted his eyes under the russet curls hanging over his forehead. After a moment, he nodded. "I'm sorry for expecting you to bear the same burdens I do and acting like the work you do isn't as important as mine. I respect what you do too."

"I need you to keep challenging me." Colm returned the arm over his face and yawned. "I do put a lot of thought into the things you say."

"That's more than I deserve."

It wasn't, but another yawn interrupted Colm's attempts to respond. Patrick crossed the floor and put out the candle, the ropes in his bed groaning as he climbed under the covers. They were both silent for a minute.

"I don't know what I can do for Henry," Colm said eventually. "It's like you said. I have the sense there's more for me to do, but I don't know what it is."

Another minute passed before Patrick responded. "Well, like you said, have you prayed about it?"

"I'll make you a deal and pray for you to know what to do in your situation if you'll do the same for me."

"Hey, it's a win for me, because it means your prayers will be focused on both of them."

If there was self-degradation attached to Patrick's statement, Colm didn't have the wherewithal to unpack it. He was too spent to do anything but roll over, pull up his covers, and fall asleep.

33

"Wait for me, Henry."

The lanky boy stepped out of the line of students streaming into the bright fall sunshine, turning aside to where Colm stood holding the door.

"I'll walk with you," Colm explained. "Sam, did you forget your hat?"

Sam reached up, touched his hair, and hurried back inside for his cap. When the rest of the students had gone, Colm made quick work of tidying his desk while Henry waited mutely inside the door.

Henry had slipped into his seat at ten that morning and had been mellow while diligently focusing on his required work. At dinnertime, he ate at his desk without lifting his head from the sums on the slate in front of him. Now he followed Colm back onto the front step, pausing while Colm locked the door.

"I suppose you need to make sure I don't get lost on the way home."

"Not really. I know you'd go straight home." Colm slipped the key in his pocket and stepped into the street. "I wanted to spend time with you."

"I'm sorry about yesterday. It was stupid. It won't happen again."

"I'm not here to preach at you, Henry. We can talk about anything you want or nothing at all." Colm gave him a reassuring smile. "I'll leave the lectures to your father."

Henry kicked at a pebble without comment. He probably wanted to forget all about whatever his father had said to him on the subject. He apparently preferred the "nothing at all" option Colm offered today, and

Colm didn't rescind it. Maybe Henry would have more to say another day, but Colm couldn't blame him for his quietness today.

He accompanied Henry through his front door, into the room where Betha sat spinning alone. She started when she saw Colm, running shaky hands over her cap and down the front of her apron as she came to her feet.

"Welcome home, Henry. Run in and get your milk from Cara."

He obeyed, and Colm glanced around the room. "Is Seamus still haying?"

"This should be his last week." She still hadn't met his eyes, cutting her gaze to the hat in his hands, the floor, and the door behind him—everywhere, in fact, except for his face. Yesterday she had all but dived into his arms, and today she seemed too uncomfortable to be in the same room as him. "Thank you for bringing Henry home."

His heart sank with the realization that she was embarrassed. Of the entire debacle or just the way she'd fallen apart, he didn't know. Either way, it was the last thing he wanted her to feel around him.

"Did he talk to you this morning?"

"Yes."

"Betha."

Still she wouldn't look at him. He wanted to ask about what Henry had said, but not when they had only a moment and Henry would be returning soon.

Colm sighed. "What can I do to help?"

"You're already helping, Mr. Gallagher. You're the only good thing in his life."

Mr. Gallagher? What the dickens had he done to deserve that kind of demotion? He took a step forward, but she didn't react, so he halted there. "You know that's not true. I'm with you in this. Let me know if there's anything you can think of that I can do."

"Thank you."

It was everything he could do to not reach out and take her face in his hands again, forcing her eyes to his. He turned abruptly for the door, away from the temptation. Footsteps sounded behind him, and Henry reappeared right then with his cup in hand.

"Good day to you both." Colm managed a smile.

"Good day," Henry returned. Betha said nothing.

Colm backed out of the house, his heart a little more broken than it had been when he arrived.

"I'm studying upstairs," Henry announced when Colm had left. Betha nodded, rooted to the floor as he retreated.

Cara wouldn't know that Henry wasn't in here with her and wouldn't dare come through the door. She looked at the still wheel and couldn't force herself to spin another inch. Sinking into her chair, she lifted the corner of her apron to her leaking eyes. Colm had to think she was either rude or addled, the way she'd just acted after everything he'd done for them. But then, he still didn't know how much it hurt just to see him here, showing compassion by bringing Henry safely to her himself. It was made all the worse by the memories and emotions of the previous day, when she'd acted like a complete muttonhead from start to finish.

Underneath it all, her heart still bore lacerations from the pain Henry had inflicted. She knew she should forgive him, but instead, she was angry. Angry! What business did she have being angry? He'd hurt her deeply by running away after all the love she'd poured into his life, and even now was upstairs so he didn't have to be around her. But he was just a boy, and she didn't want the anger. She wanted to be a shining example of the lovingkindness God would have her reflect. The fact that she was angry at Henry made her angry at herself. And of course, she'd long been angry at Seamus and Cara.

I'm sorry for being angry, she told God as she valiantly wiped at her face with her apron. *I don't know how to stop. Jesus, how do You love so well all the people who hurt You?* How did He continue to love *her* so well, showing her compassion and gentleness when she was too often like Henry, running and hiding away instead of spending time with Him? She didn't know, but she couldn't summon love like that in her own strength. She could barely even string together coherent prayers anymore.

The afternoon faded away as she remained slumped and idle in her chair, too weary and heartsore to even think overly hard. She didn't feel like herself anymore.

After a while, she realized that Henry had never come back down and went upstairs to find him. He was on his bed asleep, his book open beside him on the bed. Without another thought, Betha collapsed into her own bed and soon joined him in oblivion.

"Ma?"

Betha blinked her eyes open to darkness in the windows. Daylight was gone, and Cara must be wondering why she hadn't been down to help with supper.

"Are you all right?" Henry asked, leaning over her with a candlestick in his hand.

"I was just really tired." Even now, she couldn't produce the energy to sit up yet. "The temperature must have dropped."

"I don't think so," Henry said slowly. "You might have a fever."

Did she? Now that he said so, she did feel more odd and achy than simply tired.

"Oh," Betha said in a small voice.

"Do you want me to get you anything?"

"A drink of water would be nice. Then you should probably see what you can do to help Cara set the table or get supper since I can't."

"I will. I'll be back." He didn't hurry to leave, and she wondered briefly if he was worried. Before she could form the question on her lips, she was asleep again.

Betha woke the next morning to the sounds of rain on the roof and Henry moving about the room. She tried to place the day—Saturday, to the best of her memory. He had a half day of school today.

"Good morning."

He was on the edge of his bed tying his shoes, but looked up at her voice. "Morning. How are you?"

Betha tried to think. She pushed herself up to sit, and her body responded. "I slept well. Still a little achy, but I think it's just a low fever."

A cup sat on the bedside table within easy reach, the tea that Seamus had brought up last night. He'd told Cara how to make it the way Betha usually did for fevers, but she hadn't felt like taking more than a few sips at the time. The good night's sleep must have helped, because she didn't feel as poorly now as she had then.

Henry looked relieved, and she felt it too. Fevers were risky. Most of the time they just ran their course, but they could be dangerous. Maybe she'd picked this one up being down at the water on Thursday night.

"It's Saturday, right?"

"Yes, ma'am."

"I hope you have a good day at school. Can you bring up a little breakfast for me before you go so Cara doesn't have to?"

"Sure."

Betha stayed upstairs all morning, dozing on and off. She felt lazy, but without the energy to work, it seemed best to stay out of Cara's way. At midday, she made her way to the kitchen to get a bowl of rice to eat and feed the chickens, but the effort wore her out, and she retreated back upstairs when she was done.

Hearing voices in the street, she looked out the window to see Colm sidestep puddles with Henry. Was he going to walk Henry home every day from now on? They said something to each other, and then Colm backed up in the street. He lifted his eyes to her window, blinking when he realized she was standing there. Recognition dawned, a smile appeared, and he waved. She waved back, unable to stop the small smile creeping over her own mouth. Then he was walking away down the street and she went back to bed.

It was midafternoon on Monday when Betha took a break from spinning to mix up the codfish pie. Laundry day was always exhausting for Cara, and more so as she neared her seventh month. Betha was only glad to be back to health and doing her part to assist again. Besides, Seamus had been threading the loom all morning, and her days of spinning in peaceful quiet were gone. Still, she was thankful no one else had gotten whatever her mild sickness had been.

She was pouring the codfish concoction into the pie pan when Henry walked in. "Ah, Henry!"

"Mr. Gallagher is sick."

"What?" Betha lowered the bowl to the table, the pie forgotten.

"They had one of the committee members substituting today, Mr. Gibson. I think he used to be a teacher, but he didn't do things the way Mr. Gallagher does."

Could Colm have gotten the same sickness she did from their time together? If so, perhaps he had a mild case too. Controlling a whole classroom with even the low fever she had would have been out of the question. Reaching for a clean cup, Betha poured Henry milk from the stone jar and handed it to him. "Do you know what Mr. Gallagher has?"

Henry swallowed, wiping his sleeve across his mouth. "No, but I think more people in his family are sick too."

If it was just a couple, the family could take care of them, but if the whole family was sick, they might need help. "Maybe I'll go see if they need anything. I'll let Cara know to keep an eye on this." She slid the pie into the hot oven, took off her apron, and hurried to find Cara.

34

Colm turned his head when the door opened, spilling light into the now-dim room. His shirt was half-unbuttoned and he didn't have even a sheet covering his trousers, but he was still blazing hot.

He'd awakened a few minutes ago and had been trying to doze back off ever since. Patrick was snoring, though, putting a significant dent in the likelihood of sleep coming easily again.

Seeing he was awake, Maisie came over to him, extending a cup. As she neared, he lifted his head as best he could to meet it. Despite the care she used, water still dribbled down his chin as he drank it in.

"Thank you," he whispered, falling back to the pillow and wiping his mouth.

Maisie soaked a rag and used it to brush the hair off his sweaty forehead. "Betha came to see you."

Did she?

"She wanted to know how many were sick and if we needed anything."

"How . . . how many *are* sick?"

"Hanna started on Saturday night, like you and Patrick. Mor started feeling poorly this morning. We put Hanna in the downstairs room with her so we can keep an eye on them together." Maisie wet the rag again, folded it, and left it on Colm's forehead.

"Just fever?"

"They feel achy and don't have appetites. It usually goes together."

Colm nodded, letting his heavy eyes fall closed.

"I told Betha we didn't need anything since there's still several of us up and about. She was worried about you," Maisie added in a singsong voice.

Colm's lips tipped up. It probably wasn't true, but it was funny to hear Maisie say it.

"I suppose I'll let Patrick be, since if he's sleeping, his body is healing, as Bridget always says. Do you think you could eat anything?"

Colm considered. "Something cold and light."

"I'll see what we can come up with. Betha said she had a fever the other day, but it just lasted one day."

It had already been two full days for him and Patrick. Thank God Betha was as strong as a horse and beat it off so quickly.

"I'll leave this here in case he wakes up," Maisie said, and Colm opened one eye to see her fill Patrick's empty cup and thunk the pitcher down beside it. "Keep drinking as much as you can."

Colm obediently lifted himself and took another sip.

Maisie moved toward the door. "If Betha could recover from this in a day, I think you and Patrick could do better at it yourselves." Her laugh trailed after her down the hall.

It wasn't until the fourth day that Colm's fever broke. Now that he felt well enough to sit up and read, he availed himself of the opportunity to review his Sunday school materials and study his new dictionary. Across the room, Patrick had newspapers open, catching the crumbs from the cookies he'd ordered from Lyla. The paper crackled, and Colm looked over to see him swipe the crumbs from his newspaper to the floor, still chewing with his mouth open.

"Seriously? I don't want mice in here, you pig."

Patrick only laughed and turned his page.

Yellow fever, the physician had said. It wasn't until several days into the sickness that the telltale yellow skin had appeared. Colm couldn't be gladder to be over the worst of it and on the mend.

The sounds of footsteps and the squeaky floorboard in the hall announced Maisie's approach. Her tread stopped outside their door, and after a pause, she knocked.

"Come in." Colm pushed himself higher on his pillows.

The door opened, and Maisie bent down for the cup she'd placed on the floor before coming in. She balanced steaming tea in each hand as she came towards him.

"How are you feeling?"

He reached out and took the cup from her. "Lethargic but lucid."

She crossed the floor, handing Patrick the other one. "And you?"

"I was wondering about some pudding," Patrick said. "I think it would be just the thing. Could you make us some? The kind with raisins?"

Maisie laughed and swatted at him. "Lyla's spent the last day in the kitchen making everything you've demanded. I think she's earned a rest."

"How are the girls?" Colm asked.

Maisie leaned against the doorjamb and let out a sigh, her face sobering. "Not well. Their cases have become acute."

"Oh no." Colm exchanged furrowed brows with Patrick. "Has the doctor seen them?"

"He was here again this morning. Most of the time, yellow fever runs about five days. He said it looked like you and Patrick had classic cases. But sometimes it develops into the more dangerous version that Mor and Hanna have now."

"Everyone else is well?"

"Yes."

"Let us know if anything changes," Colm said, his calm voice not giving away the worry that had taken up residence inside. "We'll pray for them."

"We can pray now." Patrick sipped his tea gingerly and settled it on his leg, balancing it with both hands. While Maisie and Colm listened, he led them in a prayer for their sisters.

When he said "Amen," Maisie headed back downstairs, but Colm remained in bed, prayers combating with the fear in his heart.

The following evening, Colm was sitting in one of the comfortable chairs in the front parlor when Bridget showed Betha in.

"Hello," he said in surprise. It was a late hour for her to be out calling, and no one had told him to expect her.

"Good evenin'." She removed her hat and handed it to Bridget before offering Colm a shy smile. "I came to sit up with Mor and Hanna."

Friends and neighbors often helped each other by sitting up with sick ones overnight, and it was just like Betha to give up her Friday night for them. "That's kind of you, thank you."

"I'm glad to see you up. The fever had you down for a while."

"I'm tired now, but I was much stronger today. I'm planning to be back at school on Monday."

"Henry will be glad to hear it. I—" She glanced around, seeing that the others in the room were minding their own quiet conversations. The family had been hushed all day, the pallor of sickness invading every corner of the house. Taking a step toward Colm, she opened her mouth to speak and then shook her head and quickly closed it. "I'm sorry to hear the girls haven't shown any improvement. I'd best go sit with them."

She made a hasty retreat, leaving Colm disappointed that she'd changed her mind about whatever she was going to say to him. He'd hoped for an explanation for her odd behavior at their last conversation or a report on how Henry had been doing in the days since he ran away.

He missed the Betha that clung to him the previous week like he was her lifeboat. He could do without this skittish version that decided talking to him was against her better judgment.

With a frustrated sigh, he braced his hands on the chair arms and pushed himself to his feet. For a minute, he stood in the hallway, picturing a long, quiet conversation with her while they kept Mor and Hanna's faces bathed in cool rags together. Then he drove the daydream away and dragged his feet up the stairs.

Colm woke up on Sunday morning to the news that Hanna's fever had broken the previous evening after he went to bed.

He leaned on the upstairs bannister, listening to Maisie and Lyla talk over each other in the telling. There was hope for Mor, although her condition hadn't changed yet. If Hanna was out of the woods, surely she would be soon as well. It was now the seventh day of her fever—far too long to be so sick.

Padding back into his room, Colm tied his cravat and grabbed his coat before going downstairs. Ava was in the foyer, preparing to leave after sitting up with Mor overnight. Colm wished her good day and went to see Mor and Hanna.

Bridget was in the sickroom, kneeling on the floor beside Hanna's trundle and listening to a story the girl was telling. She sat in the middle of her bed, surrounded by the disheveled covers, her hair in two frizzy braids. When she saw Colm, she lit up, breaking off her story, and extended her arms to him.

"Colm! I'm going to be well."

"So you are." He leaned down and gave her a hug. "I thank God to see it." After a glance at Mor lying still on the bed, he looked at Bridget. "How is Mor?"

"She's very sick." She didn't say more, but he could hear the deep concern in her voice and knew Mor was running out of time to turn a corner.

Straightening, he came around the bed to her side. Her skin was sunken and sallow, and he noticed with dread the dark blood stains on her nightgown sleeve and pillowcase.

"She's been vomiting?"

"For a couple days now."

"Oh, Mor," Colm whispered, reaching out to brush her shoulder. He should have been in to see her sooner.

Her eyes fluttered open at the sound of his voice, and she stared at him with bloodshot eyes.

"Should I give her a drink?" He looked around, finding the cup on the table.

"It's willow bark tea. She should drink as much of it as she can," Bridget said, leaning back on her heels.

Bracing an arm around her shoulders, Colm lifted her light form, feeling like he would break her. Her lips moved in response to the cup, but only a small amount of liquid passed through them. He lowered her back to the pillow and found a rag crumpled on the bed that he used to wipe the tea from her chin.

"I'm going to church with Father and the others," he told her, sweeping the hair behind her ear. "I'm praying for you, Mor. I love you."

She only looked at him, but when he squeezed her hand, she gave the slightest squeeze back.

"Keep fighting." He gave one last pat of her hand. "I'm off to find some breakfast," he said, returning to Bridget and Hanna.

"Lyla made pancakes. Have a good morning at church."

Hanna reached a hand out. "Come see me when you get back, Colm."

Colm squeezed her hand with a smile and a promise.

35

Everything felt surreal as Colm fitted the key into the schoolroom door and turned it. He'd missed an entire week of school for the first time in his career. More than that, he was coming back a changed man. The Colm that had locked the door a week ago Saturday afternoon had been whole, back when time moved, the earth spun, and he had something in himself to offer his students.

Time was frozen now, and he was numb with shock and grief. He probably should have let the committee know to send Mr. Gibson to substitute again today, and he would have, had he not already missed an entire week. He needed to see the kids. Besides, he was utterly useless at the house. He knew this because Patrick hadn't gone into work today, and he was being utterly useless.

He stood with a hand braced on the desk as the students arrived, dully returning their enthusiastic greetings. He didn't know how bad the substitute had been, but the children had obviously missed him, which meant something.

When the sound of Miss O'Neill's bell upstairs rang over the classroom, all of his students were in their seats, watching him with expectant eyes. As the last echoes of the bell faded away, Colm cleared his throat.

"I'm glad to be back with you today. I hope you were good students while I was ill last week and gave the teacher your best, as you give me. Although I am thankful that God saw fit to bring me back to health, today is a difficult day for me." He licked his lips, working up the courage to say the words aloud. The students sat spellbound.

"My sister died yesterday."

He still wondered how it could be true. He still felt stunned, the way he and his brothers had all been when Bridget came into the front parlor in late afternoon and made the announcement. It couldn't be real. All he wanted was to go back in time and erase the answer to be something different.

He blinked, and none of the students moved. This was the point where he wanted to offer them something spiritual and lasting, and tell them about the hope he had in Christ. That Mor wasn't really dead forever but had simply moved to her eternal home ahead of them.

His brain failed him at forming thoughts into words. The students were waiting, and he couldn't get out the one thing he wanted them to know.

"I know death has touched all of our lives in one way or another. I will be sharing in the Sunday school about what death means and how we can have eternal life. I would love to see you all there."

That would give him six days to pull his thoughts together and have something cohesive to share.

"Will the monitors rise and retrieve their cards."

With a muted shuffle, the monitors quietly obeyed. The scene felt disembodied to him, like he was outside of himself, in a dream. Colm's eyes followed Henry passing his desk as something concrete to focus on. He hadn't been here for Henry or even praying for him over the past week like he wanted to be, and he wondered how the boy was faring. He ought to call on him, and he was desperate to see Betha. Not until he could think clearly, however.

Help me through this fog, Lord, so I can lead my class today.

The monitors returned to their seats, Colm took a deep breath, and class began, with or without him.

Colm put off calling on Betha as long as possible.

In reality, it was only two days, but he couldn't wait any longer. Waking or sleeping, his only thought was her, and he couldn't be right again until he'd seen her and said what he had to say. She would be getting the new Colm, the grief-stricken one who could no longer look at the world the way he used to.

It is what it is, he said to himself as he reached into his pocket. His fingers found the paper he'd stored there with his notes for in case the fog didn't lift and he forgot any part of what he wanted to say.

He'd been a very patient man, but patience wasn't the only virtue out there. There was a time to wait and a time to act, and he was done waiting.

He could only pray that Betha would come to agree.

Between picking green beans and churning butter all morning, it was after dinner when Betha finally sat down to her wheel. She still had cheese to make before week's end, which Cara had seemed genuinely interested in learning from her.

Cara came in to dust and sweep the front room, and she and Seamus kept up a lively conversation on all the news and gossip Seamus had brought back from McColgan's the night before. Betha worked steadily until Henry came home from school and Cara disappeared back into the kitchen.

After answering all her questions about school and how Mr. Gallagher was doing, she sent him to the kitchen for a roll with fresh butter. A minute later, he passed through again, taking it upstairs to study.

A couple hours had passed when movement caught Betha's eye out the window. She looked up to see a figure standing in the street, a man in a black top hat and a long black coat facing the house.

"Colm," she whispered, her wheel coming to a standstill. Her heart thundered in her tightening chest. How long had he been standing there?

Hurrying to the door, she opened it and stepped outside. He removed his hat when the door opened, and now she could clearly see the grief lines on his face. He took a deep inhale and let it out, as if seeing her brought him inexplicable relief, ending in a tremulous smile.

"I'm so sorry about Mor," Betha said, feeling like she might cry.

Colm nodded, looking like he might cry too. "I didn't really think she was going to die. I talked to her that morning."

"I don't think we ever think someone that young is goin' to die."

"That's why I'm here." Colm took a step toward her, making some kind of plea with his eyes that she couldn't understand. "I needed to see you."

"I'm here," Betha said to reassure him, because he looked afraid that she might run away. She would be here as long as he needed her to be.

"It could have been me. That's what I keep thinking. I had it too. I don't know why hers worsened but I recovered. But now she isn't coming back."

Betha had nothing intelligent to respond with. She didn't want to think about how close the world had come to losing Colm Gallagher.

"That morning when I saw her, I told her I loved her. I didn't know it would be the last time I'd ever speak to her." Colm's eyes glistened with unshed tears, breaking her heart. "All I can think about is how short and uncertain life is. And how I've never told you that I love you."

Betha started at the unexpected turn of conversation. The sight of him squinting in an effort to keep his composure nearly did her in.

"I love you, Betha. I want to marry you. I know you've had reasons why you were unwilling to consider marrying me, but would you reconsider? We could buy a house nearby. Henry will still be with me at school for most of the day, and you can still spend time with him throughout the week. We could take him to church with us every Sunday. Will you think about it?"

She wanted to tell him she would, but she was crying, wiping at her face with her fingers. He was right. Life was too short to not make sure loved ones knew how much they were loved. Could he be right about Henry as well? She had been there for him every day, and yet he'd still grown distant and even run away. Her plan hadn't worked; maybe it was time for a new one.

He moved toward her, wrapping his strong hands around her shoulders. Betha would have leaned into him, but they were on the front step of the house, in full view of the whole street. "I love you too," she sniffled right before the door widened behind her.

"You're welcome to come in, Colm, and offer for her in the parlor, properly."

Colm dropped his hands as Betha turned around. "I wanted a chance to talk to her privately first," he told Seamus.

"I wouldn't call the street private myself." Seamus stepped aside, and Betha walked past him into the house with Colm behind her. They followed Seamus into the empty parlor, and he closed the kitchen door.

"If you want to discuss her dowry, she hasn't one," Seamus said, stopping in the middle of the room.

"I don't," Colm returned. "I can provide for her. I just want Betha."

Betha's heart tugged her in two different directions. Could she truly be free to accept Colm, trusting God that she would still have a relationship with Henry from a couple blocks away? What would he say when he heard? But Seamus couldn't spare her from the weaving business. Her heart plummeted with the realization that he could never keep afloat without her spinning for him.

"I'm needed here, to spin." She looked at Colm in despair.

Seamus gave her a strange look. "I'm not holding you down, Betha. I'd have one less mouth to feed and would pay for anything you spun for me in Colm's house. What Colm said outside is true too—you'd still see Henry."

Betha felt like both crying and laughing. How had she always viewed herself as so indispensable to Seamus only to discover she was completely dispensable to him? She wasn't sure whether he was being thoughtless or magnanimous and if she should be offended or overjoyed.

"Do you want him?" Seamus asked uncertainly, indicating Colm with a tilt of his head.

"Oh, I do, very much!" Betha exclaimed, wiping her face with the apron corner she'd been twisting in her fingers. Colm beamed at her, and she thought her heart would gallop away.

"I'm just surprised and confused . . . Mor just died, and seeing you for the first time after that . . . and I'm so sad and trying to think about Henry and what he needs, and I wasn't at all thinking about marriage until two minutes ago. I do *want* to marry you, Colm, I only need time to get my thoughts straight about whether it's really the best thing for everyone."

"I know; it's why I only came to ask you if you'd reconsider. We can talk about it."

"Can we talk now?" She looked at Seamus, wondering if he needed to be shown the door himself or if he'd take the hint.

He took the hint. "I'll be at the loom," he said, stumping toward the front room and shutting the door behind himself.

36

Nerves assaulted Betha the moment she was left alone with Colm. Was this really happening? Was she allowed to finally feel everything she'd wanted to feel and denied over the last year? The sheer strength of her feelings scared her, and she feared what Colm would think of her if she let them all out. But then, he'd seen her fall apart at the docks and yet was still here.

He crossed to where she stood, taking her shaking hands in his in an instant. "Betha," he murmured, then chuckled and shook his head. She couldn't breathe. "Oh, Betha. I fell in love with you the first day you stepped inside Oliver. You intrigued me from the very beginning. I only grew to love you more in every conversation we had after that."

He slid his arms around her, as if realizing what she needed, and this time, she sagged against him. The Lord only knew how happy she would be if she never had to leave the safety of Colm's arms again.

"Do you really think Henry will be fine if I leave? He's had so much change lately, and he struggles yet."

Colm rubbed a calming hand up and down her back. "You could ask him. He's had several months to adjust to his father's marriage now. Seamus might be ready to have his household to himself."

"Without me in the way, you mean."

"He knows you aren't in the way. I think it's been good that you've been here, but that doesn't mean there might not also be good if you left. It could be the same for Henry. He relies so much on you. Maybe he and Cara will be able to grow a relationship if they're forced to. Maybe he'll learn to lean on God in new ways. You wouldn't be abandoning him or leaving altogether."

"Would you want me to still spin for Seamus?"

"You're welcome to do so, but my salary will support us. We would have him weave what you spin for our household anyway."

It all sounded too good to be true. *Is this real? Is there any reason I should turn him down? Is it really this easy, Lord?* It wasn't actually easy; it had taken all the events of the past months to bring both her and Colm to this moment.

"I love you," Betha murmured. "I'm a wee bit awestruck. I didn't know I *could* love you, and now that I am allowed to, I think I could burst from it all."

"Losing Mor woke me up and made me realize I didn't want to wait forever. Besides, perhaps I could make an even bigger difference for Henry if I married you."

Betha had never even thought of the situation in those terms before. Why had she thought that she alone could be a help to Henry? Recent events had revealed how wrong she had been about that.

She'd been comfortable snuggled against Colm's chest, but now she shifted, tilting her face up. The look in his eyes turned her insides molten.

"Betha Gallagher," he whispered. "I would be the happiest man alive if I had you for my little Irish wife."

Hearing her name paired with his produced goosebumps on her arms. "When, exactly?"

"As soon as I can buy a house."

"What if I knew of one in the neighborhood that was for sale?"

"Then in a couple of weeks."

Betha thought of her chickens and the garden, and all the pickled vegetables in stoneware jars in the cellar, and the huge barrel of lye soap, and the fresh crock of butter and the cheese she was still needing to make, and how in a couple of weeks, she would have to start all over again making all those things for her own house. The thought of it all being for Colm pumped joy through her whole self.

"If you still want to marry me after kissing me, then you can have me. In a couple of weeks."

Betha had never seen Colm move so fast. His hands went from her back to the sides of her face in an instant, burrowing his long fingers into the hair behind her ears. Betha's heart tripped. And then he lowered his dimples toward her, meeting her lips with his. He kissed her, and it was the most right thing Betha had ever felt. God had picked this man for her, and the time was right to accept the gift.

At first, she had her hands wrapped tightly around his middle. Then she moved them around his neck, clasping them together and pulling him closer. If she was afraid of him pulling away too soon, she needn't have worried. Colm drank her in like a man who'd been waiting a full year to do so and didn't move an inch until she'd been good and truly kissed.

"I think," he said, planting a kiss on her jaw, "that I"—he moved his lips up, closer to her ear—"would still like to have you." He kissed the tender spot under her ear.

"Are you sure?"

"I'm sure," he murmured. "I think I shall never move from here."

"You can't buy the house from there," she reminded him.

"Do you mean the house where we shall live together for always?"

"Yes."

Colm's face appeared before her again. "Then I shouldn't waste any time." He picked up her braid, held the end of it up to his nose, and took a deep inhale. "You'll have to tell me where it is so I can go buy it."

"And I need to go talk to Henry."

"Don't forget that you already accepted, no matter what he says."

"I agree with you, Colm. I think our marriage can benefit him too."

He kissed her again, then stopped with a hand against her cheek and studied her. "Mor ought to see this, what she brought about. It isn't fair."

"'Tisn't," Betha agreed. "I can't believe she's—"

A knock on the door interrupted her, and Cara called from the kitchen. "Are you done?"

Betha separated from Colm in an instant, smoothing a hand over her hair. "Yes."

The door opened, and Cara came in with a tablecloth in hand. Colm removed his hat from the table, and Betha hurried over to help her spread it out. "Am I to congratulate you?"

"Yes," Betha said, eyeing Cara's middle. She wouldn't be here to help with the baby. She could come over, of course, but she was abandoning Cara to all the household responsibilities right before her confinement.

"Congratulations," Cara said, grinning. "It took you both a long enough time to decide to get together."

Betha stared at her, speechless, hoping she wouldn't remember the comment about graduating from the school of *The Virginia Housewife* in time to make a joke about it in front of Colm.

"Thank you. I should go find Henry."

Colm allowed himself to be escorted to the door. "Can I come back and get you tomorrow evening so we can tell my family together?" he whispered. Betha nodded, once again saddened at the thought that Mor would not be there to share in their joy.

As she watched his jovial form walk away down the street, she still wondered if she could be dreaming. Ava had passed up the opportunity to be courted by Colm or his brother because she wanted a love like the fairytales, and in doing so, she had opened the door for Betha to find it.

Henry stopped by Colm's desk the next morning on the way to his seat. "Congratulations, Mr. Gallagher," he said just above a whisper.

Colm had been watching for him, anxious to know how he had taken the news. Now the grin on Henry's face answered all his questions, easing his worry away. He'd already come into school feeling a hundred pounds lighter this morning, and now his heart positively soared.

"Thank you." He reached out and twitched the front of Henry's cap affectionately.

"I nearly knocked Ma over with a hug last night when she told me. I had *hoped* you liked her. It made me really happy to hear you asked her."

"And here I was afraid that you would be angry at me for stealing her from you," Colm said, twisting his lips.

"Oh, I am! Dreadfully!" Henry gave a light laugh and tripped away to his seat, leaving Colm shaking his head after him.

Ava and her mother were at Colm's house getting supper set out for the family and everyone else there when Colm left to retrieve Betha. Since Mor's death four days ago, the house had seen a steady stream of guests, and church friends supplied meals to feed an army. As few Gallaghers had appetites, most of it was used to keep the company fed.

Reverend Breckinridge had come calling the night before, giving Colm the perfect opportunity to have a quiet conversation with him out on the front step before he left. If everything else went according to plan, he would marry Colm and Betha at Second Presbyterian two weeks from Saturday.

Once Colm had Betha tucked into his side, assuring him that she hadn't changed her mind, they took a detour past the house for sale.

"I'll go ask the bank about it tomorrow," he said, shading the sides of his face to peer in a window. It was bigger than he'd expected for the neighborhood—it wasn't even a row house—but maybe that meant they could stay in it longer. Betha's eyes widened into the size of teacups at the sight of the cultivated garden, which included berry vines and rose bushes. Then she saw the chicken coop and gasped in delight, and Colm knew it didn't matter what the inside of the house looked like; he would be buying it either way.

This time when she clutched his arm for their walk to his house, everything felt different. Rather than wishful dreaming and hopeful uncertainty, he had love declared and accepted. It changed everything. Betha had worn a brave face as long as he'd known her, but this was the first time he'd seen her well and truly happy. He would have wondered how it was possible that she could get all that merely from being with him, except he felt the same way—stupidly happy.

Supper had just been called and everyone was moving to their seats in the kitchen when he arrived. Besides the cooks, the only other outsider present was Ezra—if he was even considered an outsider anymore. He'd spent nearly the whole week glued to Maisie's side, looking miserable while Maisie periodically burst into tears. No one was taking Mor's death easily, but Maisie was taking it worst of all.

Colm and Betha left their wraps in the hall, and he grabbed her hand again before making their entrance into the kitchen.

"Betha!" Lyla saw her first, and Ezra paused with Maisie's chair half out when Maisie turned around at the exclamation.

Quickly, before he lost control of the situation, Colm called out, "We're to be married!"

He watched in satisfaction as bedlam broke out and he and Betha were assaulted with hugs and congratulations. Betha seemed to have an abundance of happy tears, because they made another appearance when Maisie and Ava locked her in on either side.

Colm had to endure being pounded on the back from all his brothers before Bridget shooed them away for her own moment with him. She framed his face with her two hands on his cheeks, smiling proudly at him before wrapping him in a motherly hug. Throughout the event, he couldn't do anything to stop the grin that had overtaken his whole face. Betha laughed every time her eyes met his. Yes—utterly, stupidly happy.

37

In the front parlor after supper, Colm took the opportunity to raise the topic of the coming Sunday's lesson while his core assistants were all together.

"I'd like to speak to all the children together this once," he told Ezra while Betha and Maisie listened in. "I told my pupils that I will be teaching about death and eternal life this Sunday. I'm taking the opportunity to share about the gospel and the hope I have in Jesus in a way that they can understand."

Ezra nodded. "Do you want to do it in the sanctuary?"

"It depends on how many children come. The classrooms have us closer together, and I might be able to hold their attention better with the more intimate atmosphere."

"Have you worked out what you're goin' to say?" Betha asked.

"I should have you look over my notes. I started writing things down, but I need to spend more time on it. I got distracted." He grinned at her. Patrick came in, and not finding an empty seat, leaned up against the wall by the window.

"I think you're the person to do it," Betha said. "Sometimes I struggle to find the right way to explain truth on their level, but you always seem to have the ability to help them understand."

"Well, I appreciate prayer about it, and we can do some of that together now. But Reverend Breckinridge said he thinks teaching is my spiritual gift, and I think he might be right."

"I would say it is." Patrick crossed his arms over his chest. "That's why I don't think Oliver is the right place for you."

"What are you talking about?" Colm scowled at him, instantly defensive.

"The Lancaster method. You're more manager than teacher at Oliver. I think that's why the Sunday school is going so well for you; you've hit on what it is you're meant to do. Teach."

"I think it's a good job for me and has taught me a lot, even if it's not perfectly ideal," Colm protested.

"Maybe so." Patrick shrugged. "But this?" He gestured toward Colm. "This changes your whole countenance."

A good deal had changed Colm's countenance that week, but he didn't say so. Even if Patrick wasn't wrong about the Lancaster method, Colm was the right person for the job. He had rapport with his students, which made a huge difference when he invited them to the Sunday school.

"The Lancaster method was the first thing that we ever talked about together and then the first thing we argued about," Betha said with a laugh.

"It's true." Colm rubbed his hands together. "Let's take some time to pray about my lesson on Sunday. It's the most important topic I'll ever speak on, and I want to be sure the Holy Spirit is leading it."

The wages of sin is death, but the gift of God is eternal life through Jesus Christ our Lord.

Colm centered his lesson on Sunday around Romans 6:23, since it gave him a clear outline for what he wanted to cover: that death is deserved but not final, and because of God's gift through the death of his sinless Son, Colm had hope for eternal life, for his sister and for himself. Afterward, a handful of students spoke to him and Betha about becoming followers of Jesus, and three made declarations of faith.

Colm was still filled with joy from the previous day as he stood in his classroom on Monday. It felt incongruous to not be allowed to read scripture to his students when he had yesterday and hearts were responding to it. He didn't think he was a Sunday-only Christian, but it felt like it today as he focused on sums and spelling words and spoke of the Lord not at all. What had always been normal before now felt laughable—that he could possibly watch students' lives be changed on Sundays and then on Mondays pretend that eternal matters didn't exist.

Patrick's words about Oliver not fitting Colm niggled in the back of his mind. He'd been happy with the way things were with his job for years. Why was it that all of a sudden, he now wondered if his days there were numbered? Where on earth would he go if he didn't teach at Oliver? The summer working in Stewart Brown's shipping office had been a nice change from the farm, but he had no intention of going into shipping year-round.

I'm making a difference here, he reminded himself as he locked the school while Henry waited. *Everyone always said so.* Colm walked him home, stopping in to see Betha only briefly before going to make a deposit on the new house at the bank.

The following Sunday, even more Sunday school children were at the service with their families. Second Presbyterian had been blossoming over the past several months, fruit from the men's prayer meetings. Reverend Breckinridge's singing schools were well attended, resulting in more cohesive worship in the services. The Sunday schools had recruited more teachers, and every week, students came and recited new memory verses.

Colm prepared to walk Betha home from Sunday school, happy to take the job from Ezra, who was driving Maisie and the dirty dishes home.

"I'm planning to go clean the new house tomorrow," Betha told him as she gathered up her books.

"I've been trying to collect furniture, but aside from buying a whole set brand new, it takes time. You'll have to get me a list of what we absolutely need to have before moving in."

"Not very much, really. A table and chairs and a bed."

"I do have those." Colm held the door as she exited ahead of him onto the church's front step.

Heavy clouds raced by, looking ready to drop their loads at any moment. The wind picked up, and store shingles banged wildly on their hinges. Colm had an umbrella in hand, ready for the pending storm. It wasn't raining yet, though, and there was a chance they would be able to make it home before it started.

"Mr. Gallagher?"

Colm turned at the unexpected voice of Peter, one of the oldest students at Oliver. Instead of going home after class like Colm thought, he had been leaning against the railing as if waiting for them. Now he took off his hat and squeezed it with both hands.

"I thought everyone would be home by now before the storm. What is it?"

"Well, I was wanting to make sure you'd heard about Sam Wilson. I wasn't sure if anyone had told you."

"No, no one has told me anything. What happened?"

Sam still had his rebellious streak and occasionally caused trouble for Henry, his monitor, but as he aged, he had wisened up some.

"He drowned yesterday, sir. In the river."

Colm froze, grasping at his books to keep from dropping them. "Drowned?"

"Yes, sir. Him and his neighbor who doesn't go to Oliver. They were fooling around together and both fell in."

It wasn't possible. Colm had lost a handful of former students, but never a current one. His students were mere children, with their whole lives ahead of them.

"Colm?" Betha rubbed his arm, a concerned look on her face. He felt sick, suddenly cold and nauseous at the same time.

"He was at school Friday," he managed around his dry mouth. "It was a normal day. I had no idea."

"I thought you'd want to know before you showed up at school tomorrow," Peter explained.

"Yes, yes I did. Thank you. And they're both dead?"

"Yes, sir."

Colm nodded mechanically. "Thank you, Peter."

Even after Peter left, Colm didn't move. Betha sank onto the concrete wall beside him, but he was only vaguely aware of her presence.

"He didn't come to Sunday school." It was the only clear thought he had. He'd shared the gospel clearly, but only to his Sunday school students. Sam had never heard it. Sam had never heard Colm speak about the Lord once. All of Henry's accusations from a year ago replayed in his mind, mocking him. His faltering words to his class the day after Mor died mocked him. His entire gospel speech, given only to his Sunday school students, mocked him.

He'd had every reason and opportunity to make sure Sam knew about the Lord, and he hadn't taken them.

"You couldn't force your students to come to Sunday school, Colm. You invited them to come hear about eternal life, but you couldn't make them care or give them ears to hear. The Holy Spirit could have prompted Sam to come, if he had been interested in knowing."

But Sam was just a kid. If he didn't come from a family who believed, where else would he hear about God? It would be up to the believers in his life to tell him. And who else would he listen to but the schoolmaster who had already earned a place of respect? So yes, Colm should have told him. He should have told all of them.

Fat raindrops plopped on his shoulders and head. Without thinking, he opened the umbrella and held it over Betha's head. The movement reminded him that he had her to care for, and he was supposed to have gotten her home before the storm hit.

"I'm sorry." He pushed off the railing, realized his books were getting wet, and tucked himself under the umbrella beside Betha, who had stood as well.

"I'm sorry for your loss. I can tell it's hard for you." Holding her books didn't leave a free hand to hang onto his arm. It was up to Colm to match her pace and keep the umbrella over them both.

"Believe it or not, I've never lost a student before." The rain picked up in intensity, running in rivulets down the sides of the umbrella. "I could have read even a short passage that morning after Mor died. It was the perfect opportunity, but I chose to leave it until Sunday, when fewer than half of the children were there. I should have said *something.*"

The noise of the rain made further conversation difficult, and he was out of words anyway. Tomorrow, he'd stand in front of his class again, this time telling them of the death of a classmate their own age. He wouldn't waste the opportunity—any opportunity—to give them truth and hope again.

Betha arrived home from cleaning the new house Monday only moments before Henry rushed in from school. She hurried to peer out the window in time to see Colm wave at her and walk away. He didn't always stop in after dropping off Henry, but today she wished he would.

"Guess what happened in class today?" Henry shifted from one foot to the other, bursting with the news. "Mr. Gallagher read a scripture passage to us. John 14—about Jesus going to prepare a place for us."

"Indeed?" Betha left the window to wrap an arm around his shoulders. "What brought that about?" She already knew but was curious as to how Henry would answer.

"Because one of the boys from Oliver died last week—Sam Wilson. He was in my group."

"You were his monitor?" Colm hadn't mentioned that the other day.

Henry nodded. "He used to give me all kinds of trouble. He told me last year he didn't believe in God, so he didn't really care about that kind of thing. I'm awfully sorry he died, though."

"So Mr. Gallagher read the Bible in class?" Betha prompted.

"Right after he told us the news. He said some things were too important to keep for Sundays."

"What did you think about that?"

"I think he's right." Henry beamed at her. "I'm glad he did it. It made me wish Sam was there to hear it."

"It's hard to imagine one of your classmates dying so suddenly." Betha squeezed his arm, thinking of how close she'd gotten to losing Henry to a departing ship and all its related dangers.

"Everyone was pretty serious today, and no one ran around or played very loudly during recess. Mr. Gallagher was quiet too." Henry pushed out of her hold and looked her over. "I think he cares a lot about us, Ma. He has a big heart."

"I think he does." Big enough that he would risk his job to tell his students about the things that really mattered in life.

Betha had accepted his reasons for not reading the Bible in class and respected him for the thoughtful consideration he gave the idea. If Colm changed his mind now, it was because he'd reanalyzed the situation and made a deliberate decision. Betha knew one thing for certain—it was not an impulsive or emotion-driven move. He had much to lose, and so did she. The thought of what could come of it was too fear inducing to consider, and as she often reminded Henry, it would do no good to borrow trouble from the future. All she could do now was trust him and applaud him for following his conscience despite the risks.

Henry left for the kitchen in search of something to drink, and Betha settled into her spinning chair. Cleaning had done her in, but at least the new house was ready now for Colm to start setting up furniture. As tempting as it was to turn all her attention to her soon-to-be new life, she knew she ought to give Seamus everything she had while still living with him. The wheel whirred to life, joining the thumping of the loom.

What had once seemed so permanent now shifted under her feet—everything from the basics of working alongside the loom to changes in Henry, Seamus, Colm, even herself. She was jumping out into the unknown, of her own choice this time. Betha's sure fingers deftly pulled and twisted the flax, familiar movements she was expert in. Too often she relied on her own capable hands, she knew. Did she have trust enough that God would carry her through the coming days, or was she counting on her own self to catch her if she fell?

Betha took a steadying breath, praying for the confidence to know that she was following where God led. He would not bring her or her loved ones to a new place only to abandon them there.

38

October 1828

"You might as well stay for supper after we finish moving things," Betha told Colm.

The wedding was tomorrow, and he had come thinking he would just pick up her trunk and wheel and go. Instead, they stood in the parlor together while Cara kept bringing them wedding gifts from the cellar and kitchen.

She plopped another stone jar on the table. "You'll take a few of the chickens, won't you? Then you can have a head start on your flock ahead of next spring."

"I would love to take some if you think Seamus won't mind. I'll have to clean out the chicken coop at the new house before I do."

"I'll take care of Seamus," Cara said confidently.

"This is far more generous than I expected," Betha admitted, gesturing to the crocks and packages on the table.

Cara crossed her arms over her chest and shrugged without meeting Betha's eyes. "Seems your family ought to give you a wedding gift, and this is what we have."

Colm stepped forward, breaking the awkward silence that followed. "Thank you, Cara. I can start carrying these out." He picked up a heavy jar and turned to the door as Seamus appeared in it.

At the sight of him, Betha lifted her hand, remembering something she'd wanted to discuss. "Seamus, Colm has to take his dinner with him to school every day anyway, so I can always pack something for Henry to eat with him."

She still felt a little guilty for taking some of Seamus's income away, knowing how tight things were, and feared him making up the deficit by putting Henry into the workforce. Cara was not reliable enough to trust that Henry would have dinner every day if Betha left it up to her. If she simply fed Henry herself, she wouldn't have to worry on either front.

Seamus thanked her, even though probably neither thought had crossed his mind. Picking up a wheel of cheese and a jar of ale, he followed Colm out to the waiting carriage.

"Does your new house have a stove?" Cara asked.

"No." Betha laughed wryly. "I think we'll get one eventually, but I told Colm I could wait for him to save up for it."

His father had asked him what he wanted for a wedding gift. He'd almost said the stove, but Betha talked him into asking for the feather mattress instead, since that was a gift Colm could use too. She wouldn't mention it in front of Cara, though, who obviously felt embarrassed that the Young family wasn't providing a more extravagant wedding gift. Besides, Cara had already taken it upon herself to share far more than was necessary with Betha about the marriage bed, and Betha had no intention of going anywhere near the topic with her again. She had never been remotely interested in what her brother did behind his bed curtains, and she could never unknow it now.

Grabbing an armful of packages up, she hurried after Seamus, anxious to escape the thoughts heating her face. Colm was holding the carriage door, speaking to her brother as he deposited his packages on the floor inside. Betha arrived in time to hear the second part of it.

"His brother, Stewart, is a good friend, and I worked for him last summer. I know it's not what you have been hoping for, but I think it would provide financial security and I highly respect the family."

"The bank?" she asked when Seamus didn't reply. He backed up from the carriage, his face serious if not also flinty, like someone who had received bad news.

Colm took the packages from her. "I think Alexander Brown would hire Seamus if I recommended him. He needs diligent, trustworthy workers, and that describes Seamus exactly." He set the things inside and shut the door, returning to Seamus. "I understand if it's not something you want to do. I considered it myself, but sometimes the money just isn't worth it. I thought you might want to think about it, though."

It was kind of Colm to even think of him and offer the information, but one look at Seamus told her the idea of it was physically painful. Betha couldn't imagine him working in some back room at a bank either.

Seamus strode ahead of them toward the house. "Let me help you get the trunk out next."

Betha shrugged at Colm. He offered his hand to her and she took it. "I didn't expect anything else from him," he said, ending the conversation.

Betha woke on her wedding day in a contemplative mood. Lying in bed, she prayed before rousing herself to her last morning of chores in Seamus's house.

Having confidence and anticipation in her marriage to Colm hadn't negated altogether the concerns that plagued her, mostly on Henry's behalf. She wanted to entrust him to the Lord and relinquish control of the outcomes, but she was finding it needed to be done repeatedly. Once had turned out to not be enough.

She prayed for Henry, Seamus, Cara, Colm, herself, and her marriage before pushing up to a seated position. Henry was awake, staring at the ceiling, but looked over when she moved.

"Good morning," she said, finding a smile for him. "I'll miss you tomorrow morning."

Hopefully, he would enjoy having his own room. He wasn't a young tyke needing comfort in the night anymore, and it was time he did things on his own. Learned to depend on God on his own.

"I'll miss you too," he said without returning her smile.

"Do you think you'll be fine? I'll be nearby when you need me."

It took replaying Colm's assurances that the marriage could be good for Henry for Betha's mind to ease back from panic and find calm. Henry needed Colm in his life. This wasn't just about the rapture coursing through her own veins; Colm's permanence in her life would be good for all of them.

"I'll get used to it," Henry said to reassure her.

All the important life lessons Betha had worked for years to instill in him flashed through her mind. What last words should she leave with him? She hugged herself with a shake of her head. It wasn't her last chance to tell him anything. She wasn't walking away from him, really.

Still, she couldn't help herself. "The Lord is always with you, my boy, and He loves you far more than I ever could. Let Him become your closest friend and you'll do well, deep down where it matters."

"I'll remember that."

Betha swung her legs over the side of the bed and stood to gather her clothes, but Henry surprised her by crossing the floor and wrapping her in a hug.

"I'm happy for you, Ma. I love you."

"I love you, too, Henry." He would never know how much, maybe until he was a parent. But that was as it should be.

The activities of the morning were normal ones, but everything felt different. Everything Betha did was for the last time and reminded her of how glorious the following day would be when everything she did would be for the first time. The same actions, perhaps, but in a different place and with an altogether different feeling. All the thoughts filling her mind kept her quieter than normal and feeding a constant stream of prayers heavenward.

As on Cara's wedding day, Betha was leaving Seamus's house sparkling clean today. Her own laundered sheets were hanging on the line outside and the last few fall beans were picked when she took off her apron and went upstairs to dress for her wedding. Once she had her hair pinned the normal way she liked, she folded her apron, mirror, and hairbrush in on the top of her satchel and carried it downstairs.

Cara took one look at her, shook her head so the curls bounced against her temples, and patted the chair in front of her. "Let me fix your hair for today. I'll make you look ravishing."

"I'm pretty sure Colm already thinks she is," Seamus remarked from the mirror where he was tying his cravat.

Betha obeyed and sat, a mixture of curiosity of what she would look like with a more modish hairstyle and nervous about what Cara would do to her. "Henry, if you're goin' to change, you should do it now."

He left while Cara placed her curling tongs in the fireplace and set to work unpinning Betha's hair. Nearly an hour later, after copious amounts of pomade and an impressive show of patience from Cara, Betha's hair looked like something straight from a fashion plate. A design of little braids with ribbon threaded through was piled on the back of her head, with a cluster of tight curls framing her face on either side. Betha stared at the mirror, still undecided if she liked it or not. Her neck ached now, but hopefully Colm would appreciate having the fashionable woman he deserved at his wedding. How Cara had managed to stand there and work for so long while so hugely expectant, Betha didn't know.

"Thank you for doing this." Betha handed the mirror back to her and stood, smoothing out the skirts of her pearl-gray lawn dress. Somehow the new hairstyle had changed her mood from thoughtful to festive. She was getting married today, and best of all, it was to her favorite person in the world.

"Mr. Gallagher is here," Henry called from the front room. How did Colm know the perfect time to arrive? Betha had assumed they needed to start walking to the church to make it in time, but a glance out the window confirmed that Colm had brought his father's carriage.

Cara and Seamus bustled around the parlor, pulling themselves together as Betha sidled up to Henry. "Do you want to start calling him Uncle Colm?"

"Yes," Henry said quickly. "Should I still call him Mr. Gallagher at school?"

"You could ask him. Do you want to start calling me Aunt Betha?"

"No." Henry furrowed his brow at her. "Should I?"

"You can call me Ma if you want to. I don't mind, but I didn't know if it was odd for you to call us Uncle Colm and Ma."

"You're still my ma, aren't you?"

Betha laughed. "Of course. Sometimes people make different choices when they're eleven than they made when they were five, and with names changing today anyway, I thought you should know that you have the choice."

She opened the door at the sound of Colm's tread on the stairs. The sight of him in his nice suit, long frock coat, top hat, and the adoring look in his eyes took her breath away. His cravat might be new; she didn't remember seeing it before.

"You look beautiful." He reached for her, and Betha let him take her hand. "Did Cara do your hair? It's very nice."

"Yes." The previous laugh still lingered on her face. "I'm afraid this is probably the last time you'll ever see it like this."

"That's fine too. I like the way you fix it. It makes me wish we had a portraitist here to capture you like this though. I'd hang it over the mantle. A big lifesize one."

"If you were ever that wealthy, Colm Gallagher, I still wouldn't want to look at an imitation of myself all day."

Seamus and Cara came through the parlor door, pulling their coats on. Colm leaned in to Betha's ear to say in a low voice, "It's a good thing I'm taking the real one home with me today then."

Betha ignored him now that the rest of her family was standing nearby. "Isn't your family coming?"

"They're already at the church. I dropped them off before I came for you." His eyes still danced, and she hoped no one else noticed.

"I didn't know you were coming for us. Thank you."

Handing him her satchel, she walked beside him into the gorgeous fall day with Henry, Seamus, and Cara following behind. The sun shone, glinting off the vibrantly colored trees, a chilly breeze fluttering their laden branches and sending leaves diving for the earth. With one last prayer in her heart that she would be a good wife for this very good man, Betha settled into her seat, ready for the carriage to take her to church.

Bridget served the wedding dinner for both families at the Gallagher home after the church ceremony. Colm ate with one arm permanently fixed to the back of Betha's chair, which put him in the perfect position to drop every thought that crossed his mind into her ear without anyone else hearing.

Betha savored each bite of the wedding cake, wondering just how long he'd waited to have someone who would simply sit and listen to all he had to say. Each time he bent toward her, it sent a tingle down her spine, cementing in her mind how glad she was that he'd picked her for this role.

"Do you want dancing?" he asked at one juncture, running the back of his finger down her upper arm.

Betha tried to clear her mind enough to review the layout of the house. Where was there room? "I'm fine without it. I will if you'd like though."

"Not really. It would just prolong the celebration."

Incredulous, Betha turned to see if he was joking. Who wouldn't want to prolong a celebration?

The heated look he was giving her chased the shock away. He was very serious.

"We wouldn't want that, would we?" Betha murmured. "Perhaps we'd best tell them I'm tired and need to get home."

"I can't wait for you to see the house."

She hadn't been in it since cleaning it. What was there to see other than the table, chairs, and bed he'd promised? Now curiosity had her looking for a way to make a demure escape.

Seamus saved them by announcing his family's pending departure. After the ceremony, Seamus had rented a buggy to transport his family to the Gallaghers'. All it took was a question from Colm now, and Seamus offered to take him and Betha on their way home, making their exit timely and free from dramatics.

Once Seamus had brought them to the doorstep, he drove away, leaving Colm fishing the key from his pocket. Betha held the lantern aloft as he fitted the key into the lock. Her heart beat fast in anticipation of the new life she would embark on the moment she stepped through the door. Inside the chilly foyer, the lantern exposed the dark wood wainscotting and shapes in shadowy corners of the adjacent rooms.

"Wait right here." Colm bent and kissed her cheek before slipping into the parlor to her right. A moment later, light shone from candles on the mantle and a round table against the opposing wall. He moved to the dining room beyond, the kitchen next to it in the back left of the house, then to the gentlemen's parlor directly to the left of the foyer, lighting candles and lanterns as he went.

"There we are," he announced, returning to Betha. He took off his hat and coat and placed them over hooks by the door, so Betha followed suit with hers.

Colm intertwined their fingers and smiled at her. "Welcome home, Mrs. Gallagher. Shall we?"

"Please!"

He started the tour in the parlor, following the same path he'd taken lighting the house. Betha stepped inside the papered room, turning in a slow circle to take in everything. Her spinning wheel was there in a corner beside the window overlooking the street. Under the window was an upholstered backless window seat big enough for two.

"That's so pretty. Where did you get it?"

"A couple of these items were handed down from the Browns, who were replacing some of their pieces. I thought you'd like that one. I'll light a fire once we settle in. I'm sorry it's a little cold still."

Betha inhaled, noticing for the first time the rich floral scent. She turned further to see the dahlias, phlox, roses, and chrysanthemums in a jar on the round table. "Flowers? You are a romantic."

"Maisie." Colm squeezed her fingers. "She helped with those. The curtains are all the work of Bridget and Lyla."

There were flowers on the dining room table, too, and on the sideboard against the wall. Another bouquet sat on the kitchen table, and more on the desk in the gentlemen's parlor. In each new room, Betha was further surprised by the amount of furniture displayed. "I wasn't expecting more than the table, chairs, and bed," she said, laughing.

"I do regret not having the stove for you yet. The sideboard was a gift from my aunt and uncle, and the parlor table was from my other aunt, my father's oldest sister. She also gave us the mirror." He pointed into the parlor, where it hung on the wall over the table. "We ought to go around and meet them all this week."

"It's all so lovely, Colm. No wonder I've hardly seen you lately. I can wait for the stove. Please don't go into debt over it."

"I won't. Come sit." He steered her toward the window seat, returning to the fireplace to light it. A few minutes later, she was snuggled into Colm's side before a crackling fire, his Bible on his knee. She liked this married life already.

"I had my level six class copy out this chapter yesterday," Colm said, opening his Bible. "I thought it would be a good place to start."

Betha looked over to see the header for the book of Psalms. "So the Bible is good and truly a part of the Oliver curriculum now?"

"For as long as they'll let me. One or two students grumbled when I gave the assignment on Friday. I'm sure someone will tell me to stop soon, but I'll include it while I can."

"I'm proud of you. I know it's not a decision you made lightly."

Colm's lips tipped up slightly before he began to read. "Psalm 1." Betha leaned in, listening to his deep cadence bathe their new home with God's Word. "Blessed is the man that walketh not in the counsel of the ungodly, nor standeth in the way of sinners, Nor sitteth in the seat of the scornful. But his delight is in the law of the LORD; and in His law doth he meditate day and night. And he shall be like a tree planted by the rivers of water, That bringeth forth his fruit in his season."

His students were blessed to have a teacher who loved them enough to give them this—truths about the God who made and loved them and how to live upright lives before Him. Betha breathed a deep sigh of contentment. How blessed *she* was to have been given this life with such a man.

39

The first week after the wedding, Mr. Gibson taught at the school again so Colm and Betha would have time to travel around calling on all the relatives. They were done by Thursday and could have fit them all in by Wednesday, but it seemed simplest for the committee to give Colm the week. Friday and Saturday were spent visiting the Browns, Breckinridges, Nevinses, and Ava's family.

"I can hardly believe my good fortune," Betha told Colm midweek after they'd settled down at home for the night. "I have brothers, sisters, aunts, uncles, cousins . . . even parents and grandparents now. It seems too good to be true."

Henry had accompanied them to Glen Burnie to meet Colm's grandmother and another round of family. Sure, some of the new relatives were challenging to communicate with, trying Colm's patience, and some were less relaxed than others. One would expect such things in families, and for so long, all of Betha's family problems had been tied up in one person—Seamus. Having variety was nice.

"You have aunts, uncles, cousins, and grandparents though," Colm replied, tucking her into his side.

"Of course, but they're an ocean away, and I've never met them." They and their problems were completely foreign to her. Occasionally she and her grandmother wrote to each other, but the letters were more factual than bonding.

When they weren't fulfilling all the required honeymoon visits, Henry came by after school to help them prepare the garden for the winter, clean out the chicken coop, and move in three hens and a rooster from

Seamus's. It provided ample opportunity for him to complain about the substitute teacher and express his impatience for Colm's return to school.

Monday came soon enough, and Colm left after breakfast, toting dinners for both him and his new nephew. Betha stood on the doorstep and watched him walk away down the street. It had been a wonderful, happy week with him around and few responsibilities to separate them. But the laundry had piled up, the house needed cleaned, and the dinners hosted in their honor had ended. Seamus had always done the shopping for his household in the mornings, but Colm would have to do his in the afternoon. Betha closed the door and slipped into the kitchen to find the slate and pencil he had left her. Her list would be ready for him and hopefully the house would be shipshape by the time he returned home.

"Mr. Gallagher is back."

When he'd been sick almost a month ago, Colm had returned to a full class relieved to see him again. Not apprehensive whispers that the boys thought he couldn't hear. He contemplated the change from his place beside the desk as he greeted the students coming in. He found himself looking for Sam Wilson's face and felt a new grief that Sam wouldn't be coming back.

Henry came through the door, and Colm noticed his tight mouth and slumped shoulders immediately. He shuffled along in a line of boys, not lifting his head until he was almost to the desk. When his eyes met Colm's, he visibly brightened. Colm would have to ask him what was troubling him later.

"Good morning, *Mr. Gallagher*."

The memory of being called Uncle Colm for the first time over the past week brought a grin to Colm's face. "Good morning, Mr. Young."

Miss O'Neill's bell rang as the last students were finding their seats, and Colm opened his Bible. "I'm sorry I was away again so soon last week. I was on my honeymoon with Mrs. Gallagher. Perhaps you all can tell me about what you learned later."

Most of the students already knew about his marriage, but they all cheered anyway. "I'm grateful to be back now," Colm continued when the class was silenced. "Hopefully that will be the last time for a while. This morning we will begin with Psalm 8."

The silence this time was deafening. A few boys crossed their arms over their chests and several frowned, but no one made a peep. Colm lifted his Bible.

"The heavens declare the glory of God, and the firmament showeth his handiwork."

For the following minute, Colm was swept up in the majesty of God, reminded of his own limitations and also his immense value to the Creator.

He finished the chapter and looked up to see a number of students exchanging troubling glances. They hadn't attended to the reading but hadn't openly disrupted him either. Many others had been listening, however, and more would have been if they hadn't been eying the angry ones. The only thing he could do was proceed for now, trusting God with whatever occurred next.

When he called the monitors up to retrieve their cards, the class seemed to exhale into the normal routine, easing away the tension. The rest of the morning passed with a tenuous peace. At midday, most of the room cleared out. A handful of boys stayed inside to eat their packed dinners, preventing Colm from talking to Henry about any personal matters.

Class reconvened, and Colm called the writing monitors to retrieve the cards to be copied for spelling, grammar, and penmanship. For the first time since the inception of Oliver Hibernian, he'd replaced some of the old cards with Joseph Lancaster's original scripture cards. How could anyone judge the success of the method when it hadn't been taught the way it was designed before now?

Most of the students set to work on their assignments, but sharp whispers arose from two different parts of the room. Boys glanced from the apparent ringleaders to their teacher as if uncertain whose side to take. More and more of the classes read their cards and figured out what was going on. Others looked confused, mostly the younger levels who were still copying single short letters or words. Colm stood behind his desk motionless, authoritative, ready.

"Mr. O'Malley? Please come see me with your class's concerns. The rest of you return to your work at once. I will attend to you shortly, Mr. McColgan."

The freckled level seven monitor approached the desk. "Some of them boys're refusing to do the work, Mr. Gallagher. Says they ain't supposed to have to do Bible stuff here."

"How many students are refusing?" Colm asked, exuding calm.

O'Malley scratched his head. "Three say they absolutely wouldn't, but there are others who might not because of them."

Colm picked up the card he had prepared for this situation. "Those students can copy this one instead today. Anyone who is willing should copy the card I originally assigned. Thank you, Mr. O'Malley. You are excused."

"Thankee, sir." O'Malley must have been expecting a row from him, because his eyes rounded. He said nothing, however, and taking the card, dipped his head and backed away.

Colm called Jack McColgan up next, repeating the proceedings. He was getting glares from other corners of the room, but no one else openly refused to study the Bible passage. Without doubt, he had a very short window of time before parents were involved in the protest against his changes. He would face the battles one at a time. For now, the class had quieted down and returned to their work. Leaving his desk, Colm offered a silent prayer heavenward and stepped forward to help his littlest students form their letters.

Betha was kept so busy all day, she didn't realize it was time for Colm to return until he appeared in the back door overlooking the garden.

"I had meant to meet you at school and walk you home." She crumpled the dry bed sheets in her arms and frowned at him. "Is it really three already?"

"I even walked Henry home."

"Oh dear." She probably looked a fright after all the scrubbing she'd done bent over the washtub and later the floors. This wasn't the view she wanted her husband to return home to. Colm didn't seem at all concerned, catching her in his arms. He planted a kiss on her lips and then her neck before picking up the laundry basket from the ground. He held it out and she dropped the sheets in.

"How was school?"

"Most of the day went well. Do these go upstairs?"

"Yes." Betha led him through the house and up the staircase, quickly bypassing the kitchen in hopes that he wouldn't notice she'd forgotten to eat dinner.

"I started the day by reading a chapter of scripture, but when I assigned the copywork using Joseph Lancaster's original scripture cards, there was a bit of an uproar."

"A bit?" Betha stopped in the doorway to their bedroom. "What happened?"

"A handful of students refused." Colm faced her in the hall, the basket clutched in both his hands.

"Did you force them?"

"No. I gave them different cards but explained that the curriculum used the ones I originally assigned."

"So you didn't punish them for refusing? What will you do if they continue to do so?"

"I don't think this is rebellion against me as their teacher. It's against God, and if God doesn't browbeat anyone into following Him, I won't either. They can copy something else."

"But you'll continue assigning scripture?" She moved inside the room, and he followed. As soon as he set the basket down, she grabbed up a sheet and set to work making the bed. She hadn't ironed them and hoped he didn't care. In autumn, she didn't have to worry as much about bugs living in the laundry, and for bedsheets, that was the main reason for ironing. There were enough chores to do without adding in unnecessary ones.

He hesitated a moment before responding. "I think I should keep offering them exposure to God's Word and giving them an opportunity to respond to it. If the Bible says the Word of God will not return void but will accomplish what it was set out to do, then all I need to do is make it available and trust God to do what He means to with it."

Betha pulled the sheet taut and deftly tucked it under the mattress. "But it caused an uproar?"

"Just until I gave them an alternate passage to study. That calmed things down."

For now, Betha thought. Even though she'd missed half the Bible Society distributions that year, she'd seen enough to know how some of the residents of Fell's Point felt about the scriptures. It made sense. The Bible wasn't a neutral book, and the words in it didn't leave room for a passive response. If a heart wasn't changed by it, it very likely would find itself in sharp opposition to it.

Her stomach growled as she plumped up a pillow, giving it a few extra hard shakes in an attempt to cover the sound before dropping it on the bed and reaching for the second one.

"Have you eaten?" Colm had unfolded the quilt on the bed but halted, concern on his features.

"Not yet," Betha said under her breath. "I'll grab a little somethin' here in a minute."

"What all did you do today?" Colm took the pillow from her. "You know the chores didn't all have to be done today, don't you?"

Well, if he put it that way, it sounded logical, but Betha had managed a house long enough to know that the work never stopped. Which was why maybe he had a point. Some of the scrubbing could have been done on Tuesday.

"For heaven's sake," Colm muttered when she didn't reply. "Come along, and I'll whip something up for you."

"Honestly, I'm fine," Betha protested, traipsing after him down the stairs.

He reached the kitchen and placed the cast iron skillet on the legs over the coals. The bowl of eggs was already in his hands before Betha could attempt an intervention.

"Sit down." He tilted his head toward the table, holding the bowl out of her reach. "When I was about nine or ten, my mother taught me that when you're hungry and don't have anything made, eggs are about as quick a meal as you can get together. It won't be fancy . . ."

Stopping with the whisk in hand, he eyed her as if having second thoughts. "You don't mind, do you? I don't want to step over you in your own kitchen, but . . . I rather do mean to. Really, Betha, you're more important to me than clean sheets."

The fight left Betha and she sank obediently into the chair. "You are a very kind man." He meant to give her a gift, and the last thing she wanted was to take that from him. Or turn him off from wanting to give sweet gestures in the future. "I've never met anyone like you."

Colm dropped a dollop of butter into the skillet and it slid across the pan, leaving a golden trail behind. "I'm not everyone's favorite." He winked at her. "I'm just glad I'm yours."

40

November 1828

Colm finished shopping for the household supplies at the local dry goods and grocer's shops without being stopped with a single confrontation about his teaching methods, and no angry parents mobbed their house that night.

The next day in class proceeded very much like the day before it, except a handful of seats were now empty. Colm read a psalm aloud to usher in the school day, assigned scripture for copywork and oral reading, and provided alternate cards for students who refused.

There were two committee members standing at the door to see him when school let out. Luke Tiernan and Stewart Brown waited until the room was cleared before entering in their frock coats and top hats.

"Gentlemen." Colm left the cards he was stacking and came around the desk, extending a hand. "Welcome."

"Colm." Stewart shook it. "I don't doubt that you know why we're here."

"I'm sure you've heard rumors about the curriculum. Good day, Mr. Tiernan." Colm shook his hand, determined to not be cowed by the man. Mr. Tiernan was the president of the committee, one of the most prominent men in the city, and as Colm understood, a devout Catholic. He was so used to conversing with Stewart that he'd gotten over the intimidation of his friend's similar status.

They may both be important men in Baltimore and controlled Colm's future at Oliver, but before God, he was equal with them. The reminder brought him peace and confidence from outside himself.

"There have been multiple complaints made this week, and one last week when you were out," Mr. Tiernan began. "We have parents prepared to withdraw their children from class over the use of the Bible as a clas book."

The news wasn't unexpected, but it still felt like an arrow pierced through him. Of his beloved students, some hearts were so hardened against God that they would do anything to avoid having to hear about Him. "That's disappointing indeed."

"Are you prepared to lose students over it?" Mr. Tiernan asked.

"Are you?" Colm returned quietly. "I am."

Stewart quirked a brow at him.

"I would not condemn a different teacher for making a different choice. I wrestled with it for a few years myself. All I know is that the man I am today can do nothing other than follow the original design of the curriculum. The Word of God is too much a part of who I am to separate from it now."

Mr. Tiernan's frown darkened his whole face. "It sounds like your mind is made up before you have even talked to us."

"I'm afraid so. I offer alternate passages to students unwilling to study the scripture cards, but I cannot be at peace with myself if I am not availing my students of the answers to the more poignant questions of life."

Remembering a pamphlet he'd read, Colm waved his hand through the air. "Benjamin Rush said that the Bible contains more essential knowledge than any other book in the world. As their teacher, would you have me withhold that from them? He believed that everyone who received early instruction in the Bible was made wiser and better by its influence on their minds. I believe he's right."

"Which Bible are the passages from? For some of the students, it is not the matter of using the Bible at all but that the passages were taken from a different Bible than the one their churches and families use."

Colm expected as much from him. "I use King James's Bible, sir. Giving the class more than one passage is disruptive to the method when the class is supposed to all be studying and checking the same thing. I would be glad to permit each student the use of his own Bible if I were teaching under a different education methodology."

"Unfortunately we are seeing that the presence of the Bible in the class is resulting in students leaving altogether," Stewart said with a placidity that Mr. Tiernan did not share. "Your efforts to better their minds with the Bible are fruitless if they're not here."

"I cannot control their decisions, only mine. And mine is to do before God what I have been put here to do: educate them and prepare them for life."

"By contravening the committee," Mr. Tiernan returned.

"I ask again; would you have me withhold from my students the most effective resources I have to help them in life? This is a free school; do I have the right to educate as my conscience and experience dictate while the students have the right to pursue education elsewhere if they don't like it?"

Colm felt his strength flagging after a long day of school and prayed for fortitude and mental clarity to see the conversation to its end.

"I would have you defer to the committee rather than your own judgment on these things," Mr. Tiernan said.

"Then let me know when you want me to meet with the committee, and I will be there."

Mr. Tiernan gave him a long look. "You do know your position is in a vulnerable place."

"I do," Colm said, although he doubted it. He had a written agreement, and they would have as much trouble finding a new teacher midyear as he would have finding a new job at the same time.

"I will want time to think this through and talk to students before we meet," Stewart said. "Expect to hear from us after a week."

"Thank you for your consideration of the matter. I'll wait to hear from you."

"Will you continue to use the Bible in the class in the meantime?" Mr. Tiernan asked.

"Yes."

The older man huffed out his breath and shook his head, but he didn't bark any commands to the contrary. "Have a good day, Mr. Gallagher."

"You do the same. Good afternoon, Mr. Tiernan, Mr. Brown."

When they were gone, Colm attacked the dust on the floors with the broom. Mr. Tiernan didn't have any actual arguments against Colm using the Bible; he adhered to the Good Book himself. His only issues were which Bible Colm was using and that the school was at risk of losing students. Concerns that weren't altogether invalid.

But that's what made the situation so sticky and why it had taken Colm so long to come to his conclusions—there wasn't a clear right and wrong. That fact allowed doubts to rise in his mind about his decision, but they were quickly dismissed. He could not in good conscience give his students less than the best education he could give. And Dr. Rush was right in his assertion that the best educations were based on the Bible. That was why the Sunday school hadn't been enough for Colm.

He wasn't the same person he'd been a year ago—before Betha had come into his life, the strain in his relationship with Patrick, the deaths of Mor and Sam Wilson, his personal investment in Henry. When he spoke to the committee, he wouldn't have more to say than what he'd already said today. The person he was today could not be separated from the Scriptures.

The school may need to find a different teacher if they were unable to change along with him.

Betha's influence shone through again when, as Colm knelt to sweep the dirt into the dustpan, he turned his heart to prayer. He was praying more now than he had been a year ago too. He prayed first for the upcoming meeting and his future at Oliver, but soon the prayers turned to the students and their receptiveness to God.

"Lord, Your mercy and compassion must be great to see hardened hearts so firmly resolved against You and still love them. You have been melting stony hearts since the beginning of time. No one who has had it done to them has ever regretted it. For the sake of Your name and our good, soften all of our hearts, mine included, that we may better know You and do Your will."

The dimming of the light in the room finally roused him from his knees. He'd missed walking Henry home and still hadn't had a chance to talk to him, although he had little idea of what to say when the opportunity arose. It was obvious that Henry wasn't happy at home, and there was nothing Colm could do to fix the situation.

Colm locked the schoolhouse door, more sure than ever of his path. This was why he gave his students their Heavenly Father's words—they gave life, whereas his own fell short every single time.

41

A line of sweat trickled down Colm's back and his throat closed up, making it difficult to speak. He hadn't counted on this.

He sat in a straight-backed chair in Stewart Brown's front parlor, grateful the committee had chosen a neutral, if not positive, location for all of them for this meeting. He'd been a guest in this room at least a dozen times, each time warmly welcomed. Around the room were seated the six officers of the Hibernian Society, each wearing business suits and averaging twenty years older than himself.

Oddly enough, he'd remained calm and confident all week leading up to this meeting. His confidence lay not in himself or in a false hope that everything would turn out the way he wanted, but in the fact that he knew he'd done well and had nothing to be ashamed of. If he lost his position over reading scripture in school, he was willing to accept the consequences. Most of all, he trusted that God was sovereign and that the meeting would result in him and these reasonable men coming to a satisfactory solution together.

But this? This irrational anxiety muddling his mind and creeping through his skin had not been part of the expected equation.

Colm recognized it immediately when his heart first began racing a few minutes into the meeting. It started when Mr. Craig cited the third chapter of Titus.

"The scriptures are clear that we are each in subjection to the powers that God places over us. By running away with your own schemes, you show complete disregard to the governing body of the school and the rules limiting the scope of classroom instruction."

Colm had experienced all the symptoms before. Twenty years ago, in front of Mr. MacMurrough's desk. He thought he'd done well before he went into that meeting too. That was about thirty seconds before he was subjected to the screaming, the twisting of scripture, the emasculating and then eventually the rod. After that, these exact maladies had been his ever-present companions anytime Mr. MacMurrough was in the room.

Colm resisted the urge to squirm against the back of the chair in an effort to stop the itch the sweat was causing. It didn't make sense. Two of the committee members, Stewart included, seemed to actually be on his side. Mr. Gibson was quiet, face unreadable. Mr. Tiernan and his colleague, Mr. Craig, were most concerned about the twenty students that had left Oliver in the past week, with more sure to follow. Only Mr. White was good and truly hostile.

Which was why Colm's physical reaction to this meeting felt uncalled for and rather unfair. It hadn't been this way when he spoke to Mr. Tiernan and Stewart at the school, but Mr. White's raised voice, the questionable scripture quotations, and the expectation on Colm to defend himself had put him right back in time. It was humiliating.

"James 3 says that wisdom from God is peaceable and without judging," Mr. Tiernan put in, pushing his glasses up his nose while Mr. White growled his agreement. "The school is currently in an uproar, with families choosing sides because of your insistence on imposing on them a Christian sect that less than half the class belongs to. That's not peaceable or impartial, so it could hardly be said to be a wise course of action."

Colm fought through the lightheadedness in an attempt to listen to Mr. White's speech about the First Amendment and the students' right to religious freedom. He was dreadfully thirsty but hated the thought of interrupting to ask for a drink of water. The man's face had been red for most of the meeting, and his bounteous whiskers quivered with feeling. Colm blinked, realizing the man was staring at him and waiting for a response of some sort.

Instead of answering, Colm used the quiet moment to beseech God for help. How could he go home and explain to Betha why the meeting had been an utter failure? She wouldn't believe the truth, because she'd never seen this side of him before. He'd thought it was gone for good himself.

Stewart replied when Colm didn't, explaining once again that no one was forcing religion on any of the students.

"They can study the alternate cards," Colm repeated. He felt defensive, but that was the ten-year-old boy in him who'd never had the chance with Mr. MacMurrough. God was his defender.

"Can they leave the room when you read the chapter of the Bible at the beginning of class?" Mr. Tiernan interjected.

"No." Colm's head throbbed. There was more he was supposed to say. He'd been prepared for this meeting. "It's not a matter of freedom of religion, because they have freedom to choose a school, and no one is forcing them to adhere to a creed they don't believe in. Oliver Hibernian can either use the Lancaster method and have me as its teacher, or be forced to follow a different education philosophy. But it can no longer attempt to keep Lancaster and me and eschew the Bible at the same time."

Mr. White swept his hand wide and Colm winced, the way he had right before Mr. MacMurrough struck him. He tried to cover it by reaching up to straighten his cravat.

"You did so for years," Mr. White boomed.

It was something Colm had to work to not regret. He'd done what he believed God would have him do then too. He cleared his throat. "Sir, physicians swear the Hippocratic oath when they take up the medical profession." He looked to the physicians in the room. "They vow to do their best with the knowledge they have to treat their patients. As a teacher, I must give my students the best education I can. It would be like a physician withholding the medicine he knows would treat his patient's ailment if I withheld the Bible from my students. I am simply unwilling to do that anymore."

A strained silence fell, thickening the air. Colm's mouth felt like cotton, and he had to focus on simply breathing.

"It sounds like we need to find a new teacher," Mr. White finally said.

"Don't be so hasty." Mr. Gibson gripped the armrests with his hands. "Mr. Gallagher's record is exemplary. His students are faring better than the other schools I'm on the board of with attendance and grades."

"Attendance before last week, you mean," Mr. Tiernan corrected. "Before the extended McColgan family spread word around the parish about what was happening here."

"Well, yes. I support Mr. Gallagher's changes, I think he's an unmatched teacher, and I vote to keep him."

"I don't," Mr. White snapped.

"Are we putting it to a vote then, just like that?" Mr. Tiernan looked around the room. "You're the one who said to not be hasty. We've heard from Mr. Gallagher tonight, but I say we take more time to sit on the matter before voting. Debate it further, give Mr. Gallagher a chance to consider what we said, see if we even know of any qualified replacements, talk to other educators to see how religious texts are handled elsewhere."

Stewart raised his hand. "I second that."

"We'll reconvene two weeks from today unless something changes before then. I'll let you know if you're needed at that meeting, Mr. Gallagher."

Colm nodded, his jaw clenched tight.

Stewart stood and made his way to the sidebar. "A drink for anyone?" He lifted a decanter.

"Water for me," Colm said quickly, trying to keep his voice low and smooth. He didn't trust himself to stand until Stewart brought him a glass and he'd slaked his thirst. Mr. White was just starting on his brandy when Colm returned his glass to the sidebar and approached Mr. Tiernan.

"Thank you for the meeting. I'll see you shortly," he said, reaching out to shake the president's hand.

When he'd shaken hands with each man, looking him in the eye, he put his top hat on and exited the room. Stewart followed him.

"Are you feeling well? You looked peaky in there."

Colm summoned up a weak smile. "I am. Just brought up some bad memories. They're good men, though, and I trust they'll make the best decision for the school."

Stewart gave him a penetrating look. "You know I'll do my best for you. I recommend you pray hard in the coming weeks."

"We are. Thank you, Stewart." Colm clapped him on the upper arm and pushed out the door.

He stopped for a moment on the bottom step after the door closed, filling his lungs with the cool evening air. Then he thought of Betha and how he was supposed to find the words to relay what had occurred. Lowering his head, his shoulders caved in and he started down the sidewalk.

"Colm."

He snapped his head up, looking around the street and finding Patrick ten feet away with the horses. "Need a ride?" His brother pushed off from where he was leaning against the carriage with his arms crossed.

"What are you doing here?"

Patrick shrugged, pursing his lips. "I know I couldn't come in, but thought . . . you should have someone here."

Colm could only stare at him.

"Are you coming then?"

"Yes." Clapping his gloved hands together to break out of his reverie, Colm strode over. "Thank you, Patrick. I didn't know you . . ."

His voice trailed off, and Patrick moved away to climb into the seat, avoiding his oddly sentimental look.

Neither spoke again until the carriage was moving. "Did they make a decision?" Patrick held the reins loosely with one hand and reached up to straighten his cap with the other.

"Not yet."

"Does it seem like they'll keep you?"

"I wouldn't count on it."

And he had a wife and house to keep. Colm shut his eyes, letting his breath out. Out of the meeting, he felt normal and could breathe again, which only made the embarrassment at his earlier performance greater. It was stupid to let such distant history affect him now. What was wrong with him?

"Do you remember Mr. MacMurrough?"

"I remember he was out to get you, but they replaced him before I moved into his class. You weren't very fun to be around that year."

That's right. At least his siblings had been able to avoid lifelong effects from the man.

"Why?" Patrick gave him a side-eye.

Colm shook his head.

"Your students are lucky to have a teacher like you when there are ones like him out there," Patrick muttered. "The board should think about that."

"It's in God's hands."

Exhaustion settled over Colm, and he looked with anticipation to unwinding in the comfort of the bedroom for his conversation with Betha.

"Thank you for the ride," he said when Patrick dismounted onto the walk beside him in front of the house.

"Of course." Patrick kept the reins in his hand as Colm made his way to the door.

Lifting his hand in a final farewell, Colm stepped into the warm foyer. The moment he adjusted to his surroundings, the sound of voices coming from the parlor jolted him out of his daydreams of a quiet, private talk with his wife.

42

Through the parlor door, Henry's black head was visible at the round table, bent over the chessboard. Colm deposited his hat and shuffled inside.

"Hello there." His tone indicated his surprise. "You're out late on a school night."

"Cara's aunt and midwife are over," Betha said easily, pushing back from the game and coming to her feet. "Figured Henry could stay with us tonight."

"Of course. As long as needed." Colm wrapped an arm around her and inhaled deeply. It was a quick hug, being in front of Henry, but enough for her closeness to thread comfort through him. "How are you, Henry?"

"I'm all right." He kicked lightly at the table leg, though, and fiddled with the pawn in his fingers without meeting Colm's eyes.

Colm wasted no time in dropping into the chair opposite him. "You look a little troubled."

"Why should I be? Ma doesn't seem to think I ought to be." Henry tossed his hair out of his eyes.

"Now, that's not what I—"

"I suppose your ma knows a thing or two about what it's like to have troubles," Colm interjected. He lifted an eyebrow and waited for Henry to nod in agreement.

"I guess I'm tired of being told how to bear up under it." Henry scowled. "It doesn't fix it."

"When she shares what carries her through her trials with me, it's meant to uplift, not pretend it doesn't hurt." He picked up Betha's rook

233

and used it to knock Henry's bishop off the board before settling in its square. Henry's scowl deepened. "None of us here can fix what's troubling you, Henry. We can't even make it seem smaller. All we can do, really, is point you to a God bigger than all of it and let you know you're not swimming this current alone."

Henry turned the bishop over in his hand, and Colm watched him turn the words over in his mind. He swallowed, set the bishop down, and moved his queen to block the king.

"It's about what's happening at your house tonight?" Colm asked quietly.

Henry shrugged. Colm and he made their moves on the board, but still he didn't speak.

"Why don't we pray about it together and then let you get some rest," Colm finally said. "The more tired we get, the worse things look usually."

Betha returned to her seat, folding her hands in her lap.

"Now I'll be praying about your da and his wife and everything that's happening there." Colm watched Henry carefully. "If there's anything else you want me to pray for, anything that has you worried, you'll have to say so, since I won't do a good job sitting here guessing at it."

He moved his rook over two spaces while giving Henry time to respond.

Henry kicked at the table leg. "Sam," he almost whispered.

"Sam?" Of course. Losing a boy his age that he interacted with every day was sure to cut deep.

"Not *for* Sam," Henry rushed on. "I . . . I guess I think about it a lot. That's all."

Colm nodded gravely. "I do, too, to be honest. I'll bet most of the class does. We could pray for them too."

Henry moved a pawn, and Colm waited. When there didn't seem to be anything more Henry wanted to add, he clasped his hands together. "Do you want to pray first or second?" he asked, because the idea struck that giving Henry someone else to pray for could help him too.

"Second."

Colm kept his prayer simple and straightforward, boldly asking God for a change in Henry's relationship with his father and stepmother, grace to bear each day, and His loving comfort for the whole class, as well as a healthy new baby in the family that night. He said "Amen" and remained with his hands folded and eyes closed.

A long moment passed before Henry started praying, and Colm relaxed.

"O Lord, please help the other boys not to be worried about dying but to trust in Jesus for eternal life. Please make the baby to be all right and for me to love it and Da and Cara. And help them to love me too. Bless us all. Amen."

Colm had heard Henry pray before, but never without the practiced words from the books or to make a request on his own behalf. He would have pondered it further, but Betha had surprised him by adding her own prayer to theirs.

She finished on a yawn and smiled at Henry, patting his hand. "Let's get you up to bed now. I'll put you in the room next to ours." She stifled another yawn as she escorted him up the stairs.

Colm pushed to his feet and set to work banking the fires and putting out the candles. He had no regrets about hosting Henry or attending to his needs tonight, but he couldn't get into the topic of the evening's meeting with Betha now. He ought to take his own advice to Henry and sleep on it anyway. The situation would look better to both him and Betha when she wasn't overtired and consumed with Henry. He wouldn't keep it from her for long, and it would give him a chance to follow Stewart's counsel to pray like his job depended on it.

Betha walked in Seamus's back door after her solitary dinner—always eggs these days, since Colm had started it—hoping that by waiting until the afternoon, she could meet the baby. Instead, she found a sweaty-faced aunt informing her that Cara was on her twentieth hour of labor. The house was quiet for the time being with the exception of Seamus's loom. He must be nearly driven mad.

Betha bypassed the delivery room, walking outside around the house and in the front door to see him. His shuttle flew furiously, focused determination on his face.

"I heard there's no update." Betha sidled up beside him.

"Not yet."

"Did you get any sleep?"

"Just a little here and there. Is Henry being good?"

"Of course. Has he been giving you trouble?"

Seamus didn't break concentration on his work. "He's not very pleasant company these days, but he's not poisoning us, so it depends on what you mean by 'good.'"

"He didn't used to be like this," Betha said pointedly. "Children don't often change in this way without a reason."

"His thinking he has a reason is not the same thing as having a valid one. I had a right to get married, whether or not he likes it. His inability to accept it isn't my fault."

"It isn't? What have you done to help him through it?"

Seamus frowned. The loom thumped.

"To make him know that you still love him even though you're adding to the family?"

Betha sighed when Seamus still didn't respond. "Whether or not it's true, he believes you and Cara don't want him, and I can't convince him otherwise. He won't simply change his mind on his own either. You have to prove it to him. And if you won't do that, you can be assured we'll all continue to lose him."

The loom stilled and Seamus pushed back on his bench. "While my wife is laboring in the other room is not the time to be coming to me with your lectures. If Henry's too much for you, you can bring him back here anytime. But he'd probably appreciate being with you for the next week or so while Cara's aunt is here helping with the baby."

Betha saw the fear he tried to cover, the uncertainty whether there would even be a baby to care for at the end of this. But if there wasn't, her house was probably still the best place for Henry this week.

"I'm happy to keep him."

"Are you goin' to make him think it's because I don't want him here?" Seamus's eyes narrowed.

Not any more than you do, Betha wanted to say. "No. It makes sense for him to stay with me."

"Thank you."

"We're praying that all goes well with Cara. Do you want me to check back in tonight? Bring you a bite to eat?"

"Tomorrow should be fine. If it comes today, we'll probably fall asleep, and I'm not that hungry."

"Sure then."

Betha pulled her shawl around her shoulders as she descended the front steps. Her prayers for Cara on her walk home quickly turned to imprecatory prayers against Seamus. How could her own blood brother be so pigeon-livered? Who cared if Henry was the product of his own stupidity—how could he so offhandedly spurn what used to be such a sweet boy?

She was spinning when Colm and Henry returned, shutting the door against the cold. Coming to her feet, she met Henry in the foyer and gave him a hug. "I've a biscuit for you in the kitchen."

He shuffled off, and she took the lunch pail from Colm. He reached for the back of her head, meeting her lips with his for a lingering kiss.

"That'll warm a man right up." He grinned at her.

"Welcome home." Betha took his cold fingers in her free hand and pressed them against her cheek. "How were things today? I haven't had a chance to hear about your meeting yesterday."

His brown eyes held hers, the grin fading. "We're losing more students every day."

"What is the committee goin' to do about it?"

"I don't know yet. They said they need more time."

Betha felt his sadness. It was heartbreaking to watch a loved one reject God. What must it be like to watch dozens of them do so before his eyes?

"We can talk about it more after Henry goes home."

She shook her head. "I was just over there and told Seamus Henry could stay with us for the next week while Cara's aunt is there."

There was a moment's hesitation while Colm digested the news.

"You don't mind?" Betha asked.

He blinked as if snapping out of a reverie. "What? Oh, not at all. Of course he ought to stay here. Well, that's really all I know until the committee makes a decision anyway. We need to be praying about what happens next."

Henry appeared in the kitchen doorway, swallowing his bite. "Is the baby here?"

"Not yet. By tomorrow, surely."

Betha didn't miss the way his lips quirked at the corners. He was excited despite himself.

"Do you think it will be a boy or a girl?" she asked.

"A boy," he said as if he'd never considered there was another option.

"I hope so too." Betha moved toward the parlor and her wheel. "Because then your Uncle Colm can teach him too."

43

By the week's end, Betha was relieved to reinstall Henry at home. He sat swinging his legs at Seamus's table, staring grumpily at her. There had been moments of light throughout the week, but handling his changing moods day in and day out was exhausting.

She kissed the fuzzy top of baby Elizabeth's head and returned her to where Cara sat by the fire dressed in a wrapper. "I can come do laundry on Thursday and bring some more food."

Cara reached for the bundle, positioning her against her shoulder. "Thank you." Motherhood looked good on Cara. Even with dark circles under her eyes, she glowed when Elizabeth was in her arms.

Betha looked longingly at Henry, her heart breaking for him. If only Cara would let him bond with his sister like he wanted. She'd been adamantly against letting him hold Elizabeth when they came the other day to meet the baby, and Betha didn't know whether to risk bringing it up again.

"Goodbye, Henry. I trust you'll do what you can to help while Cara can't be up much."

"Yes, ma'am."

"I left a stew in the kitchen for tonight," she added to both of them.

He nodded, so with nothing else to say, she headed into the other room to find Colm.

"She's so pretty," she gushed to Colm on the walk home. "Did you see her little apple cheeks? They look so much nicer on her than on Seamus."

Colm shot her a grin, but his shoulders were tense and his hands in fists at his side. She hadn't stayed to hear what he'd been talking to Seamus about and wondered if it was the source of his unease.

"What is it?"

"I have a meeting tonight with the committee."

She'd been too caught up with Henry when they got home from school to give Colm much attention. Now the tone of his voice shot needles of fear through her middle.

"God's in control." He squeezed her hand as if he could read her thoughts. "We need to pray when we get home."

Were things worse than she'd imagined? "How many students have left, exactly?" Nearly every day, he reported more gone, but she'd never stopped to ask about numbers.

"Most of them."

"Most of them?" Betha's voice rose and she stared at him in shock as panic rose. "What do you mean, most of them?"

Colm swallowed hard and looked away down the street. "We'll talk about it at home."

Betha's stomach was in turmoil by the time she was seated across from Colm at the parlor table, her hand in his. His touch was supposed to bring comfort like usual, but with the seriousness in his eyes, it would take a lot more than that to quiet the storm raging inside.

"Betha . . ." He worked his jaw forward and back and lifted a hand to his forehead. Running it down his face, he blew out a breath. Had he been holding things back from her? Or was he finally free in Henry's absence to feel the full effects of the pain he'd been suppressing all week? "I taught thirty students today."

Thirty? Out of a class of a hundred and seventy? "Oh, Colm."

"I didn't . . . I didn't expect this. When I made my decision to incorporate the Bible. Not a response this extreme. I'm grief-stricken," he added, shaking his head on the last note.

Betha covered his hand on the table with both of hers. "If they ask you again to leave the Bible out, will you consider it?"

"I can't." His voice cracked. "A hundred and seventy boys and their families will then know that the Bible is important enough for me to prioritize reading it to them but not valuable enough to actually make sacrifices for. They'll know I say one thing but act differently, and that Jesus isn't precious or powerful enough to sustain those who choose to honor Him. I could no longer teach them because they would no longer respect me. It would have been better if I'd never brought the Bible in."

Betha furrowed her brow, processing and then accepting his words. "Do you regret it?"

"I do, in a way. I could not have done otherwise though."

Betha knew it was true, and that more than anything, she wanted a husband who lived out his convictions to honor God in every sphere of his life. But dread and profound grief pressed in, choking out whatever affirmation she would have wanted to give him. A tear slipped down her cheek, and before she could stop the flood, her eyes brimmed with more. She pressed her eyes closed as tightly as they would go.

"Pray with me?" Colm whispered.

Betha could only nod.

They prayed for an hour, until darkness settled in around the edges of the room and the fire in the hearth provided the solitary light. It was suppertime, but Betha didn't move to make anything to eat and Colm didn't ask her to. They sat in the silence, hands clasped on the table, and watched the fire. From time to time, Betha reached up to wipe tears away.

"If I leave now, I can get Maisie or Bridget to come over and be with you when I go," Colm said.

"Not tonight." They fell silent again.

At a quarter to seven, Colm heaved to his feet and retrieved his coat and hat. Betha leaned on the doorjamb and watched him ready in the foyer. He gave her a long look and bent to kiss her cheek. Swallowing over the lump in her throat, Betha waited at the open door while he strode confidently down the street. When he was out of sight, she returned to collapse on the window seat and let the tears flow.

The door clicked and Betha jumped, stabbing a needle into the pad of her finger. She dropped Colm's shirt onto the seat and bolted to her feet as she stuck the bleeding finger into her mouth. Colm blew into the foyer and shut the door behind himself.

"You're back so soon!" Wrapping the corner of her apron around her finger, she hurried to meet him and take his hat.

Colm hung up his coat and turned to her. "Here I am." He looked lighter than he had when he'd left only an hour ago, the weight pulling on his shoulders nowhere to be seen. Betha's heart lifted in hope.

"What happened?"

"Thank you for praying for me." He stopped in front of her and took her hand in his, smiling down at her. "I could tell God was with me."

"Did something change?" Her heart rate increased as she studied his face for the answer.

"I do not teach at Oliver Hibernian anymore."

"Colm?" The air left Betha's lungs and confusion swept over her. She took a step backward.

Her instant reaction made him hesitate. "I resigned," he said, softening his tone.

"Resigned?" The tears that had dried up now pricked her eyes again. She searched for the truth in the situation, because surely the betrayal she felt couldn't be true. "What do you mean? We prayed and . . ."

Colm opened his mouth, then closed it and led her by the hand back to the window seat. He knelt on the wooden planks before her as she sank onto the seat, gasping for breath.

"There was no way left for me to stay." He lifted her knuckles to his lips and returned her hand to her lap. "Can't you see that? It was impossible to return to the way things were, and if I continued with the way things are, I would be withholding an education from my students. The committee will get another teacher who will follow the rules and then the boys will know how to read when they do get a Bible. When they do want to know about God."

"Were they going to let you go if you hadn't resigned?"

His eyes cut away briefly. "I don't know."

"You don't even know, Colm?" Betha sobbed. "They could have wanted to keep you, but you resigned before they had a chance?"

His brows furrowed and he straightened on his heels, studying her. Was she being so illogical and erratic that he didn't know what to do with her? Because right now, her heart felt cut down the middle. She was bleeding out, left in the horrible, sticky aftermath of a massacre.

"You promised me." Her voice wobbled and her chin did too. Colm lifted his hands to either side of her face, gently wiping her tears off her cheeks with his thumbs. "You *promised* me that you would be there for Henry every day. You made me believe I could marry you because Henry would have you. You promised me," she repeated, weaker.

His hands fell away when she leaned forward and covered her face, weeping. Colm pulled her against his shoulder and she dropped her forehead on him as the tears fell.

"Betha," he whispered, his own voice breaking, but she couldn't listen to him.

"We had him all week, and he was already so difficult. He's pulling away from the Lord and from us. He needs us more than ever right now. How could you resign?"

"I thought you knew when we prayed before I left tonight. We asked for the Lord to direct the proceedings and that He would give us the grace to face whatever happened. By the time I was on my way there, I had complete confidence that the only way forward was to leave the school. There wasn't anything left to do. There was no reason to waste the committee's time. I didn't feel anxious or fear them at all when I told them."

His wording seemed strange. Betha leaned back to look in his face, wiping at her eyes to clear them. Colm dug in his pocket and handed her a handkerchief. His face was so pure, so handsome, so broken.

"I'm so sorry I hurt you," he whispered, and his eyes shimmered. "I thought you understood it, too, before I left."

"I think I understand leaving the school, but leaving the school means leaving Henry, and I don't understand that. How could that be what God wants?" Betha thought of where she left Henry sitting on Seamus's chair, sullenly kicking at the ground, and couldn't imagine telling him his Uncle Colm had resigned. "You thought you'd be more anxious? In the meeting?"

He pressed his lips together and nodded. "I was the last time I met with them. But this time I had so much peace, it could only have come from God. I think it's because we prayed beforehand."

Betha wished she could have a fraction of his peace. She looked at her finger that had stopped bleeding and wondered when her heart would stop feeling like a battlefield. Another tear trickled down her face, and she let it.

She had prayed and worked so hard. She'd spent years teaching Henry the things of God, being an example for him, battling on her knees for him. How could she be here now, having lost everything she'd fought hardest for? Weariness blanketed her. If God was sovereign in determining the outcome of Henry's life, were all her efforts meaningless? Did any of it matter at all?

Colm rolled to a seated position and tugged at her hand to pull her onto his lap on the floor, but she stood, shaking her head. "I just want to go to bed."

For a heavy moment, they held each other's sorrow-filled gaze.

"I'm sorry, Colm. I'm not angry at you anymore." Betha took a slow, tentative breath. "I promise I'm trying to let him go, but . . ." Sobs threatened to choke her again, and she pressed the handkerchief to her eyes.

"But you're angry at God?" Colm finished, compassion in his eyes.

"Mostly Seamus. But I am, if I'm honest. And I'm exhausted."

Colm nodded and draped his empty arms over his knees. "They agreed to let me teach for another week or two while they look for a replacement. I need to say goodbye to the students that are left. Will you manage if I go to school tomorrow?"

She had to be. It didn't matter if she wanted to curl up in bed all day with Colm tomorrow; she couldn't possibly deny him one of his last days with his beloved boys.

"What were you doing tomorrow?" Colm scrambled to his feet, suddenly alert.

"Wednesday. Mending and spinnin'."

"You don't have to work tomorrow. If you need to take the day with the Lord, we'll be fine. I can buy supper on my way home."

She probably needed to keep her hands busy while spending the day in prayer, but it was so kind of him to make the offer, Betha stood on tip-toe to kiss his cheek before turning to drag her heavy heart up the stairs.

44

Betha sat on the edge of the bed in her nightgown as sunlight streamed through the window. She could hardly imagine the believability of sleeping so late or the fact that she now lived with a man who told her to spend the day in prayer instead of work. The thought made her laugh out loud to the empty room.

They'd woken together before daylight, and Colm had made love to her, seeming to need reassurance that there was nothing lingering between them. But then he'd insisted she stay in bed while he dressed and left for school. She'd actually fallen back asleep.

Now, feeling physically refreshed, she saw the wisdom in it. She had a lot of ground to cover with the Lord today, and now she felt almost capable of facing it.

She dressed, threw her hair into a quick braid, and found the now-cold coffee Colm had left in the kettle. Her stomach growled, reminding her that they'd fasted through supper. Embarrassment threatened at the sight of Colm's egg remnants stuck to the sides of her cast iron skillet, and she sternly dismissed it. Her husband's priorities should be hers as well, and he prioritized a spiritually healthy wife over one that made him breakfast.

She fixed a bowl of porridge and sat down at the kitchen table with her coffee and Bible. For a long minute, she stared at its faded, nicked cover. What was she hoping would happen today?

"Lord . . . I want my heart to align with Yours. To trust You with Colm's and my future and believe You when You say that You have Henry in Your hands. And to understand what my place is in it. Whether the things I've done on his behalf really has been a misdirected use of my time and whether it matters."

Maybe she could spout quick answers to those questions now, but she'd search for the truth of what God said about them until she found it. She couldn't be at peace with herself, the Lord, or the situation until she was very sure of God's view of things.

Picking up the cold coffee, she cradled it in her hands to sip it. "I know I've no right to be angry, and I'm sorry. I want to trust You enough to release everything back into Your hands while still fulfilling the duties You've given me. I can't bear the thought of Henry rejecting You and letting this bitterness in his heart destroy him."

With her heart humbled and laid out before the Lord and a growing hunger to spend time with Him, her day had a clarified sense of purpose. Reaching out, she opened the Bible, desperate to begin.

Colm leaned back against the edge of his desk and stared at the empty seats. In a very short time, he would no longer have a place in this room. What was it that Jesus had said about putting new wine in old wineskins? Colm related to it. The new thing God had done in his heart over the past year didn't fit in his old life, and his old life didn't fit him anymore.

Somehow he had missed Jesus saying how profound the grief would be in the transition. New beginnings were supposed to feel joy filled, weren't they? Instead, it had been death upon death for him lately, and the way ahead remained completely dark. He had broken his brand new wife's heart, for pity's sake, and doubt about his decision to force the Bible on the students plagued him. Where was the way out of this?

Henry had been at school today, and they'd spent dinnertime talking about the new schooners down at the shipyards while ignoring the pain each other tried to hide. The missing friends, neighbors, and relatives in the classroom surely hurt his remaining students as much as it did him. Still, Colm couldn't bring himself to confess his resignation to his students yet. Not when he and Betha hadn't come to terms with it together. He'd have to do it in the next couple of days, though, before the boys found out about it elsewhere.

Pushing off from the desk, Colm retrieved the broom and swept slowly, as if in a trance. He returned his books to their shelf, raked the sand tables smooth, and straightened the monitor cards into order on their nails. Walking up and down the rows of benches, he straightened them, thinking of the boy who had occupied each seat and offering up prayer after prayer for every one. He ran his hand over Sam Wilson's desk and his heart ached.

"You're faithful even if I made a mistake with all of this, Lord. If You're leading me out of here, then You must have a place prepared for me to go and someone else to take my place. May they find You during their service here the way I did."

A new thought struck. Grabbing his coat up, he locked the school door behind him and headed resolutely toward the office of Stewart Brown, who had always been so supportive of him. In the coming days, he'd need to make a list of possible schools to apply to and figure out his options as he waited on God to direct his path. In the meantime, work at Stewart's shipping office would, Lord willing, keep food on the table. Betha shouldn't have to worry about that, too, just now.

"Maisie!"

Colm quickened his pace down the street to catch her, but she halted at his call and turned with a happy smile for him. He reached her, stopping to catch his breath.

"What are you doing on this side of town?" she asked.

"Just out on an errand. Are you going home?" He relieved her of her vegetable basket and fell in step beside her as she resumed walking.

"Yes. I've missed you. Are you coming over soon?"

Colm glanced at her out of the corner of his eye. "Is supper tonight too soon?"

"Not soon enough." Maisie sauntered along beside him. "I've wanted to talk to you about something."

"Would tonight be best for that, or now?" His own news would probably upend the evening's discussion, but he had time now before he needed to see how Betha was doing.

"We're alone now." She looked up and down the street, but no one was in hearing distance.

"Over here." Colm led her to a row of three stumps in front of the barbershop and straddled one, setting the basket down on another. With effort, he put his own troubles and the damp chill in the air out of his mind to give her his full attention.

Maisie sighed and lowered herself onto the seat beside him. "It's about Ezra."

Colm stiffened, giving her a look of warning, but she laughed and waved her hand at him. "He didn't do anything. He's been amazing. Perfect."

He waited while she studied the seams on her gloves. A couple walked by a few feet away. When they were gone, Maisie said, "I think I was wrong about him. He's a good man. A worthy one."

"What about his freckles? And awkwardness?"

She breathed out a giggle. "I think he's outgrowing some of the awkwardness, or maybe I've gotten used to it. The freckles—I can't imagine him without them."

"What do you need from me then?" Colm asked in amusement.

"Do you . . . do you think he'll give me a second chance?"

He blinked at her timid question. "Maisie, he's been giving you a second chance for an entire year. He's been affixed to your side like a burr. A man would have to be smitten to wait as long as he has."

"He never stopped, did he?" Maisie groaned. "Even though I told him not to be in love with me."

Colm wanted to shout with laughter. "If I told you right now to stop loving Ezra Wright, would you be remotely tempted to do so?"

"No." Maisie shoved at his knee.

Colm couldn't stop. "If he walked up right now and told you to stop loving him, would it go any better?"

"I see your point." Maisie grabbed her basket and shot to her feet.

"What are you going to do about it now?" Colm asked from his perch.

"Do?" She halted before taking two steps in her escape.

"Will you tell him?"

She gaped at him. "I couldn't *tell* him. I am a refined lady, Colm Gallagher."

Ah. That's where he came in.

"I suppose Ezra will have to simply figure out that your affections have changed himself and work up the courage to try again."

"I suppose so." She smirked at him.

Fine. He'd put Ezra out of his misery the first chance he got, but he wouldn't tell Maisie that.

"I have to talk to Betha about supper, but we might be over."

"There will be enough if you do." Waving her hand behind her, Maisie ambled off.

Colm stood, leaning back to stretch his back. Betha was at home waiting for him, and he felt anxious to check on her. Hopefully the extra time he'd given her hadn't made her feel abandoned on top of everything else.

I don't have comfort and answers for her, Lord. Helping Maisie was easy in comparison. He stuffed his hands in his pockets and started the long walk in Betha's direction. *If You want to use me to encourage and strengthen her, You're going to have to do the work, because I'm still reeling here myself.* What did he know about how to lead a wife through heartbreak caused at his own hands?

Before Colm had closed the front door, Betha appeared in the parlor doorway. She was in her simple day dress with the apron pinned over it, her hair in the braid she only wore at home anymore. The sight of her was comforting and welcoming, softening the jagged edges of the burdens he carried. She came willingly to him, so he wrapped her in his arms and inhaled deeply.

"How are you?" With his face buried in her hair, the question came out muffled.

"Thank you for giving me today," she said instead of answering. "I needed it. I did some mending while praying though."

Colm kissed her temple and released her. "Do you want to tell me about it?"

"It might take some time." Betha pursed her lips, studying him. "In some cases, I think I ended with more questions than answers. It was worth it to take the time to surrender things to the Lord and put everything back in its proper place though."

Lifting a hand, Colm stroked her cheek with his thumb. "I had a thought on the way here. By the way, Stewart said I can work for him until I find a new position. That's where I've been. On my walk, I was thinking about the people in the Bible who faced dark nights in their lives and how God always gave them a dawn after it. Job. Hannah. Joseph. Naomi. There's story after story of periods of joy coming after intense difficulty and loss."

"Some of the ones in the New Testament died in the middle of their dark night though." Betha's brow furrowed. "Stephen and Paul. They didn't see the dawn in this life."

"Ah, the most glorious dawn of all. The one that never ends." Colm smiled, stroking down her jaw until he tapped her chin and let go. "One day, God will take away all the sorrow. He promised. Everything that breaks our hearts here is temporary. Every misstep we make is redeemed. We have hope." Unshakeable hope, because it hinged not on their strength or circumstances, but on the promises of the God who never failed. Whose love was deep and wide and firm.

Betha crossed her arms to hug herself. "If it was anything less than Henry's soul at stake, I'd agree that it's temporary. But this is eternal, and I'm not the one who can determine his eternal resting place."

"He's put his faith in Christ, hasn't he?"

"Seamus did, too, at this age."

The weight of the reminder hung in the air between them. Colm could see the reason for her fear. Confessing Christ was not the same thing as truly surrendering one's life, and neither of them could judge the heart of another.

Betha took a deep breath and let it out. "That's what I spent all day talking to the Lord about. I studied the Bible and found repeated reminders of our responsibility to instruct children in the ways of God and to love, love, love. Not once did God say that I can save another person or guarantee their future."

She hesitated as if she had more to say, but Colm didn't have a response anyway.

"I keep trying to let him go and release him to the Lord. But . . ." Her words slowed down as she carefully chose which ones to give voice to. "I still have a sense that we're in a spiritual battle, and walking away isn't the right thing to do either. That God places people in each other's lives to fight for them. That trusting God with results doesn't mean we ought to give up."

"You think we have more to do."

"Yes."

Colm nodded. "I've thought that too. I had begun to think lately that marrying you was what God meant."

Silence fell for a minute as he began to work through everything she said and the implications of it. There were no conclusions to be had in this moment, though, so he lifted his head. "We need to spend time praying about it. I don't know the answers, and it would be valuable to create a daily discipline of surrender in the meantime." Surrender was too important and necessary to rush past, and he was a long way from mastering it.

"You don't have supper either," Betha said, looking at his empty hands.

He winced. "I have a plan for that, depending on if you're up for visiting my father's this evening. If you'd rather a quiet evening at home, I'll figure out a different plan."

"You'll make eggs?" Betha's grin was a welcome relief after the tears of the night before. The faith that allowed her to smile through the questions and darkness was inspiring to him. "It would be nice to spend time with your family tonight. I've a loaf of bread left we can bring. Should I change?"

"No. You could do this, though." Sliding an arm around her waist, Colm spun her around so her back was to the front door and his lips captured hers.

45

Betha was hanging laundry in Seamus's back yard the following Thursday when Henry found her. He plopped on the bottom step and swiped a pebble from the ground without offering a greeting.

"How was school?" Numb from handling wet laundry in the cold, Betha's fingers fumbled with the pin.

When Henry didn't answer, she glanced back at him and gasped.

"What happened?" His shirt was untucked from his trousers, streaked with dirt, and missing the bottom button. His swollen lower lip bore residue of dried blood. "Did someone attack you?"

"Not really." Henry tucked the pebble into the slingshot in his hand and sent it flying toward the empty garden.

"Don't frighten the chickens. It doesn't look like you just fell." Betha shivered from a gust of wind and quickened her movements, reaching for a pair of stockings from the basket.

"I got in a little fight."

Betha gaped at him, the stockings forgotten in her hand. "At school?" And on the day before Colm left Oliver Hibernian forever.

"On the way home."

"So Uncle Colm wasn't there to see it?"

He shook his head.

Betha couldn't fathom it. Henry had never been in a scuffle in his entire life. He was always the boy who turned the other cheek and was considerate of others.

"Whatever was it about?" Another gust sent dried leaves scuttling across the yard, reminding her to finish her work and return to the warm house. She pinned the stockings on the line.

"There were some boys who don't go to Oliver anymore sittin' there being good-for-nothings when I walked past. They called me a name, and it made me mad."

"And the only thing you could think of to do was become violent?"

"It made my blood boil. It was the same name Cara called me." And which he had obviously never forgiven her for, if he was bringing it up now. He crossed his arms and scowled at the ground.

"What's happened to you, Henry?" she nearly whispered to the diaper in her hand. Where was the boy she knew and had loved all these years? Would she ever see him again?

"I'm sorry it happened again. Sometimes people just feel like being mean, and there's aught we can do to change them. I don't suppose getting in a fistfight will make them feel less like being mean the next time." Grabbing up a petticoat, she pinned it with aching fingers. "Do you think some of those boys will come back next week when the substitute takes over for Uncle Colm?"

"A lot of them will. Did you tell Da he quit?"

"I haven't." She'd been unable or unwilling to attempt a normal conversation with Seamus lately. Maybe she wasn't much of a better example of how to treat someone who angered her than Henry was. "Have you?"

"No. He doesn't really ask me about anything. As long as I'm at the free school, I don't think he cares who the teacher is."

"I do. Uncle Colm and I are both very sorry that he's leaving you. He felt it was the right thing to do for the school, though. If I talk your da into sending you wherever Uncle Colm teaches next year, would you want to do that?"

She glanced over to see him give her an odd look. "Ma . . . I don't think I'll be in school next year."

"Why?" Betha asked, even though the dread in her stomach answered the question for her.

"I think Da's going to indenture me soon. I'd give anything to go to school with Uncle Colm instead." And just like that, his sullenness gave way to the old vulnerability he'd always had with her. All those years building a relationship where he was loved and safe weren't completely lost.

She nodded slowly, her mind racing with ideas of things she could do to fix this. Which meant she needed to get home as soon as possible and hit her knees with Colm to seek the Lord's face. Before she took matters into her own hands and made a mess of things again.

"I'll pray about that," she said simply. What she wanted to say was "I'll pray that God will open another way," but if He didn't, would that further destroy Henry's already weakened faith?

"How are things with Elizabeth?" Tucking the empty basket under her arm, Betha stopped beside him.

"She's a really sweet baby, and she likes me." Henry grinned. "Cara doesn't want me around her much, but sometimes she can't help it when she's trying to make supper and the baby's crying. I talk to her and play with her and then she's quiet so Cara can work."

Tears burned in the backs of Betha's eyes. "You're a sweet brother, Henry. I'm proud of you." She tweaked his cap. "I think I'm goin' to head home to Uncle Colm now. No more fights, all right?"

"Yes, ma'am."

Depositing the basket inside, Betha kissed Elizabeth's head, gave a hurried goodbye to Cara and Seamus, and bolted down the street. Anger propelled her forward, away from the burning desire to confront her brother and his wife again. It was pointless. Her time would be much better spent in prayer, taking up Henry's guard alongside Colm.

Colm handed Betha his dirty dishes as she cleared the table after supper on Monday. She appeared to be struggling more with the report of his day at the shipping office than he was. Her jaw was tight, and she didn't meet his eyes as she filled the dishpan.

"It's just temporary, Betha," he said softly. "Thank the Lord He gave us the Sunday school so we can continue teaching these children in the meantime."

"Do you know where you might apply to work next year?"

Colm leaned back in his chair with an exhale and fiddled with the corner of his napkin on the table. She wanted a way out of this. He didn't blame her, but more than anything, he didn't want to do anything without the Lord guiding it.

"I considered going deeper into the philosophy of education and teaching teachers, but I don't think there's anything like that in Maryland right now. I'd enjoy that though. Just think of how large the impact could be if I influenced a hundred teachers to prioritize the Bible in their classrooms."

Betha turned from the dishpan with the pensive look still firmly affixed to her face. "We aren't responsible for our impact. Anyway, what would you need in order to do that?"

"A teacher's college." Colm laughed at the opportunity that didn't exist. "Where teachers are actually trained for their job instead of simply given a general education, like I was. But you know I would miss being around boys every day. McKim's is a Quaker school. I wouldn't be asked to leave the Bible out of the classroom there. I don't know yet if they'll have an opening next year, but I think they would be my first choice."

Betha nodded but still didn't relax. Colm pushed to his feet and reached out to touch her sleeve. "It will be all right, Betha. I don't want to be a merchant forever either, but I've done it before, and I'm grateful to have work right now. Please don't let it make you anxious."

A knock on the front door interrupted before she could respond. Colm gave her an encouraging look and left to answer it. Swinging the door open, he found Seamus on the front step in his woolen cap, his hands in his coat pockets. He wasn't smiling.

"Can I talk to you?"

"Absolutely!" Colm overcame his surprise and moved aside to allow him entrance. "Betha's in the kitchen, but I can light a fire in the study."

Seamus waved a hand. "The kitchen's fine. She can hear." He kept his coat on to follow Colm down the hall. When they reached Betha, she stared at the intruder without a greeting and dried her hands on her apron.

"Something to drink?" Colm asked.

"No, no. I was, ah—I need to talk about Henry."

"Have a seat," Colm said, but Seamus didn't move, so they all remained standing in a triangle around the table.

"I'm out of options." Seamus's shoulders dropped, the lines on his face deepening. "It's pointless to start Henry on weaving. It will never make enough to support him, and it won't keep us from bankruptcy. We need the income from his indenture before the cotton mills ruin us altogether."

Betha nodded, tight-lipped, but neither she nor Colm indicated amazement. It was a long time coming.

"There's no other way for us to keep going. The indenture will give our household income and will provide room and board, eliminating the expense of keeping him. You see that, don't you?" He was looking at Betha, seemingly desperate for her to understand. "I know how you think about it, and I've done everything I can to avoid this. There's only one way I can think of to keep him in school."

Colm held his breath, waiting.

"Before I sign a contract, I thought I should offer his indenture to you. I know it's an expense, but . . . I thought you'd like to know first."

There was silence while Seamus worked his cap in his hands and Colm and Betha stared at him.

Betha cleared her throat. "You mean we could buy your son from you, raise him in our home, and rather than using him for income, allow him to finish his education." Her voice was flat, and it wasn't a question. It was exactly what Seamus meant.

253

Something flashed across his eyes. "I've always thought you were his mother, Betha. Cara isn't, and she never will be. I'm not asking you to do anything you don't want to do; I'm informing you that these are my final two options and giving you the first opportunity to take him before I send him to a stranger."

"I can't, Seamus." Betha's voice rose and her eyes filled with tears. "I would accept your horrible proposal and gladly take Henry in—if Colm thought it was the right thing to do—but we can't afford his indenture."

Seamus looked around the room in confusion. "I know it would be a chunk of money, but I thought you . . ."

"I don't teach at Oliver anymore," Colm said softly. "Our finances recently dived significantly."

"You don't?" Shock and fear passed through Seamus's eyes. "When did that happen?"

"Friday was my last day. I probably won't find another teaching position until next school year."

"Was it about the ruckus with the McColgans? I heard about it at the pub. I thought it was a fool thing to turn preacher on the kids, but I wouldn't have gone through the trouble of trying to find a new school over it. But that clan from the parish doesn't take kindly to anyone meddling in their ways."

Colm pressed his lips into a line, not anxious to revisit everything he was trying to put behind him. "I didn't know that Father Michael was Mr. McColgan's brother or that the whole community would follow suit when their extended family withdrew their children."

"The papists are as thick as thieves like that. Who's teaching the school then?"

Their community was closer knit than the Irish Protestants, Colm would give them that. "They have a committee member substituting while they look for a new teacher."

Seamus stood, shaking his head. "I didn't know they'd dismissed you over it, but I guess I should have figured it would happen. Henry didn't tell me any of it."

For a fleeting moment, Colm wished more of his students' parents were as aloof as Seamus, instead of pulling their children out of his school, but the issue about Henry remained unsolved. "We would be thrilled and honored to have Henry live with us. He always has a home available to him here, and I'm happy to take on his expenses. But unfortunately, Betha's right; we can't afford to pay for his indenture."

Betha wiped at her eyes with the corner of her apron. This had to be convincing her further that Colm's resignation was a mistake. How were they to know that less than a month later, they would be offered the opportunity to buy Henry from Seamus? What would he have done if the offer came a month ago? Would he have had the resolution to quit his job then? He shuddered at the thought.

"Would it help at least for us to take him?" Betha asked in a small voice. "Would you allow us to provide his room and board without the indenture?"

"It's not enough." Seamus looked as defeated as Colm felt, his words a husky whisper. "I can't keep weaving."

Colm knew the grief he felt, only on a smaller scale. He at least had hope that he could teach again. They remained silent, each in their own thoughts, searching for a solution. And in his case, surrendering Henry's future once again into God's hands.

"I wanted you to have him," Seamus finally said. "I trust you. Maybe more than I trust myself. But if you can't buy his indenture, it's the end of weaving for me. Alexander Brown offered me a job at his bank."

"Did he?" Betha's head snapped up.

"With Henry's indenture, I could avoid having to do that."

Colm didn't move a muscle, praying harder than ever.

"The pay is good?" Betha asked.

"Enough for now, if I didn't have Henry. But opportunity to move up later."

"If we take Henry, we're keeping him," Colm said, still frozen in place. "We'll raise him. He won't go back and forth depending on how your finances change, and you won't be meddling with our guidance."

Seamus frowned. "Even with an indenture, I'd still be his da. He's not up for adoption."

"Still his da, but I'll be the one raising him. You'd have to agree not to pull him in two directions."

"But you'd still have to work at the bank for that to happen," Betha reminded Seamus. "If you indentured him as you originally suggested, you could keep weaving."

Seamus inhaled and exhaled slowly. "I do love him, Betha. He would have a chance with you."

"A chance?"

"To grow up right. Be educated and choose his career. To have faith."

A tear trickled down Betha's cheek, and the sight of it caused the lump in Colm's throat to grow. He spoke up. "You would be willing to work at the bank to give Henry that? If you are, we would do that for him." He watched the war inside play out on Seamus's face. Giving up a beloved livelihood was no small thing; Colm had never seen a man do such a thing for his son. His prayers quickly changed from "Thy will be done" to "Lord, please give us Henry."

"Don't say that if it's not what you want or if you're just trying to appease me, Colm Gallagher," Betha burst out, her whole body shaking. "This changes everything."

Colm crossed the floor in two strides to press his palm against her cheek and look her in the eyes. "You ask what I want? I'll tell you truly. I want you to be who you are. And you, Betha Gallagher, are Henry's mother, and you always have been. It's killing you to be away from him. We prayed, and we gave Henry to God, but how can a mother truly let her son go? You weren't meant to leave his life."

"I will," Seamus said firmly. "I'll speak to Alexander Brown tomorrow."

"And that's final?" Betha asked, as if she was still too frightened to hope.

"I promise."

Pressing her lips together, Betha looked up at Colm for a long moment before moving toward Seamus and crushing him in a hug. "Thank you," she whispered tearfully. "Thank you so much. May God bless your sacrifice."

With an exhale, Seamus patted her back. Even his earlier look of defeat had been replaced with something lighter. Maybe the knowledge that he'd made the right decision brought peace that had hitherto escaped him. "You're good for him, Betha. You're good to my boy."

"When should we get him? Can I be the one to tell him?"

He scowled and stepped back. "Don't you think I should? You're always trying to get me to—"

"No. If it comes from you, he'll think you're trying to get rid of him, because it's what he already believes. From me, it will sound like he's wanted. I think that's what he needs right now."

Seamus shrugged without arguing. "You always seem to think you know what he needs."

"I'll be over after school tomorrow then." The tears were gone, and Betha's eyes now sparkled with joy.

Seamus stopped in front of Colm, his hand outstretched. "I'm indebted to you for this."

Colm couldn't disagree. Taking on another man's son was a huge commitment. But it was one he'd made when he married Betha, not today, and it was Henry. It was worth it.

"Thank you for trusting us with him," he said, unable to verbalize more.

When Seamus was gone, Betha flew into Colm's arms. "How can I thank you? Can you believe he would make a sacrifice that big for Henry? I didn't think he would do it. I can hardly believe it's true, but I'm so happy."

Colm cradled her in his arms, smiling down at her in the flickering candlelight. "It's hard to believe, but I thought there was something in him that would do it. He's been selfish, but he's not altogether a cold-hearted villain."

"He's wanted to be able to start clean with his new family with Cara ever since he married her. I wasn't sure how you would react when he suggested dumping his son off on you."

"Hey." Colm cupped her chin in his hand. "Henry isn't his bastard son. He's Henry, a member of our family. Whether Seamus views it as dumping, I don't. Seamus gets what he wants and we get what we've wanted all along, and it's God we thank for answering our prayers. I'd never even hoped enough to ask God to give him to us before. It seemed too far-fetched a dream, or maybe too selfish."

Betha tightened her arms around his middle. "I don't know what I did to get such a good man. But we do have a lot of thanking to do. And then start praying for wisdom in raising him."

Colm didn't want to take a single step without asking God for help, but they also weren't starting from scratch. He'd been raising boys for six years, and Betha since Henry was a baby. Perhaps God had been preparing them to take him in all along.

"We can afford him, can't we? On your retail salary?"

Colm almost opened his mouth with an answer about numbers and wedding gifts, but suddenly Patrick was in his head, stopping him. "I think we can trust God with that, don't you? We released him to God, and God was working it out all along for us to have him. He knew everything with the school would be happening at the same time, even though we didn't. I think He is going before us to make a way."

He could hardly fathom the work God had done over the past two years. Instead of floundering in uncertainty the way he was when he met Betha, he was now rooted, his faith flourishing. All while his circumstances looked more unstable than ever. He was like a tree planted by the rivers of water, with visible fruit that God was bringing forth in his heart and life. And now he had the opportunity to graft a vulnerable young man into his home, the faith that God had grown in him now nourishing another.

The journey would be long and probably challenging, but he knew now that it wasn't something to fear. Colm pressed his lips against the corner of Betha's mouth. "How do you like the dawn?"

46

Betha could hardly contain herself the following day. The breakfast dishes were neglected while she freshened up the room Henry would occupy. Occasionally, she burst into songs of praise and then laughed out loud at how Methodist she sounded. Her prayers swung back and forth between joyful eulogies and sober pleadings for the grace and insight to fulfill her responsibility to Henry.

It was different, being Henry's ma up until this point. She'd accepted being thrust into the role happily, but it wasn't something she'd chosen. The prayers for wisdom she offered were in moments where it was needed, never in a larger sense for their relationship as a whole. Now she was fully and officially being given the duty of raising Henry to adulthood. What's more, it was while the boy was at the lowest point of his life. It would no doubt take time to undo the damage from the past year and convince him that he had a place to belong where he was truly wanted.

She waited until he'd be home from school but hopefully hadn't left to play yet before she took off her apron and made her way the few blocks to Seamus's. After a light tap on the front door, she opened it and peered inside to avoid causing a disturbance if the baby was sleeping. Seamus was standing by the loom studying it, his back to her.

"Hello," she said, shutting the door. She took another step before realizing he was running his calloused fingers over the freshly woven linen. He didn't turn when she stopped beside him.

"I talked to Alexander Brown this morning," he said, his voice gruff. "He said I can start immediately."

"What did you tell him?" Betha asked, suddenly fearful that he'd changed his mind.

"I said I would."

He leaned forward, resting his forehead on the beam, and closed his eyes.

"Leave the loom up. Maybe you'll still end up weaving sometimes."

"I'm goin' to sell da's," Seamus said with a heavy exhale. "I might sell this one too."

Betha touched his sleeve. "It's a wonderful skill you have, and you're good at it. We can still create beautiful things that bring us joy even if it doesn't bring in enough to support our families. Surely you can still weave for your family. Don't get rid of it in a hurry."

"Maybe. I'm sure Cara would appreciate having the room available if I'm not using it during the day."

"I'm sorry, Seamus. It doesn't seem fair, and it breaks my heart too. I wish I could have saved your livelihood for you." She had hope that working for Alexander Brown would be good for her brother and one day he would be thriving and happy again, but this moment wasn't the time to say so. The sounds of the baby fussing and Cara calming her in the other room reminded Betha of her errand. "Is Henry home?"

"I think he's out back."

Betha gave his arm a light squeeze and backed up.

"Betha. I was able to weave beautiful linen because you spun beautiful thread. We did good together."

"We did. I was honored to work with you. Da and Ma would be proud." She gave him a sad smile before walking away.

A thunking sound met her ears when she opened the back door, followed by the squawking of chickens. Henry had a row of pinecones set up on the cellar door and stood several paces back, shooting them down with pebbles from his slingshot. His face was a thundercloud.

Will You bring him back to us, Lord? The cold bit her face as she stepped down the stairs and jammed her hands into her coat pockets.

"What happened that you're taking out on the pinecones?"

Thwack. A pinecone went flying, leaving debris in its wake.

"I didn't know you were coming over today." Henry's nose and cheeks were rosy against the dreary gray sky, and the bruise around his lip had purpled.

"I have something to tell you. Something important. But you seem rather perturbed at the moment."

Thwack. "Ma, there is nothing wrong with me wanting to play with the baby. She isn't going to catch my disease by being around me."

"You don't have a disease, Henry."

"That's how her mother treats me!" His voice rose, his face deepening its scowl as another pinecone went flying. "She hit me today."

"She *what*?!" Betha blanched.

"I picked up my sister when she was down in the cellar, and when she came back up, she almost dropped her jar, she was so furious. She came over and snatched Elizabeth out of my arms and smacked me upside the head and told me not to touch her. It's not the first time it's happened. Hitting me."

Betha couldn't see straight for the rage that encompassed her. For a minute she considered punching something or obliterating a few pinecones with a slingshot herself. She couldn't get Henry out of this house fast enough.

"You have every right to touch your sister," she said as calmly as she could manage. "People can't rightly own other people. A member of a family belongs to everyone and no one."

"I know, Ma." He looked at her like she was stupid for even having to say it. "What did you come over to tell me?"

This was hardly the note Betha wanted to tell him on. She'd had a speech prepared that had nothing to do with Henry deserving a safe environment to grow up in, and now she couldn't remember a word of it.

"Your da, Uncle Colm, and I met and talked about the best way we could take care of you."

Her words captured his attention, because he lowered his slingshot, interest replacing the crossness in his eyes. "You did?"

"We were all hoping to figure out a way that you wouldn't have to be indentured. And I think we found one."

Henry twanged the slingshot mindlessly with his fingers. He seemed to be holding his breath in anticipation.

"Uncle Colm and I have a place for you at our house if you'd like to continue your schooling. If you move in with us, it would be forever."

Henry's lips parted. "Forever?" he breathed.

"We all agreed." Betha took a step toward him. "Uncle Colm and I are hoping you'll decide to come. I've missed you unbearably. I hate to take you from your new sister, but you'll just be a few blocks away."

"Da will let me?"

He reminded Betha of herself the night before, too frightened to hope.

"He loves you, Henry. He promised me he wouldn't stand in your way."

Dropping the slingshot, Henry flung his arms around Betha's middle. In an instant, her eyes were filled. She'd almost grown tired of crying lately but couldn't wish away how her heart felt full to bursting.

"You'll come then?" she asked with a tearful laugh.

"I will. I will, I will!"

"If you move in with us, we'll be terribly strict. No more fights after school. You'll have to eat your dinner while it's still hot. No more leftover crusts of bread by yourself instead of dinner. And you can't scare my chickens with your pebbles, or they won't lay."

Henry squeezed tighter, and she couldn't breathe. "I'll do anything you say, Ma."

"Then let me breathe, please?" she gasped.

He released her, allowing her to absorb what he'd just said. "That's the thing, my boy. You don't have to do anything to be allowed to stay. You don't have to try to earn it. It's settled." She dipped her head, making him look her in the eye. "You can live with us because you're my boy and Uncle Colm and I want you there."

"Yes, ma'am. When does it start?"

Betha lowered herself to sit on the step, and Henry sat beside her. "I thought Saturday would be good. We can get you all set up and then can start our new week fresh, goin' to church and Sunday school together."

Henry gave a huff. "Sometimes I don't want to go to church anymore."

"I know." Reaching out, Betha took his hand in hers. "We'll go anyway, because we're weaker when the devil gets us off by ourselves. Like a predator trying to get his prey away from the rest of the herd. But I'm sorry it's been so hard for you. It won't always be like this, and no matter what, Uncle Colm and I will be there for you."

He leaned his head against her shoulder, and Betha rested hers on his cap. She simply held him, shivering in the cold, wondering with gratitude at the God who invented love, created families, and never left His children alone.

47

Betha quickly shut the kitchen door against a blast of snow flurries, giving one last shiver as the residual heat from the hearth coals made its way to her limbs. She'd meant to be home an hour ago, but at least she always put beans in the dutch oven before leaving for the Bible Society.

Depositing her basket beside the door, she used a poker to move the lid off the pot. The beans had long since finished cooking and were still plenty warm. She gave a quick stir with the wooden spoon to ensure nothing had stuck to the bottom before peeling off her gloves and unwinding her muffler. Surely Colm was home from work, even though he hadn't come when he heard the door.

She removed the beans from the coals and coaxed the fire back to life to chase the chill from the room. With that done, she carried her coat and hood to hang by the front door. The sound of voices reached her, sparking curiosity. Poking her head into the study, she found Colm and Patrick sprawled in the chairs, deep in conversation.

"Hello there. I'm sorry I'm late."

They both came to their feet, and Colm came to kiss her cheek. "I would have started to worry, but I knew you were with Ava, and I could smell supper. I stirred it once for you."

"Thank you. How are you, Patrick? It's nice to see you here."

"I'm well enough. Your home looks lovely."

Guilt pricked at her. They'd been married over a month and still hadn't had anyone but Henry over for a meal. She turned stricken eyes on Colm. "I feel awful. I never even thought about it, but we should have had your family over by now. I could never really be free to invite my own guests when I lived with Seamus, so it never crossed my mind."

"You've had plenty else on your mind," Patrick interjected easily. "It's hardly been a normal first month for you."

"We should do that, though, shouldn't we? We could have the young people over sometimes for little dinner parties."

"With Henry living here, I think the boys will become frequent visitors as well." Colm gave her a reassuring smile. "There's plenty of time to make up for our oversight. Shall we have supper now?"

"It's just beans with a hambone, but there's plenty. Do you want to wait for me to whip up some corn cakes?"

"You don't need to worry about it." Colm led the way down the hall. "Patrick can always eat when he goes home if he doesn't like it."

"Maybe next time?" Patrick looked at her hopefully.

She shooed him into the dining room. "I'll bring in supper, and then you can tell me how you've been. I've not heard any news from you lately."

A moment later, she had the beans on the table and set to work spreading the place settings.

"I've been mostly busy with the newspaper office and the freedmen's society." Patrick straightened his jacket and smoothed his waistcoat. "Sometimes I find more tangible ways to help those who are new to freedom. It's still hard to know when to get involved and when my presence will bring greater risk. More often than not, my work is behind the scenes instead of directly with those in need."

"That must be a sacrifice for someone who loves people as much as you do." Betha placed a bowl in front of him.

He lifted a shoulder. "I have to remind myself that it's not about me and the priority is to protect those in danger. I do rather hate it though."

"Sounds like it's good for you," Colm put in. Betha shot him a withering look.

Patrick inhaled. "And in my free time, I'm chaperoning Ezra and Maisie."

"That might not be for much longer." Colm accepted a cup of ale from Betha and met Patrick's curious look. "I had a little chat with Ezra after Sunday school this week."

"Should I be concerned?" Patrick asked Betha. She smiled and shook her head.

"I think there will be a do-over of the proposal soon. One that has the confidence of a man who knows his affections are returned." Colm lifted his cup as in a toast. "I'm sure it will go much better the second time around."

Patrick let out a whistle. "So our little sister will be married soon. And you two becoming parents"—he glanced at Betha—"or continuing, rather. Which puts me behind, I suppose."

"It's not a race." Betha took her seat and scooted her chair in. "The only time we are all on is God's. You just worry about what He's given you to do now. The work you're involved in might not be possible when you're married."

"I hope I'll be doing even more when I'm married." Patrick lifted his chin in defiance. "I could do so much with a partner."

Colm raised a hand to calm him down. "She only means it might not look exactly the same. I'm starving. Bless the food, Patrick, so we can eat it."

April 1829

Betha studied the granite building before her, praying that this was yet another of Colm's brilliant ideas.

"Are you nervous?"

"Nope." He squeezed her hand and turned a dazzling smile on her. "Mr. McKim seemed kind and encouraging when I met him. He's the son of the founder, who was a member of the Hibernian Society. And we've been praying about this."

"And they won't try to use their power over you to get you to act against your conscience?"

"Mr. McKim told me that the role of a teacher is to serve his students, not try to control them. He strikes me as a pretty humble man. I think we'll agree on a lot of things."

Betha tilted her face up, using her hand to shield it from the sun. "You've only become more confident since the Oliver committee challenged you, and yet you view your own position of authority as an opportunity for humility. Henry."

He'd walked on ahead but now turned around when Betha called him. "What do you think? How do confidence and humility work together?"

He only stared at her, but she knew he was thinking it through.

"Humility and confidence go together," Colm answered for him, "because trust in God is the only way either one is possible."

"You'd have to trust God to really be humble," Henry said, crossing his arms over his chest. "Someone who knows God's taking care of them doesn't have to try to work things out or get all the attention for themselves."

Emotion rose in Betha at his answer. Not every day with him was easy, and he didn't always engage in conversations of faith, even after spending the last few months in their house. But when he did, he was thoughtful and displayed startling insight.

She swallowed hard. "And confidence?"

He shook his head, stumped. Betha looked to Colm for the answer.

"Any true confidence is confidence in God, not ourselves. He's the only one who won't fail. When we're confident only in ourselves, it's pretty shaky—false confidence—and we know it. You can tell it's false confidence when it's accompanied by pride. Humility and confidence go hand in hand as natural results of a growing faith in God."

"I think you're right." She nodded to the building. "Are you ready to take your trust in there and see if they've decided to hire you?"

"More than ready. It shouldn't take long, then we can go to Maisie and Ezra's for supper."

Betha reached out to straighten his cravat and gave him a smile. "We'll be here praying for you."

When the door had closed after him, Betha's attention lit on her own church across Great York Street with the yard beside it. It would make an ideal location for wandering around and praying while waiting for Colm. Before she could step onto the dirt road, a farmer came down it herding a handful of cows. She let them pass before proceeding with Henry by her side.

They strolled through the garden path, basking in the sunshine. The calendar said it was spring, but the weather had been slow in catching up until now. Soon the asparagus would be up at Seamus's and she'd be getting her own garden in for the first time.

At the thought of Seamus, she peeked at Henry sauntering beside her. "Do you want to go visit your da soon? You've not seen him or Elizabeth lately."

A shadow darkened his brow, and he gave a noncommittal shrug. He never wanted to go whenever she asked. They'd hosted Seamus and Cara for supper a handful of times, and Betha stopped by almost weekly to help with chores, drop off thread for Seamus to weave up for his family or hers, or hold the baby and visit with Cara. But it would take a miracle to convince Henry to keep putting his heart on the line for his father and sister.

Betha almost opened her mouth to advocate further for the visit but then closed it. It wasn't really her job to coerce him into her point of view. In her home, Henry was instructed in the ways of God, subjected to the spiritual disciplines, and loved warmly. She prayed often about the rest, but that was as far as her control extended.

"When I talked to your da the other day, he said you were welcome to come use the loom this summer while he's at work. He'd thread it up for you. Might give you something useful to do while school's out."

"The money would help, wouldn't it?"

"It would, but Uncle Colm could probably find something else for you to do down at the shipping office if you'd rather."

"Maybe I will. It's not the weaving I mind. And it's just for a little while."

Betha prayed for Colm's meeting as promised and then leaned on the stone wall and watched passing traffic. Henry's stomach rumbled beside her, making her wonder if they should go along to Maisie's and let Colm find them there.

"There he is." Henry leapt to the ground from his perch on the wall. Sure enough, Colm had exited the school and was looking up and down the street for them. Betha trailed behind Henry, arriving too late to hear whatever he'd asked Colm.

"If we want a place to put down roots, I think we've found it," Colm announced to both of them. "As soon as enrollments begin for next year, we can get you registered, Henry."

Betha exhaled and took Colm's hand in hers. "Congratulations. I don't doubt you'll serve them with humility *and* confidence."

Henry was still staring at the Greek-style building. Colm kneaded his shoulder affectionately. "I won't be teaching your level next year, but I'll be in the same building."

"Couldn't I stay at Oliver?" Henry asked timidly.

Betha frowned over his head at Colm in confusion. Colm looked surprised but not upset. "You like the new teacher there?"

"My friends are there. Ma makes sure I study the Bible at home anyway." He'd noticed Betha's frown, so she smoothed it away. "If you can't be my teacher anyway, I'd rather stay with my friends," he continued. "You won't even miss me since I live with you."

"What about the boys who called you names at Oliver?" Betha asked. "No one knows those things about you here."

Henry made a face and shoved his hands in his pockets. "They can say whatever they like. It doesn't bother me so much since we prayed about it."

Colm's mouth ticked, a smile tempting. Betha held her breath, unsure of what to say and afraid of blurting out the wrong thing.

"I think . . ." Colm slowly began, "I wouldn't have to worry about you staying there since your Heavenly Father is making it clear He's taking care of you. You're right—we'll be home together with you every night and praying for you. We should give your ma time to think about it though."

266

"I did." Betha hooked her arm through Colm's and propelled him down the street. "Uncle Colm can't share about the Lord there anymore, but I think you should stay with the friendships you've built, Henry. They'll probably need you."

Henry tripped along beside her, turning to send a grin her way. "Thanks, Ma."

"We're only deciding for this year," Colm warned. "We'll decide for next year when it comes."

Henry dipped his head and nodded, and Betha tightened her grip on Colm's arm. By God's grace, this man was on Henry's side with her, and Henry finally had a chance to thrive.

"Did you see the *Thomas Jefferson* is in port this week?" Henry asked Colm. A rooster crowed nearby, and a carriage clattered by next to them. Betha exhaled, surrendering her worries, and listened to stories of schooners all the way to Maisie's house.

About the Book

When I sat down to write the story of the Young siblings' parents (from my Finding Home series), I realized that Henry Young's story didn't begin when he met his children's mother. In order to understand how his family's roots were woven as they were and why their story developed as it did, I had to go back to his childhood and his own father.

Going back thirty-five years in history and moving to a different part of the country brought a series of fun challenges for this historical fiction author. It involved erasing a lot of technology that the Young siblings used in their story—the telegraph, photography, railroads. Chicago itself wasn't even incorporated yet! I found myself in an era where *stoves* were the new technology, for pity's sake.

Weaving Roots centers on the real history of the Oliver Hibernian Free School in Baltimore. It was incorporated in 1824 by John Oliver of the Hibernian Society, who established it with the Lancaster education model and stipulated that the Bible not be used as a classbook. Many of the Hibernian Society committee members were religious, including shipping magnate Stewart Brown from First Presbyterian and Luke Tiernan, a Catholic. The minutes for the society committee meetings includes a note that for a brief period of time, the Bible was introduced into the curriculum, but after the student body was reduced to "mere skeletons" as a result, it was removed again. The teacher at the time was William Gibson, whom I honored by naming the fictional committee member/substitute teacher after. *How* it all unfolded is not recorded and is purely my own invention.

Second Presbyterian Church's history is written almost exactly like it really happened, including the men's prayer meetings with First Presbyterian men, as well as the singing schools and Sunday schools instituted by the pastor, John Breckinridge. All of these events took place during the time of the Second Great Awakening and were likely a direct result of it.

Anti-Catholic sentiment was high during the period of *Weaving Roots*, and Presbyterians made up the largest population of Irish immigrants to America in the years before the Great Famine. The celebration of Guy Fawkes Day in coastal cities would have been even more common when Colm and his brothers were growing up and although it was in vogue in America during this time, it was later eclipsed by the arrival of Halloween.

As usual, this book would not have been anything close to the quality that it is now if it weren't for the incredibly talented team of people behind me.

My critique partners, **Jennifer Q. Hunt, Amanda Chapman, Rebekah Gwynn, and Scott Gwynn** get all the credit for the amount of thoughtful guidance they provided at every stage of this story. They push me to higher and better work, and I'm deeply grateful for the investment they make in my writing. Each have different highly valuable skills they bring to the table.

Joanne Bischof brought her professional eye to the first couple chapters, and I'm so thankful for her insights.

With deep thanks to my beta readers, **Carrie Cotten, Bonnie McGraw,** and **David Wood**, for your attention to detail and every effort you put into helping this story shine;

To my editor, **Jessica Barber**, for perservering through this job and doing such careful, thorough work;

To my cover designer, **Hannah Linder**, for your patience and talent creating the beautiful "face" of *Weaving Roots*;

To **the staff of the H. Furlong Baldwin library** at the Maryland Center of History and Culture for all your help during my research visit, and to **Ciaran Toal** of the Irish Linen Centre & Lisburn Museum in Northern Ireland for answering all my weaving and linen questions;

To all the **Christian Mommy Writers** and to **my family** for your unfailing support, encouragement, and prayers;

To **my kids**, for their excitement about my writing, even with all the sacrifices it costs them of my time and attention;

To my husband, **David**, for continuing to make space in our lives for this endeavor and for being a better romantic hero than any I've ever written;

And to **God**, for the way You stretch and grow me, meeting me through each story I write and revealing more of Your goodness to me. I was brought to tears rereading a section of this story tonight because it was just what I needed at this time in my life, and You knew that.

I could not keep writing if it weren't for **my readers**, whose kind words, purchases, and recommendations to friends keep me and my writing going. Thank you for every review and share! You'll never know how valuable they are to your favorite authors.

About the Author

Heather Wood grew up in the Chicago suburbs, loving history, classic literature, writing stories, and Civil War reenacting. After obtaining her bachelor's degree in Bible/Theology from Appalachian Bible College, she settled in Virginia with her husband, David. Her early passions fuel her writing today, although she spends most of her days now working to infuse her love for God and good literature into the hearts of her four children.

I would love to have you visit me online at
my social media accounts @heather.wood.author or at
www.HeatherWoodAuthor.com
where you can sign up for my newsletter and receive news of sales, giveaways, and new releases in your inbox about once a month.

If you enjoyed Weaving Roots, please leave a review wherever you review books! Indie authors rely on reviews for our work to get noticed.

Read More by Heather Wood

Until We All Find Home

When Justin Young is reunited with his orphaned siblings during the American Civil War, he decides to bring his widowed sister and younger brothers to live with him in Chicago, desiring to give them a home and a family. But he soon discovers that sometimes love is more painful than it is healing as he faces his own inadequacies. Along their journey toward reconciliation with God and each other, the siblings and their friends learn that real love often looks like the hard work of granting grace and second chances to other hurting, imperfect people with whom they have nothing in common. In the end, they find that when they come home to God, He gives them the courage, freedom, and grace to come home to the people they've come to love.

Until We All Run Free

Jed and Jack Young may be brothers by birth, but as orphans, their separate upbringings produced polarizing results. Now that the Civil War is over, the brothers look forward to settling into the next chapter of their lives and learning to walk in their new faith. Each brother's ideal happily ever after is the other's worst nightmare, and when that nightmare becomes their own reality, their relationship is threatened. Mary Pierce has a picture-perfect life with three daughters and a loving husband. When tragedy strikes, Mary has to lean on God in deeper ways and learn to navigate a painful new path. Faced with their greatest fears, Jed, Jack, and Mary must anchor themselves in the unchanging character of God. As they overcome sin, learn everyday obedience, and find peace in surrender, they discover there are no dark corners in their lives that God's grace won't illuminate and His power can't resurrect.

Until We All Share Joy

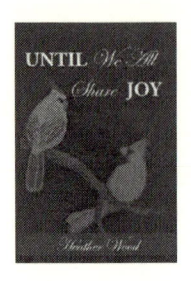

Titan Dinsmore loves his family, but as the youngest of five, he craves his older siblings' respect—and a little distance. A chance meeting at the train station with a forlorn young lady turns into a growing attraction between them. But Titan quickly learns there is a difference between wanting to be treated as an adult and truly stepping up to lead. How can he help tenderhearted Nora see beyond her father's abandonment and rest in the love of her Heavenly Father? And will his secret plan to restore her family for the ideal Christmas together win Nora's undying admiration or only lead to greater heartache?

This warm stand-alone Christmas novella highlights a lesser-known member of the beloved Dinsmore family in the *Finding Home* series. With all the charm of a Victorian Christmas and yet the realities of navigating difficult relationships in a Christlike manner, this book is one to be savored throughout the holiday season and beyond.

Until The Light Breaks Through

Jack Young's past comes back to haunt him in the third installment of Heather Wood's Christian family saga as the Great Chicago Fire threatens to destroy everything he loves most.

Newly graduated from seminary and on the cusp of taking a pastorate in Kentucky, Jack discovers devastating consequences of the licentious life he put behind him six years ago. To move forward, he must go back. But each encounter with his old life brings lasting reverberations for his future and further chips away at the peace he's pursued so desperately all these years. The revival of an old friendship sparks feelings he's worked hard to keep dormant and challenges his determination to reject anything that could come between him and the Lord again. When the city of Chicago burns to ashes, it leaves his family tragically altered—and Jack more unsure of his place in God's plan than ever.

Made in the USA
Middletown, DE
20 June 2024